Series One:

A WORLD BEYOND OUR OWN

Book One

James Marcus

A World Beyond Our Own
Copyright © 2018 by James Marcus

All rights reserved. No part of this publication may be reproduced, distributed, or transmitted in any form or by any means, including photocopying, recording, or other electronic or mechanical methods, without the prior written permission of the author, except in the case of brief quotations embodied in critical reviews and certain other non-commercial uses permitted by copyright law.

Tellwell Talent
www.tellwell.ca

ISBN
978-0-2288-0375-1 (Paperback)
978-0-2288-0376-8 (eBook)

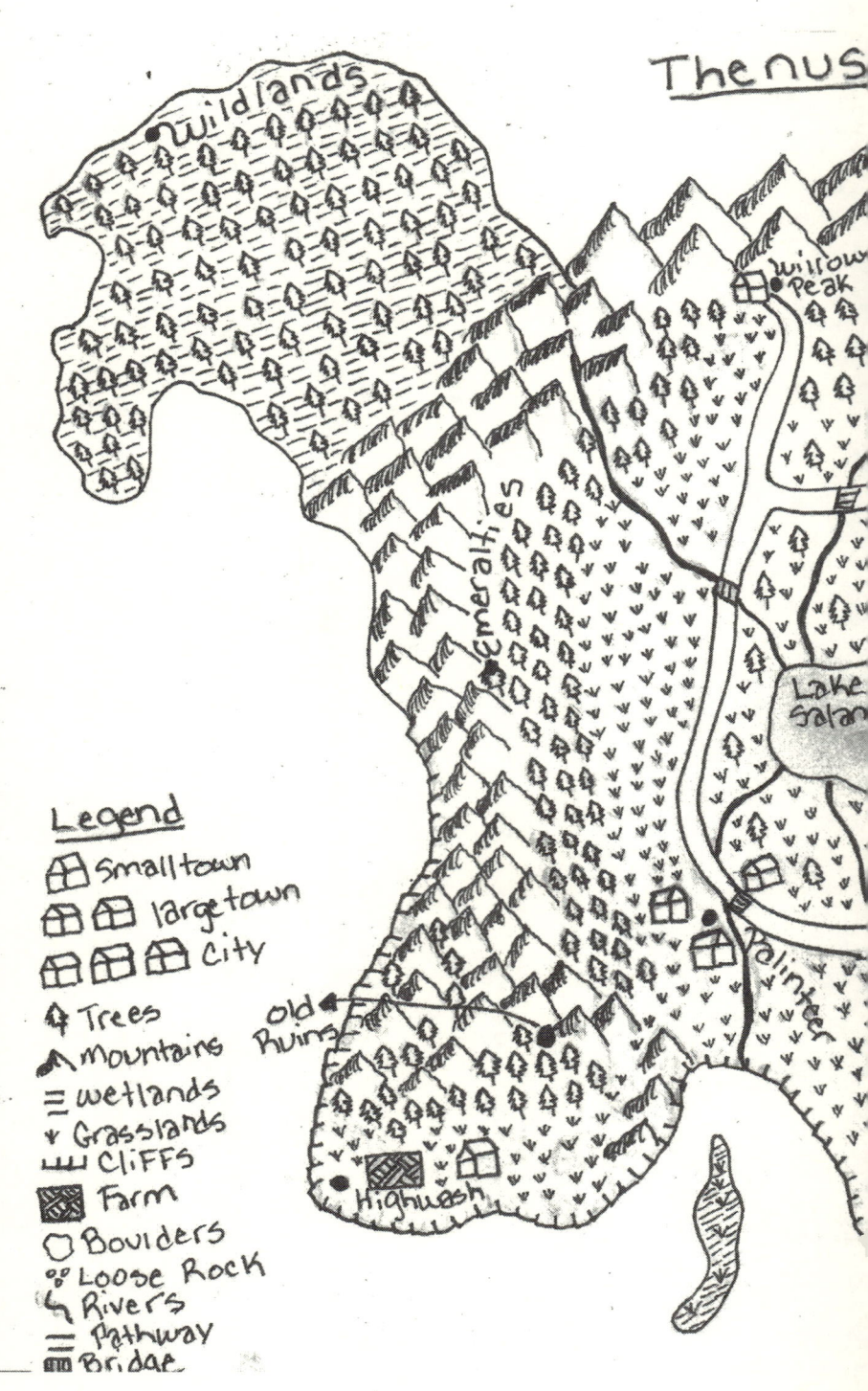

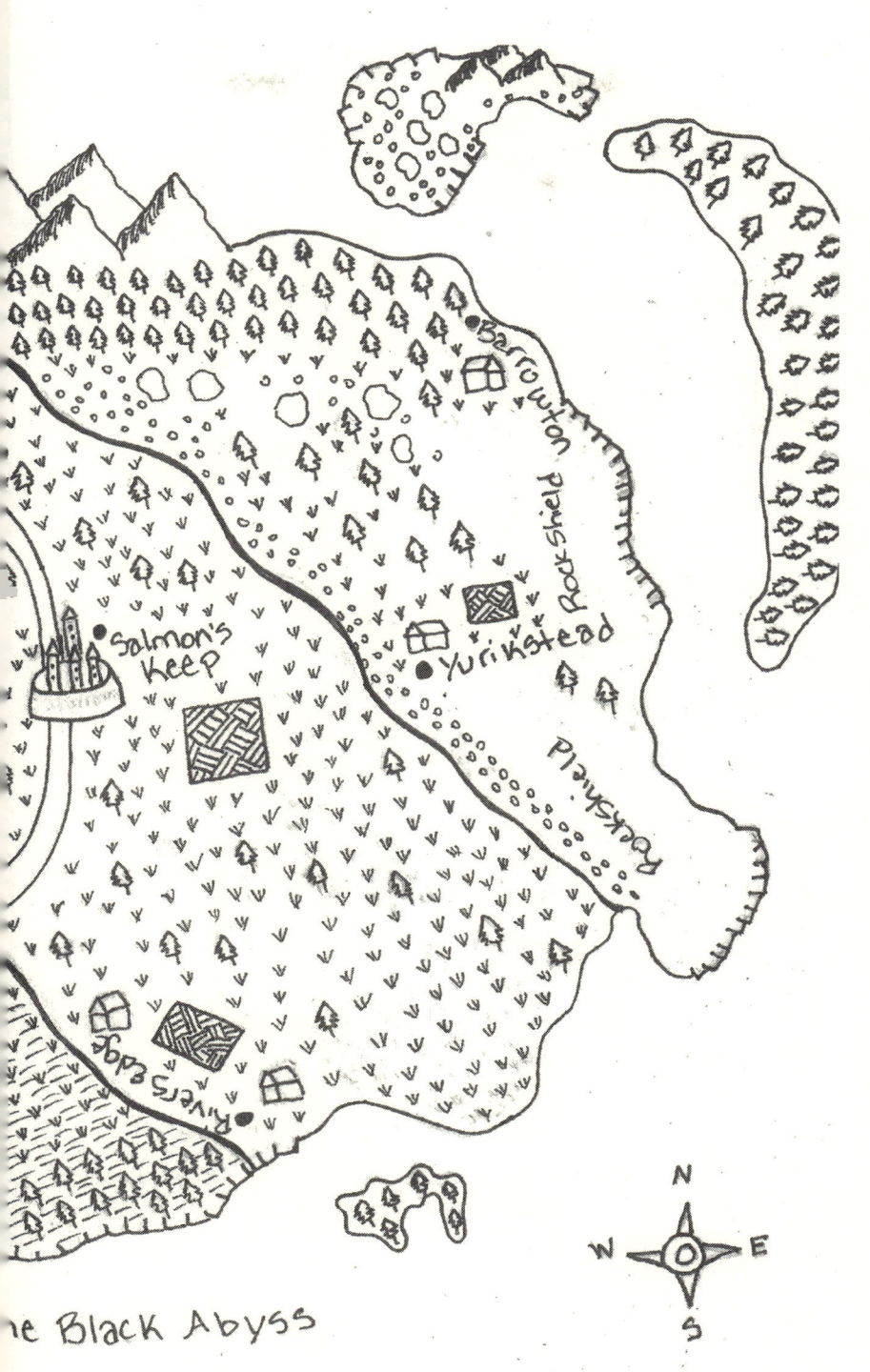

So it is said that the universe was born in a single day.

Magic. Commoners know magic as an ill omen, a few haunting nightmares told by elderly folk, or legends taught by religious sanctions. Some well-read folk—though not often found among common people of Thenus—might stumble upon scholarly work describing in detail, encounters with men who could perform incredible feats.

Many people know of old fables depicting magic users, called Mages, who are said to have stolen powers from beings beyond comprehension. These magic users are said to be lone wanderers who live in the high mountains or deep woods. At times they venture into cities and towns and kidnap kids by hexing their minds. The kidnapped children are then brought back to the Mage's home and raised to be Mages themselves, continuing the cult for generations.

Now these are only legends, and most common folk of Thenus have never even heard of Mages, never mind actually having met one.

It could be fairly simple to find a Mage—though you would need some uncanny luck to stumble into a village so small, and some thick legs to be able endure such adventurous hiking. But, if one were to hike long enough, they would eventually stumble into Highwash.

The village of Highwash rests nestled between a vast prairie field edged by a forest rimmed by mountains to the east and cliffs that drop off into the cold Black Abyss to the west. A village as small as Highwash could only be stumbled on by sheer luck. It is so small of a village it only housed around forty-five people; most were small children and young adolescents. A few village Elders lived amongst the youth, either teaching lessons or carrying out daily necessities.

Now, in regards to magic, the people of Highwash have a much different take on what magic may be and how it should be used. To hear and read legends is one thing but to get to know the villagers of Highwash was a privilege beyond words. I shall first introduce my dear friend Marius when he was a young lad around the age of sixteen.

I

Marius blinked as the morning sunrays glimmered through the clouds past his eyes. He had his thighs bent parallel with the ground, toes pointed out, sweat running down his forehead, his brown hair caught in the sweat stuck to his face. He had picked a miserable spot to do his horse stance this morning. His ears tuned to seagulls cawing, the ocean waves crashing against the cliffs walls, the slow melodic breathing of his classmates standing beside and behind him. The sun pierced Marius's eyes again. He brought his attention to his feet planted on the bedrock, legs shaking. Marius hated horse stance.

The horse stance is an exercise for beginner Mages. Students have to stand with bent legs in a squat position, legs parallel to the ground and knees beside the body. This is an energy building exercise, its purpose is to build energy within the body which is stored to use magic to manipulate matter. Horse stance is preferably practiced daily for an hour at sunrise.

Marius hated horse stance, but here he stood. Finally Elder Macaro stood up from sitting behind them. He was a tall, bald man descending from a line of fathers native to Arngrimir. His face was blank and had soft features, a white beard rimmed his chin. He did not say much of a word, but picked up his neatly-stacked sewn sandals, put them on his feet and started down the hill towards the village of Highwash. Marius and the rest of the students followed Macaro back towards the village.

Not much was said at times, all students knew the daily routine, and for young apprentices the routine never changed. Apprentices were made to wake up at dawn, do meditative stretching, then horse stance at sunrise. Following horse stance was breakfast. After breakfast the disciples would be led to train and be taught the way of the Mage by their current Elder. Marius' current Elder was Elder Macaro, he had trained under Elder Macaro since he was a little boy.

Marius stood up, slipped on his leather sandals as well, and followed the line of students down towards the main hall, with him falling last in line. The Elder could hear all the classmates' childlike talk as they walked down towards the village.

"One day they better make something different for breakfast!" Mathius shouted so all could hear. "I'm tired of cooked wheat and milk."

Marius' class consisted of seven classmates. Marius was last in line, only of the age of sixteen. He was tall and lean, with long brown hair that fell to his shoulders and was usually either tied back in a ponytail or left hanging; usually the latter as it always fell loose when he was training. Yuri, second from last, turned to face Marius as they walked down the hill, the knee-high brown grass tickling their shins as they walked on. Yuri's black hair was darkened from his sweat. He didn't say anything, just gave Marius a look of acknowledgement.

Ahead of Yuri and Marius was Mathius, Daniel, Cynthia, Reggard and Clive.

As the group waded through the grass they approached a dirt trail that led towards the village of Highwash. As they approached Highwash, Marius could see the rim of the wooden shack houses forming a circle around the town's main hall. The main hall was a small, thin tower, roughly four floors high it barely stood over the surrounding buildings. As they entered the town the ground became hard and firm from years of feet treading on it. Small pebbles crunched into the dirt as Marius stepped on. The group entered the circle of houses and turned left to follow another dirt trail

Highwash was a simple town. If a commoner were to visit, one would notice quite a few peculiar things about the place. Firstly, the size of the town: even a small city would dwarf Highwash. Secondly, one used to the hectic marketplaces out west in Central Thenus would feel a bit underwhelmed. Instead of the Vatican ruling Highwash, Highwash ruled itself. Making Highwash a very friendly, open place. The only sense of monarchy in Highwash was the fact people sought advice from Archmage Nathaniel. Highwash was a self-sufficient democracy, which is enough said as is. But the biggest, most extravagant detail about Highwash was the fact that magic users were common place.

The group continued under Elder Macaro's lead, following a trail that took them going north out of town, opposite to the main hall where breakfast would be served. Instinctively Marius knew he was not getting breakfast today, he wondered if the rest of class had picked up on the matter yet.

Elder Macaro continued on for almost thirty minutes. The trail wove through high grass and thicket bushes until it lead them to a clearing of beige, sand-like dirt. Seven huge logs with the circumference about the size of a man's face were in a circle, placed to stand straight up, perfectly plumb.

The morning sun had now risen above the eastern mountains revealing its face among strings of cloud.

Elder Macaro turned to the group and finally spoke up. "Why did no one ask where we were going?"

Asking rhetorical questions was not uncommon of Macaro. He chuckled loudly as the class sat in silence; his blue eyes crunched from smile lines, leaving his pale expression blushed. "Did not one of you think not to ask? Were you afraid of what the answer would be? Or did you already know?"

Again he only received subtle blank nods. Macaro continued talking.

"Never be afraid to peer, a Mage should always be at an intellectual advantage. Now, Mathius, why is that?"

The Elder's gaze pierced Mathius as he replied to his questioning. "A Mage should always be aware, not only of the physical environment, but of the energetic environment."

"Why?"

"So a Mage always has advantage over the environment."

Elder Macaro turned towards the logs placed in a circle, gesturing towards them. "Today we start the first day of the Trial of Apprentices. Every twenty years we run the Trial of Apprentices for our current apprentices. To graduate to Adept level, one must complete each task."

The students stirred under their skin. All of them wanted to move up to Adept level, the next level of their Mage schooling.

"This trial consists of four tasks. These tasks shall test every aspect of each of you: the mental, the physical, the emotional, the energetic and the spiritual. To move up the tier of Mages you must pass each test. Now, I shall warn you, these will be no easy tasks. Study and practice with vigilance for the next year as these tasks take place."

Mathius and Daniel looked very excited, their broad shoulders puffing at the excitement to show off.

"The first task shall be a test of mental discipline. You say you are tired of milk and oats, Mathius? Well, you will wish you had some after I say what this task is. Each student shall headstand on top of their own log for two days, without food, water or sleep. A Mage shall be strong internally and externally. This task shall represent and test our ground chakra, our will to survive."

Mathius laughed hearing the description of the task Macaro had set forth. "What's the purpose of this?" he asked with a hint of mockery.

"Meditation," was all Macaro said to answer.

The group of students walked forth silently, each picking a log to headstand on. Yuri chose to be beside Marius.

Marius himself was beyond nervous, he hadn't expected this earlier when they hiked to the spot, he thought they would be training or something along the lines of that. But two days on a log?

Who the hell designed this? He found himself thinking. As he approached the log he'd chosen, his stomach growled.

"Don't worry, Yuri, no mind, no mind." Marius chanted to Yuri mainly to calm himself.

"I hate when you say that," Yuri growled as he kicked dirt up at Marius. As children Yuri would often say such remarks before fights and training, and others had grown to mock him for it, mainly Marius.

"This is shit," was all Yuri had to say about the task at hand. Obviously they both felt similar about this task.

Each student climbed up their respective logs, placing their heads on top of the log. From here they pressed their legs up into the air, arms at their sides, heads balanced on the logs.

"In two days, following sunrise, I shall return. Breath peace, my children."

Elder Macaro turned his back towards them and started back down the trail. Soon his footsteps were no longer audible. Only the susurrus of distant waves crashing into the high cliffs could be heard. All was silent. The first task had begun.

The task was meant to test each student's will to live and their attentiveness to survive. The first task was designed to bring each student into an almost death-like state, caused by a lack of food, water and sleep. Marius guessed this was why Macaro had given them naught to eat the night prior.

The children didn't know but Elder Macaro had looked back as he walked down the path back to the village. He disliked raising children under this path. He understood the path was meant to achieve enlightenment and mastery of self, but to leave kids behind to the possibility of death brought him close to tears. Not that this task itself would kill them, they'd simply fall, but the fact of what awaited them if they passed all four tasks... But it was their time now, they weren't little kids Macaro had to raise anymore, soon their wings would spread and they would fly. He loved each of his disciples as if they were his own children. Each one he knew and felt a different appreciation for. He feared to lose any of his students and thought about each of them as he returned to the village.

The eldest of the group, and the natural leader, was Mathius. Mathius was tall, reigning from Northern Thenus. Mathius wore a long, tied-back ponytail, and his hair was shaved at the sides of his head. Most students mocked him about his appreciation of aesthetics and the time he spent on his hair. Even Macaro thought it was silly. Among his classmates Mathius had the most skill in martial arts, being the strongest fighter among them, he studied diligently, but he believed himself to be greater than others because of his skill. His broad shoulders and thick build matched his mocking attitude, but Macaro knew it was sourced from insecurity of envy towards his superiors which clouded his vision. The Elder feared for Mathius, his yearning for greatness sometimes became his flaw. Ultimately his flaws came from his line of thinking, believing that his Elders were somehow greater than him.

Second was Clive, twin brother to Cynthia. Matching Cynthia, Clive had olive skin, brown hair that fell to his shoulders in curly locks and deep green eyes. Clive had a short and stocky build, and what he lacked in physical strength he made up for in mental fortitude. The Elder thought of him as one of the most cunning students of the group. Most days Clive spent his time alone reading in the library above the main hall, studying the beastiaries, manuals, and maps. Macaro had no fear that Clive would not make it.

Third there was the female of the group, Cynthia. She was Clive's younger sister. She had long dark hair cut at shoulder blade length, short, and lean she was. Cynthia was one of the Mages who seemed unconnected to the path; she had high levels of qi but was also unable to control it. Elder Macaro worried that she would not survive the Trial of Apprentices. Maybe it was from the fact she was among one of the only females in her group of students that caused her to feel disconnected to her home. Thinking of Cynthia made Macaro think of times long ago, "it's much harder to steal a man's daughter than it is their son." As well females tended not to take well to the path of a Mage, their bodies tended to be more sensitive to qi and martial arts. But nonetheless Cynthia had accompanied Clive when he was taken. Together they were almost like a package.

Daniel came after Clive and Cynthia in age. The Elder could best describe Daniel as a young wolf in a pack; he was always trying to get ahead of the pack. Initially Daniel didn't respond well to training when he was a young child, but through perseverance he climbed his way to become one of Macaro's top students. His magic abilities were focused and his martial art techniques were always true to form. His short black hair, strong features and broad nose reminded Macaro of his father who had passed away a long time before. Daniel was always seen to be following Mathius.

Fourth in age, Yuri was the cunning but rebellious kid. Hard to give orders to and even harder to get to sit down, Yuri was one of the Elder's least favourite apprentices. Though the Elder thought Yuri was one of the most powerful Mages of his class, his fiery nature always put him at odds with Macaro. He had deep brown eyes and an olive complexion. Yuri was tall, a couple inches above Marius' height. Yuri and Marius were the best of friends, they could not even remember the start of their relationship as they were both raised from an early age at Highwash. The Elder worried for Yuri, his uncontrollable qi was thought to bring his demise.

Then there was Reggard. Reggard was another powerful Mage, just with untapped abilities. Though quiet and soft spoken, Reggard was thought to be the most powerful Mage in the group. He stood out from the group the most, not just because of his outward personality and his constant desire to joke, but as well as his looks. He had blonde hair that fell in stringy locks on his head, and a stubbly blonde beard to match.

The youngest of the group was Marius. The Elder was most interested in Marius. He was one of the youngest apprentices ever to be put in the Trial of Apprentices. Though Marius did not lack qi, willpower or strength. The Elder worried if Marius would even be able to survive the tasks. Even much older, and stronger apprentices had lost their lives to the Trials.

The Elder shook his head to shake the thoughts of doubt about his students. He hated losing apprentices, worse off losing ones he thought not ready for the Trial.

"Well shit, huh?" Mathius joked after the last whispers of Macaro's footsteps disappeared into silence.

The class laughed, but again they fell into an eerie quietness. And there Marius stood, not on his feet but upon his head. All seven of them, their heads stacked upon tall logs. Only thirty minutes had passed since Elder Macaro left them alone when Marius finally realized the intensity it would require to overcome this challenge. Two days he would have to hold this headstand upon a teetering log.

A great fear channelled in Marius. Closing his eyes, he focused on his breath and the qi moving up and down his spine. Marius tuned his attention outward, he could hear small birds humming, the wind softly moaning against dry grass, the distant crash of waves, the beating sun on his chest, his classmates breathing in front and around him. Everything was still. He had chosen the most western facing log, the rising eastern sun was blazing into his face.

Marius thought about the sun—called Sol by Mages—and about what kind of being was immersed inside of it. The sun with its unwavering will, intense heat and its purity, that which lights the world, that in which bears life. What type of being could possess such power?

Mages follow an angelic path of spirituality and magic. The Mages of Highwash believe that magnificent angels exist in the outer plane, in the nonphysical world, or as commoners call it "space." To them the sun is an omega being; a being beyond comprehension, that which is the source of all life and qi. The sun is said to exist and not exist at the same time. That duality is said to create the immense energy of the sun. The sun is said to be the creator of this world, that the world is all the sun, that with the sun's thought we exist and that death is just rhythmic patterns of the sun's thought. The Angelic path is the path of a Mage, which he is taught to follow all his life.

The sun peaked high in the sky, it had reached noon of the first day. The heat of the day had finally reached its peak and it had been hours since Macaro had left the students to hold headstand. Each one of them held strong, only with slight quivering in their breath at odd times. Marius would find himself lost in thought, thinking about the sun, his classmates, these trials and breakfast. It was only the first day and he was doubtful he could make it to nightfall, and what about sleep? Once doubt would creep in, Marius would go back to focusing on his breath.

Eventually Marius' legs went numb, all the blood descended into his heart and head. The air crisped as the day went on, the sun drying out the shrubbery and plant life. The sun descended slowly around Marius' body. By sunset Marius was worn. He could not feel his feet, his head was aching and his whole body was trembling. At this point all Marius could do was tune his attention inward. He would sometimes peer out his eyelids to see his fellow students; they seemed to be trembling as well. For the last time, Marius peered his eyes open, viewing the black sky opposite of the setting sun. He closed his eyes and drifted off again; his body soon became cold with the coming of night.

Mayura. The internal void. The opposite dimension of space. Space is outer and expansive while the void is inward and compressive. Using the void was a style of meditation Mages of Highwash used to endure situations which would normally kill a human body. This style of meditation involved the user to drift their attention into the body and the mind, which is an endless void of thought and consciousness. Tuning the mind into the body distorts the mind's perception of the body, so any physical trauma may not be perceived by the body as the mind is attuned to lower levels of consciousness than physical reality.

The cold of night grew further on. Stars lit the night sky and the mountains to the east could be seen as a black silhouette against the night sky lit up by the stars and moon. The seven of them would not of been able to see the view of the mountains from their alcove in the high grass.

For Marius, reality was already growing distant; his body becoming fatigued and worn from the opposite flow of blood. Clive started to sway passing into sleep.

"Clive, don't fall," Cynthia whispered as she stood next to him. "Clive!"

Clive came to attention; a thanks could be heard from under his breath.

The night carried on into the dawn. Each student growing more cold and weary before a trickle of sunlight peeked over the eastern mountains.

Marius was very tired, every moment he could feel himself swaying. Lack of sleep, thirst and hunger he could deal with, but the ache in his body from being in headstand for almost twenty-four hours was becoming unbearable. Each student looked as if they were suffering a great trauma.

The first day had passed and each student was still standing strong, none had fallen. The point of this task was to test each disciple's ability to turn their mind inward. The first day was intended as a prequel to the second day, where the real test would occur.

Now, with each student weary and burnt, their mental limits were about to be tested.

Marius could feel an ache emanating from his head all the way up to his feet. With each breath he took the pain intensified. His feet felt cold and numb, along with a sensation of featherweight.

The morning sun rose over the mountainous horizon. The wind grew from the shift of heat. The light slowly started to spill over the earth, piercing Marius' eyes. Closing his eyes in response to the sun's light, Marius drifted inwards. The light sensation continued growing in his feet, it grew when he closed his eyes, the feeling spreading down into his legs.

Marius noticed his senses increasing, he could hear everything, the birds waking up, the waves against cliffs, the wind against the trees, insects crawling. But more particularly, he could hear each of his friends' breath and the pulsating of their hearts. The more he focused into the pain, the more his sensations grew. His own heart rate began to slow. He could feel the pulse beat slower each passing minute. The pain from his head would shoot into his nerves from his neck all the way down his spine. He could no longer feel his feet.

Marius started to wonder about Yuri, he could hear Yuri's breath and heart, but he wondered much more than that of his vital signs. How was Yuri holding up? Once his mind slipped the pain would increase, the sharp, lightening-like pains would shoot into every nerve, leading to him starting to fall but catching himself with his arm on the log. Repositioning himself, Marius focused on his breath, again aware of his heightened sensations.

The pain continued to grow until it started to consume Marius' body. He could feel every cell in his body vibrating and pulsing, like a rhythm or a hum, a slow, steady hum. He could feel his nerve cells vibrate as high-energy freeways vibrating at the highest frequencies in his body. His muscles could be felt as long vibrating bands; his bones, the lowest of frequencies, humming ever so deeply. His organs each felt synchronized in their rhythm, humming together in a harmonious tune.

The pain began to turn into a feeling of immense awareness. Soon the feeling grew outside of Marius' body. It started as what he thought was his skin burning, but soon it expanded ever outward, noticing this Marius realized it was the air molecules vibrating at an extremely high frequency. Lost in these sensations, Marius began to move beyond time and thought. The ever-expanding air took him far into the sky, feeling the slow empty void of space, seeing the distant stars, tiny dots illuminating space and the universe, yet up close the most immense beings to exist.

That is the irony of life: the non-duality of all things. What appears to be small is actually large. And what appears to be large, as in a mountain or the ocean, is actually very small. What was pain at first to Marius, slowly, with a change of mind and different perspective, became a pleasure.

The slow rising sun rose again over the horizon, this time poking Elder Macaro in the eyes as he practiced horse stance over the ridge above the towering cliffs that led into the ocean's abyss. With a gentle eagerness, Macaro stood up and headed for his students. The two days had passed and he wondered about his disciples.

Step after step Macaro led himself back to the village and through it, back to the trail which led to the standing logs. As he came to the clearing Macaro let out a sigh of relief. All of his students remained in headstand, none, to his knowledge, had fallen, and none had died from exhaustion. His students had passed the first task.

Aware of their Elder's arrival, the students jumped down off their logs. Reggard rubbed the top of his head, spreading his hands through his tough blonde hair. Clive and Cynthia were exhausted and not much of a word came out of their mouths. Mathius acted as if the task had been a breeze.

"The first task all of you have endured."

A World Beyond Our Own

Just as soon as the Elder began to congratulate them, he noticed in his peripheral vision that one student had not come down. The Elder turned his body towards Marius still standing on the log, his head on the log, his legs floating high, a gentle smile across his face.

Amazed the Elder walked over mumbling, "Of course.".

"Marius, you may come down now." The Elder spoke again.

Marius' eyes slowly opened revealing a glow in them similar to his smile.

"It's over? Did we end early? I thought we were doing two days?" Marius asked as he flipped off the log.

Again the Elder's eyes lit with surprise. He had taught many students through out his years, some had even failed, unable to endure the task, but for a student as young as Marius to have completed the task, while reaching "Mayura," the internal void, was quite remarkable. The Elder knew Marius was unaware of the significance of this so he said little more about it.

"It has been two days, Marius, you should mind paying more attention if you're unaware of such," replied the Elder.

Though the Elder's answer was a lie and untrue with his thoughts, he felt as if Marius should not know of what happened until he had been separated from the group.

Marius continued to smile and moved over to stand beside Yuri. Yuri looked at him with amusement. The students hushed as the Elder began to speak again.

"I'm impressed. You all completed the first task. I've never had a class where all the students got through it. Now come," Macaro said while gesturing his students to walk with him. "The last thing you all need is another lecture from me this moment. Come, come, let's get some food and discuss matters."

The Elder turned and started down the trail, his students following. Each one stumbled through the rocks, tired and worn. The Elder brought them into the village centre and into the town hall.

The great wooden door that led into the tower pushed open, and through they went.

Inside the first floor of the Highwash hall was a large circular room with steps down into a round, flat level at a lower elevation than where they had entered. The room was dimly illuminated by candles placed all over the floor, and some candles hung from metal chalices. This is where the Archmage would come to meditate at night.

The Elder walked down the steps hands folded behind his back, span and sat down cross-legged on the floor in the centre of the room. His students followed him but instead sat on the higher steps around him.

Once the students had settled a middle-aged woman with deep brown hair came out with platters and served all the students bread and warm milk.

The Elder piped up with conviction. "Now everyone, confident and collected we may be, after the first task we must not lose our diligence. Each task shall be a surprise, each shall be more challenging than the last, each shall test our limits more than we can imagine. We shall train for these tasks as well. Starting tomorrow we will learn new elemental magic to use. That is all I shall say for the second task. Now, before I let you guys leave to rest, the Archmage would like introduce himself to all of you."

Marius perked up in interest. The Archmage was Highwash's hidden gem; Nathaniel was his name. The young apprentices had never met the Archmage. For the past twenty years or so, Nathaniel had been preoccupied with his studies, so he was rarely in attendance and never in Highwash, so an excitement brewed among the students.

A wooden door opened up opposite of the door they'd entered, and out came a large, robed man, with slicked back black hair curled down his head, and a thick beard hung on his face. Immediately his presence filled the room. Marius instantly recognized the man as Ralis, another Elder who taught at Highwash. Though he himself was often not in Highwash. Elder Macaro stood up, a puzzled look upon his face, the man began to trot down the steps while Macaro started upwards meeting him halfway.

The man's low voice could be heard. "Nathaniel hasn't returned."

"That's not a good sign," replied the Elder in a more hushed voice.

"The western mountain range is where he had been looking, I'll try to find him there. There's notes spread in his chambers."

Suddenly Ralis gazed at the students. Marius could tell he realized everyone could hear him.

"No good can come from this. I'll head out tonight, I just need to muster my horse and gear," Ralis said changing the course of the conversation, now alert of the students' budding ears.

"Thank you Ralis."

The man turned and started back for the door he came through, and Elder Macaro turned towards his students, "Well I guess we are not meeting the Archmage today. Alright, you may all go to the dining house, I'm sure you are all hungry and that little loaf didn't fill you much, so give Mirane a visit, she shall know I have sent you."

They all stood up and started to leave, but, before Marius could start for the door out, the Elder asked for him.

"Marius may I see you?"

"Yes."

"I would like to have a word with you later, come by my quarters after you eat."

Marius was hesitant to answer and only responded with a slight nod.

"Alright, I'll be seeing you, go now go with your friends." The Elder finished and patted Marius on the back leaving Marius by himself.

A candle in the corner blew out. Marius left the hall and caught up to Yuri and the group who was closing in on Mirane's dining house.

"What did Elder want?" Yuri asked.

"I don't know, he didn't say in particular. He just said he wanted to talk to me after I eat."

"Now that's weird," Yuri snarked.

The group approached a large, round, wooden house about twenty yards from the main hall, they swung the door open, and a long single table with food and drink was set for them.

Marius' mouth dropped. There were platters of cooked eggs, bread, berries, apples, beets, carrots and a couple pitchers of wine.

Eagerly they started eating and drinking. Mathius, holding a wine pitcher, got up from his seat.

"Be merry today my friends! This all might be our last good feast!"

"Aye!" chanted the rest, and Mathius poured himself a glass of wine and started to drink it with wine pouring down his face.

A feast like this did not come often, Marius thought to himself as he grabbed a plate of boiled eggs. Let alone the dining hall empty of the other students so Macaro's class may enjoy.

The group continued on with their merry feast. The majority of them all caught in eating and drinking. Then came the dancing, first it started with Cynthia, grabbing Clive out from his seat bringing him to dance. Then soon Reggard and Mathius joined in. Marius and Yuri instead were locked in a drunk conversation.

"What do you think the Elder could want from you? You weren't that much of a smartass when you stayed on the log," Yuri exclaimed. "And what was with Ralis, barging in like that? They got me all excited to finally meet the man himself, Nathaniel. Nope! In comes his lesser." Yuri continued on without pausing to receive an answer to the first question.

"I did not stay on the log on purpose, I honestly didn't know he was there," Marius said as he grabbed for another glass of wine.

"And to inquire further, what about the Archmage? To say he was going to be introduced to just whip that from under our noses!" Yuri continued on, his voice raising. "Well, I at least say we should find out where Ralis is going. I would like to receive my honour of meeting the Archmage!"

"I would rather not stalk an Elder deep into the woods late at night, Yuri," Marius said, looking at Yuri with a slight look of disbelief.

"You're being a baby. C'mon, lets sleep now and get back by early morning for lesson. Actually, I don't care if you come, I'm going. Either meet me by our oak tree at sunset or I'll see you tomorrow."

"In your drunk reverie you create the wildest of plans, you know that?" Marius said to Yuri as he grabbed another apple off a platter.

Yuri started up, standing, he guzzled the last few bits of wine in his glass.

"You're actually going?" Marius asked with a mocking laugh.

"Of course, I wouldn't speak of it for naught."

"Alone? You know Macaro would kick your arse if he caught you?" Marius said spilling some of his wine in laughter. "Alright, alright. I might come. I know nothing I can say will persuade you not to go. Forcing me to come you may be, but I'm not a fool to let you get killed by Ralis."

Yuri smiled, wine dripping down his neck, he waved goodbye to his fellow classmates explaining how he was tired and headed out the door. All the while Mathius laughed at him for being a baby. Marius frowned knowing it would be much harder for him to leave now for the same reason.

"Sitting alone?" Cynthia, Clive's sister came over to Marius and took a seat beside him. The noise of their friends echoed in the background. "Why did Yuri leave? Unlike him, usually he's the one to stay and drink." She chuckled.

"He left to sleep, that idiot, he wants to follow Ralis after dark," Marius said, grabbing another sip of wine.

"Well, you better go with him!" she said as a huge smile appeared on her face. "Now, c'mon, get up and dance! I didn't come over here for no reason."

Then Marius found himself getting dragged by the arm by Cynthia into the side of the room where his friends were dancing. Reggard's soft angelic voice rang through the hall as his fellow students danced to his voice.

From the stars the world was born
Elements creating all that exists
From the mountains, to the trees, to the air that we breathe
From the blazing sun, the waters run from river to sea

Fire burns like passion yearns and anger churns
Water flows like a song from the heart and rushes
 great wrath destroying all in its path
Earth roots like the deep rhythmic sound of feet hitting the ground
 and rumbles and grumbles trying to hold itself down
Air floats freely like a passing thought and can blow with
 great power making even the bravest cower

Beasts and man roam the land feasting off the world itself
We fight for life, we have will to survive together we will thrive
We are no assassins but warriors of compassion
We train until we feel the pain of our fists get-
 ting sore for fear we run into a manticore
But for now we will forget about our stances
 and have some fun with dances

"Come on, Reggard! Can't you think of anything better?" shouted Mathius, laughing as he drank some more wine.

"Show me your musical genius then, Mathius!" Reggard countered, grinning.

Talun is smelly and queer
He is a fat old fart
The only lady he's ever had is a mare

"Oh, that's just mean, and it didn't even rhyme!" Cynthia exclaimed.

Mathius snickered and everyone laughed as they drank and continued to dance.

Hours passed until it reached midafternoon, and, slowly, the food and wine disappeared off the table. The dancing had calmed down and everyone was enjoying the last bit of remaining food.

Thinking of Yuri, Marius tried to think of a way to exit. *I must leave now*, he thought, no... that didn't sound good. Marius found himself saying the same line as Yuri to the group finishing with, "I'll see you all tomorrow!"

No one seemed to notice that Yuri had said the same thing a while ago. Cynthia, Clive and Reggard wished Marius a good evening, while Mathius and Daniel gave him half-hearted looks of dissent, wishing the party would continue longer.

Drunk and full, Marius stumbled out from the dining house. He remembered he had to visit Macaro, so he started off towards the Elder's house. Marius had known Macaro since his earliest memories, but he had never ventured into his house. A curiosity to see how the Elder lived grew inside him.

Marius approached the Elder's house; it was similar in design and shape as all the other houses in Highwash. A tall wooden door marked the entrance, while the house was made of wood and nails. While the Mages at Highwash had advanced magic and study, their scientific and engineering systems were very rudimentary.

A few knocks later, and Elder Macaro swung the door open greeting Marius with a smile.

"Marius, my dear boy, I thought you would have stayed longer with your friends, the chance to feast as such won't come for a many of moon cycles," the Elder chuckled at the end of his sentence, gesturing Marius to come inside.

His house felt unique but looked nothing unique, it was one floor with a small sleeping cot clung to the wall, a few padded cushions on the floor to sit on, and in the corner a shrine containing a few flower petals and a beaded necklace, a lone window opposite to the door, and a rickety-looking chair placed for one to sit on and gaze out such window.

"Please sit down," the Elder said, again gesturing Marius to make a motion. Marius sat cross-legged on one of the cushions and the Elder sat on his cot staring deeply into Marius' eyes.

"Now you must be wondering why I brought you here to talk. Perhaps you know?" He raised his hand slightly, signalling Marius out of shyness and to speak.

"No, I don't know."

"You remember all my lectures on Mayura?"

"Yes, Elder, of course," Marius answered, still in great confusion; being drunk did not help the matter.

"How did you feel during the first task?" the Elder asked again, changing his line of questioning.

"Good, well, I mean it was obviously a challenge, but I felt I handled it well, do you think so? I didn't mean to insult you if that's why you brought me here, I honestly did not know you had arrived!" Marius rebutted quickly.

"No, no, you did not insult me, Marius, just the opposite, in fact, you have opened my eyes to a hidden talent inside you. You obviously understood my lesson on Mayura, many don't."

The Elder stood up and gazed out his window, "It's been a long time since someone as young as you has been able to reach Mayura."

"Then why were you angry at that moment?" Marius said cutting off his Elder.

"Angry, ha. My dear, Marius, rash I may have reacted, but in all sincerity I was covering my surprise from you. You are young, Marius, do not try to compete with the older children, do not get lost in competition, stay on your path and all your strength shall come, do not force yourself to grow, but allow yourself to flourish. I fear for all my students, the tasks are not easy, definitely not easy for someone young such as you."

The Elder walked over to where Marius was sitting, and sat down in front of him on his knees and placed his hand on Marius' shoulder. "Do not take me wrong, I have much confidence in you. Train valiantly, do not let pride get in your way, follow your heart, and, most of all, protect your friends."

The Elder stood up. "You may leave."

Marius got up and started for the door, but before leaving he turned to his Elder and said, "Thank you."

II

Marius awoke in his tiny wooden house, still slightly drunk and very full. Tired, and sighing as he was, he still got up. He slipped on his leather sandals and headed outside.

It was evening, the stars could be seen over on the eastern edge by the mountains while the western sea was blanketed by an orange hue. Regretting his decision of agreeing with Yuri, he headed for the oak tree he and Yuri played around when they were younger. It was on the eastern border of town, and Marius had to put quite an effort to be unseen. Stepping with a silent swiftness, Marius' Mage skills kicked in. Dark like a shadow, Marius skirted across town.

"Just in time, Ralis is about to leave," Yuri whispered in a low voice as Marius approached the oak tree.

"Why is he leaving at night? And he said he was headed for the eastern mountains, that's a week ride on horse? There's no chance we can follow him to his destination."

"Calm down, Marius, you over think. I want to catch his horse's scent and follow him for a few hours to see his trail."

"For what use? Just to get in trouble?"

"Ever heard of the word 'curiosity?' This is obviously much bigger than we think."

"Alright, I'll follow you for a bit, Yuri, but I must come back to village before sunrise. I'd rather not miss Macaro's lessons."

Yuri and Marius headed off into the east away from the village trying to catch where Ralis would be departing from. The evening glare diminished further, the blackened veil of night covered their movement. They headed for the most likely place Ralis would be departing from, the stables out east of the village by the farms, but through fields they would have to tread. The main road could not be taken, as they would be seen too easily. They knew little of Ralis and they knew only so much of the forest. Their lack of knowledge made Marius grow uneasy as they treaded through thick fields of high grass, around the odd trees that grew every so often.

As they approached the road nearest the stable they kept cover in the grass.

"Let's wait here, see if we can catch him leaving," Yuri whispered.

"And what shall we do if he had left? Not like we know which horse or which direction," Marius replied back.

"Shh, do you see that?" Yuri commanded, placing his hand on Marius' chest.

In the distance was a small elderly man leading a great black horse out of the stable with a small rucksack attached to its saddle, he was holding a lantern which had caught Marius' and Yuri's attention. The man continued to lead the horse out of the stable but the horse seemed to refuse leaving. They could hear the old man bickering to the steed.

"C'mon, you stubborn mule! By fuck sakes!"

"He is no mule, Talun, just a bit finicky with the idea of leaving you," Ralis spoke as he appeared out of nowhere and chuckled at the man's frustration with his horse. "Thank you, Talun, I wish you a goodnight."

Ralis then stepped up onto the horse, adjusted himself, and grabbed the reins. The horse began to trot off. Talun the old man stepped back inside looking slightly embarrassed.

"That was our cue, lets go!"

And before Marius had a say Yuri was running through the field, running fast but silent, parallel with the road. Marius, disgruntled, ran after him in the same style. Already Ralis' horse had picked up speed, and Marius and Yuri were losing distance, fast. Soon the road forked, forcing them to leave the cover of the field and into the road to check Ralis' horse's tracks.

Yuri and Marius eyed the ground. There were many footprints of different kinds, but their trained eyes could catch the difference between the freshest horse prints and the oldest, and clearly they could see Ralis was headed up the northeast road.

Again Marius and Yuri started running off into the fields, which were now becoming thicker and untamed with more saplings and trees poking out of the ground.

Of all the warriors across the land, Mages were considered the deadliest, but not just because of their skill in combat or usage of magic and elements. A Mage's versatility is the reason of their infamy. Not only are Mages trained to fight and taught the ways of magic, they are also taught the ways of stealth. The deadliest foe to a Mage was himself—and not just metaphorically; the power Mages wield could be a source of compassion and power, or a source of destruction and force. That was why much importance was placed on the angelic path.

At Highwash, Mages followed an angelic path, a path that followed principles of peace, compassion, love, honesty, discipline and virtue. But it wasn't to be assumed all Mages across the world followed such paths. As for Marius and Yuri, they followed the path like their fellow classmates with a blistering dedication.

The sky twinkled with waves of blue stars, and white auroras overhead as Marius and Yuri continued to follow the road.

"Yuri! Let's get out of this field onto the road, there's no risk of being spotted this far from the village, we're wasting the night in these fields." Marius shouted to Yuri ahead of him.

"Would you quiet your arse? We can still be heard!" Yuri said as he headed towards Marius annoyed but nevertheless agreeing with him.

But just as they turned to towards the road, Marius felt a warm, wet feeling come over his right foot.

"Blech! What is this shit?" Marius said too loudly once again.

"Quiet your arse, I said! Probably just some horse dung or some other animal's excretion."

Marius bent over trying to wipe off the vile substance he had stood in.

"Yuri, produce a flame so we can see what this is."

"Why? So Ralis can spot us out? Oh, maybe to start a wildfire in this grass? It's shit, Marius, get over it."

"Stop being a smartass! This shit isn't coming off my foot as easily as some shit would."

First a spark popped out of Yuri's hand, then in the palm of his hand a ball of fire appeared. Yuri's whole figure lit up. Looking down to see what was on Marius foot, he jumped. It wasn't shit that Marius had stood in, but a pile of decaying flesh obviously from some manner of beast's feast.

"Aaah, damn, even grosser," Marius exclaimed as a stream of water emerged out his hand to wash the gross goo off.

"What the hell could've caused that?" Yuri asked as he began to bend over and investigate the corpse. If anything could be made out from what the giant pile of decaying matter was, it would sort of seem like a donkey.

"Never mind that, this is a mess, we won't get anything out of this and we've wasted plenty of time, let's get going." Marius jumped to his feet and got back on the northeast road.

Marius and Yuri continued on. The dry road had barely an indent of Ralis' horse, and if anything looked good it was too mixed up in older prints to make out a direction Ralis could be headed.

"Nothing. I can barely make out any prints," Yuri said, beginning to get frustrated scouring the ground looking for any sign of fresh prints.

"Let's continue forward for another hour. If we see no signs, let's head back. He must have known he was being followed," Marius said.

The two of them continued running on the road. The trail grew harsher with larger stones appearing on it and the bush began to creep from the sides onto the road. Branches of tall willow trees enveloped the road. Soon another fork appeared in the road.

"Which way?" Yuri asked Marius.

"I thought you were leading? Well, I know the road that heads east from here heads back to ocean, this northern road heads to the Wild Woods, but that's a week's hike from here. Let's turn back Yuri, nothi—"

A large, sharp shriek pierced the silence of the night, interrupting Marius.

"What was that?" Yuri asked, bending his knees, anticipating danger.

"I've never heard a noise like that, not any animal or beast I can recognize," answered Marius.

The large shriek came again; this time a horse could be heard shrieking as well.

"No time to wait to see—let's go!" Marius said as he charged off down the northern road.

Yuri followed right behind.

The night was silent again, and as the two of them ran on no screech was heard and nothing was seen.

"Wait, what's that there?" Marius stopped running and pointed to the side of the road.

There on its side was a saddle, and attached a leather rucksack. The bushes beside the saddle were ripped open leading a hole into the bush off road.

"Come on, we will see the prints off road!" Marius ran forward into the bush scanning relentlessly his eyes darting, scanning every nook and cranny, his ears deepening their sense for noise. He could hear ruffling, a man struggling, something big stepping.

"C'mon, Yuri! Someone's in danger!" Marius yelled as he sprinted through the bush, webs of branches and leaves tangled at his feet slowing him down.

Following the damage and clearing in the bush, they were led to a little clearing among the willows and bramble. Directly in front of the clearing was the horse Ralis had rode off on and in the clearing was Ralis, crouched low, walking in a circle around the clearing. Opposite to Ralis was a giant, winged beast, it walked on all four feet, wings above its massive shoulders, its face was long and disgusting, its mouth revealed large sets of sharp teeth. Its grey skin was coated in waxy scales, its feet bore huge talons like an eagle, its wings were web-like, like a bat. Its tail was long and spread off into three others with sharp talons on the end of each.

Ralis looked injured, his right hand pressed against his stomach.

Marius and Yuri, still untrained to kill beasts, jumped into the fray without hesitation. The beast, surprised by the pre-emptive strike from two foes he had not been aware of, stalled backwards. Marius shot flames out his hands, scalding the side of the beast, while Yuri ran in front of the beast to grab its attention.

The beast swung its tail wildly at Marius, almost hitting him across the face, all the while Yuri ducked under the thrashing claws, smacking the beast under its chin with a high, roundhouse kick. The beast span aggressively, spreading its huge wings, smacking Yuri in the chest and knocking him onto the ground.

Marius ducked under the wings, predicting such a move from the monster. But the monster was fast, and even though Marius was quick he was not yet quick enough for such a beast; its large talons ripped into Marius' right leg. Marius fell onto the ground, a searing pain in his leg.

Ralis jumped in out of nowhere, his hand lit with energy as he smashed his lit fist into the beast's body. Ralis' blow knocked the beast on its side. The beast was up quickly, but so was Ralis ready. The beast swung at Ralis and, gracefully, the Mage moved out of the way.

Marius struggled to get up; he managed if he didn't put much weight onto his right leg. Ralis and Yuri continued to fight the beast.

At this point the beast had been ignoring Marius, as he seemed gravely injured, and now the beast's backside was facing Marius. Fire erupted from Marius' hands again, scorching the beast from behind. The beast screeched loudly, its high-pitched screech ripping through Marius' ears. Its tailed lashed out at Marius but he dodged each talon-like whip. The beast began to get exhausted from the constant attacks from its foes; its wings sagged down, its reflexes becoming worse and worse.

Lightening bolts ripped out of Ralis' hands, the beast yelped and jumped, almost preparing to flee, but, before it could, Ralis was in the air, his fist lit with energy before the heavy blow smashed the beast's head into the ground. The beast's feet wiggled and squirmed for a second before it became still, its breath silenced. Marius sat down tired and injured, Yuri came up beside him to check his wound.

"You two! Name yourselves now!" Ralis commanded, anger erupting from his voice.

"First tell us what that thing was, then we shall give you our names!" Yuri shouted back.

Lightening shot out of Ralis' hand and hit the ground away from where they were crouched. Ralis was obviously not in the mood for games.

"I am Marius, this here is Yuri. We are students of Elder Macaro." Marius spoke up interrupting Yuri before the situation grew worse.

"Then why are you out here trailing me? I sensed your presence following me long ago."

Neither boy spoke.

"Answer!"

Marius looked at Yuri, as this was all, of course, Yuri's idea. Yuri cleared his throat and began to speak.

"Well sir, my friend and I here were simply indulging in some endeavours to feed our curiosity."

Ralis did not look amused. Marius elbowed Yuri in the side.

"We are very sorry, my friend here wanted to see the Archmage very badly, I came with to make sure he caused no trouble. We shall be on our way back to Highwash, as I said, we are very sorry and should not have followed you out here." Marius gave Yuri a cold stare as he said this.

"Bahaha!" Ralis spat out as he laughed.

"What's so funny?" Yuri asked Ralis.

"My packhorse is dead, I need something to carry my gear. Or not something—now it's closer to two *someones* to carry my gear."

Marius and Yuri looked surprised and nervous. They both hoped the same thing: that Ralis did not mean what he just said.

"As punishment for your insubordination you shall come with me; you shall carry my gear and be my servants for the next two weeks as we hike northeast towards the Emeralties, the northeast mountains. Now, what would have taken me four days on horse, shall take us two weeks on foot."

"What about our lessons? And we are not the ones who killed your horse. In fact, I believe you owe us one for saving your life," Yuri spat back.

"Yes, you did not kill my horse, but you did not save my life. In fact, you've caused the death of a very beautiful manticore mother hunting for her nest. Before you two interrupted I had planned to bend its will and send it home, but that all changed when you two came charging out of the forest. I had to quickly put it down in order for you two not to get killed. So, I believe I owe you nothing. You shall serve me for now until we return to Highwash in a month's time. I shall send word to Macaro. And for your lessons, well, we shall have a lot of time so you shall learn on the journey."

Ralis whistled a soft tune and raised his arm; a crow flew down onto his hand gazing at Ralis, ready for an order. Ralis whispered something to the bird and it was off, flapping its wings, launching itself into the air. Then Ralis raised his left hand, an orange stream of light ran over his body and his own injury healed back to fresh, new skin. He then pushed his hand in Marius' direction and an orange ball of light was sent at Marius inducing the same light over Marius, miraculously healing his deep gash in his leg from the manticore's talon.

"Well, Yuri, you may go and grab my pack off the saddle that fell just outside the bushes, Marius, you are obviously good with fire, you will help me incinerate my horse."

Ralis and Marius stepped over to his horse; it had bled out from a huge wound in its side. Ralis crouched down beside the horse and started to pet its head. He than stood back up and flames sparked in both his hands. Marius readied his flames as well.

"I will miss that stallion," said Ralis before he immersed the horse's corpse in flames; Marius joined in as well. Flames absorbed the horse's body and by the time Yuri had got back with Ralis' pack the corpse was nothing but ash.

"We shall leave at once, continue on for another mile, then we shall take rest for the night, come now." Ralis started out of the woods for the road.

Yuri gave Marius a fearful look and the two of them followed Ralis. The three of them hiked of another hour in silence until they hit a clearing beside the road.

"Rest here." Ralis stopped in the clearing beside the trail and sat down, and then lay down on his back, the grass tickled his back through his shirt. "Set up my bed please." Ralis commanded them.

So Marius and Yuri opened Ralis' pack and took out a small, folded up leather mat. They unfolded it and Ralis lay down on it, and soon passed into sleep. Marius and Yuri sat further away from where Ralis slept, both without a bed, and not much food to nourish them.

"You idiot, now we will miss lessons and maybe even miss a task," Marius said as he gave a burning look at Yuri. Yuri didn't say much but just lay down on the grass.

The morning sun peeked over the eastern mountains. The morning was humid and damp. Marius lay still after the sun started to rise, waking him up. He slowly got up into a seated position, tuning to the environment around him. Yuri was still a sleep beside him; peace rimmed his face. The prairie fields that rimmed the road they had taken shelter on the night before softly swayed with the gentle breeze. Close to there makeshift camp, Ralis could be seen meditating in horse stance. His eyes opened once Marius had sat up.

"Up too late, up too late. Macaro must take it easy on you all. Both of you up, horse stand and build your qi until I prepare some food. From then we shall head out, we shall not break till sundown," Ralis said as he left horse stance and went to rummage through his gear.

Yuri, yawning, slowly sat up and went off into the bush to relieve himself. Marius started in horse stance and Yuri joined him soon after.

Twenty minutes swept by and soon Ralis called them over to have breakfast; it was nothing exciting either. As soon as they came over to where Ralis was seated he presented some pieces of bread he had of obviously ripped off a loaf he had packed and some wild berries he had just picked. Not a word was said over breakfast. The group soon gathered Ralis' gear, which took no time at all as neither Marius nor Yuri had packed anything. Starting off, they headed east towards the mountains again. Marius' mind quickly drifted towards the thought of water.

"Don't worry, I'm not an idiot, we shall reach a plentiful stream soon," Ralis said as he looked at Marius, obviously reading his mind. The sun crawled overhead and the day became drier and crisper as the summer's air cooked and baked the ground.

They reached the small stream, which was fed from the mountains by midday. Marius and Yuri eagerly gulped down a few mouthfuls of water with their hands while Ralis was patient and calm and filled up his canteen. It seemed as if his composure never changed. The three of them sat quietly on a dry rock bed beside the stream.

"What are we going to practice today?" Yuri directed his question at Ralis, breaking the silence.

"Not today, tonight we shall practice. You two are very dumb for following me out here. I've already received word from Macaro. You're lucky he is unlike me. I am strict with my students, I would not let them continue the tasks with such disobedience."

"I blame this kid!" Marius yelled as he kicked Yuri lightly in the leg. "I came so this kid didn't end up dead."

Yuri stood up, a furious look growing on his face. "All my fault! Weren't you even slightly curious? Or are you just dumb and don't think for yourself, obey, obey, obey, is all you think, Marius!"

Marius stood up in response. "I actually care about our path, Yuri! I get you don't like authority, I get you hate being told what to do. Look past yourself and onto the others who care for you! You could've got yourself killed, maybe by that manticore, maybe by Ralis."

Ralis sat quietly as the two of them bickered, listening with intent.

"You think of me as a baby, Marius! I'm older than you, stronger and faster! If you didn't want to come, you didn't have to! You probably didn't even consider my safety, only your hard on for Cynthia!"

"Enough!" Ralis piped up, though he sat motionless. "Enough of this stupid banter! You two are like crazed men in a whorehouse fighting for a fresh one! Yuri, being older doesn't count for anything, your friend obviously deeply cares for you if he risked his schooling at Highwash to come with you this way. The more I hear from you two the less I like you. So please shut up. Solve this like Mages do and come with me." Ralis got up and led them to the road close to stream.

"This shall be your first lesson with me. Marius and Yuri, you both are second level Mages. You should both understand how to manipulate matter, particularly air. So, Yuri, if you're stronger, I want you to hit Marius while he holds up a shield with air. If you are stronger than Marius, Yuri, you shall be able to break through his shield. If not you shall look like a moron."

And there stood Marius and Yuri across from each other on a dirt road. Marius stood in horse stance, a shield of air held in front of him. The shield wasn't visible but all three of them could sense its presence. Yuri stood cocked and ready.

"Now, Yuri, may you?" Ralis commanded. Yuri stepped his right foot forward leading with his fist heading straight for Marius' face.

BAM

A huge bang screamed through the air. Both Marius and Yuri were on the ground. Marius had blood coming out of his nose while Yuri held his hand groaning in pain as he rolled on the ground.

"You see, anger and pride can get us nowhere, you both get hurt in the long run. Stop your bantering. For Marius' sake I'll send word to Macaro to delay the second task until we arrive back at Highwash. Only for Marius' sake," Ralis said as he walked over to Marius who was sitting up holding his nose. Ralis held out a hand helping him up, then did the same for Yuri.

"Yuri, you are not to blame. Childishness and egotistic nature are natural and common in youth, especially young Mages."

"My hand, I can't move it, what happened?"

"Your hand is broken, Yuri."

Ten days passed and the trio kept hiking eastward. Mages, powerful and intrinsic, were still bound by the laws of physics. Mages, unfortunately, could not teleport, though whole lives had been spent dedicated to finding such a way, however, no Mage had yet been able to find a one. So the trio continued on.

The prairie field eventually lost its low elevation and started climbing upwards as they turned northward. The shrubbery of the flatlands slowly turned harsher and thicker, soft grass became thorny raspberry bushes, small thicket bushes became large ferns, and small willows became an abundance of thick pine and fir trees. The clear roadways became rough and unmaintained, the sides of the road being swallowed by bushes and grass. The forest always retakes the land.

As the road became unclear, Ralis led them forward. Ralis obviously had hiked the route before; his knowledge of the land was natural. Without much food or water, the trio had to survive on the land as all they had was Ralis' packed food and canteen for sustenance. The prairie field was an abundant source of food with many streams, wild berries and small mammals to feast on, but by the fourth day of hiking, as the trio hiked further northeast, the land became harsher. Streams of the prairies merged into larger, steeper, fast-running rivers. Though the rivers held salmon, the steep ravines down to white water rapids were too dangerous to tempt descending, so the trio was left to scavenge the forest.

"You can turn molecules from the earth and air into water, can't you, Ralis?" Asked Yuri, drudging Ralis' gear up the steep forest bank, sweat poured down his face even though the forest foliage blocked out much of the sunrays.

"I can."

"Well, let's get on with it. I refuse to carry this up this bank until I get some grub and some water to drink."

"Or we can continue hiking. Above this ridge there's a waterfall where a nice alcove of water has formed. We shall stop there."

When they finally hiked above the ridge, the boys' suspicions of Ralis' deep knowledge of the forest was confirmed. Exactly as stated there was a deep pool flooded by a waterfall which fell from a large rock cliff. Yuri quickly dropped Ralis' pack and slammed his head into the pond.

"Why couldn't you just make water then? It would save an enormous amount of time if we didn't stop every now and then to find water and food," Marius pried Ralis, finally getting over his fear of Ralis' intimidating presence.

Ralis gulped down a few mouthfuls of water from his canteen before he spoke. "Nature has a way of making such things much better."

Marius didn't continue on with his questioning.

All three of them sat there by the pond and munched on a loaf. Yuri talked most of the time, either questioning Ralis or stating his opinions about certain members of Highwash to Marius.

"Where exactly are we headed? These mountains stretch far from what I've seen from maps in the hall. How will we find the Archmage in here? It's nothing but ferns and trees."

"He obviously won't be hiding like a hermit in the woods. And if you paid any attention in geography you would note a key point of interest lies inside these Wild Woods. The Emeralties hold a massive site of ancient ruins. We know little of who dwelt there, all evidence seems to be swept away, though by analyzing the stones the ruins are built in we have estimated the ruins are about a hundred thousand years old. Nathaniel has taken quite an interest to these ruins of late. So we head there, and, with deductive reasoning, if by chance he is not there, well..." Ralis suddenly stopped speaking and did not resume but just gazed at the water, an intense focus could be seen on his face. Both Yuri and Marius looked at each other with faces of confusion silently agreeing not to question further.

The group gulped down a couple last mouthfuls of water, gathered their gear and headed out. The forest became more treacherous as they hiked on; the ground became unstable and loose, and stones and dirt tumbled down the slope, bashing into trees with each odd footstep. Even Ralis started to look somewhat exhausted.

"Night is coming, it will be unsafe to travel further. Stop here for the night." Ralis said as he looked around, scouting a soft mossy patch under a few fir trees, which looked cozy to rest on for the night.

The three of them rested in the pitch-dark forest. No light from stars could leak through the forest canopy. Marius could make out nothing in front of him. He could only make out his surroundings with his hearing. Yuri sat beside him munching on some loaf. Ralis was in front of him.

"Tonight we will cover more martial art techniques. This place serves perfectly. Today's lesson is about sensing an opponent's energy, not just in everyday life, but in a fight. If used effectively, one can predict any upcoming move. Only the most efficient Mages have mastered this technique. Through the first task you would've both sensed the vibrations of matter and life. Now, imagine if we could reach that state of meditation during a fight. Yes, I know, how? Danger is opposite of meditation, that, of course, is blatant; but without focus and attention a fight against any advanced Mage is a certain loss. Here is a perfect place to try to learn as one of our senses is out. I obviously can't see you both, and obviously you cannot see me. So, Marius, stand and try to hit me."

"I'll try, but I can't make out where you are."

"That is some of the challenge, yes."

Marius got up and looked for a feeling of Ralis' presence. He could hear Ralis breathing, but could not sense his exact location. Marius did not hesitate, he performed all the exact movements Macaro had taught him since he was a kid. Strike left, roadhouse kick right, hook kick, tornado kick, pirouette back, duck, dodge, strike right. But each hit Ralis dodged and parried with his arms. Even though Marius could not see Ralis' face, he knew a smirk was upon it.

"Now for my turn." Ralis suddenly struck out of nowhere, smacking Marius right across the temporal bone.

Marius tried every counter attack and dodge he knew but Ralis was there every time bashing him in a undefended zone. Soon Marius lay on the ground, bloody and bruised.

"Get up, and again," Ralis commanded, spreading an orange hue over Marius' beaten body healing his wounds. Surprise swept over Yuri's face, finally seeing the results of the tussle.

Marius stood, ready again.

"Hit me." Ralis commanded.

Again the same result, Marius, unable to break any of Ralis' parries. The same result happened when Marius was made to defend from Ralis' blows.

"This isn't a matter of skill or technique. I'm using the same level of martial arts as you. No matter, we will practice until you guys learn. We still have a couple nights before we reach the ruins."

The same deep orange light spread over Marius body. Ralis called over to Yuri.

"Get up, Yuri, your turn."

Elder Macaro looked out onto the setting sun. It burned the sky into a crimson red as the sun set in the west over the ocean. The jagged Emeralties could be seen as a black silhouette to the east. He sat cross-legged on the ground next to a fire near his house.

"Contemplation covers your face, Macaro, miss your students do you?" Mirane said as she approached. Her dark hair, tied back into many braids, bounced gently as she walked. A tight, neatly trimmed leather dress outlined her figure. At first Macaro did not respond. After much time he began.

"We are too strict at times, Mirane. I see these students, their children-like minds. Not knowing where or whom they come from. And then I think why do we raise such people any more? We've long hid from the Vatican." He stood up at this point and peered out into the distance sunset. "Much time has passed since we have come out here. I am starting to wonder if the Vatican is no longer looking for us and choosing bigger prey. So why such discipline to our children, as if we are training warriors? As if we continue to live in fear, trapped in chains of a cycle that cannot end? To not punish them would be contradictory to our way, but to what end of punishment? Truancy and abandonment is rectified with banishment. Where would they go? Out there into the world? Into the clutches of who knows? But that's the case with all apprentices, I guess. Still young kids, not well trained to defend themselves, but with potential—the best weapon."

He then looked at Mirane. She thought maybe he expected an answer, maybe he did not. What answer could she give? A cook at Highwash; an apprentice who never made it to Adept level—why was he asking her opinion?

She answered nevertheless. "I don't think you will have to punish them at all. I believe Ralis is acting on his own accord with the punishment. Assuming I know Ralis correctly."

Macaro chuckled slightly. "That is true. And if Ralis does get to where he is going. Who knows what Nathaniel may decree?"

They sat silently, both in thought. They both had known Yuri and Marius since they were little.

"And the Vatican, I have never seen or known. I live day-by-day, Macaro. You know this. Don't fear what is not here. A waste of energy, might I say. You should focus your attention on your current students."

Macaro put out the fire and went on his way thanking Mirane for the talk. Mirane just stood looking out in the distance.

The trek proved to be more treacherous than the young men imagined. Ralis did not seemed phased at times, but they lagged behind at many moments. The forest twisted and turned, every odd moment their path led to thick bushes and impassable fallen logs. The trees seemed to get larger and taller as they continued their hike through the Wild Woods.

Occasionally Ralis told them stories of many things about the Wild Woods. He spoke about the trees and the fauna, the way to move at night, stories about nights he had spent out in the forest, but most times he barely spoke.

At night they continued to train under Ralis' wing. They improved on their magical abilities, and Marius even parried a couple of Ralis attacks in the dark. And on the fourteenth day, as Ralis predicted, they arrived at a great gorge set between two massive jagged cliffs. Outlining the steep rock faces were tiny pine trees, which had weaved their way into survival. As they entered the gorge they approached a steep drop off into a dark cave. The hole was covered in a dry moss but the cave itself felt damp. They crouched down further to get a good look down into the pit.

"You're telling me he's in there?" Yuri asked in a sarcastic tone.

Ralis said nothing and raised his hand. A white light appeared in the palm of his held out hand. The white ball glowed bright and filled the cavity as it slowly glided across the cave. The cave was old and cavernous-looking and led to a great big door made of stone. Outlined and trimmed with great big stone columns was a stone door cracked open by which looked to be opened by a great force. Ralis jumped down into the pit, which was now illuminated by his Mage light. Yuri and Marius followed.

"When we enter here you are both to follow me and stay by my side. These catacombs have hardly been explored. So stay behind me and don't lose sight of me. Is that clear?"

Both the boys nodded.

Inside was nothing but blackness. The only light to be shown was from Ralis' Mage light, or Marius' flames that he would occasionally conjure. Though Ralis would bite his ear off every time he did so. Ralis sometimes would state he could sense living presence around. Twisting and turning through hallways, Ralis led them on. It was cold and damp and fear slowly crept down Marius' back. He had never been to such places before. The darkness caused him a great anxiety. After an amount of time unknown had passed, unknown because the trio no longer had the sun to track time they stopped to rest. Ralis let his light dim and soon all became black. The darkness, however, definitely did not shut Yuri up.

"Do you even know where we are?" Yuri said pointing his head in the direction he thought Ralis would be.

"Quiet, and speak softly, you idiot." Ralis said as he hushed him. "I have less than a clue to where we are, and the last thing I'd like to do is to illuminate this whole place to show everything here where we are. Things could dwell here that are much worse than a manticore. But I do know where Nathaniel is. He's here. I can sense him. That's what I've been following. He has clearly left signs, but the closer we get to him, the less I can sense him. Something even more powerful is covering his energy. So, please, by all means, just let me meditate and focus."

Yuri and Marius sat there quietly while Ralis meditated. They couldn't find the will in themselves to calm down and meditate. The place crawled with eeriness. Small noises of scratching and scuffling could be heard, but the noise was ever so slight, even with their improved hearing, they thought they still could be imagining such, soft noises.

Ralis soon commanded them to get up and depart. And then, after what felt like days' worth of hiking, the trio went on, the two boys stumbling down stairs or into what seemed to be massive columns. They soon came to what could be made out as a crypt. Tall cement caskets stood upwards. The only reason they could make out the details of the room was because candles sat lit in each corner of the room. In the middle of the room sat a man in cross-legged position. His long flocks of black hair were tied back into many braids. He looked tall and muscular, even though he was seated. He didn't flinch when they walked in, he sat frozen, his eyes gazed forward waiting, only he spoke.

"Ralis, a pleasure." Nathaniel's eyes darted past all three of them. When he stopped at Marius, Marius could feel his eyes being pierced by their gaze. "How impeccable your timing. And two boys, how you knew I do not know, but that is exactly what I needed." The man quickly sat up greeting all three of them in a very eccentric manner you would not expect from a Mage. "My, you must of read all those signs correctly to find me here. Why have you come? Has something happened back at Highwash? Or wait, did you coming looking for me, how long has it been since I departed?"

"Three months, Nathaniel. Exactly the same amount of time you said to go look for you. Did you intend to call me here? With all those obvious signs you left, plus the clues in your room you blatantly left it looked as if you were calling me here."

"No, no, just simply a safety measure. Were I to go insane here I'd at least have a well-enough Mage come and find me. Back-up plans, remember this, boys." Nathaniel raised his hand pointing his finger at both of them obviously joking. "But, Ralis, you did perfect, exactly what I needed is multiple people. Come, come, I'll show you all. Come, no time to hesitate now I've been pondering too much. And before I forget, boys, who are you?"

"I am Yuri and this is Marius, we are students of Macaro."

"And why did you bring these two bright young'uns, Ralis? Never mind, never mind. Let's be off now. C'mon."

Nathaniel led them down more twisting hallways. He cast many lights that floated above them all. Yuri and Marius felt way more relaxed in these ruins with the Archmage. His eccentric attitude they interpreted as confidence. His stride was long and swift. Everything about Nathaniel fuelled both Yuri and Marius' imagination about him. For both of them it was their first time ever meeting the Archmage.

The Archmage led them into large, long hallway that ended abruptly in a large chasm.

"You see, this chasm is obviously a trap, but also the only way forward I have found. Now, here is my idea. Why I need more than one person is quite simple: I just would like one of you," Nathaniel pointed at all three of them, "to jump down into the hole and see what lies further. I couldn't do this myself, as a trap a single person alone cannot escape. Actually I'll need you up here, Ralis, to help rescue if the need arises."

Ralis looked serious and tense since they had met up with Nathaniel. But only after Nathaniel had requested such a task of one of them did he speak out his mind.

"Elder, you wish to risk the lives of our students? For what? What could lie here in these ruins of such significance that one of our children should have to pay such a price for?"

"Ralis, always feeding your altruistic pride. What is magic without risk? What is science without endeavour? One viewpoint can be, yes, we are putting these children's lives at risk, but aren't we all at risk all the time? Death is inevitable, Ralis, of that I'm sure you are aware. So let's not here today cast the fear of death over our own students."

"Just because something is inevitable doesn't mean we should seek it."

"Well, what do you two think? Do you wish to explore? Do you wish to possibly be part of a tale of discovery that changed the world? Or would you, like Ralis, choose to rather fear initiative and action?" Nathaniel loomed over both Marius and Yuri, his once-eccentric attitude becoming intimidating.

Marius spoke firmly before Yuri could get a chance to say something stupid. "A couple questions before I jump down into anything. First, what could possibly lie down in there?"

"Possibly anything, maybe nothing. Highly likely to be something, not something good."

"That gave me nothing."

"Ask smarter questions, apprentice."

Marius thought for a second. "What do you know for certain about that pit?"

"A magical presence. That is all that is certain. I cannot be sure of what lies down there as the magical field distorts all other presences of energy."

"Secondly, what do you know of this place? I could hear things crawling and breathing earlier, obviously creatures den here. What is it?"

"That I do not know, not once have those creatures shown their face to me. I feel as if my presence provokes fear in them. Though, in all likelihood, they're probably large arachnids or insect-like crustaceans. Creatures like that avoid light and heat at all costs, both of which I emanate."

Nathaniel's face changed and he began to rant. "But these ruins I know much of. Many a times have I come here since my days as an Elder."

A face of shock appeared on Ralis' face as he suddenly interrupted. "What do you mean 'many a times'? This place has been off limits since…" Ralis suddenly went quiet, and then started again. "Since you became Archmage."

"Which then leads to my third question. You know there is a trap inside there, but you can't sense anything because of what's beyond. If that's true, then I am assuming you know of the trap because you have been in there. Assuming that, I would believe that you have been in there many times, and you placed all those clues to get people to follow you here to then enter the trap only for you to get what's on the other side?"

Silence always looms after such a question. Marius didn't know why he asked it, maybe it was because Ralis jumped in while he was asking questions, maybe it was hunger and thirst, or his lack of sleep causing irritability from the want to go home. He stood frozen waiting for answer he didn't want.

Ralis thought to himself a hundred different scenarios. Could Marius be right? Was Nathaniel, his mentor, truly attempting to gain power from the loss of another's life? It couldn't be true, he thought. It did make sense though. Nathaniel would be gone for long periods of time and would never describe his errands. This was also the first time he had ever left any clues to where he had headed. Of course all the Elders knew of this place's existence, but none assumed Nathaniel's business was to scour here for many moons while sealing it off to any other interested Mages.

"Your doubts of me are certainly justified, Marius. There is a trap in that pit. But I have not been in there. Never have I had the means to enter, because I cannot sense what lies in the tunnel, thus I would not enter. Now we have the means to explore further, and you would try to conspire against me. I am your Archmage, Marius, would I truly lead you down a terrible path? Whatever happens in there, Ralis and I will be there to counteract the trap."

Marius looked over to Yuri who stood idle. He looked anxious and excited but also covered in a gleam of fear. They stared into each other's eyes for what felt like a minute. Yuri nodded. Marius then looked back at Nathaniel.

"Fine we shall."

Marius and Yuri headed forward. Yuri gazed down into what looked like a long, dark tunnel. After further investigation, the floor of the hallway looked as if it was smashed down into the dark tunnel.

"Well, volunteer, you can go ahead first," Yuri said as he gave Marius a slight nudge forward, and they started climbing down broken cement slabs into the dark tunnel. The light dissipated and soon they were in darkness.

"I just didn't want to say no to the Archmage."

"Ha, even after accusing him like that!"

"I'm just very frustrated, Yuri, I want to go home. We have been travelling for two weeks, I thought finding the Archmage would be enough to turn back. But of course our journey continues."

Marius' sentence got cut off as he stumbled on broken concrete when they finally reached the tunnels floor, but he quickly regained his balance.

"Into darkness now, into void, where are we even headed here? And a trap? Well, our second test I guess it seems. I wonder what the class is learning anyways?"

Yuri almost tripped on another concrete stone. "Jeez, I can't see shit."

Fire lit in Yuri's hand, his face illuminated by the fire as he stood still staring at Marius.

"Marius, I'm sorry, alright. This was a mistake, we shouldn't have followed Ralis. I'm lucky we both didn't get slaughtered by the manticore. Thank you for following me and risking yourself for me. But now we're here, ok? Let's get this done, deal with this trap and get home."

They continued on for about five minutes using their conjured fire as a light to guide them.

"Do you hear that?" Marius whispered as he listened intently.

They both cut out their conjured fire. Blackness saturated their view. In the distance a slight crunching sound could be heard. They stopped walking forward, listening, anticipating any movement from whatever was there. But nothing was moving, only the slight crunching sound could be heard. They stepped forward silently and slowly, afraid to stumble in the darkness. They didn't dare conjure their fires. The crunching sound became rapid clicking and scuffling.

"Things are moving, to our left and to our right, we are surrounded," Marius whispered to Yuri.

"Has Macaro taught us any ways to light up this room? I don't recall and I can't cast Mage lights like what Ralis or Nathaniel cast," Yuri whispered as they both crouched down closer to each other.

"No, but we can conjure a firestorm if it comes to it. What do you think is around us? Is this the trap? I don't recall a lot from Macaro's beastiary lessons."

They both crouched, huddled together in the darkness. The clicking noise growing louder and clearer and ever more often, sometimes at rapid pulses. They were surrounded and they knew it.

A light hovered above Ralis' head while he stood there, focused on his hearing. The hallway was dim and nothing could be heard from the tunnel. Nathaniel paced back and forth rubbing his fingers against the wall.

"What did you send them into?" Ralis turned to Nathaniel. It sounded as if he'd wanted to ask that for a while. "It's been half an hour and not a noise has even come up that tunnel?"

"Do you not trust me, Ralis?"

"Trust is a matter of reassurance, which you have not assured me of. Many things about your story don't add up, clearly there's more to this than you let on?"

Nathaniel slowly walked over to where Ralis was standing. "So in short you do not trust me. But the matter at hand does not require your trust, Ralis. In fact it does not require your presence at all. Most important of all, I don't answer to you, Ralis, your constant questioning only bothers me, only irritates me."

"What are we now? Are we switching to believe as the Vatican does? You've sent two of Macaro's apprentices into a tunnel which leads to angels-know-what, and that I'm not supposed to question? The Nathaniel I knew when he first picked me off the streets would not condemn any apprentice to a fate unknown. The Nathaniel I knew would allow for such questions and answer them honestly."

Ralis stared deep into Nathaniel's eyes, as they stared long at each other. Nothing could be seen, a human was not behind his eyes, this was not the Nathaniel Ralis knew he suddenly realized.

"What is it about humans, why do they carry so much fear? Fear for each other. Fear of loss and death, or guilt, disease. They find something to fear in all aspects of life. But most of all humans fear themselves, is that the root cause of fear? The doubt? To not know what lies behind each second, an end possibly around every turn of every moment. Is that why, at all costs, they prevent it? Never mind that rambling, it comes to you, Ralis, and the fear that just stuck through you."

The clicking grew in numbers, it echoed against the unseen walls of the dark cavernous tunnel.

"Alright I have a plan," Marius whispered to Yuri.

"Let's hear it."

"I'll use a spell to reveal life, in doing that this place shall illuminate somewhat, I don't know what we will reveal, so be prepared. Revealing the sound might prove to our advantage, it also may be our disadvantage. So shall I?"

"Yes, do it, Marius."

Marius quickly readied himself. A pink glow lit in his hands, he span around and whipped the light into a circle. The light then spread through the room. The light did not illuminate much as the purpose of Marius' spell was not to illuminate the room but to reveal the source of the unrelenting clicking. The pink light stuck onto many forms as it spread across the room. The dark shapes moved rapidly around them.

"There's about thirty of them, they seem not to like the light. We are definitely surrounded." Marius confirmed. The dark shapes, irritated, moved more rapidly, the clicking sound grew louder and sharper. "They are trying to confuse us, scatter us, that is our weakness, we must not break from each other."

But before Marius and Yuri could decide a further plan of action a giant shape leapt towards Yuri. Yuri dodged to the left, spinning, and while launching a blast of energy at the unidentified foe. The blast lit up the dark shape and finally the source of the clicking was revealed: A large insect stood in between Marius and Yuri. From the quick blast of light they caught a glimpse of the monstrous beast. About waist high, covered in thick, grey scales, a large spider-like, crustacean-looking creature stood. It walked on its four back legs and its two front claws were shaped like long spear-like hooks, capable of sheering prey apart with its long serrated blade.

At the sight of it, Marius stumbled backwards, a mistake as natural. As he stumbled back in horror he felt a long pincer-like claw slash towards him. Marius rolled out to the side, glanced in the shoulder by the claw as he was not quick enough to fully dodge the creature's strike.

Everything slowed down in the dark cavern. Adrenaline coursed through Marius' arterioles, spreading to each organ and muscle, each cell in his body. And then he felt it: the same feeling as on the log, the same feeling as the first challenge. He felt everything.

Marius felt another claw reach for him as another creature pounced towards his position, he span to the left dodging and blasting a wave of fire into the beasts mandible. But before he gave another blow he was forced to pirouette out as two of the spider things leapt towards him.

Surrounded they were, and Yuri had yet to announce himself, Marius feared the worst. Two balls of flames lit up in Marius hands as he spun wildly conjuring a firestorm. Fire ripped from his hands igniting the closest creatures to him. Fire spread across the whole room making it smell of burnt tissue.

Most of the creatures fled. Presumably from the heat and the light, Marius thought. To where they escaped he did not know.

Some of the spider things, the ones closest to him, lay burnt and wriggling. All went black in the room again.

"Yuri!" Marius yelled.

A low grumbling was heard close to him. Marius ran over to the source of the noise. Marius knelt down as to what he sensed as a living being. He then conjured a ball of light, which hovered over him. The light spread a blue glow over Yuri's body, as he lay there awake and motionless, many gashes and wounds lay across his sternum and abdomen. The blood soaked through Yuri's cloak, his eyes rolled back as he started to lose consciousness.

"Shit, shit, shit." Marius began to panic seeing the blood pool on Yuri's robe. Instinctively he grabbed his friend into his hands and started to drag him towards what he thought the exit. But as soon as he started walking, holding Yuri, an intense pain stabbed his right shoulder, causing him to collapse and drop Yuri. Clicking. Clicking again once started back into the cavern.

"Shit, shit, shit." It was him or Yuri. Thousands of different versions ran through his head of the scenario. He was wounded, barely able to fight with his adrenaline now dropping and his body starting to register the wound in his right shoulder. Yuri was wounded even worse, and barely looked alive. No he thought, he wouldn't leave his friend and nor were they going to die today. He stood up grabbing Yuri's chest with his left arm holding Yuri at his side he slowly started stumbling again towards what he thought was the way they had come from. The clicking started to come even closer. But Marius had little speed. Exhaustion setting in, his legs burned from the weeks of endless hiking. His arm pierced with a pain that grew and grew with every step. He collapsed and fainted.

Ralis had not a clue about the next few seconds, all intuition seemed to leave him for a brief moment. Before he could react,

Nathaniel had leapt up, rebounded off the wall, spun and heel-kicked Ralis in the chest. The concrete floor jarred Ralis' head as he smashed down upon the ground. Another kick had started to come down towards his head. This time Ralis reacted in time, rolling out to the left and springing up.

"Nathaniel, stop!"

Nathaniel laid down two spinning kicks, Ralis dodging them both. He span to face Nathaniel, his fists in the air, his stance grounded.

"I am not bound by the rules of your kind, Ralis."

Nathaniel's face had become sinister, his intent was to hurt, his provocative to kill was clear through the glare in his eyes. Nathaniel leapt up into the air, striking two kicks towards Ralis head. Both deflected, Ralis span a kick underneath his foes chest, his intent to wind Nathaniel. Nathaniel took the kick straight into his sternum. He looked up, unphased, as he locked his hands around Ralis' foot. Nathaniel's right fist and right elbow, slammed in unison down the tendons of Ralis' quadriceps. Ralis quickly jumping from his standing foot and booted Nathaniel's face while Ralis continued his jump into a back flip landing on his feet, his left leg weakened from Nathaniel's strikes.

I can't fight him, he is too powerful and a much more skilled Mage, I won't win this by fighting, Ralis thought.

"Ralis, my boy, pass me the lock picks."

Ralis quickly swung his rucksack off his back and rummaged inside, looking for his father's tools. He placed the bag on the harsh stone floor of the sewers. Ralis could barely see inside, so he felt with his hands. His father dressed in black robes stood over him, his blue eyes the only facial feature to be seen under his hood. The other two men that held torches were Hungo and Thermus, two burly men in dark cloaks similar in fashion to his father's. All three men wore small daggers attached to their waists. They were silent as Ralis rumbled through the bag. What was a few seconds felt like minutes. Drips of water could be heard falling from the stone ceiling. Moisture filled the air.

Drip.

Drip.

"Hurry, boy," Ralis' father commanded.

"Why bring an eight year ol' young'un anyways, my lord?" Thermus questioned. His voice was deep and resonating even for his attempt to whisper.

"Yes, why wrap up your boy with such shit, my lord?" Hungo added.

Ralis' father didn't answer. He just held out his hand and took the lock pick gear from Ralis. He began to open the wooden door, they stood by. If one were to have seen them they would've looked very odd standing in the sewers, crowded around like a group of bards. But very unlikely anyone saw them opening that door it was the sewers after all. The wooden door swung open. Ralis was handed back the lock pick gear. Ralis put it in his pocket this time, as they walked through the door, with the burly men pushing past him. They kept silent as they tiptoed down the length of the damply-lit sewer channel. Ralis held his hand up and felt the brick wall to navigate his way behind his father and his men, his fingertips collected water as he stepped on.

"Stop here," his father whispered. The group stopped just before a large metal grated door. "Ralis, the lock picks." His father held out his hand and, in sync, Ralis handed over the lock picks. Minutes flew by as his father tampered with the lock.

Memories are such funny things. Unreliable and inconsistent but as well the basis of a human's personality and traits. We cease to remember the most important of events, only but the faintest details, while the most mundane of memories we hold onto for the rest of our lives. This was one of Ralis' earliest memories. When I got to know him better he would always rant about this specific moment. I also believe he isn't too fond of this memory because it's one of the only clear memories he has of his father.

After a long period of silence, the door creaked open and Ralis' father handed him the lock picks.

"From here on we remain silent. Hungo and Thermus, you two are responsible for hauling the barrels back to the ship. We need thirty, any more is unneeded but welcome, just don't risk the job. I'll get us into the cellar. Ralis follow behind us and don't make a noise."

Hungo and Thermus nodded in agreement and the group set out. At this point of the journey they had obviously reached the sewers beneath the building they were attempting to rob. Ralis knew his father was a thief, it never needed to be said, it was one of those unspoken things between a father and a son.

Two left turns and one right turn led them up a brick stair set which was centred beneath a large wooden door. A cellist and violinist could be faintly heard reverberating from the wooden door. Many voices spoke, almost as if a feast was being help in the building above. Ralis' father reached underneath his cloak to reveal a long, steel pry bar, around the length of his forearm. Obviously meant to rip open the door latches which looked unpickable. The day of the theft was obviously planned specifically on the day of such a feast to cover the noise of the thieves bashing through this cellar door. Hungo took the pry bar and smashed in between the door and its brick framing, making no hesitancy when the noise screamed down the sewer channels. A couple bashes and then a large *bam* from Hungo and Thermus tore the door from its seams, and they were in.

A musty smell of wine and mildew hit Ralis' nose, his ears sensed the intensity of the noise from the party which the door was muffling. It seemed as if no one upstairs had heard a thing. The feast continued. Glasses and silverware clinked above. The muffled rabble ensued.

Slowly they entered the room. Ralis' nose did not betray him. The cache they were robbing today was obviously a rich noblemen's wine cellar. Hungo and Thermus each snuck in, their footsteps fell like feathers, surprising for their size. Each grabbed the nearest crate of assorted wines, each bottle rattled as Hungo stacked multiple crates on top of each other. Anxiety grew over Ralis, every noise they made seemed oddly loud to him. The burly men started hauling crates back to ship while his father and him were positioned behind the cellar door to act as guards. All was quiet and the ball continued above them. Suddenly another door could be heard swinging open from within the cellar. Ralis and his father instinctively leant closer to the cellar door focusing on the noises within.

"A prudish and immature action, by my wish I never brought Marcella to such a gathering," a soft tender male voice could be heard.

"You must stop controlling her, Joshua, she is your fiancé, you must stop worrying about an odd man's feeble to attempt to flirt with her," a deeper voice responded.

Some of the conversation skipped past Ralis' ears, muffled by footsteps.

"Where is that vintage plum grape? I'm sure we could not of drunken it all already!" The footsteps pattered out of the room.

"That is not a good sign," Ralis could hear his father mumbling to himself.

Many minutes went by, while Thermus and Hungo had yet to return.

"You see, son," Ralis' father turned to him and started speaking in a low voice. "This is why you never hire idiots. Come, follow."

His father backtracked their path they'd come in with intensity, but no sign of Thermus of Hungo showed. Not until they turned a corner a little ways away from where their boat was docked, by the sewers main drain way in the port. A lone wine bottle sat broken by the stonewall. Its smell dampened their nostrils in a flower-like fragrance. Ralis hated the smell of wine. They both leant down to see the broken bottle obviously shattered from being dropped. Then the footsteps could be heard. Deep, monotonous, rhythmic.

"Good attempt, a failure nonetheless." A man gowned in white sewn robes loomed before them.

Ralis focused his sight on the man's face but nothing but a silhouette was returned to his eyes. Ralis backed away towards the wall, while his father slowly stood up from his crouch, his gaze fixed on the robed man. Fear shot first down his spine then down his legs, shooting a wave of weakness throughout his whole body, to a point where in one instance Ralis almost collapsed. Before he knew it his father was reaching his hand inside his own robe attempting to pull out a knife.

"A mistake." The robe man leapt forward at his father and, before Ralis could figure out what he was doing, Ralis found himself long lost in a network of sewer tunnels, out of breath, dry mouthed, with legs quivering like thin branches in a storm. Once he realized he had fled the scene—that he had run instead of helping his father—he collapsed on the ground, sobbing. Fear overtook him and his vision went black. What was a boy supposed to do?

The same fear overtook Ralis this day. He stood there frozen, staring deep into Nathaniel's eyes. Nathaniel danced forward, his footsteps grazed across the floor, sprinting at an unnatural speed whilst leaping up for a kick aimed high at Ralis' head. Ralis barely reacted in time. If not for the fact he was trained to fight as a Mage, he would have been dead. Ralis stumbled to the right, swiftly spinning to catch himself. But Nathaniel moved at a freakish speed, before Ralis could finish recovering to face his opponent, a dash of strikes rippled into his chest. Winded he stumbled back.

"Why are you doing this?" Ralis spat out blood as he attempted to spit out barely audible words. Nathaniel stood before him, but before he had time to reply a young boy holding a slightly taller, scruffy and very bloody boy came feebly running up the tunnel entrance screaming, "Run!" And, following the two injured boys, finally fully visible from the dim light of Nathaniel's set torches were these large arachnid-like creatures. Nothing fancy, just waist height, with four back legs covered with tiny hairy spindles. Its two front pincers were coated with nasty-looking barbs. The whole creature's appearance was awfully grotesque. It took Ralis half a second to even get his mind wrapped around such an odd scene, but once Ralis understood the immense gravity of the situation he leapt up and grabbed Yuri from Marius' approaching hands.

Nathaniel was nowhere to be seen, and, before Ralis had a moment to think, he was sprinting though the ruined tunnels holding Yuri over his shoulders, Marius panting at his tail. The creatures scurried fast on their limber legs behind them. Craving the scent of fresh blood. The tunnels seemed endless; some hallways were now dark, abandoned to darkness by the flickering wall torches.

They soon came upon a great stone hall, with a vast dark abyss that hung in the sky as the ceiling was too high to see. Skipping over stone benches, Ralis and Marius sprinted to a bright glow emanating from the end of hall. As they fast approached the glow its shape formed into a doorway. Light blistered Marius' eyes as he left the stone doorway and entered onto a sharp cliff based upon a mountainside. The evening sun faced them; a sun too bright for such creatures of the darkness.

Ralis laid Yuri down on to the granite surface. It was a flat and wide granite slab which formed a cliff with the decaying mountain face. While Ralis performed healing magic on Yuri, Marius rested. As he lay there, resting his head which ached from the stress from the intensity of the past events, Marius could finally get his head together.

First his surroundings hit him. This was not the same entrance that they had entered the ruins. Finding the door way was obviously a fluke, the rapid sprinting could have taken them miles off course. And where was Nathaniel? Marius vaguely remembered seeing him sprint off inhumanely fast when he arrived at the tunnel entrance. Marius walked over to where Ralis was healing Yuri. Ralis looked shook, his face was pale white and his hands shook as the orange light radiated from his palms.

"I can't heal this energetically, this requires physical manipulation to remove these barbs. I can get him standing, but I can't guarantee he will make the journey back," Ralis spoke as he examined Yuri.

Yuri's eyes looked dim with life, they flickered open and closed, barely focused on anything. His robes were ripped open and his abdomen revealed nasty claw marks with barbs stuck in the coagulating blood and scab tissue that was forming.

Ralis turned to face Marius, "I'm sorry." He took a long pause and looked away at the setting western sun. Its rays lit up the landscape. Rolling hills of golden grass could be seen slowly turning into a silhouette; the sun fading behind the expanse. "I'm sorry, about your friend. My intuition felt as if something was off when we arrived here. Nathaniel confirmed that."

Marius almost interrupted, his mind coming with new questions every second.

"But yet I reacted too late. Do you see, Marius, why being a Mage is more than fighting and magic? I could have saved your friend's life."

"He isn't dead yet!" Marius exclaimed, cutting Ralis off.

"True." Ralis turned to Yuri and knelt beside him. "I doubt in his condition he could make the journey to Highwash on foot. My point being is that being a Mage is about reacting—reacting fast and swiftly—knowing the correct course of action. But that requires wisdom."

Marius pushed Ralis. "Enough of your depressing talk, my friend sits here injured while you talking about depression. Think! You're an Elder!" Marius was becoming frantic. Seeing his friend lying there groaning.

Yuri looked misshapen and not himself. Marius paced, back and forth a few times, his head spinning with a storm of a headache.

"You said you could get him to walk! Alert Macaro, communicate to a bird, send it to him, they can send people to meet us at a halfway point."

Ralis turned to face Marius his eyes wide with shock of not thinking of such a simple solution himself, but as well, his eyes filled with doubt. For the first time he doubted himself. Ralis looked out west, the sun was half set, leaving a orange hue on the sky. He lifted his fingers to his lips and whistled a tune, a bright tune that made even Marius calm down some.

A large sparrow fluttered over Ralis' head. He gently held out his hand and the sparrow landed on his arm and it interlocked its gaze with Ralis. The bird remained still for half a second, and then flew off towards the setting sun.

"It's done, now we just hope it reaches Macaro sooner than later."

"How long could it take?" Marius said as he stepped closer to Ralis.

"Depends on its flight path, the sun is setting, as well an owl could easily take it out. Macaro will send a bird in response, but that could take a fortnight with how far we are from Highwash. So we won't know if he received the message for a bit. You get some sleep, Marius. I'll tend to Yuri, he will be conscious by morning, I promise to that at least."

Marius nestled down on a patch of yellow grass imbedded in the rough granite face. It was harsh but soft enough to support his back. It took him what felt like hours to fall asleep. In his sleep, dreams took over his mind, dreams where Yuri died of malnutrition and where Nathaniel was his best friend.

Marius awoke covered in sweat, gazing up at starry night sky. He was cold and the fact his robes were damp with dew didn't help the case. He sat up and gathered his surroundings. Ralis had passed out beside Yuri, he must have passed out while performing healing spells thought Marius. The fact Ralis had not set up his camping bed proved his theory. This frustrated him, as he wouldn't have minded using such a mat.

He stood up and got into horse stance. Before he could even reach a meditative state, the sun started to peek around the eastern mountain ridge. The sky blended from night to day.

Ralis awoke, but didn't assume horse stance. He immediately went to wake Yuri. Grabbing a canteen from his bag, he held the lip of the container to Yuri's mouth.

"Where am I?" Yuri awoke, water dribbling down his chin.

"Silence, and feel yourself, you are injured you must first know that. We must walk miles down the mountain, you have till the sun peaks over the ridge to recover enough to walk, then we descend."

Yuri didn't say much as he sat beside Marius. He slowly chewed on a chunk of bread Ralis gave him. His robe was now tied back on, his wound not visible. Marius could sense Yuri's distress, although it was not visible on his face; Marius could tell by Yuri's demeanour, which was usually extroverted and loud. After the quick breakfast, Ralis announced that it was time to depart. Ralis gracefully stood Yuri up by holding underneath his armpits.

"How does standing feel?" Ralis asked.

Yuri simply nodded as his feet found his natural balance.

"Good then," returned Ralis, answering Yuri's silent gesture.

The three of them set off. Slowly at first, as they had to descend the side of the granite face, where the door of the ruins was set upon. They climbed down the right side of the rock face, which was the only face that was not completely vertical so it was an easier decent for Yuri. It was rough as well, with many places to catch a foot or to place their hands.

"Where are we, Ralis? We obviously didn't come out the same way as we entered." Marius asked as they hiked downwards. Their feet snagged between ferns and roots as they climbed.

"We must be further south than the doorway we entered the ruins from. Look at the sun." Ralis pointed at the thick forest canopy above them, directing their gaze towards thin glimmers of glowing rays from the afternoon sun. An almost impenetrable blanket of pine and fir needles covered the three of them. "You see its angle? It's slightly lower than in regards to when we were hiking upwards. We must be miles off course."

Marius gave Ralis a distressed look, worrying about Yuri's chance of survival. He didn't express his worry to not discourage his friend.

"Let's not worry about where we are exactly yet. Once we get out of this forest, we will have a clear view of where we are. Come on, no standing around until sunset, make haste," Ralis commanded. He set off down the half beat trail, pushing past heavenly fern leaves, with Marius and Yuri at his tail.

Marius looked worriedly back at Yuri who walked behind him, his face was pale and his eyes filled with exhaustion.

The night came over them faster than what felt like normal and evening was already upon them. They had not fully descended through the thick forest as Yuri's slow pace held them back. They camped by a small stream. Ralis gave his mat and blanket to Yuri and sat down close to him. Marius sat in front of them.

"May I have some loaf?" Marius asked Ralis, the question brought on by feeling his stomach growl and clench. Ralis answered, Marius eyes fighting to see his face with the sunlight dimming.

"Sorry, I gave the rest to Yuri, he will need it more than you."

Yuri was asleep at this point in the evening.

"There's no more food?" Marius asked in dismay.

"No, there is not, sadly. I'm sorry I never planned for a month's hike. I had a horse, remember? I also never planned to have two additional companions."

"Why didn't you turn us back? Why wouldn't you have turned back yourself?" Marius grew impatient with Ralis' constant emotionless, logical way of speaking.

Ralis sat quiet for a few seconds, his face further retracting from Marius' view every second as night took its full swing.

"You feel what it feels like to slowly lose a friend?"

Marius was stunned by such a question and froze. The thought of losing Yuri for real never occurred to him. Any challenge, he thought, together they could overtake.

"Nathaniel is my friend," Ralis continued. "A greater friend to me than I was to him. And when one's friend disappears for months, you naturally set out to find them. And, naturally, when one's friend is missing, you tend to act irrationally and irresponsibly. You two also dragged yourself into this. I was angry with you two for following me. If I could see the future, or even slightly come close to predicting future events, I'd have sent you back and headed here myself. Even two weeks change what you know. Enough now, you're a Mage like me, trained to withstand days without food. Relax. And sleep." Ralis finished his lecture and lay down on his back.

Marius lay down as well. His mind fluttered with thoughts, about Nathaniel, his friend Yuri. Was he a good friend to Yuri? Was this his fault? Was Yuri trying to show off because of Marius' performance during the first task? No, that couldn't be. Marius barely did much. Was it the private talk with Macaro? Marius thought he guessed he would never know. He fell asleep to the guilt of Yuri's injury, his stomach churning and rumbling. His final thought became *This journey back is going to suck,* as he drifted asleep.

They awoke to the sound of chirping birds and the stream they'd camped beside gently trickling. Yuri was the first to wake;

he could feel the wound on his side now and he groaned loudly as he sat up.

That groan is what started their morning. Ralis performed some energy work on Yuri, holding his hands on his stomach and over the wound, attempting to reduce the pain. Setting off for another day's hike, they gathered some water from the stream, filling the two canteens Ralis had brought, and filling their stomach with water they headed once again downstream. As the hot summer sun reached its peak, they had finally descended enough where the ground's slope softened and the bush thinned out. Thin stalks of yellow grass started to blend in with the green needles of all sorts of different shaped trees. This was the farthest east Marius had been.

Ralis and Marius kept pace most times, easily agile enough to manoeuvre between rocks and stumps without stumbling, often moving at a quick jog. Yuri, on the other hand, stumbled often and moved slow. At some moments Yuri's willpower would give out, so Marius and Ralis would trade supporting him around his shoulders.

Another day would pass until they left the slope of the mountain behind them and entered the flat plateau of the plains.

"We're in for a storm tonight," Ralis said, pointing up at the sky which was finally in view as they escaped the trees darkness.

A grey torrent of clouds overtook the view of the eastern horizon; dark masses of grey and black, it looked as if death was taking over the bright summer landscape, and would eventually consume the whole of the plains.

Marius knew these storms well. He had been in Highwash longer than he could remember and during each of his sixteen long summers a massive storm would inevitably blow in from the east, drenching the landscape with a downpour to match all the winter storms there could be.

When Ralis pointed out the storm, all three of them felt the same emotion at once, they linked like brothers at that moment whether they knew it or not. Each of them had the same thoughts. Thoughts of fear and a feeling of their dropping hearts. The wind was already starting to pick up a bit, trees swaying gently, but ominously. Ralis stood fast and ready.

"Ok, if we want to survive, we turn back now. If you remember up the ridge we just came down, there was an alcove in a rock face. We could camp there and make it through the night."

Ralis didn't wait for an answer. Grabbing Yuri he headed backwards up the hill back up into the forest. Marius didn't oppose, he simply followed behind Ralis, thoughts on his friend, who he worried deeply about.

The three of them barely made it to the alcove by nightfall. The wind had picked up to a threatening pace, a wolf howling as it blew through the sky. They sat nestled together by a fire. The alcove was a little deeper than they remembered—the first time they saw it they simply strode by. It was wet and moist inside but it was large enough to fit the three of them. The wind chill still bit them, but it gave shelter from the rain.

Under the alcove, they waited. As it grew deep into the night the storm intensified, rain dropped from the sky and pounded the trees and ground. The beating of the rain trembled their eardrums. Flashes of lightning ever so often would wake Marius from a state of delirious half sleep. Another one had just woken him and the accompanying roar of thunder startled him. Yuri was beside him shivering in his sleep. Ralis had wrapped his robe around Yuri, to act as a blanket for him.

Ralis sat up seated meditating beside Yuri. The fire lit up Ralis' bare upper body. He was covered in dark brown bruises across his chest and back.

"How did you get those bruises?" Marius asked, whispering quietly. Marius examined Ralis as he sat there unmoving, not answering the question he had placed. Marius began to wonder what went on while he and Yuri explored the inner tunnels of the ruins.

"I'm worried, about your friend; he has fever. This storm might delay us by a couple of days, and then we must reach the crossroads, which is still a long journey."

Marius stared out of the alcove blankly. The rain that gathered on leaves and branches dropped down with an intense velocity. He didn't want to believe Ralis, but a part of him thought, if the storm persisted, Yuri might not make it. He banished those thoughts from his head. Nothing was said after that. The conversation dying before it started, the situation as awkward as it would be. Marius drifted away into a restless sleep. Thinking of Ralis, how he has been silent and not himself since leaving the ruins; thinking, as well, of his friend.

Morning's benevolence came, relieving them of the onslaught the sky had given them the night before.

A stroke of luck, thought Marius as he awoke to Ralis packing up, readying to depart. Yuri was the last to awake; forcing himself up, he got to his feet and returned Ralis' robe. The night had not been kind to Yuri and he looked more exhausted then rested. Marius held him by his shoulders and looked him in the eyes.

"Can you walk, Yuri?"

Yuri simply gave a half-hearted nod and leaned on his friend.

Ralis reacted impatiently, pressing urgency and haste.

A dim and mucky morning awaited them as they set off. The trails were soaked, coated with needles and wandering branches. The storms aftermath left an ominous feeling on the valley. The sky was coated in a light grey haze with the remaining clouds grazing by. Erosion caused by the sudden rush of water from last night's storm, had changed the landscape dramatically. Trails they had hiked the day before were no longer accessible, resulting in the group veering off course and traversing south and east along the mountainside in attempts to find a stable path down into the valley.

Waves of hunger hit Marius, the odd berry or fruit scavenged as they hiked did not satiate his stomach. Irritated by the set back of the storm he tramped as he walked on.

By midmorning they reached a section of forest that seemed safe to descend and started down. The trail they had chosen was flatter than most sections of terrain on the southern face of the Emeralties. Marius was glad for that as it made the hike less enduring for Yuri, but left his feet sodden and wet. Tiny rivers of water dribbled by them, embraced in gravity's clutch.

Halfway down, Marius spotted a clearing on their right which had view of the whole valley and into the plains. He demanded to rest there, claiming Yuri needed rest, but in reality it was more for his case. So they rested, finishing up what there was of the water they had collected over the course of that day. The valley looked disturbed, damaged from last night's wave of constant rain and wind. The wind still gave the odd gentle howl, a simple reminder to all creatures of its power. Marius and Yuri were seated sipping on water while Ralis scanned the valley intently. Ralis knelt down slowly, his eyes caught on something in the distance. Marius felt his anxiety and grew tense.

Ralis whispered to himself. Marius sat up to see what disturbed Ralis; focusing on the distance, he realized what. Beyond the tree line a small brigade of men were camped about fifty miles beyond the forest in the valley. Tents and horses could be seen, but Marius could not see detail in their banners or ornaments; they were too far away in the distance to be fully seen. Ralis estimated the group to be about forty men large.

"I believe its men under kingship of Salamon. I know no other who rules Thenus. We continue onwards, with caution. I do not know their intention or why they are here. I'll support Yuri, while you scout a ways behind me, Marius. You must ensure we are not being tracked by anyone. Do you understand, Marius?" Ralis grabbed him by the shoulder as he said this.

Marius nodded, though inside he was slightly confused by Ralis' intensity. He had studied about the men from the western and eastern continents but had never known anyone from outside of Highwash. *They must not be followed.* The words spun circles in Marius' head as they continued the descent of the steep muddy trail.

Marius followed roughly fifty feet behind Ralis, while Ralis carried Yuri. It was silent expect for his own footsteps. He kept his head raised as he walked, watching and listening for anyone who could flank Ralis as well himself. Hours went by and the trail thicket became thinner and flatter. After hours of navigating through fallen logs, steep cliffs, roots, boulders and eroding trails, Marius was glad to be off the mountain pathway. The trail had led them before a quiet stream which fell down a gentle hill which then flattened out to the plains of Highwash. The camp that was seen before was in clearer view, but so were they.

"We must plan carefully," Ralis said as all three of them crouched low behind a bush of ferns. "These men are who I assumed. We must be diligent with our planning, if we are too slow, and hike too far south and east, we may not meet Macaro in time."

"Won't Macaro wait for us?" Marius interjected.

"Of course, a day or two Macaro will camp out at the crossroads, but if he grows impatient, as we are his friends and students, plus he knew where I was going. Meaning he might attempt to follow or backtrack our steps. He may even send a party to look for us, which would be the worst situation as, unfortunately, nowhere on Thenus seems out of reach from Men, but I cannot know for sure."

"Back to what I was saying before you kindly interrupted," Ralis said, looking at Yuri, preparing for honesty. "If we hike around to avoid being seen, it increases the risk of you not returning." Ralis paused for a second, gulping, did he really look a student straight in the eyes and say what he said. Did he really doubt himself and his ability to save Yuri? "I'm sorry, Yuri, that came out somewhat wrong. It's a hard and long hike if we travel further southeast."

Ralis stood up and looked at the surroundings in detail. Scoping through his mind. Marius and Yuri sat gazing at Ralis, wondering his state of mind.

"If we head directly west and then cut north around the encampment, that leaves us with harsher terrain, a greater chance of being caught, but it would prove a shorter path. If we stick to the trees we should have well enough cover to get by unseen."

Ralis stepped over to a lone tree and whistled the same soft tune. A crow, this time, swept down and perched itself on Ralis' arm. Ralis whispered it secrets and it flew off.

"That was to Macaro, to warn him of this encampment."

The three of them hiked north, again off route; this bugged Ralis. Fate seemed to want the boy. They drudged on. The flatter ground of the hills was swamp-like and muddy after the storm.

Water soaked into Marius' feet, his toes felt corrugated and pruned. Trying to think positive, Marius did feel grateful for the flatter terrain, not necessarily for himself, but for his injured friend's sake.

Yuri stumbled often, clutching his hand over his wound. Ralis or Marius would simply help him up and they would continue on. By evening they had made it no more farther than they had the previous day before the storm. They made a sleeping area within a section of bush.

"No fires," Ralis commanded as he stepped away, determined to find some wild berries or fruit that they could eat. It was just Marius and Yuri now. Marius looked over at his friend who lay there. Yuri looked cold, his face dim and pale, irritated whispers of breath passed Yuri's lips—a sign of some injury to the diaphragm.

"Yuri, look at me."

Yuri looked up at Marius, his eyes blinking for a second before opening halfway. "You're going to make it. No matter what. I'll carry you myself if I have to, ok?"

"You won't have to," spoke Yuri.

Marius smiled at the remark.

III

The morning came, its sunrays which peeked through clouds above the eastern Emeralties mountain range woke Marius.

Groggy and hungry, he sat up. Awareness filled his body with senses. He was so sore and bruised, so he moved slowly as he prepared for another day of hiking.

The night before Ralis had only managed to gather some berries and water to eat, making all three of them low on energy. Yuri seemed the most impacted by hunger, his movements were slow and deliberate. Before departing Ralis asked Yuri to see to his wound. As Ralis opened Yuri's robes, Marius caught a glimpse. The wound was covered in congealed blood and scabs. Yuri grimaced at the sight of it.

"Fucking bastards," he muttered under his breath.

They still had to travel further north to traverse away from the encampment of soldiers before they could head east towards Highwash; this meant an additional day of hiking.

The long August summer was slowly turning into a dry September. Marius spent the morning pondering on as he walked. His mind stuck on what lessons they had missed at Highwash; they must have been hiking for about three weeks now.

About midmorning, Yuri collapsed into the grungy ground, being clipped by a tree root as he stepped. This woke Marius up to reality and away from his sombre thoughts. Slowly, with a struggle, Yuri pushed himself up onto his feet, covered in dirt. They continued on. Marius held his position behind Ralis again while Ralis walked ahead with Yuri. The day grew hot, with the sun positioning itself directly on top of Marius' head for a midday torrent of sunrays. Ralis still avoided turning west out of the forest cover and into the fields.

Why would he delay? thoughts of irritation ran through Marius' mind.

Maybe it was the midday heat of a steaming August day, maybe it was hunger. But Marius started to get irritated. Rashness filled his veins, his steps felt like anchors ramming the ground. He wanted to run forward to Ralis and demand that they turn west, for Yuri's sake. *Enough,* thought Marius. But he continued on. An hour of walking and debating occurred in Marius' head, but his inner quarrel stopped when unfamiliar voices rang into his ears.

"There's been no sign of them for days," an accented voice rang through the hills, it was a sharp and rhythmic accent that pronounced every syllable perfectly—that of the northern men. Marius ducked down into a bush vanishing out of sight. Listening intently.

"Tsk, shame, too, I would like to get out of these woods. Utter filth these forests." Another voice disturbed the air.

Marius focused his vision down to where he had last spotted Ralis; he couldn't see him.

Be calm, Marius thought. He listened and felt. Not the air, not the wind or the sounds of birds. He wasn't listening for those. He listened for heartbeats, for the sounds of breathing. To his left were multiple voices, contracting hearts and the inspiration of diaphragms. Three men were on his left. Downhill he could hear the tiny beats, one had to be Ralis with its slow methodical pumps. He focused harder, his senses expanding through the trees, and that's when he felt it.

"Stay still. Do not move or show your self."

The words generating the command in Marius' mind were not of his own, but of Ralis'. Now Marius understood Ralis' plan, he was reading Marius' mind to gain a wider field of perception; that is why Ralis sent him to trail behind.

Ralis' was in his mind again. "If we want out of this, you must do all that I say. Flank to the right behind some of those bushes and sneak down to me. Do this when I say so." A pause. "Move now."

Marius cut right, keeping himself in a low crouch moving on all four of his limbs. His training was coming back to him. He remembered all about Macaro's lectures on stealth, that mimicking the movement of a monkey or cat will decrease your odds of being detected. He also remembered the endless hours of a game Macaro invented where the object of the game was to be the first out of your class to catch a hare in the field on all fours.

Marius steered straight under a log into and down through the bushes which outlined the trail they were on. He headed for Ralis' position down trail. Weaving his way through needles and grass, orienting himself towards Ralis' energy.

"Stop there." The words drummed through his mind.

Marius froze in position, but left himself light and limber ready to move.

"They are moving towards the path we were on, listen."

The accented voices grew louder once more, Marius leaned through the bushes, gazing through grass and fern to observe them. Thin slits of light between the grass blades allowed Marius to see the three scouts. They were tall men with a warm, light complexion. The three men wore light armoured leather, worn turn buckles around their chests to support a sheath at their waists. The sheaths supported small, short swords at one side and horns on the other. One man carried a crossbow and wore a quill on his back. He had brown chestnut hair unlike his two other comrades whose hair was golden blonde.

"It's crucial you remain unseen, Marius. If they blow that horn, the whole valley will hear. A company of horsemen would be here within the hour scouring the valley." Ralis' thoughts summoned fear in Marius.

"There ain't nothing here. Come on, let's head back to that river at least, come! What do you say, Folcest?"

"One more mile north and we will turn back." The one with the crossbow spoke with a more brooding voice. He must have been Folcest.

"Another mile, argh! Damn this whole search. We will be out here for months," one of the blonde men spoke. Marius couldn't make him out looking through the grass blades.

"I've been dreaming of warm soup and my wife's touch for days now, men. Just shut up and hike on, our jabbering won't find any signs of these Rangers any sooner now." Folcest spoke again, irritation vibrated with each word. The men continued hiking downwards towards, where unknown to them, were Yuri and Ralis.

Ralis' voice cut into Marius skull again. "Stay there, be silent, they are heading towards me, let me handle this."

Marius looked down towards where he thought Ralis was positioned. Nothing moved, no one could be seen, not even a grass blade or fern ruffled. The men made it further downhill. Their voices ceased to speak.

A hand placed itself on Marius' shoulder, he jolted to this touch. It was Ralis kneeling behind him with Yuri at his side.

"Shh, we make our way behind them. We must keep track of them to not lose their position, but we cannot be seen."

Marius and Yuri were led by Ralis. Together they hiked slowly, in a half-crouched stance, following the three scouts. What seemed like an hour went by and their slow pace was made even slower by the group of scouts scavenging the hills. Marius had a hundred questions about the foreign men but decided silence was a greater priority. Ever so often Ralis would stop and wait for a few minutes, gathering his whereabouts. To Marius Ralis looked worried; he didn't wear it on his face, Marius could just feel it. They followed Ralis until they hit a ridge that overlooked a steep muddy bank and a stream. Marius observed the scouts resting down by the stream. Obviously the badgering had forced their commander to finally stop and rest, as Folcest, the one who bore the crossbow, looked frustrated while his two comrades had splendid looks of relief.

At least some people were getting rest, Marius thought. The three of them were nestled above the scouts on a bank. Trees and dense weeds covered them from view, but the bank down into the ravine was nasty and muddy and led into a rocky shore before the stream. Ralis gave silent hand signals to Yuri and Marius, directing them to traverse across the bank with him and not to head down.

Marius stepped forward following Ralis and Yuri even though thick weeds and trees were on his left, he felt the ground could give out any moment with him plummeting downwards into the ravine. But before Marius knew it, it was not he who was falling but Yuri. The ground seemed to slip from under Yuri's weak step and he collapsed, starting to roll downwards catching weeds and thorns on the way.

Ralis and Marius both ran down the bank after him, it was less stable than Marius thought and he went plummeting down the bank as well, thorns and needles rattled his skin. And then a face full of mud and gravel. He stood up quickly and looked up, Yuri was in front of him lying in the riverbed. Marius' own descent was cut short by a tree; Ralis was not to be seen. Marius' heartbeat started rising.

"Boy! You mind telling me who you are, eh?" The man called Folcest sat a far distance away from him on a rock, his crossbow held out firmly, pointing directly at Marius.

Marius froze and listened. He could potentially dodge a shot from the bolt if he reacted in time when he heard the trigger pull, but that required intense focus.

"Who the hell are you, boy?" the brown haired man yelled again. But before another thing could happen, Ralis came behind that man, appearing almost out of thin air and grabbed the man's head, breaking his neck.

The other two blonde scouts shot up from their stone seats, one went for his horn, the other grabbed his sword. Ralis was faster, his hand already had the small dagger the man he'd killed had worn on him and he threw it directly at the man reaching for his horn.

Blood squirted in the air, the dagger had been precisely thrown into the man's neck. The other scout leapt at Ralis, sword in hand. Ralis quickly stepped to the side, grabbing the scout and twisting behind his back, while slitting his throat. The last scout fell to his knees and ended up with a face full of mud. Blood covered the streambed.

Yuri was just getting up, his mouth hung open witnessing such a bloodbath. Marius stood there shaking. His limbs felt like water and he knelt over not resisting the vomit that left his mouth.

IV

The rest of the day was spent silent. Marius and Yuri were too shocked by what they'd seen; they didn't speak a word. Marius spent the whole of the afternoon in his head, replaying the events that occurred over and over. The swiftness and speed of Ralis' kills, how they stained no regret on Ralis, and the smell as Ralis burned the bodies. Marius' whole life he was told never to kill; that a Mage's purpose was to bring light to the world, not to destroy life. Ralis' actions shattered that vision. He witnessed an Elder kill. Dealing death was against the code of a Mage.

Around midafternoon they finally reclaimed trail and started heading east, but they soon camped as evening took the sky. They camped in between some trees and bushes nestled in high grass.

"No fires tonight. We cannot afford being seen." Marius shook hearing Ralis' voice, he imagined it demonic and evil.

"You killed those men," said Yuri in a rough voice, he sat up a bit, resting on his elbows. Both Marius and Yuri stared dead into Ralis' eyes.

"Yes, I did." Ralis spoke calmly. "And if I did not, a many of things could have occurred. One being that horn being blown. A whole mass of armed soldiers would have headed towards the noise. We all would have been slain. Worst of all—" Ralis hesitated for a second gathering his thoughts. "Worst of all, they would have discovered that we are not who they are looking for. Which would be a bigger discovery to Salamon's men. Not only would our lives have been at stake, but all of our friends as well."

Marius cut him off. "You slew those men in cold blood! Any kill is a murder, which... which is against our code as a Mage!" Marius shook as he talked. The memories of the scouts' death replayed over and over in his mind.

"I am not a Mage, Marius," Ralis answered. All grew quiet to that answer. The evening light was dimming and so was the conversation. What Ralis had said brought a thousand questions to both the minds of Yuri and Marius.

"What do you mean you're not a Mage?" Marius bravely asked the question that both him and Yuri wanted to ask.

"That's a very long story, and I guess you both deserve the truth after what you've seen me do; but I will not tell that tale now, for we need sleep and rest. Tomorrow we must press forward, time is of the essence. So, sleep. That will be a story for tomorrow."

Ralis lay down on a soft bed of grass. He seemed unaffected by the day. As if he had seen death's icy grasp before. The night grew dark and the stars showed their tiny faces, covering the sky with endless sparkles and streams of light. Marius lay there staring at the stars, his mind restless and his body shook.

Who was Ralis? Marius thought over and over. Eventually his mind started to fade into sleep, and he was left with a single thought before he drifted into his subconscious, *Who am I?*

"You're trying too hard, Mathius."

The sun was dimming into an afternoon hue. Macaro had taken his students, with the exception of two, to a single oak tree in a large expanse of golden grass on the outskirts of the Highwash village.

"How am I trying too hard?" Mathius shot back, obviously frustrated from his lack and not directly at Macaro. Macaro knew this, he knew Mathius well.

"Stop for a second and listen, nothing but air stands between you and the tree. And we all know the composition of air, don't we?" Macaro looked back to his other students who waited patiently in a group off to the side. They nodded in agreement and recollection. "Air contains hydrogen, oxygen, some nitrogen and other elements. This works well for you, Mathius, as the concentration of oxygen and hydrogen together out weigh the concentration of the other elements. If you focus your energy not on hitting the target, but on directing the energy you will hit the tree. That does not require effort, Mathius. You know this all though. Try again."

Mathius bent his knees, building energy and directing it towards his hands. He felt the heat, the waves of current that jolted up his nervous system into his arms. Bending his left arm and extending his right, he released the energy.

Bam.

A lightning bolt shot from the air around Mathius' hand into the grass left of the tree, missing the shot. Mathius stamped his foot into the ground angrily.

"Raah, fuck! I can't control the bolt, it always hits the ground."

"Your mistake is a simple one. Understand that the air is no different than you. The same molecules exist in you that exist in the air. *Munto un tin*, the objective of the first task. Cynthia, your turn."

Cynthia's head popped up to her name being called. Her brown hair swayed as she walked forward. She was excited for this challenge, she was good at energy work it was her skill.

"You have heard what I told Mathius." Macaro directed his words at Cynthia and waved his hand towards the lone oak tree. "Go ahead."

Cynthia stood in horse stance readying herself. She started from her centre, focusing on the strings of energy that wrapped around her pelvic floor. She directed the energy up her arm and into her hands. She held it there, focusing, letting the energy build in her palms. She thought to herself as she moved. Left arm bent and in, ground legs, extend left hand and exhale.

Bam.

Another bolt of energy surged through the air, moving from molecule to molecule in the air snapping into the ground.

"Close, very close." Macaro smiled a little as he spoke. The bolt had hit the ground right to the left of the tree. The grass smelled burnt and fell to black ashes in the spot Cynthia hit. "Now, children, see that energy expressed in its rawest form is very volatile and uncontrollable. From this distance I've set you at, it is nearly impossible to hit the tree. So, Mathius, Cynthia, do not be upset. You have simply been set up. That is why, as Mages, we tend to use mechanical energy in the states of matter. Water, Earth, Air. Energy moves slower between denser particles, so they tend to be more controllable. Fire and lightning cannot be directed well. Understand when and why to use a certain element in a given situation."

A raven flew down out of nowhere, cawing as it descended from flight. The raven landed on Macaro's shoulder. Macaro stood there for a second and the rest of his students stood gazing at him. It looked as if Macaro was having a silent exchange with the raven. Then the raven flapped its wings and took off into the air. Macaro looked at his group of students.

"Lesson is dismissed for the day. At sundown I expect you all to come to the great hall. We all have something to discuss."

Macaro walked away down the hill, he wore a grim face. Mathius looked at Daniel, and then to the rest of the class; all of them wore the same face of confusion and worry.

"What do you think Macaro interpreted from that raven?" Daniel said as he made a gesture to touch Mathius as they walked back together to the village of Highwash. The group split up into sections as they headed back, Mathius with Daniel, Cynthia with Clive and Reggard.

"I bet it has something do with Yuri and Marius," Mathius answered back, his statement mocking the two missing students.

"I still can't believe they would sneak out like that, I mean what idiots they are. They know how Macaro would react." Cynthia looked over giving Daniel a sharp look as he spoke.

"Agreed. I hope they don't get exiled from Highwash, speaking honestly though."

The conversation was cut short as Mathius reminisced about moments with Yuri.

"Is something wrong, Mathius?" Daniel asked noticing his friend drop into silence.

Mathius' answer came late, "No, I'm just thinking. Yuri, I understand would do such a thing, but Marius? I'm surprised Marius got caught up in that. What do you even think they're doing now?"

"And that is what I can't wait to ask them," Daniel said, smiling.

The sun was setting. It looked gorgeous to Patrick, more gorgeous than his love Elizabeth. The ball of fiery light setting behind the western Emeralties stunned him. Patrick stood there gazing in awe at nature's occurrence that was before him. In all his fourteen years, a sunset still amazed him.

He looked down at the city below. A city of marble stone was before him, tiny specks below were carts and townspeople, hustling and bustling in between buildings. Each building was handcrafted by the best masons and architects you could hire in Thenus. The city itself spanned onward in a circle, which was surrounded by a large wall of marble. The evening sunrays illuminated the stone with an orange hue. Patrick was on a balcony on the tallest tower there was in Thenus, his country. Salamon's Keep.

The sunset was merely a distraction—a distraction from his worries. Patrick originally came out on the balcony to debate within himself, but the sunset seemed to bring an answer to Patrick's internal dilemma. He turned back from the balcony, entering the tower through a large wooden door. Its handle was detailed in a spiral fashion forged from iron.

Everything in Salamon's Keep was aesthetic. It was hollow inside the tower with halls and stairways that filled the walls like an ant's hive. Inside the hollow centre of the tower stood a great marble statue. It was of a man standing tall holding a sword atop his head within his right hand. Patrick had seen this statue since he was an infant and was no longer baffled or mystified by its massive size.

He headed left up a flight of stairs and climbed floor after floor until he reached his father's floor. Five guards stood out front, each holding a lance, all in silver armour enrobed with a golden flower on its chest. The king's guard bowed as Patrick walked forward, and one opened the door. Inside, his father sat in his study, his back turned to the door, focused on readings.

Lord Salamon's study was not as impressive as should be for a king, Patrick always thought. His father insisted on no decorations in his study, stating that his study "Was for thinking only, because not all places gold can take you." Only a few books were sprawled in randomly placed shelves. His desk was massive and made of oak. Patrick's father himself was old and grey. Long grey hair was tied in many ponytails down his back forming an intricate V-shape. His face was large and round and bore a large grey beard.

"Father, may I speak?"

"I cannot see you at the moment I'm afraid, Patrick." Salamon didn't even gesture to turn his head as he spoke.

"Please, Father, let me speak, I shall be quick."

His father stood up and turned around to face Patrick giving him a nod.

"Brother has not returned in months, I ask permission to take a battalion with me west to the Wild Woods to search for him."

"Permission denied. Is that all?"

"Father, he is my brother. I have to—"

Salamon cut off his son. "And I am your father and you are just a boy. You are fourteen years old. And I don't trust any fourteen-year-old boys to run a battalion, not even my own son. Your brother can handle himself, trust me. Now please leave, I must return to my study." Salamon sat back down and began again.

Patrick stood idly for a second, annoyed and irritated, but then left with haste. His older brother, Sebastian, had been gone for months on an attempt to find the criminals that labeled themselves the Rangers. His father's spies had picked up sources of people affiliated with the Rangers and ordered a search, sending Patrick's older brother, but it was unlike his brother to be gone for so long. This worried Patrick, but also a weird happiness grew in him. The thought of his elder brother being slain in combat excited his ego. It would mean claim to the throne was his.

Patrick stormed down the stairs, his footsteps intent on finding the kitchen; he would order the cooks to make him a fine meal, a custom of his when he was frustrated by his father's lack of approval.

Later he sat eating his meal of soup, braised pork and some fine cheese and bread, brooding and brooding over his brother. Father always trusted Sebastian, always favoured Sebastian. His older brother's face and figure flashed through his mind; his narrow face and large shoulders. His gleaming armour dressed in red outlines, displaying his role as lord commander. Patrick also loved his brother. To this day Patrick retained vivid memories of his elder brother. He remembered training in the fields and swimming in the streams on hot summer days. The most vivid memories were of him and his brother playing with their sister at the stream. There was always a dilemma in Patrick's mind, his emotional state towards his brother always fluctuating from love to jealousy. The jealousy of his brother originally stemmed from the fact that Sebastian's figure differed than his.

Sebastian grew up more like his father in build; he had a large, broad back and huge arms and legs—that of a warrior. Patrick was more like his mother, thin and lean with wiry hair. Patrick also had his father's round face. The thing that bugged Patrick the most was the recent arrangement of Sebastian's wedding. During early spring his father arranged the marriage of Sebastian Salamon to Elizabeth Cascichelli daughter to Vincent Cascichelli. Most of the details about her family name or line were irrelevant. But dear Elizabeth was only fifteen. Not only that but she was in love with Sebastian's younger brother, and the marriage was set for the next spring. So, constantly, day after day, these thoughts consumed Patrick's mind. Elizabeth had been his crush since he was a child. Both he and Elizabeth grew up with the idea they would wed. Not until the reality of adulthood hit them did their childhood dreams dissipate.

Patrick Salamon got up from his chair, not even the faintest thought of cleaning up after himself occurred to him, and he left hastily. A decision had been made. Patrick stormed out of the dining hall, set on his course. Patrick loved his brother—no doubt about that—and that was the decision that he'd made: to love, not to hate.

Patrick headed down the tower, through marble corridors and stairs illuminated by metal candle ornaments placed in perfect sets of four on either wall. Knights, servants and barons became more clustered the lower he descended down the tower.

The amount of people was caused by the bottom level of the tower being a courtroom. Large oak benches circled the bottom floor around the walls, all centred to face the room. In the centre, between the legs of the statue, chains hung down coming from the knees. This was obviously placed to intimidate, as the chains were for restraining the accused. Knights walked randomly about the halls, almost looking as if no one was really accomplishing anything.

As Patrick passed groups of knights and lords, each one bowed slightly to him. Turning down the main hall that left the tower courtroom he headed towards a great curved wooden door. Each door panel had a picture of a red flower engrained on it. As Patrick approached the door a group of knights made signals to each other and opened it. It opened easily, considering its massive size, only taking two knights to open the door.

The whole city of Salamon's Keep was a marvel of engineering and architecture. It was said the first king had built it along with Thenus' finest engineers and architects.

Patrick stepped outside the tower, he had spent all day inside the tower. Easily done as well since the tower was massive in size and it required an effort just to descend or climb to any floor. But the engineers who built Salamon's Keep remedied its size with a chained pulley system elevator which was able to bring goods to any floor.

Feelings of relief quenched Patrick's anxiety as he stepped outside into the cool air of the evening sun. But his anxiety grew back as he stepped on towards his destination. The streets were loud, and citizens moved sporadically. Some gave stink eyes to Patrick, while others bowed as he passed by them. Because of the city's mixed feelings towards his family, Patrick always requested a company of guards to accompany him in the streets. Patrick was a good enough swordsman to hold off most untrained folk, but still the guards helped soothe his anxiety.

Soon his path took him to a large barracks; the building was large and made of stone marble. It stood four stories high and to the left of it was an area fenced off with wire. The fence outlined the border of a training yard where Patrick spent most of his time learning swordplay. His entourage of knights dispersed beside the barracks, awaiting his next command, while Patrick went inside the building though a rectangular wooden door. Inside the building on the first floor was a room with hundreds of glamorous swords and armoury.

"Hail, young Salamon." An old bearded man knelt low as soon as Patrick entered. "What brings you here to my lovely depot?"

"Have my armour shined, and my sword ready by tomorrow's morn, please and thank you, smith."

"At your service, lord."

The old man bowed again and retreated somewhere in among the sets and displays of armour. Patrick departed at once from the barracks, issuing his knightly escorts to follow once again. This time he was headed to the stable which was slightly south of the barracks. By the time he arrived at the stable the sky was starting to grow dim. The stable was much more impressive than the barracks Patrick had visited. It had three main wings, all which held about forty horses. He headed into the left wing and was greeted by the smell of must and fecal matter. Patrick paced about the stables searching. Soon he was greeted by a familiar voice.

"Patrick! What brings you here?" She swung her arms around him grasping him in a firm hug. She smelled of horse, but Patrick didn't mind.

"Elizabeth, may you see that my horse and six others be readied for departure by tomorrow morn?"

"Of course, Patrick, though it is very late to request such a thing, but I will at once, my lord." Elizabeth turned to start gathered saddles but stopped in mid-motion. Her blonde hair swayed as she spun around to face Patrick again. "Where are you headed, Patrick?" Concern filled her face. She didn't need to ask.

"Don't go find him, Patrick. Sebastian will be fine."

"Elizabeth, I must."

"Did you tell your father? He, naturally, declined your request, didn't he?" Elizabeth held Patrick close, grabbing him by the waist. "Listen to him for once and don't go."

Patrick pushed her away. "You're his fiancé, Elizabeth. You understand why I can't let him get hurt, don't you?"

She looked down not meeting Patrick's eyes. "Yes."

"Then please have the horses ready."

Patrick turned to leave, but Elizabeth grabbed his arm and swung him around. They interlocked in a kiss. It ended as fast as it started and they stared into each other's eyes for a moment, but, hastily, Patrick left before a word was said. Elizabeth turned to gather the equipment for Patrick, a tear running down her cheek.

Later that same day, as the sun descended behind a curtain of cloud and sea, the students of Macaro headed to the great hall. Inside Macaro greeted them. It was just their class and Macaro. Candles flickered around the great hall, while the students sat at the steps that led down into the centre of the room where Macaro stood. When the students settled Macaro began to speak.

"An unfortunate event has beset some of our fellow students and we must act accordingly. Yuri has been maimed and is deeply wounded. I shall depart tonight with a rescue party. I am to head east on horseback and meet a fellow teacher at the crossroads. I need three more of you to come with me to bring horses and supplies. One of you who come may also have to hike back to Highwash—that may be a necessary burden. Now I must ask the question: Who am I to take?"

Macaro glanced at each of his students. Every one of them raised their hand.

"Cynthia, Clive and Mathius, you three shall accompany me. The rest of you continue your training and wait for us to return."

Later that evening, when the sun had descended, Cynthia, Clive and Mathius waited patiently outside the village stable. They had readied four horses, gathered medical supplies and were waiting on Macaro to depart. The old stablemen Talun stood by with them, awkwardly creating silence.

"I hope my horse Ralis took comes back in one piece." Talun looked at the three of them as he spoke, none of the students responded.

"Ahem," Talun cleared his voiced.

Mathius kicked some dirt waiting in the silence growing more awkward.

"Good, thank you three for the haste." Macaro appeared out of nowhere, he swung a rucksack around a grey mare's neck that the students had readied.

"Why are you leaving at night?" Talun asked.

"The sooner we leave, the better," Macaro answered gracefully. "Thank you for the horses, master Talun. I'll be sure to return them in good shape."

Cynthia gave Clive a glance of worry. Clive knew Cynthia the best out of all of the students, he knew Cynthia since he was a young infant—they were siblings, after all—and Clive knew her facial expressions. He knew what she looked like when she worried or when she hid her emotions.

Soon they were on their way. A starry night hung above them, while Macaro cast a ball of light to illuminate his field of vision. Macaro led the group. The roads were dry again; the summer air had absorbed all the water from the past storm, the ground looked as if it had never occurred. *Click, clack,* the horses trotted on. The sounds of crickets could no longer be heard.

Clive brought his horse around from the rear of the group up to Macaro's horse.

"Why did we leave at night?"

Macaro stared blankly ahead as if he had not heard the question. Clive's face crunched in confusion.

"Sorry, Clive, I was in deep thought," answered Macaro as he shook his head awaking from his self-induced trance. "Yuri is deeply hurt, I have seen his wounds through the raven's eyes, and so is my friend. I wanted to leave at once."

Both Clive and Macaro sat in silence for a second, thinking about their friends.

"Macaro, how are you going to punish Marius and Yuri, if I may ask?"

"You may ask, Clive. But in truth, I haven't made much thought into that. I have a feeling the situation might be punishment enough."

"What do you mean by that?"

"It is going to be a curious few days, Clive," Macaro said, ending another conversation in rhetorical speech.

Clive reared his horse to slow down and drifted back from Macaro, creating distance between him and Macaro again. Clive hated how Macaro was; his metaphorical speech drove Clive to frustration. Clive deeply worried about his friends and wanted clear and concise answers. While Macaro rode in thought and Clive brooded in anger, Mathius and Cynthia kept pace behind.

"How are you so good at energy work, Cynthia? Your accuracy and flow is impeccable," asked Mathius as he rode alongside Cynthia. Although Mathius couldn't quite see it, Cynthia blushed at his remark.

"It isn't all too hard, actually. It's really all about conceptualizing where you want the energy to go—less about effort, more about mindfulness," answered Cynthia.

"That's why I prefer fighting to magic. I'm more about effort." Mathius erected his spine straight as he talked. The horses trotted on.

"Well, actually I feel they're one and the same in that aspect. Fighting is similar to magic as movement is simply a transference of energy, same as magic."

"I suppose you're right," Mathius said after going quiet. "But that doesn't explain how you were so close to hitting the tree."

"Just good luck, I guess."

Mathius scoffed at Cynthia. Elder Macaro squeezed his thighs around the horse, urging it to go faster than a trot, and the three students followed along.

Along the ridge of the hill a pair of unseen eyes watched the four of them travel. Hidden by spells of his own and the cover of darkness, he watched.

The sun rose casting an early morning light while Ralis stood out on watch. Grass covered him from sight in most directions. From the trail, Ralis couldn't be seen blending in with the golden grass in his brown garments.

The group had a hard time making any distance. Every so often a group of four or five riders would storm the trails and prairie hills. Ralis assumed the cause was the trio of scouts he had killed, which he insistently blamed on Yuri and Marius. Ralis stood watch, while Yuri and Marius rested. Marius held a canteen to Yuri's lips as he sat up resting on a large boulder. Yuri's fever had grown in intensity, which also hindered their progress. Marius looked behind him, hearing Ralis' footsteps coming towards him.

"Marius, come please, we need to talk."

Marius simply nodded and started to walk with Ralis who took him to the side in the grass. Yuri didn't seem to take notice.

"We're still a day out from the crossroads. That's if we hiked at a decent pace. Unfortunately, our situation besets us, as you see. A group of Salamon's just rode north past here which leaves us with a window of an hour, I estimate, to get moving. We either head out now or your friend doesn't make it. He needs medical assistance, actual medical assistance."

Marius gulped at Ralis' statement.

"Go, and get him up."

Marius started over towards the spot where Yuri rested on the boulder. The thought of waking Yuri from his rest to hike bothered him. Yuri looked frail and his skin colour was pale. Marius knelt down beside Yuri, placing his hand on his shoulder.

"Yuri, we have to get moving." Marius shook Yuri as he said this. Yuri remained unresponsive to Marius' request, his eyes staying closed. "Please, Yuri, get up. You have to."

As Marius said this, Yuri's eyes flickered open, showing dim signs of life within him. Before anything could be said, Marius grabbed Yuri underneath the arms and hauled him up unto his feet. "Get up. We have to leave now and I am not leaving you."

Marius supported Yuri underneath his arm and essentially dragged Yuri who could barely lift his feet over to where Ralis was standing. Ralis had gathered what remained of their supplies in his pack and was waiting patiently.

"The trail looks clear, let's move."

And so, slowly, they continued westward once again. They had made headway in the last few days before Salamon's patrols started making rounds. The summer air was less humid, as August passed into September. The reduction in heat made the hike easier and less unbearable, but Marius was still exhausted. Four weeks of endless hiking, continuous sweating, minimal food and overloaded nervous stimuli were taking a heavy toil on Marius. Yuri took the worst end of the stick. Yuri would sometimes collapse over, sometimes passing out, or sometimes vomiting up blood. As well Ralis' healing spells seemed to prove less effective each time he used them.

"C'mon, Yuri, we have to get off the main road," Marius said as he grabbed Yuri from flopping over. Marius carried him over to the side into the tall golden grass that lined the roads sides.

"Ralis, Yuri needs to rest. For at least a bit."

"No." Ralis stepped towards Marius and looked daggers into his eyes. "We go as far as we can before nightfall, no rests, no stopping. Carry Yuri if you have to, as you did make that promise to him, did you not? But otherwise another night or two and the sickness will claim him."

Marius didn't hesitate, he grabbed Yuri from under his waist and hauled him over his shoulders. Yuri was heavier than he usually felt, but Marius assumed it was his hunger that made him weak. "We will trade, don't worry, but let's please make haste."

By evening they had successfully avoided two of Salamon's patrols. One of them they nearly escaped out of sight into the bush as the grass covered and muffled some of the horses sounds and vibrations.

"I predict, if everything plays out according to plan, by tomorrow we will arrive at the crossroads. I hope Macaro is there. If not... "

"He will be," Marius said, which was more of an attempt to convince himself of it than Ralis.

"Such confidence. I hope you're right, Marius." Ralis took off his robe as he said this, and picked out a small rag from his rucksack. He dampened it with some conjured moisture and wiped his chest.

Underneath the full moon light, Marius noticed what Ralis was wiping. His chest and abdomen had signs of bruising and massive contusions, which bore signs that Ralis had been healing them. Instead of the contusions being black from clotted blood vessels, they were brown and pale. Signs of healing, a natural rate of healing wouldn't yield results this fast, almost improbable without good nutrition and rest. Obviously, Marius concluded, this is what he was doing when he would step away to find food.

"What are those bruises from?" Marius rose his hand pointing as he asked.

Ralis didn't answer at first, obviously gathering his thoughts to answer appropriately.

"It wouldn't be in my authority to say," Ralis looked up as he said this. His face finally revealed bits of worry; his frown lines could be made out more clearly.

"What kind of answer is that? You're injured and you're not in the authority to say what happened? Whose authority is it?"

Ralis chuckled hoarsely. He looked back down and continued cleaning his wounds. "Something weird is going on at Highwash, Marius. Something is severely wrong with Nathaniel, our Archmage, as you have clearly seen."

Ralis let Marius ponder this for a second then continued talking. "Now you understand the repercussions of this, don't you? Surely, if I were to tell the other Elders of Nathaniel he would deny such things. And me telling you this puts you in an awkward situation, since now you know."

"What do I know?" Marius was surely confused at this point. He wondered if all Elders talked like this. "Are you saying Nathaniel attacked you?"

"Not directly, because, if I did, that would put us in an awkward place. Wouldn't it?"

Marius sat and thought about what Ralis had said. Surely Nathaniel had reached Highwash now. Now he did know. But did he believe that Nathaniel attacked Ralis? The wounds on Ralis definitely provided evidence.

"Sometimes it's better not to ask questions."

Marius had one more question; he wanted to ask it badly, but after what Ralis just said, he was unsure of himself.

"Go ahead and ask, I can see you yearning to." Ralis smiled for the first time that night. Both Marius and Ralis locked eyes for a second.

"What is wrong with Nathaniel? He is your friend, isn't he?"

"And that I do not know, Marius." Ralis stood up and wrapped his cloak around him. The night had grown very dark now. Only the moon's rays showed. "Rest now, please, we have much to accomplish tomorrow."

And another night was spent sleeping in the backcountry. Owls hooted and cicadas chirped and buzzed for a few hours before Marius fell asleep. And before Marius knew it, it was morning. The sun rose again once more. This morning hunger gripped his stomach hard. A large fist of pain sat in his abdomen. Marius lay there in agony for a few moments before gathering his will and slowly sat up. Marius looked to each of his friends. Ralis stood crouched amidst some grass observing the forward expanse of hills. Yuri sat up with his head in his palms rested on his knees; he didn't look good at all.

"Alright. We lie a couple miles east of the crossroads. I doubt Salamon's riders will come out this far west. But we will move forward with caution and stay off the main trails. If all goes well we should arrive at the crossroads by midmorning," Ralis announced.

Marius nodded but Yuri ceased to respond. Yuri just sat there with his head in his hands moaning.

"I think I'll carry him today," said Ralis as he approached Yuri, hauling him up over his shoulders. "No time to waste. Let's be off."

And without wasting anymore time the trio set off, hopefully for the last time this journey.

Highwash valley was gorgeous this morning thought Marius as they hiked on. The sky held a bright blue glaze as the sun rose high. The valley looked gold and green in all directions. Looking backwards to the east, the Emeralties held their peaks high. Although this journey proved treacherous, Marius was once again awed by nature's power and beauty.

By midmorning they could see the crossroads in the distance. Five people could be seen at the crossroads. As they approached the figures became clearer. Some were of people, who Marius could make out as Macaro, Mathius, Clive, Cynthia and another figure whose back was turned to Macaro and he could not make out. Around them were horses and tents on the side of the road.

Once all of the people were clearly visible Marius heart dropped: the fifth person, who Marius had not recognized, was Nathaniel. Macaro saw the three of them and started sprinting towards Ralis, who carried Yuri. Within seconds, Macaro reached

Ralis and swiftly they traded Yuri. In the distance Marius saw Mathius and Clive put the finishing touches on a mare's straddle and stirrups. Marius just stood there, shocked by the emotion that spun around him. Macaro set up a horse immediately, he hoisted Yuri on top of the horse that Mathius and Clive set up. Placing Yuri upright in front of the saddle, he jumped on himself and kicked his legs.

"Nathaniel, I leave this to you. Move, horse, heya!" And Macaro was off and Yuri with him. Marius watched as his friend rode out of view.

"Marius, where the hell have you been?!" Mathius stomped over towards Marius with Clive following tail, both looked awfully grumpy.

"Across the whole valley and back," Marius smirked at his remark, and then started bellowing with laughter. To his surprise Mathius and Clive started roaring with laughter as well. Mathius ran up to him, embracing Marius in a hug.

"My god, Marius, you've had all of us worried sick. What did you do to Yuri?" Clive approached as Mathius let go of Marius.

"And why didn't you bring me, asshole?" Mathius scoffed pushing Marius.

"Leave Marius alone he's been through a tremendous amount, as well as Yuri," Nathaniel approached, his skin glowed, his eyes pierced hard into Marius' skull. Something felt off.

"You two," Nathaniel pointed at Mathius and Clive, "ready a horse for our dear Marius."

Nathaniel placed his arm around Marius' shoulder and started to walk him towards the other side of the crossroads where the horses were hitched against a maple tree. Beside the horses was Cynthia. Her brown hair swayed in the wind as she looked at Marius. She looked away once Marius met her eyes, obviously she'd been staring. Nathaniel rambled something in Marius' ear but his mind was elsewhere. Cynthia looked back at Marius and a huge smile appeared on both of their faces. She looked beautiful, and Marius reacted instinctively, leaving Nathaniel's arm he ran towards her. They embraced in a hug. Marius could feel her heart beat against his chest.

"You were supposed to go to protect Yuri," said Cynthia, speaking into Marius' ear.

"Things got out of control." But before Marius could say anymore Nathaniel had caught up to them.

"Now, now, have patience, love birds. Let's get Marius back to Highwash. Ralis, ride with Marius here back to Highwash. The other two shall have horses, as for myself, I will hike back."

Marius had forgotten slightly about Ralis since the commotion started. He had remained quiet the whole time.

"At once, Marius."

Ralis hopped onto one horse and gestured Marius to hop on behind. Marius got on at once, Ralis' stern face told him not delay with any goodbyes. Ralis nudged the horse on and they were off. Looking back, Marius could see the three of them watching their departure. Once they were out of range, Marius began to pry. He knew he shouldn't, but a part of him just needed to ask questions.

"Well, that was awkward," Marius spoke, trying to bring up the topic gently. "I mean I didn't expect Nathaniel to be there."

"That was one alternative I'd considered. It seems to me that Nathaniel was quick to return to his role as Archmage, doesn't it?"

"Yes, it does."

Marius waited a bit before asking, wanting it to seem like he had thought of the question spontaneously. "Why was Nathaniel never around when I was younger?"

"You're wrong about your accusation, but slightly right. Nathaniel was around at times. But… he seemed to be always obsessed on something. Usually he was off exploring or investigating, as he would say. But even when he was at Highwash, he locked himself in his study."

Ralis went quiet for a second, as he usually did, preoccupied by thought, of events that had passed and events to come.

"But, to answer your question, I don't know why, Marius."

The horse trotted on while they talked, ignorant to the conversation. The afternoon sun held high and Marius was glad to be on a horse and off his feet for once.

"You said Nathaniel was your friend, and you also said you aren't a Mage. So how did you meet Nathaniel?"

"Marius, your persistence bugs me. But I guess I at least owe you some truth since what's happened. How can I keep this simple?"

"Hunger, that's what drives the impoverished. You see, controlling the food supply is what is most important."

Two aristocrats talked as they walked through set up stands, each bartering different food. It was a gorgeous summer day in Palinteer. A modest civilization west of Salamon's Keep, ruled under the Salamon family reign. It was one of those days where everything is pleasing and the mind is free from anxiety, though usually provided that you have some form of wealth.

Unfortunately for Ralis, he had not accumulated much wealth. Being a kid on the streets didn't bear well with making a great fortune. Ralis watched these two aristocrats from a distance, blending in with the hoards of a crowd. He watched and listened, the traits of any good thief. The words of his father rung through his head, "A thief's greatest ability is in his ability to observe."

"I dare say, you hold harsh opinions of the poor. I feel that if we were to educate the poor we could lift them from the depths of their misfortune," one of the aristocrats blabbed on. He was dressed in silk white robes which matched is pale skin. "Look, on paper Palinteer is one of Salamon's richest and wealthiest towns, but in person this place is a mere shithole. The dock is pungent with trash, the streets are littered with poor, beggars at our feet everywhere." He pointed as he talked.

"No, no. That would be a crude mistake, the poor must remain poor. Keeping the poor poor gives us a steady supply of food and soldiers." The two of them chuckled. Moving on they continued checking stands of barter.

Some sold apples and lycas, others sold vegetables. The variety of foods was insurmountable. Palinteer was the centre of trade for Thenus and provided ample opportunity for young orphans like Ralis. Ralis wove through crowds, invisible, as no one gazed upon the poor, especially the ones who begged, the ones who stole. Weaving through he stalked the two men like a snake, slithering. Two years of stealing, two years of begging and evading guards, two years of death knocking at your doorstep. Those two years had taught Ralis much. Taught him how to steal.

He followed and followed, until the marketplace narrowed in between log buildings. The ground changed from tiled stone to dirt. The aristocrats talked on oblivious to their stalker. And then he saw it the perfect moment. They had left the main centre of the marketplace and were headed down side streets, the amount of people thinned out making it ideal to pass by them as they turned a corner. The two aristocrats turned down another side street just in time to hit a crowd surrounding a vendor in which they could not glimpse what he was selling. It must've been something good, thought Ralis, maybe even good enough to steal. He told himself to focus, stay on target, and, right when the two aristocrats merged with the crowd, he sped up towards them. Weaving his steps between fellow men and women, he soon reached the aristocrats who were turned away from Ralis, walking forward down the street. They stopped for a second gazing at a lonely stand, marvelling its wares.

"Here we have a rare honey made from winter climate bees native to Arngrimir," the salesman who looked old and suspicious pushed hard to sell the two obviously wealthy men his items.

"How could you have shipped such a honey, across sea? The war between Salamon and Arngrimir has been boiling for centuries. Not one ship has passed in years," one of the aristocrats spoke intensely.

Ralis paid no attention to their banter. His focus was on a coin pouch that hung on the aristocrat's waist.

"Some traders I know have tie-ins with Arngrimirian's themselves."

"I hardly believe so."

"Hey! Wait! God damn! Blasted thief! Thief!"

And, before the aristocrats knew it, Ralis had snatched one of their coin purses and was off sprinting though the street. He wove between two people, skipped behind a stand and turned right down a narrow alleyway. He didn't look back, he only focused on what was forward.

Sprinting down a cobbled alley, he turned right down another street that led behind buildings.

"Catch that blasted boy!"

Ralis could hear cries in the distance behind him. The voices fuelled him to keep running. Turning left Ralis headed down another empty alleyway. He quickly turned right again to head into a nook he'd noticed in between two houses. Turning sideways, he squeezed into the nook, the wood of both houses scratching his skin and scraping his ragged robes. The nook led back into another marketplace, it was less busy than the central market, but, nonetheless, Ralis had many people to blend into. He turned his running pace into a walking pace and held his head down. It seemed like a successful catch.

Later that evening Ralis sat under the wooden docks of the harbour. Palinteer's incredible economy was because Palinteer was situated beside a large river. This enabled a huge port and harbour to be built on the edge of the city.

Ralis sat beneath the wooden docks. His small, childlike frame enabled him to crawl beneath the wooden planks and logs which held the massive wooden beams that supported the dock. Freshwater barnacles littered the damp logs. Underneath the dock was Ralis' sanctuary; it had become his home ever since his father passed away.

"Holy crap," Ralis whispered to himself as he counted his loot. He counted and recounted and his tally was ten silver coins and three gold coins. This meant supper was waiting for Ralis, not just tonight but for many fortnights. And after waiting for hours until dusk in the damp under space of the docks, Ralis had grown very hungry. So, leaving the sanctity of his hovel, he headed for the eastern market away from where he'd performed his thievery. The way brought peace to Ralis, finally masking his constant anxiety. The evening was upon the town, bringing an orange hue after the day's sun.

"A little boy shouldn't be stealing."

A voice from behind Ralis made him jump. He quickly turned around to see a large man with braided hair behind him. He instantly reacted to start running, but it was too late. The man had grasped his arm, his grip unrelenting.

"A little boy should not have to be stealing at all. Where are you parents, boy?"

Ralis was frozen with fear, his arms shaking violently. Ralis had witnessed the punishment for thievery many times.

"Has a crow stolen your tongue? Where are your parents?" the man asked again.

"My... my father is dead."

"And your mother?"

"The same."

The man grew silent for a second and his grip on Ralis' arm eased slightly. "I'm sorry to hear that, young lad. Come, please walk with me."

The two of them headed down the streets, Ralis had not a clue of what was happening. He was afraid, but the man's demeanour felt relaxing. Ralis had just become aware of the man's features as well. He looked different from the guards or most men. His hair was black and long, wrapped in many braids.

"My name is Nathaniel. I witnessed your event today, the one at the market." His face was stern as he looked at Ralis while he said this. "I don't approve of stealing, but I also don't approve of orphans abandoned to steal on the streets. Now, I will be straightforward with you, little boy. First, what is your name? Absolute apologies, I told you mine but forgot to request yours." The man's face froze on a blank staring facial expression, telling Ralis to answer quickly to avoid interrupting his rant.

"My name is Ralis."

"Unique name. Now, as I was saying, I will be straightforward with you. I know of a certain community who would rather use your talents for better uses. I'm sure you would testify that yourself. Isn't it ironic that you're living out your father's fate, the fate of the thief? I'm sure you, too, believe that you could achieve more?" His face froze again unmoving, waiting for a response. Ralis was confused, how did he know of his father, was this the man that…? It can't be… that man never saw… he'd been crouched in the corner. He didn't see.

"No, I am not that man, nor have I ever killed."

Ralis shook terribly. The man knew what he was thinking. His heart started to race, his legs naturally starting to back him up.

"Now don't fret so easily, I can hear your thoughts. Let's keep it at that for now, and it's not as if your situation is not grim. Any day now you shall be caught stealing, a matter of probability. The situation is not your fault, I know, but it does further my point. Can you read, Ralis?"

"No, I can't." Ralis looked down thinking the man would think negatively of him.

"Well, you can if you have the will to. I offer you this: Come with me and I'll take you off the streets to a place where you will have a family, a place to learn and a place to make an impact rather than spend the next of your years behind bars. What do you say?"

"See, naturally, I refused. A weird man appearing out of nowhere offering me a way out really seemed too good to be true."

"So, how did you end up with him?" Marius asked as the horse trotted on, he was so interested in Ralis' story he had forgotten his hunger and thirst, but the sudden surge of it reminded him swiftly.

"I'm done with storytelling, Marius. This day has been awkward enough, I'd rather not continue to bring up my past."

"You can't just leave me there, with that kind of ending," Marius complained.

"Unfortunately, Marius, I can."

The two of them rode into Highwash just as evening approached. As soon as they reached the centre of the village, Macaro insisted Marius go see Mirane.

Marius spent the following days in bed. Macaro insisted, again, that Marius should rest from training for at least two days. Marius argued, claiming he was fine, only a few bruises bugged him, but Macaro did not budge, arguing that Marius must regenerate his qi. Apparently weeks of malnutrition have a negative impact on ones qi.

Staying in bed bugged Marius, mainly as he was separated from Yuri. He wondered what state Yuri was in. Macaro and the others who visited him regularly stated that Yuri was recovering quickly, but Marius still wanted to see him for himself. Marius also had not seen Nathaniel or Ralis since he arrived at Highwash.

On the second day Macaro came in and placed his hand on the blanket above Marius' belly.

"Good, you seem to have recovered fast. You should get up now and do some training, maybe even some energy work. It's about midday. At sundown, please visit me at my quarters."

Without allowing a word from Marius, Macaro headed out of the small cabin Marius lay in. Marius didn't get up for a bit. He contemplated what Macaro would tell him tonight.

I assume he will bring up my punishment, which could be a number of things, ran through his mind.

Marius put his worries aside; thinking of Yuri, he sat up. He was stiff from the days in bed but soon enough he was out the door. Its rough metal hinges creaked as it opened. The September sun laid its beams upon Marius' face as he exited the cabin. It was warm, and Highwash was inviting. It was good to be back from such a treacherous adventure. First he needed to find Mirane. She cooked for students at Highwash but she also was a master healer, and she would be in charge of Yuri's care.

Mirane's cabin was close to where Marius had stayed. It was large and square with trusses that peaked high at a sharp angle. Marius knocked on the cabin's wooden door. Shuffling could be heard from inside. The door swung open.

"Yes, Marius! I've been expecting you. Macaro said you would be coming by. Yuri is up, so it's a good time."

Mirane opened the door, her hair was let loose and she looked awfully tired. She took Marius' hand and led him in. Inside many beds were lining the perimeter of the hut. Yuri lay on one of the beds. Medical equipment, herbs and liquids were placed in many locations in the room, allowing Mirane easy access to them. Yuri was up and looking better, his skin had obtained most of its colour back and his face looked spry. He was shirtless except for bandages over his left abdomen. His veins looked blue and constricted on his right chest.

"Yuri."

Marius walked over to his friend, overcome with emotion. Both of them froze for a second, both not knowing how to react to such a situation, they looked as if they were going to hug, but then didn't.

"I made it back, see?" Yuri chuckled as he talked with a ton of sarcasm.

"We had to carry you though."

Both of them laughed awkwardly.

"So how do you feel, what's the damage?" Marius slowly asked.

"Nice way to ask gently. Worst case scenario, I lose some feeling in my right abdomen, best case scenario, it's just a nasty scar. I'm not fully recovered yet, though, Mirane says training should be rejuvenating, no energetic practices for a week. It may help with healing."

They both were still for a second, both not knowing what to say.

"I'm sorry Yuri, I shouldn't have let you get attacked. There was just so—"

"Marius. You got me out of there, you guys got me home. What more could I ask?"

"Well then, I'm sorry I didn't see that coming." Marius stuttered for a second before continuing. "I have to train anyways, now—Macaro's command—back to training again."

"Hopefully," Yuri responded dully.

They held a long stare. Then Marius thanked Mirane for her care of Yuri and himself, and left. Marius started to head towards a section of granite slab that met the ocean waves. The spot he had in mind was where his class usually went to practice horse stance. Marius loved the spot and practiced there privately.

Waves crashed and clashed with the rock wall when he arrived. The torrent of noise always calmed his mind. The large amounts of noise drew his focus on the sounds and not his mind. Today the noise was especially useful. His conversation with Yuri had been weird and indifferent.

He began his training with basic movements; first horse stance, then Marius moved on to basic fighting positions and flows. The basic fighting stances were meant to cover all skills a Mage would need. Marius practiced these with much repetition; he assumed his classmates did as well. He then moved into more complex kicks and strikes. Hours went by as he moved from fighting to energy work. By the evening he had covered most skills and he ended in horse stance.

It was time to see Macaro. Marius started his way back to Highwash, the small trees that occasionally came into view awed him. He thought that this might be the last time he would witness them.

"Come in."

Marius heard Macaro's voice as he knocked on Macaro's cabin door. Marius opened the door. Macaro sat on a rickety, wooden chair looking out a lone window.

"Sit down, please." He gestured Marius to sit on a stool.

Marius sat down, shuffling his legs, he prepared for what he knew would be an awkward conversation.

"We as Mages rely on something much larger than energy, and that is trust. It's the bond that holds us together, it's the bond that unites us as friends and companions." Macaro began talking, but did not change his stare out the window. "Trust is what forms all of our relationships here at Highwash. That's why I instil a sense of great obedience in my students towards their Elders. But there always comes a time when a student disobeys an Elder's command and the trust is broken."

Macaro finally turned to look at Marius. "Do you not trust me, Marius? Do you not trust my teachings? Do you not trust the warnings I heed?" He waited for an answer from Marius and got nothing but silence. "Then why was it necessary to follow Ralis?"

Marius began to speak, ready to talk about how Yuri was planning on going anyways and his intention was to bring Yuri back—but that wasn't the truth. So he stopped himself from speaking it. "I'm sorry Elder. We…"

"I will talk with Yuri later. Please speak for yourself. Why did you follow Ralis?"

Marius thought for a bit, deeply trying to find a rational explanation Macaro would believe.

"I would want to tell you that I went for Yuri's sake, but, honestly, Yuri had made me curious. He assumed something was up when Ralis interrupted our lesson. And more, he pressed the fact that we had never seen or met the Archmage—which is odd enough for growing up here. So I followed Yuri, justifying it with the fact I wanted to protect him. Which, as you see, I failed."

"Ralis fully briefed me of what had occurred over the last weeks; he has told me an awful lot. Also much about Nathaniel, our Archmage. Which leads me to ask: what did Ralis tell you?" Macaro's face was slightly inquisitive. A chill shot down Marius' spine, he did not know how Macaro would take the answer to his question.

"I was told Nathaniel had attacked him. He had bruises, and I had asked—more than asked, actually—more like inquired."

"And what do you think of that story?"

"Well, it has evidence to support it. Ralis' wounds are one. As well Nathaniel was never to be seen when we fled the ruins."

"Nathaniel had ran into me, he was on his way to get help from Highwash," Macaro said, deflecting some of Marius' argument.

"Yuri was gravely injured. You would think an Archmage would have stayed to help with his superior healing skills. Plus, he fled before we physically left the ruins, he fled right when I came up from the tunnel entrance from the ruins."

"What tunnels?" Macaro's face frowned to this.

"There was a collapsed portion of the ruins which led to a long stretch of tunnels. Nathaniel sent us down there knowing those beasts lurked down there—another reason why I believe he attacked Ralis. He must've known of those creatures, or else why did he send Yuri and I down there?"

"That is interesting."

Macaro stood up and turned himself to gaze outside the window again. It was not glassed, just an opening in the wall, so he put his hand on the wood that separated inside and outside.

"You may go, Marius."

"That's it? No punishment?"

"Why? Do you want more of a punishment then you have had?"

And before Macaro completed the sentence Marius had left his cabin.

VI

"There is a sword greater than all other swords, a strength that can lift all others, a state of mind that trumps all anger. What I speak of is compassionate nature. Form follows function. We purify our minds with study, study of self, the world, nature, martial arts and the stars. We purify our bodies with practice and correct eating. We purify our soul with meditation. All to meet the ends of creating a pure vessel, to transmit compassion. A Mage can find him or herself practicing for many years and still miss the most important point: Compassion for others, compassion for ourselves. That is our way of being... Mathius please pay attention."

Mathius woke suddenly with an embarrassed expression and drool on the side of his mouth. The class chuckled. The event slightly alerted Marius; he, too, found these lectures boring and struggled to keep awake.

"Now see, young children, we may never use our skills to kill another. May we never strike any blow without necessity. I know I say this every lecture, but the point must be emphasized: If we let our mind wander, our feelings get out of control; one may be so easily tempted to use their skills when flustered or angry. Now today's lecture is on star constellations."

Lectures from Macaro were always held in the main hall and the hard floor always grew uncomfortable during them. The students sat on the circle of descending stairs, while Macaro stood in the centre. He paced as he talked, not out of anxiety, but out of excitement.

Astronomy lectures were Marius' least favourite, to say the least. He always complained and complained to Yuri about them whenever they studied it together. Marius removed the memory from his head and refocused on Macaro's lecture.

"There are many local star clusters we can't see. The fact that we are located in the northern hemisphere means we cannot view any stars below our horizon."

The lecture droned on for another hour until they were dismissed.

"We will have a lesson tonight, please meet me by the logs," Macaro said as he dismissed the class.

It had been two days since Marius had talked to Macaro about his punishment. Yuri and he seemed to somehow have avoided Macaro's retaliation, as if Yuri's injury deflected such scrutiny.

"Now we know of southern star clusters, aren't you thankful?" Yuri joked as he walked up from behind Marius, both of them headed out of the hall.

Marius laughed reading Yuri's hints of sarcasm. They exited the hall into the midday sun. It was a cooler day than most. The fall had slowly been starting its approach.

"How do you think we got off that easy?" Yuri asked Marius when they were well away from the hall.

"To be honest, I have no clue. What did Macaro say to you?"

"Well, he droned on about trust for a bit, my injury, how I should be thankful of Mirane and Ralis—"

"Speaking of Ralis—have you seen him lately?" Marius said cutting Yuri off.

"No, I haven't seen him." Being cut off bugged Yuri, but he let it go; if he had continued he would have said how Macaro told him to be most thankful of Marius.

"Well, we have a bit of time. Let's check around for him, I've been wanting to thank him for a while now."

So the two of them roamed around the village of Highwash. They first visited the stables. Greeting them there was Stable Master Talun. He was old and everyone found a great awkwardness in his being, but his way with horses matched no others in Highwash. Talun stood in a stable beside a horse, combing the mare's fur.

"Shouldn't you two be in a lesson?" Talun greeted them bitterly, and then quickly changed his expression to a happy smile. "Jesting, I'm just jesting ya. I don't get much visitors here, only when someone wants a horse. Wait, don't you even start about asking me for horses, I ain't allowed to loan apprentices horses, Macaro's command."

"No, don't worry we don't want a horse, we were actually just coming by to ask if you have seen Ralis?" Marius said.

"Of course, silly me, expecting youse young'uns to be visiting me. Ralis, the fella had just stopped by recently, asking for a horse and whatnot. And I said, Nope! I said, Not after the last horse you got slaughtered. He didn't take that too kindly and stormed off somewheres. I'm sure he will be back for a horse. I mean I'm going to have to give 'em one eventually, but to witness his face was worth it." Talun chuckled hoarsely to his own comment.

"Well, do you know where he was headed after he left?" asked Marius.

"Not sure where he went. But he did seem in a hurry that's for sure. How about this? I'm liking you two, good mannered. So I will have to eventually give him a stallion of mine, but how about I delay it till this afternoon. If you understand me?"

"We understand you clear," responded Yuri.

"Good, come here when the sun's about three quarters set."

The boys thanked Talun and set off back towards the village. The sun was bright and the day was cool. So the two of them decided to spar. Yuri and Marius were often sparing partners and today was no different.

"Where do you want to train?" Marius asked as they walked around the centre of the village. None of their classmates were around, presumably training, they thought.

"Let's head to the cliff's edge? I like the scent of the salt," Yuri responded.

"Yes, you've told me before. I was thinking the fields, but I don't mind the cliffs. Easier to bash your head into the rock, I guess," teased Marius.

Yuri chuckled and gave Marius a slight push, and they started their way to the cliffs.

They arrived out of breath and sweaty, Yuri decided a race would be fun. Huffing as he talked, Yuri hollered over the sound of the waves. "What do you want to practice?"

"I was thinking we could just spar, you haven't sparred in a bit as you're injured. That would be a good way to start, don't you think?"

Yuri responded by quickly stepping into horse stance, his knees bent and ready. Marius responded with the same. Stepping side to side, they both walked, circling a small space. Yuri boldly stepped his right foot forward in an attempt to make the first move. With his left he sent a roundhouse towards Marius' jaw. Marius easily dodged the kick, ducking underneath it and sending a strike at Yuri's body. Blocking the strike, Yuri sent his right arm down. Jumping up Marius sent two kicks to Yuri's chest, the first kick Yuri dodged, the second connected. Yuri groaned, winded, but that did not stop him from reacting. As Marius landed from his kicks, Yuri sent an elbow to connect at Marius' head. Marius quickly raised his arm to block the elbow but was unable to react in time when Yuri grappled him, delivering a suplex to Marius and slamming him into the ground. Marius was up fast, delivering a swift kick to Yuri's head as he was crouched. Yuri rolled to the side dodging the kick and both of them were swiftly back on their feet. Pacing in a circle.

Later that afternoon the two of them talked on as they walked back towards Talun's stable.

"I believe I won that one," Yuri boasted as he hopped forward on the dirt pathway.

"I'd have to disagree, I held back because of your injury," Marius said jokingly.

Marius and Yuri always had competition between the two of them. Whether it was energy work, physical competitions or the Elder's approval, both of them wanted to be on top. It was a friendly competition and it never developed much animosity between them. They both were in laughter as they approached Talun's stables where the old man could be seen talking with Ralis and setting up a saddle on a grey mare. It was tall and burly but obviously aged.

"Now, this is the best you will get after last time's catastrophe."

"Well, I thank you, Talun." Ralis nodded as he said this.

"Aah, the two fellers." Talun hollered over for Marius and Yuri to come to them as he noticed them approaching. Ralis looked at them sharply and swiftly, then turned away quickly. Both Marius and Yuri thought that was weird of him, his hesitancy was unusual. Yuri started talking before Marius said a word.

"You never visited me while I was healing." Yuri said it mockingly, his intent to get a laugh from Ralis. Ralis, unfortunately, did not laugh.

"I didn't think you were that attached to me," Ralis said without looking at the two of them.

"No... but I..." was all Yuri could say before Ralis objected.

"No. See? That clears the air."

"But I thought you'd at least come to check how I was doing."

"See, following me in the first place was your fault. I got you home safely, what more did you except of me?"

"I don't expect anything more... just... what's gotten into you anyway?" Yuri asked.

Marius thought an awful answer awaited them.

"What's gotten into me is that for some unknown reason you two fancy following my steps. I don't find it flattering you investigated around to find out I was leaving."

Ralis stood up from tying the horse's tethers and hung a large rucksack over the horse's rear.

"That wasn't our intention. We just wanted to come find you." Marius began talking but then his tongue froze midsentence.

It did seem slightly absurd that Yuri and him went to find Ralis. It began to be apparent that Ralis never acted out of friendship, but out of obligation.

"But we get it, Ralis, we will be going. Come on, Yuri."

Marius grabbed Yuri by his shoulder and started to steer him to leave, but then stopped in his tracks.

"So you're leaving?" Marius asked slowly.

"Yes," Ralis said as he led the horse out of the stable.

Talun looked depressed as he realized he had to part with another one of his horses.

Both Yuri and Marius left without saying another word. It was only till later that evening Marius realized Ralis left without ever finishing his story.

VII

A dark red hue filled the main hall; the light flickered fast from the unkept embers, fading. The room was quiet and the group of students sat on the circled steps waiting for Macaro to speak. The mood was slightly grave, everyone had heard the whispers of Ralis' sudden departure. Ralis did not teach much at Highwash but his absence was never the less noted.

"A gracious summer we have had. Filled with adventure, only a single storm and many beautiful nights," Macaro began to speak. "And now, as we approach the change of the season, we enter in autumn. The season of change, of hibernation, and the entering of the great sleep. For you, all though you enter a time of change yourselves, a time of change and challenge. The time is approaching for the second task, a task that will unite you all in a common cause but only to separate you and pit you against one another. This task represents the physical adeptness of a Mage and will challenge each of you so."

The class stirred at the words Macaro spoke.

"The world is not as romantic as one would like to think. Reality bears harsh realizations, and the world outside Highwash is not exempt from the reality of life. Beyond the eastern mountain range, lies the rest of the continent of Thenus."

Marius' mind drifted off to the maps he had studied. He thought about how far west Highwash was and how small it looked compared to the rest of the pages. He remembered how much Yuri hated studying the maps of the world, how he claimed they were useless and triflingly boring. They had interested Marius. *Who had written such maps?* he wondered, it would seem that only a bird could see such a view of the lands, which led Marius to conclude that there was a high probability of error among the maps and charts of the world, and that the truth would be far more exciting than staring at maps. These tasks were his way to explore. If he passed each task he would move up to the position of an Adept Mage and be allowed the privilege of leaving Highwash.

"I have had long talks with Mirane, countless discussions on whether or not to burden young children with the truth."

Marius became aware again and focused on Macaro's words.

"Each of you, remember our teachings, of love, of respect, of family, honour, integrity and, most of all, compassion. Keep those ideals in your hearts. I say all this because there is an unfortunate truth that we are burdened with being warriors of the light. We're not the only Mages that live in Thenus; there are our brothers and sisters."

Macaro seemed disturbed as he spoke, his voice was slow and methodical, as if he chose each word very carefully.

"But they've been guided down the wrong path. Now this brings me to the purpose of this task: Each of you must be able to defend themselves and each other. You will all be split into groups of two and fight each other until the other submits, or cannot stand."

The classmates looked at each other, stunned.

"One who wishes you pain will not grant you an easy fight. Find no sympathy for your friends during this task, as your enemies will not be so kind."

Cynthia raised her hand.

"Yes, Cynthia."

Her soft voice chimed up, "These Mages, what's so different about their path?"

"Their path embraces dissolution of compassion and embraces death and control. Pain and fear are their tool."

Silence as loud as shouts filled the hall.

"Now, moving on, in two days the task will commence. I will suspend lessons until then. Do what you must to prepare. These are your two days."

It was evening, the sky was a dark red and the air outside the hall was brisk and cool. The cold air filled Marius' lungs as he and the other students left the great hall after the lesson.

"Are you nervous, Cynthia?" Marius could hear Daniel break out laughing as he hollered.

"I think you're the one who's nervous to get beat by girl," Cynthia countered.

"If only that was the case."

Daniel and Mathius chuckled as they splintered off from the group headed towards their own destination.

"What arses they are," Cynthia remarked as she caught up to Marius and Yuri who walked together.

"They're only joking, don't mind them. Though they did bring up a good point, I wonder who we'll be facing, and there's an odd number of students in this class, so, I wonder how Macaro will fill that space," Marius said.

"Probably some other student. It doesn't matter anyways, I honestly don't have a clue what to except. And does he really expect us to pummel the crap out of each other?" Yuri scoffed as they continued onwards.

Their destination was Mirane's dining hall, where food was being served most times of the day.

"Apparently he does," Cynthia said coldly.

"Just treat it like sparring, because that's exactly what we're going to be spending these two days on," Marius joked trying to lighten the mood.

The three of them went silent. All of them felt uneasy and anxious about the upcoming task. Facing any one of their friends at anything more than sparring seemed very harsh for a task. Marius' thoughts wandered as they walked. The village was always peaceful at this time of day; many of the Elders were off in meditation or eating, classes were over and most wildlife started off to sleep. This was Marius' favourite time to think, the quietness of evening. He wondered whom he would fight in two days. He wanted to fight Cynthia and Yuri the least. He could not bear to harm them for real, they were his greatest friends at Highwash. Marius also disliked the idea of facing some of the older students. Mathius and Daniel were much older and stronger than him and would prove a great challenge, and, in the depths of Marius' mind, he thought it to be most likely a loss. In honesty, all of Macaro's students were going to be a challenge, each of them were fierce combatants.

The three of them approached Mirane's dining hall. The door was open and many students were inside, some Marius recognized as Adepts or other apprentices. Reggard and Clive were both seated at a long table in the far left corner. Marius and Reggard met eyes and Reggard waved the three of them to come and sit.

"This second task is a bunch of shit, huh?" Reggard asked them.

"Yes, I have to agree. His words were 'until they cannot stand,' I don't think I could fight any of you with the aim to hurt," Marius said, answering Reggard.

"Agreed."

The bangs of Reggard's rough blonde hair swung to the side of his face as he turned to Marius. They sat silent for a second, but before long Reggard and Clive were arguing about who would most likely fight who, breaking the depressing silence. Marius, Yuri and Cynthia all sat quiet for similar reasons; all of them were absorbed in their mind anxious of the upcoming task.

The forest loomed before Sebastien. Old pines and fir trees filled their surroundings all around him and his brigade. Sebastien led the force on horseback through the treacherous forest. Sebastien disliked coming out this far west. The mountains of western Thenus proved unsettling, the mysterious woods had led his troops and himself in circles; maps proved incorrect. And still they had not seen any sign of the Rangers. The path he currently rode could barely be considered a trail. Bushes reached out to snare his feet with every step his horse took. Even his stallion had hard times traversing the forest so used to riding the eastern plains. The sounds of hooves clattering against the ground awakened him from his thoughts.

"Lord Salamon, if I may?" A lone scout approached Sebastien on horse.

The scout was coated in sweat which soaked through his arms of Salamon's scout troops. A dark leather suit embroidered with steel buckles, now damp and rank with sweat from his harsh ride to the front.

"Yes, you may. What is it, scout?" Sebastien replied as he halted his horse.

He swung himself off the horse to greet the scout who had done the same. His armour clattered as he stepped off his horse. The scout was obviously admiring the armour's craftsmanship.

"Some of the scouts have noted a clearing among the mountain ridges just five leagues north of here, sir." The scout bowed as he spoke.

"Rise, and speak, what is your name?"

"Sir Ramsely, my lord. Just northwest, a path has been located which my scouts believe will further penetrate the mountain range. It needs further scouting, but my scouts have already established a camp just before and are investigating as we speak." The scout bowed again.

"That is good news. I'm getting very tired of aimless wandering, Sir Ramsely. Come, accompany me back to the main force. We will decide our next move there."

The scout nodded in agreement and hopped back on his horse. Sebastien did the same.

"So, Sir Ramsely, has there been any leads on the rangers, any recent news?"

"None whatsoever, my lord, these renegades seem awfully good at reconnaissance. They obviously change location daily. Clearly they're covering their tracks."

"Well, Sir Ramsely, that may be a lead in itself." Sebastien chuckled lightly as he spoke. "Stop calling me lord as well. Here in the forest no one 'lords,' only the forest rules."

"Truly spoken, my..." Ramsely smiled and laughed. Their horses trotted on while old crows cawed away.

"I am a Salamon, yes, but that does not make me above nature, above the gods does it? No. We are all bound to nature, Ramsely."

The scout rode silently for a bit, in awe of what he was hearing. "Have you spent much time out in the woods then, Salamon?" The scout said breaking the silence of their slow trot.

"Yes, I have. Hunting is a pastime of mine. My father would go out regularly, he would bring my brother and I on long journeys out west here in these woods. I guess that's partly why he entrusted me with command of the search." Sebastien looked down slightly in thought about his father, he rubbed his stallion's mane feeling the softness of its fur.

The scout cleared his throat. "Why are we in search for these Rangers, my lord? I mean, I respect any command from my lordship, but these Rangers seem like common rabble, why waste time on bandits and rebels? Why, we have Arngrimir at our shores."

"Questions I ask myself, Sir Ramsely." Sebastien did wonder why his father was so set on this vendetta against these Rangers of the West. They were known for small raids of travelling merchants and supply garrisons, but nothing severe.

"Why are you so kindly, my lord?" The scout asked reprehensibly.

"I try not to be like my family. I view common men no worse than me, most of all in places like this. My father always taught me that nature shows man's true nature, that no man is above anyone here. So you see, Sir Ramsely, we are all brothers out here in god's domain."

They rode silently for the rest of the journey through heavy bush and thickets of trees, making their way back to the main force. When they finally reached the main force, Sebastien noticed unrest among his troops. All appeared normal, many men were busy in discussion, under tents mapping routes or gathering gear and preparing to move forward from this camp. Many troops were mounted on horses ready to move.

"Sir Ramsely! Sir Ramsely!" A lesser scout could be seen running up towards Salamon and Ramsely.

"Yes, squire?" Ramsely spoke attentively intending to impress Lord Salamon.

"Scout Major Harding asked me to escort you to him at your arrival, err, Lord Salamon," the squire bowed as he acknowledged his lord. "Your presence will be welcome as well."

The scout waved them to follow. They both hitched their horses and started to follow the scout.

"What's this about, scout?" Sebastien asked weaving in and out of frantically moving soldiers.

"I don't know the news, my lord. I was only asked to come find Sir Ramsely at his soonest arrival, but word is some news has gotten everyone ready to move onward." The scout huffed and puffed in between words his pace quickening. "It sure has gotten folks frantic."

Sebastien did notice a vibe around camp, and no sooner did he arrive at Scout Major Harding's makeshift command tent did he find out why. The scout that led them to the tent opened one side of the flapped entrance and waved them to go in. The daylight lit the inside of the tent, casting a red hue that penetrated through the tent. A lone desk was placed in the middle with many papers scattered among the desk. A large map was placed on top of papers and was obviously the paper of interest.

"Aw, yes, Lord Sebastien and Sir Ramsely." Major Harding bowed as they entered.

The major had a deep dark brown hair colour and an awful-looking complexion from many days in the sun.

"Come in at once, dire news has reached us, some of my scouts were sent out east through the valley. Actually I'd best not tell this tale. Squire! Sorry, m'lord, I have not yet to learn everyone's name. Yes, squire!"

The young squire that guided them to Harding's tent burst through the flapped entrance bowing ready for a command.

"Squire, see that Sir Christian and Sir Alec come here at once," the major commanded.

Before long two more scouts marched into the tent, one looked feeble and small while the other one tall and rugged.

"Scouts, tell Sir Ramsely and Lord Salamon here what you told me."

The feeble looking scout began to speak. "Well, sir, two days past my trio of scouts came past a large riverbed, we went there to rest and to wash. But as we stayed there we noticed these scorched into the ground."

The tall scout pulled out three metal chains with Salamon's crest of a rose on each of them. Sebastien took them and placed them on the table.

"These are signets, anyone who bears arms for Salamon are given these," Sebastian claimed. He stared at the signet necklaces, deep in thought of what it could mean. "They have charcoal stains on them, as well, signs of combustion, meaning these were burned. There were no corpses near where you found these?" Sebastien asked to the two scouts.

"No, my lord. We scoured the surroundings, but nothing was to be found, we barely came across the necklaces in between the rocks of the riverbed."

"Major Harding, are any of your scouts unaccounted for?"

"Many. But we have had no word from a certain trio of scouts we sent out west a month ago. It seems too long for them to have not returned."

"Sir Ramsely, ride out to the western camp, find out if the missing scouts have returned or not. You may take men with you if you need. Make haste, autumn approaches and our return to the Keep is within a month's time."

Sebastien gave Sir Ramsely the necklaces as he gave the command. "Present these to the major there, he might recognize their names."

Sir Ramsely gave a bow and left the tent. Sebastien gave Harding a nod and left as well; his mind in spirals about the burnt necklace. They'd been out in the western woods for nearly six months, yet just now before the winter, a lead had been found. Sebastien gave the ground a smug look as he walked in thought, wondering what it all meant.

"Dammit!" Yuri screamed.

It was the second time Mathius had knocked him down on the ground with a winding kick. Yuri clutched his scarred abdomen, pain seared through his chest. Even though the wound had healed over, he still felt pain there.

"You're still healing, Yuri, don't take it so hard," Marius said as he walked over to help Yuri up.

A few of Macaro's students had decided to spar. So Marius, Yuri, Mathius and Cynthia were practicing in the autumn sun. They still had another day to recover before the second task, so they decided today should be spent on sparring.

"Injured or not, I won't hold back on you, Yuri," Mathius said "You could've easily stepped back by pivoting your left foot to avoid that kick."

"Going to start teaching now, huh?" Yuri grumbled as he finally stood his ground. "Come on, again."

"I'm not fighting you again. This is not the time to get injured," Mathius said as he grabbed his robe that had been lying on the grass. He swung the robe around his shoulders and began to walk back to the village.

"What an asshole," Yuri spewed when Mathius was out of earshot. No one else responded to Yuri's comment.

"So, who's up for another round?" Marius asked them.

"I'm in," Cynthia answered.

"No thanks, I'm going to get some water from the well. If you want to find me later I'll be in the fields practicing forms."

"Oh, come on, Yuri, stay for another round!" Cynthia said attempting to empathize with Yuri.

"No. My side has been bugging me, this blasted wound. Fucking bugs."

The two of them let Yuri go. Then it was just Cynthia and Marius.

They looked at each other oddly, with slight interest. They hadn't had a moment alone since Marius had gotten back from his accidental journey with Ralis.

"So, you want to spar?" Cynthia winked at Marius as he spoke.

"I was actually thinking about what Yuri said, why don't we practice partnered forms? It would help with the second task." Marius gave her a slight smile responding to her wink.

Cynthia really liked Marius, but she didn't know why at times. She thought other boys of the group were more skilled at fighting, or better at manipulating elements. But she just felt something different about Marius: a gentleness that the others did not have, a way of looking at her and seeing past her attitude, her skill and her fire. Cynthia remembered things that Marius did not even recall. She remembered when Macaro had first brought him to Highwash, just a little babe with bright eyes. She remembered when he first arrived he was in tears, calling for his mother. Cynthia was only little herself at the time, but she still remembered that day as vivid as when it happened.

"I would love that, Marius," Cynthia said as she stepped to the side, widening her stance and raising her arms to either side of her.

Marius did the same and stepped beside her, widening his stance and raising his arms, his right hand touched fingers with Cynthia's left hand. They moved in unison in a circle, stepping lightly, and then they crossed forearms and stepped closer to each other, spinning rapidly. There in the autumn sun they danced, they moved slow, like the water that trickled downwards from the streams near them, moving like the wind with such grace.

Yuri's side still hurt from the blow he received from Mathius; the blow only increased the pain Yuri felt from his old wound. Troubled memories crossed his mind, but he eagerly blocked them with distracting thoughts.

He knew my wound hadn't fully healed, and he specifically targeted me there, Yuri thought to himself.

Yuri's fist clenched to the thought of the match he just had fought against Mathius. Yuri wanted nothing more in that moment other than to get Mathius as his opponent for the second task and face him fully healed. The pain in his side made him limp a bit as he walked on towards the well. He could see it in the distance—the large circle of perfectly built stonework. It was said the well fed off sources of fresh underground rivers that flowed all the way from the eastern Emeralties. Macaro had told Yuri many times that this well had the cleanest water in all of Thenus. After spending what seemed like forever pulling on the crank that lifted the bucket from up out the well, Yuri agreed with Macaro that it was the cleanest water he'd ever had.

"Injured? I saw you limp over here from the distance."

Yuri jumped when he heard the voice. He turned quickly to face it. Nathaniel stood over him, leering deep into Yuri's eyes. Yuri could hardly stand to look at Nathaniel directly.

"And jumpy?" Nathaniel laughed at his own comment. "Tell me, Yuri, what happened?" Nathaniel's face remained strangely cold as he spoke.

"Some of the students and I were practicing sparring for the upcoming task—" Yuri began speaking but was cut off by Nathaniel.

"And you lost, I assume?"

"Yes."

"To whom?"

Yuri felt obligated to answer, this, after all, was the Archmage of Highwash. "Mathius."

"Yes, of course, the eldest student. Who else was there?" Nathaniel asked continuing to pry.

"It was myself, Mathius, Marius and Cynthia."

"That must hurt then? To have your friends watch you get beaten down and to stand idle." A smug expression grew across Nathaniel's face.

"It wasn't like that, we were just practicing for the fight." Yuri disliked this attitude from Nathaniel.

"Practice is merely an imitation of life, emotions do not flee in practice. Would true friends stand idle in any situation? Practice is just as real as life."

Yuri stood confused for a second, unable to grasp or conceptualize what Nathaniel was saying. "What do you mean by this?"

"Your friends may not be there for you in times of need. Maybe that is the true lesson of this task."

"My friends would never abandon me," Yuri defended.

"You seem so sure, you thought Ralis was your friend, and he left without a second thought. You decide for yourself what to think, come to rely on yourself. Think for yourself."

Yuri was left there, stunned and in awe, as Nathaniel walked away. Doubt spread through his mind like poison but he brushed it aside.

He gulped down some water, dropped the bucket down the well and started towards the fields. At first Yuri intended to go to the fields to review his forms, but the unwanted talk with Nathaniel had left a mark upon him. Anxiety kept reeling inside Yuri, so he decided to go back to where Marius and Cynthia were last. He thought he left on slightly negative terms so returning might be in his favour.

Yuri thought about Marius, how Marius carried him back when he was injured, how many times they had laughed together. Marius would never abandon him, he thought. And Cynthia, Yuri cared for deeply. He had always had an attraction to her, but he never claimed the courage to speak of it to her, and only told Marius of his feelings. *She would never betray me either.*

A smile grew on his face in thought of his friends so he picked up his pace to ensure he did not miss them. He waded through tall grass, it prickled him through his robes as he ran through it. As he approached the spot they had sparred in he could make out some figures in between the blades of grass partially covering his view. As Yuri reached out his hand to move aside the last length of grass, he caught view of the figures fully. A jolt of shock rippled down his spine, and his face blushed red to the sight of Marius and Cynthia locked in a lover's kiss. Yuri turned and disappeared in the grass.

Yuri's room was small, contained in a wooden shack formed similar to the size of a shed, he sat on his rickety bed lost in lonely thoughts. It was near evening and he had come to his room to be alone.

A knock came at the door.

"Yuri, are you in there?"

It was Marius.

Uncomfortable feelings plunged through Yuri's stomach, but he started to breath to remain calm. "Come in."

"We went to go find you in the fields, but we couldn't find you." Marius began as he entered the room.

"I just went for a walk, my injury was acting up," Yuri lied.

"Oh." Marius looked deep at Yuri's face and recognized his sombre look. "You alright?"

Yuri's insides clenched. He looked at Marius and anger swelled in him; he could not bear to look in Marius' eyes.

"Nathaniel came and talked to me when I went to get water," Yuri admitted, avoiding the topic of witnessing Marius and Cynthia's kiss.

"That's weird. I haven't seen him in days. What did he want from you?" Marius sat down next to Yuri on his bed.

"I don't know, he ranted a bit, but it didn't make much sense."

Marius sat quietly, waiting for Yuri to say more.

"He mentioned Ralis."

"What about Ralis?"

"How we thought he was our friend and that he left so swiftly. But that's gotten me thinking, honestly."

"About why exactly Ralis left?" Marius said finishing Yuri's thought.

"Yes."

"I've been wondering that, too."

Both Marius and Yuri sat silent for a bit, until Yuri broke the silence.

"We should find out."

Marius gave Yuri a devilish look in reaction to his comment.

"And how would we find that information? It seems it has left with Ralis."

Yuri got up and headed out of his room. It was evening, an orange splash could be seen entering the sky by the approach of the sunset.

"It may not all have left with him," Yuri said as he walked, his destination unclear to Marius. Marius followed behind Yuri,

"Where are you going? What's this idea of yours now?"

Yuri spoke as he walked on. "Ralis' quarters, he must have left something behind, maybe a clue."

Marius stopped in his tracks. "But why investigate? Maybe Ralis was right, maybe we should stop putting our noses in places we don't belong."

Yuri stopped dramatically and turned to face Marius. "Something's up here, Ralis wouldn't leave for no reason. I can feel it, Marius. Whether you believe me or not, I'm going to search."

"Yuri, don't. What if you're caught? You'd be banished. What would I do without you here?"

"You have Cynthia."

Yuri's face scowled as he spoke. Marius had never seen Yuri so angry before. This had been the first time they had ever truly fought.

"What does that mean?"

Yuri turned his face so Marius could not see his eyes water.

"I saw you two in the bush today."

Yuri stormed off before Marius could say anything more. Marius stood alone wondering if he'd made a mistake kissing Cynthia. He could still feel her lips on his.

Marius felt himself floating. Lost in nothing but darkness, emptiness and void. He opened his mouth to scream but no sound could

resonate. Not in the void. He floated there, alone, unable to move or understand. Suddenly, out of nowhere, a great being stood over him. It engulfed his whole vision. Bright blue lights rippled past him. They froze over him but all was still, he could not see what was there beyond the light. If he looked, it blinded him.

The brightness grew and grew, until all Marius felt was incredible heat, but instead of burning he could feel his whole being vibrate. Before the brightness could swallow him Marius awoke, sitting up and covered in sweat.

He lay down, exhausted from his dream. It was night time, he could tell by the fact no light came up from under his doorway.

Good, Marius thought, he could get some more sleep before the second task. Marius felt exhausted and lay there trying to fall back asleep, but visions of blue light burdened his mind.

Morning came and with it light filled in Marius' bedroom from under his doorway. *Today was the day,* Marius thought as he woke, *the dawn of the second task.*

Marius was slightly tired from his restless sleep, but it didn't matter, he sat up, dressed in his robes and was out the door in seconds from waking. Thin strips of clouds lined the sky casting a shadow over Highwash. It was a brisk autumn morning. There would be no breakfast this morning; Macaro wanted the fight to be raw and harsh. *An enemy will know no boundaries to pain. And neither should you*; Macaro's words ran though his mind. All the students were meant to meet in the great hall the morning of the second task, and so Marius approached the great hall doors, ready to fight.

Inside all of his classmates were waiting. He seemed to be the last one, and apparently everyone was just as anxious as him. Macaro stood in the centre of the circle, as usual, he nodded, welcoming Marius as he entered the hall. Cynthia waved to Marius and gave him a gentle smile, Marius scanned the room and his eyes met Yuri's, who had obviously watched him enter, they glanced away as swiftly as their eyes had met. Yuri and him hadn't talked since they'd fought. He hoped he wouldn't have to fight Yuri on this day, it would hurt their relationship more to physically hurt each other after such an argument.

"Good morning, everyone. I see you all look avid and ready for the second task. You sure should be, the first task was a surprise, but the second I have given much time to prepare for. Today shall certainly be an important day for all of you. Each of you will fight, but only half of you shall move on."

The class stirred as Macaro spoke.

"I know you're all anxious to find out who each of you are fighting, but first we must go over some ground rules. The match shall continue until an opponent has been defeated and lies unconscious or until an opponent yields. Both circumstances would mean death for the losing party. No magic shall be used throughout the fight, if any magic is used, it qualifies as disqualification from the fight. This fight is to test purely the art of hand-to-hand combat. Now, each of you fight well today, fight as if your life depended on it. And remember this key mantra." The class started to say the mantra with Macaro. "We are the pillar in the ocean torrent, we are the light in the darkest of nights, we are the sword, the staff and the shield, and alone we stand as an army."

The class finished chanting, Macaro bowed and began to speak. "Clive you shall be fighting Reggard when the sun is at thirty-five degrees, Yuri you shall fight Cynthia when the sun reaches forty-five degrees, Daniel you shall fight a student from Mirane's class at noon, Mathius you shall fight Marius when the sun lies at one hundred and twenty-five degrees. Each of you come to totems at your designated time, for now the morning is yours. I shall see each of you soon." Macaro bowed and left without saying another word.

The class all stood still for a moment each contemplating their coming fight.

Shit, ran through Marius' mind, he was up against Mathius. Mathius was Macaro's best fighter, but at least he didn't have to fight Yuri or Cynthia, Marius could at least hurt Mathius without guilt. Marius left without speaking to his friends, he wanted to remain focused for the coming fight and headed to his bedroom to meditate. Marius thought if he could focus enough and study Mathius' style in his mind, it would be his best chance to defeat him. He could not doubt, but, most of all, he could not hesitate.

Deep in meditation, Marius began to focus on his feet. He could see his whole body as a mirror image, all of himself was strung together with cords of energy in all different colours. He remembered the words of Macaro's talk with him. Mayura the internal void. All consciousness stemmed from it.

The first task had left a mark on Marius, he could feel it every time he meditated. He was more sensitive after the first task, while in deep meditation he could feel the energy outside of himself, the deep rumbles of the earth, the vibrations in the air, the rapid movement of particles around him, unrelenting and unpredictable, all around him centres of energy smaller than a single grain of sand, vibrated, all held together by the strings of life. His own thoughts started to become physical waves of geometric spirals. Every thought Marius had engulfed him. He felt deep love for someone, he felt blades of grass tickle his arms as he ran. *What was he running towards?* he thought, *Was it for love?* And he could see her, the girl he loved, but she was with another man.

Marius was ripped from his meditation. He understood what he'd seen. It was himself kissing Cynthia through another's eyes. Marius sat their blankly staring at the door.

"I am a pillar in an ocean's torrent, I am the light in the darkest of nights, we are the sword, the staff and the shield, and I alone stand as an army," he chanted to himself, not to gain confidence to fight, but to cover his guilt.

Marius stood up and took a deep breath in. It was time.

The fight was to be held at the same place the first task was held. Everyone at Highwash called the spot "the logs." The name, however conventional it was, did not relish in the spot's importance. The logs were said to be placed there long ago by the first Mages who came to this land; many rituals and gatherings had, supposedly, been held there, but now it was used as a spot to train or meditate, and usually only the Elders used it.

Marius walked the forested path to the logs. Highwash, although primarily composed of plains and grasslands, still held pockets and groves of trees. Marius looked up to see the blue sky as he walked, it gave him hope. He let the cool wind blow over his face, red and brown leaves fluttered by as he took in the air. As he walked on, he could overhear chatter. Listening closely, he could recognize some voices of his classmates. The trail made an abrupt turn at the end leading to an open spot amongst the bush and grass.

Seven perfectly cut logs stood tall, around them stood his classmates as well as some Elders and others Marius did not recognize. Marius could make out Yuri in the crowd, he was bruised and bloody, but Cynthia was nowhere to be seen. The circled group hushed to silence when they caught sight of Marius entering.

Mathius stood at the other end of the circle, he was shirtless and shoeless, wearing nothing but white cloth pants. Marius walked further into the circle, just passing two logs, and stopped to wait. Macaro came out from the circle of people and nodded to both Mathius and Marius.

"Marius, Mathius, you two are my children, whatever happens today know that you shall always be my children and I shall think no differently of you. Ready yourselves. I wish you both the strength to endure." Macaro bowed and left the circle back into the audience.

Mathius immediately began stepping into horse stance, his legs bent. Marius did the same, bending his legs and crouching low, he raised his right arm out behind him then brought it back towards his chest, gathering his breath.

Macaro kept his breath stable trying to remain calm. *Who would attack first?* The question was answered immediately.

Mathius spun his back leg forward reorienting himself closer to Marius. Marius changed his stance in response, but Mathius was already on him with a right spinning back kick, his heel aimed for Marius' head. Macaro held his breath for an instant, but luckily Marius had predicted the kick from Mathius and ducked to strike Mathius from under, leaping up onto his hand to keep his chest low whilst delivering a kick to Mathius' chest. Mathius stumbled back a little, but re-focused his breath centering his stance. Mathius reacted fast, his fists were like flashes of light, one strike headed for Marius' right temple, but Marius deflected with his right elbow, a second for Marius' left forcing Marius to duck down into Mathius incoming right knee.

Marius felt Mathius' knee crack into his nose. Pain rushed through his face, but Marius had little sensitivity to pain, he flipped back into his hands to escape from Mathius' grapple and gave him a swift kick to the chest. Both stood their ground, crouched, arms raised. Mathius sent a heel kick straight for Marius jaw, but Marius easily stepped left to dodge the kick, allowing Marius to kick out Mathius' knee of his supporting leg and forcing Mathius down crouched.

Macaro was surprised by Marius' prowess. As Mathius was sent down to the ground, Marius gave another kick to Mathius, jarring his skull. Marius was about to be upon Mathius in a ground grapple, but Mathius rolled to the side and sprang up to his feet, blood dripping down his forehead. The intensity of the match grew further. Mathius launched himself at Marius and the two of them exchanged fists, both parrying well to the opposing strikes. Mathius, again, launched a kick aimed at Marius' side, but this one connected, slamming Marius clean in the ribs. In that little second of Marius becoming stunned, Mathius spun around him to his back, grappling Marius' waist to deliver a massive suplex into the ground. The crowd gasped at the blow.

Marius' head spun circles after the suplex Mathius had given him. Marius had to act fast, before he knew it Mathius was on top of him, brutalizing him with smashes to his face. Marius forced his body right while hooking his legs around Mathius' back to bring him in close so he could no longer strike. Marius held with all his life, hugging Mathius into his chest, he could feel Mathius struggling to root his feet into the ground.

"Ragh!" Mathius roared as he lifted Marius into the air preparing to body slam him.

Marius was too fast for that though, unhooking his legs from Mathius' waist, Marius brought his legs to his chest and kicked off Mathius with both legs, flinging himself into a back handspring. Marius was back on his feet, assuming horse stance. Mathius gathered his breath and gave Marius a slight half smile.

It's all in your breath, move with Mathius, not against. Water flows down with gravity, not up. Flow like water, Marius thought in his head.

Mathius began to side step, circling Marius keeping his body low and centred. Marius kept his position, waiting for a move from Mathius, *React only to his movements.*

Mathius lunged towards Marius with a flying knee but hit nothing but air as Marius swiftly ducked to the side, spinning to deliver a kick to Mathius' back as he landed sending Mathius flying forward, stumbling. This gave Marius an opportunity to get on Mathius and, leaping, he grappled on top of his grounded opponent.

This surprised Macaro, Marius was doing supremely well against Mathius. Despite the difference in age and skill, Marius was putting up a great challenge. Maybe the time he spent with Ralis had taught him much, thought Macaro as he watched the two of them fight.

Marius was on top of Mathius who lay prone. This was an unexpected turn of events. Marius locked his arms around Mathius' neck attempting to get him into a choke, but Mathius sent his elbow flying backwards to smash Marius in the mouth. Blood filled Marius' mouth, but this didn't deter him. He held fast, beating his knee into Mathius' side, he felt ribs and flesh crack under his blows. Mathius' yelled and struggled to move but Marius kept up the pummels. Reorienting himself, Marius grappled Mathius' face and smashed it into the ground, then directly kipping up to get back on his feet. Marius spun to face Mathius.

"Give in, Mathius," Marius said as he stood ready to face Mathius again.

"Not a chance."

Mathius pushed himself up quickly and was back on his feet. His face was bloody with a broken nose from being smashed into the ground.

A mistake, Marius, Macaro thought as he witnessed Marius let up his hold from Mathius. Marius' heart was too big at times, letting off Mathius was a sign of weakness, but a great sign of compassion. Too bad this task does not require compassion. Mathius spat blood out onto the dirt, then got low to the ground, extending one foot out, chest high with both his arms positioned in front of him. With a gentle wave he signalled Marius to attack.

Marius leapt high into the air, aiming a heel kick towards Mathius, but the change of Mathius' stance cut Marius off guard as he missed Mathius, allowing Marius to get caught by a parry and multiple strikes to his abdomen. Blood shot up from Marius' esophagus into his mouth, and before he could recover, Mathius kicked out his feet from under him, ending with Marius' back slamming into the ground with a thud. Marius would not give up so easily. Exploding off the ground, he kipped up to the left to avoid a drop kick headed for his face.

Anger filled inside Yuri watching Marius fight. He didn't know exactly why but he felt disturbed as he watched. Thoughts fluttered into his mind of his fight with Cynthia, it made him wish Marius had been chosen as his opponent instead. Yuri thought that if he had won the second task his pain would be released, but now that his vision had taken reality, his feelings were far from what he had imagined they would be. For the first time at Highwash Yuri felt alone.

Macaro stood close to Yuri and could sense his anxiety. Macaro stood awkwardly for a second, relating to others was one of his many faults. He was tempted to read Yuri's mind, as he easily could, but reading another's mind was always accompanied by guilt. Talking seemed the most logical approach. "Yuri, are you feeling alright? I can sense you, you're uneasy." Instantly Macaro realized his approach was too forward.

"I am not uneasy, Elder." Yuri repressed anger that flew up from his stomach, pushing it back down he refrained from acting out in front of Macaro.

"I'm sorry, Yuri, it was not my choice to put you up against Cynthia, that was up to the angels."

Yuri froze, uncomfortable by Macaro's truth. But then thoughts fluttered into his mind about Ralis and how he'd argued with Marius about investigating his old quarters. And it just happened to be a perfect moment.

"Elder, may I leave this conversation?" Yuri said turning to face Macaro asking him directly.

"Yes, you may."

His question struck a chord of sorrow in Macaro. Macaro was left standing there amongst the crowd, watching Yuri disappear into the grass that bordered the logs. Macaro wondered what he did wrong, why did some of his students always get taken by despair. Was it their fate, the trial they must face? Or did his own actions or lack of reactions cause this within Yuri?

The fight was dead even. Frustration was filling inside of Mathius and Marius could sense it. Mathius stepped right and then flanked in towards Marius. Countering, Marius stepped left and raised his leg. As Marius predicted, he blocked a kick aimed for his ribs, stepping his raised leg back he lifted his other to kick Mathius. Mathius dodged right and then launched another kick, at Marius.

The clash between them erupted with power. Each of them fought ferociously, each of them deeply focused.

That was when Marius started to feel it again—Mayura, the internal void. He could feel the essence of the atoms that vibrated near him and beyond. He was able to counter each of Mathius' strikes better than the last. As his focus increased, so did his awareness, he could feel each individual who stood among the audience, and he also felt pain, absence, hurt and distrust. Feeling this, Marius turned to look at the crowd, an automatic reaction from realizing Yuri had left.

Then everything dispersed, he could no longer feel the atoms and energy of life. Multiple blows struck Marius. His head echoed and his jaw hurt, and in the next moment he was on the ground. Soon his mind was blank and coveted by darkness. A deep heaviness covered him in the dark, and among the darkness a large light stood above him, a great being. Fear rippled through Marius' mind, he could feel the creature's malicious intent. It began to speak loudly. Its voice hurt Marius as it spoke.

"I see you."

VIII

Marius' eyes flickered open, light filled his eyes and his awareness came back to him. His head hurt, so he reactively went to feel it, he could feel bandages covering the side of his head.

"Calm, child."

Macaro sat at his bedside, he rested his hand on Marius' stomach. Marius calmed significantly with the sight of Macaro. Looking around he noticed he'd been lying in Mirane's medical cabin.

"I lost, didn't I?" Marius asked.

"Yes, you did. Though that is not what I am here to talk about." Macaro went silent for a moment. "You went unconscious for a while, Marius."

Marius did not respond, he couldn't think of what to say, Macaro sensed that and continued talking.

"You muttered many things in your sleep. Some words were not of the language of men, they were in a language I could not even articulate. Mirane sent me here when you first started uttering in your sleep. Do you remember what you saw in your dreams, Marius?"

Marius tried to think back to his sleep, the memories of the dreams seemed more distant every second. That wasn't a good sign.

The Mages of Highwash practiced an angelic path of belief, they believed harmony with themselves and the environment is the key to happy and healthy lives. One key practice to harmony was dream watching. Dreams showed a Mage many things: the future, one's true emotion towards past events and one's place within the universe. More importantly, dreams connected one to the higher universe, where it is believed that humans could contact celestial beings. It was said that, if one cannot remember their dream, they were out of sync with the universal harmony of life.

"What do you remember? Anything at all would be of importance, Marius," Macaro pushed for an answer. With all that had being going on, from Nathaniel acting deranged at moments to Marius speaking unfathomable words, something—even anything—of a clue would be helpful.

"I remember it being dark, and I was afraid, as if it wasn't my choice to be afraid… there was a bright light." Marius struggled to remember his dream, "I think it spoke… but I'm unsure of what."

"Ominous," Macaro said, speaking mainly to himself. "Keep track of your dreams from now on, Marius, and let me know of what you experience."

Macaro sat up beginning to gather his cloak. "You should get moving today, you have been stagnant since the fight."

Macaro nodded to Marius and left Mirane's hut, leaving Marius alone with his thoughts.

He had lost the second task. The reality of it slowly settled in. What did it mean for him and his training? A cold feeling slowly washed through Marius' body. He had lost. In no vision of the future he had, he never thought he would lose this task. Marius decided to stay in Mirane's hut for a bit longer. Facing his classmates would be an embarrassing moment anyways, he thought.

Mirane's hut door opened up, the sound awakened Marius from his deep thought. Expecting Mirane to enter Marius cleared his throat, but unexpectedly it was Mathius who entered into the medical hut. Marius lowered his eyes in shame.

"Macaro said you'd be up," Mathius said as he strutted in.

"What do you want, Mathius, are you here to rub in your victory?" Marius spat out coldly relishing in his envious thoughts.

"Well, no matter how badly I want to, I came for another reason."

"And that is?" Marius asked.

"You should have won, Marius." Mathius went silent for a moment, Marius refrained from saying anything, wanting to force Mathius into continuing. The silence grew and Mathius continued.

"You had me, and you knew it, too, but something weird happened in the match, you stopped fighting, you didn't react. You stopped fighting, Marius. Which means I didn't win fairly."

"You won, Mathius, don't be so cocky as to analyze how you won," Marius said, looking away from Mathius.

"I know I won, Marius. I just want to know why you stopped fighting." Mathius frowned and headed out to leave Mirane's hut, obviously angered by Marius' attitude.

Marius didn't say anymore to Mathius as he left. Marius was now in a horrible mood, Mathius' unexpected arrival irritated him. But that was the fuel Marius needed to at least get up and leave Mirane's.

Macaro stepped onwards up the circular staircase of the main hall. The staircase was dusty and dimly lit from candles that struggled to hold on to their ember. He approached the top of the staircase and came up to a wooden door. Macaro raised his hand to knock, but then hesitated for a second. He made up his mind and then knocked. Nothing stirred inside the room so Macaro knocked again.

"Yes, Macaro." Nathaniel's voice echoed deep from within his chambers.

"May I have a word with you?" Macaro asked gently.

"I'm a little busy at the moment, Macaro."

"It's urgent, Nathaniel."

No response came from behind the door for a second.

"If you insist, then, come on in."

Macaro opened the door and light from inside the Archmage's chamber filled the stairway as he entered. The room matched the shape of the main hall; the walls were circular and made of stone masonry, a metal chandelier hung from the ceiling, spreading light across the room. A massive bed stood in one corner of the room, while a desk was placed opposite to the bed. The walls were surrounded by dusty bookshelves with books splayed across the room some open some closed. Nathaniel sat at his desk, with papers spread across, which Macaro could not get full sight of.

Macaro stood by the door and began to talk. "It's about one of our students, Marius. He has been unconscious the last few hours, but in his sleep he was disturbed by some kind of nightmare."

"And what is uncommon of that Macaro?" Nathaniel reacted bitterly, surprising Macaro.

"If you'd let me continue I can tell you. In his sleep he spoke a language that has not been spoken by man for thousands of years, he spoke in angelic tongue, Nathaniel." Macaro started to pace as he talked.

Nathaniel perked up with intense interest hearing what was being said, "How are you sure of this, Macaro? Are you sure the words weren't gibberish uttered in a state of delirium?"

"That could be, yes, very likely a possibility. But the articulation seemed almost perfect, almost ethereal. That's why I came to you immediately, Nathaniel. You are the expert on angelic tongue."

"Do you remember what he said?" Nathaniel's head raised and his fist clenched unbeknownst to Macaro who continued to pace in thought.

"I can't utter the words, no, but I could remember some of the meaning. He said something on the lines of, 'I see you, you are mine.' That's about all I could understand." Macaro turned to face Nathaniel who still sat at his desk facing the wall.

"It sounds a little sceptical, Macaro, I wouldn't spend much more thought on this."

"A little sceptical? How would a child of ours pronounce angelic words, let alone words we ourselves cannot speak? I understood little of what was said, yes, but that does not mean that we should not investigate."

Suddenly Nathaniel's fist slammed in the desk. His voice became dark and twisted with malicious intent. "Macaro, trust me when I say leave certain things alone, darkness lies in the deepest of places, do not tempt to bring it upon yourself, let alone those you love. Now, leave me be."

Macaro stood frozen for a second. This was unlike Nathaniel. He bowed slightly and left without a word, something was definitely not right in Highwash, and definitely not right with Nathaniel. Deep meditation seemed the only answer.

Marius wandered aimlessly through the village of Highwash. A wicked vibe had taken over the village. The sky was eerie and dark. Aimlessly Marius walked, as if he was not himself, as if he had a clear direction but it was not his own, as if something was guiding him against his own will. Through the field he walked, crunching grass with his footsteps, the further he walked on, the more the air grew dark and misty. Soon Marius had found what he was looking for, Cynthia and Yuri lay naked in the grass, giggling with glee. Marius stomped over to Cynthia and lifted her off her feet by her hair. Yuri had disappeared and it was just himself and Cynthia. Raising his fist he beat Cynthia over and over, smash after smash. Her face began to crumble around his fist.

Marius froze as he took control.

"What have I done?" As soon as he realized what he had done, he held her broken body close and cried. As he hugged her, he began to feel cold powder in his hands. Opening his eyes, he noticed Cynthia had turned to ash. Marius began to scream. Darkness overwhelmed him and soon all was black.

"Your mind shall be mine, your actions my tool, your words my own."

Marius jumped out of bed, covered in a cold sweat. He was shaking.

"Fuck!" Marius screamed and smashed his fist into his pillow. That was the third night in a row that he had a nightmare. Crashing into his bed, he wallowed in pity for a moment. His sleeps had been nothing but a torrent of nightmares ever since the second task. Sleepless and anxious Marius decided to get up and leave his shed. There was no chance he could fall back into sleep.

It was early morning and the sun had not yet poked its head over the eastern Emeralties mountain range. At first Marius just walked on, the dream replaying in his mind over and over again, slowly losing more detail and vividness every time he ran through it again. So with the early morning at his hand, and no one awake but himself he headed to the coast, to the rock cliffs he loved to train on. The air was brisk and cold, autumn mornings always tended to be cold and dry. But the cold didn't bother Marius, he was used to the weather in Highwash, he did sleep in it every night. Marius laughed at his own thoughts, recalling stories from Macaro about Arngrimir, the neighbouring continent which was said to be colder than even the most northern part of Thenus. Macaro always would say that Highwash is warm compared to winters in other lands. Some folk would even say Arngrimir is always in winter.

In no time Marius was at the rocks. He started the same way he always did, in horse stance, which then led into his martial art forms. Each form represented an aspect of nature. Horse stance represented the horse and its power that comes from the legs, and so horse stance trained the legs. Some forms train one's physical strength, agility or speed, each targeting a specific skill. Daily practice was necessary to become a skilled Mage. When the sun beamed over the mountains to the east, Marius moved onto his elemental skills.

"Marius, up early to practice?" Macaro stood behind him. It seemed as if Macaro had been watching him for a while.

"Yes, I am, couldn't sleep," Marius responded, surprised by Macaro's appearance.

"Well, good to see that losing the second task doesn't deter you from training," Macaro said approvingly.

Marius wanted to tell Macaro of his dream badly, but how? He could barely remember any details of it, what was he to say, that he had had a bad dream?

"Why don't we run through basic forms together, Marius?" Macaro smiled at Marius as he asked.

And so Marius spent the morning with Macaro and they practiced until the sun rose high in the sky.

Later, Marius wandered back to the village, breakfast lingering in his mind. He walked to a shack close to the main hall which served dried wheat with some water or milk every morning. For meat they needed to hunt the local forests or scavenge for berries and fruit. The only edibles they grew at Highwash were wheat and gourds. Everyone called the kitchen "the grub," since it mainly served oats, which got very bland to eat day after day.

Marius entered the grub and saw some of his classmates inside. His eyes locked with Mathius who sat at a table at the far end of the room, he ate with Daniel and Reggard. He stared for a bit then continued to converse with his friends. Yuri sat with Clive at a table opposite to Mathius, but Cynthia was nowhere to be seen. Marius had not seen her since the second task.

Marius then decided to be brave and sit with Yuri and Clive.

"Marius, how are you?" Clive instinctively asked as Marius approached. They were good friends as well, and it was likely that Clive had no knowledge of the conflict between Yuri and Marius.

"Well, I lost the second task, so not the best," Marius chuckled as he spoke to lighten what he said. Yuri didn't react to Marius' approach.

"Come, Marius, sit down with us. And don't worry about your loss. We all saw your fight. You must have heard the talk among Highwash?" Clive asked.

"No, I have not. What have they been saying?" Marius said.

"Well, your fight was incredible, Marius, no one thought you stood a chance against Mathius." Clive froze for a second, realizing what he had said, but then continued when Marius did not react. "You fight like a demon, Marius, now everyone is talking about you."

"By the way, Has anyone seen Cynthia around lately?" Marius said changing the subject.

"Yuri should explain that one," Clive said harshly, then out of nowhere he stood up from his seat and left. Yuri had not said a word yet.

"So, what happened?" Marius asked him.

"She got hurt in the fight against me. She's at Mirane's quarters. Mirane is attending to her most of the day at the moment, that's why she's not in the medical hut."

"You hurt Cynthia. Damn, Yuri." Marius sat frozen for a second.

"It was a fight, Marius, you know what Macaro asked of us."

Marius started to get angry listening to Yuri speak. "You hurt Cynthia?"

"She wouldn't give up, Marius, what was I to do?"

"Damn, Yuri." They both sat in silence for a second. An old lady who served oats walked by and served Marius a bowl of oats. He didn't notice at all who served him, let alone that there was food in front of him.

"I searched Ralis' quarters," Yuri said breaking the silence.

"And did you find anything?"

"No, not one thing. It seems Ralis cleared out everything, or took all his belongings," Yuri said, with slight disappointment.

"Or, he didn't have much to begin with," Marius said finishing Yuri's sentence.

There were only two routes in and out of the valley the people of Highwash lived in. A coastal mountain trail that ran north from Highwash up towards the northern Emeralties, which then turned east into the mountains and through a wretched pass that would lead to the forests of the eastern face of the mountains. The second route was east, and it twisted and turned through the densely-forested valleys that the eastern Emeralties formed.

Ralis knew both trails equally well. He knew the northern pass was safer during dry seasons as the spring run-off cut the pass off, and winter made the pass impassable. Ralis' purpose was safety and reconnaissance; his mission was to find out why Salamon had sent a troupe of armed men to the valley. Macaro didn't want him to go, but it was his own mission. So, Ralis spurred his horse on heading east towards the mountains.

The last conversation raced through Ralis' mind as he rode on. *Stay here, Ralis, you are needed at Highwash.* Ralis shook his head, clearing his thoughts. He must be focused.

The eastern forest loomed in the distance beyond the fields he rode. By the time he reached the woods it was nearing evening. Ralis dismounted his horse at the break before the forest. Taking his sack off the horse, he took everything he would need for a solo journey in the woods.

"What shall I do with you, mare?" Ralis placed his hand on the horse's forehead as he spoke, feeling the horse's thoughts. "Run back to Highwash. Talun will be very happy to get you back. The least I can do is get you back there."

And as the command was issued the horse kicked up and ran towards the west, back towards Highwash. The rest of Ralis' journey was on foot now, he had wished to keep the horse but there was no way a mare could ride the terrain of the Emeralties.

His first objective would be to obtain some height; he needed a clear visual of the forest and mountain range and night would not aid him in this task. Ralis needed to move fast, at least to reach a position of height before nightfall, in that way he could start again tomorrow morning.

Into the forest he went, this time without the burden of two young apprentices, this time he could truly move as a Mage should move. He moved like a leopard, his feet never to make a noise, running through the forest as silent as night. Grappling onto some branches, he pulled himself into some trees. A Mage trained years for the ability to climb, so he could move like a monkey, swinging through trees, kicking off branches to leap to the next tree. A Mage must be home in nature as power comes from the essence of earth.

He held onto an oak tree, in the distance he could make out what looked like a cliff cut out by a landslide that had occurred, it looked perfect to gain a view of the valley and forest below him. Ralis jumped down from the tree he was perched on and made his way toward the eastern ridge of the cliff that looked safe to climb.

The view from the face of the stone cliff looked beautiful, the fields glowed as the sun set to the west and the valley loomed before him in darkness of the east. He could not see far, so Ralis decided to wait there until morning. Slowly the sun drifted beyond the horizon, the light fading away, leaving Ralis in total blackness. Clouds covered the sky so no stars showed their light. The autumn night was cool and crisp. No sleep would arrive for Ralis tonight, so he meditated into the night.

You are needed at Highwash. Macaro's words floated across his mind, bringing him back to the conversation he had had before he departed. Macaro stood before him, they were in Ralis' quarters.

"You are needed at Highwash."

"We have Salamon at our door, Nathaniel clearly denies this, despite my council, and you would do nothing, Macaro." Ralis stopped packing his gear to look at his friend standing in his doorway.

"We cannot be rash, the situation needs us to remain calm, it requires us to be subtle, and it requires us to stay hidden. If you are seen—or worse, caught—imagine the nightmare you would bring upon the children, Ralis."

"If they already know we are here, we are already doomed," Ralis said.

"And if that was the case, you would still leave and abandon us on our own?"

Ralis turned around again to pack his gear, he threw his knife into his bag, which was placed on the bed.

"It seems I cannot convince you to stay. Then I wish you the best of luck, Ralis. Do remember to stay hidden."

Macaro turned to leave but before he left he said one more thing. "Remember compassion, Ralis. You are not to blame for your father's death."

The conversation still stung in Ralis' mind. He told himself he would not regret leaving.

Night turned into morning and, deep into meditation, Ralis could feel the warmth of the rising sun on the back of his neck. He knew this meant the whole eastern valley would be lit up. He got up and stood at the cliff's edge, staring down into the valley. A northern mountain and southern mountain face, created a deep valley into the east of the mountain range, he could see the forest twist and turn into the depths of the mountains. Ralis could also see the camp Salamon had sent, they had moved from the open space from before and into the cover of the forest.

Long Ralis stood and watched the woods to the east. He studied the movement of the camp by the signs of the woods. No birds floated over a large section of forest, indicating something startled them there. The camp must be centred there, Ralis thought.

It was time to move. Ralis climbed down the cliff face, and headed down the slope into the valley. He needed a closer look at the camp. Ralis knew the tactics of Salamon's armies; they often set up many camps during woodland expeditions or foreign ventures with the purpose to scan more terrain at once. To coordinate the movement of camps and to communicate information between camps, they relied on scouts to move from camp to camp with information. Scouts were trained in wild terrain tactics and reconnaissance, as well as the standard military training, the perfect targets for Ralis. All he needed to do was find and track a scout. They knew much and were easy prey.

By midday Ralis had surveyed the forest around the camp, and deep into the valley. He traveled carefully, ensuring he was not seen. By studying the forest floor Ralis could see the markings of travelling scouts everywhere: cut branches, deep indents in the ground, crushed bush—all were signs of humans travelling. All he had to do was to wait.

And so he waited, high in the cover of a large dense fir tree. Hours went by and the only living things to move about were small mammals and birds. Patience was one of Ralis' many skills. When one spends the majority of their life as a thief they grow a huge tolerance to waiting, waiting to eat, waiting to drink and waiting for the right opportunity.

You are needed here at Highwash. The words floated across his mind once more. He shook his head, shaking off the thought. Focusing his mind he listened to the sounds of the forest. Light clanging, metal on metal, maybe chains. Footsteps. Only one set of footsteps. Ralis opened his eyes and started to move amongst the tree branches towards the sounds. The footsteps grew louder, the jangling became clearer in expression the closer Ralis drew towards it. It was gear, a belt, a rucksack, jangling as a scout walked onwards. Ralis looked up to ponder the distance between him and the camp. It seemed far enough.

Sir Ramsely walked through dense forest and bush. He swore underneath his breath as vines tangled at his boots. It was cold and damp deep in the bush.

"Shit! I wish the western camp wasn't actually this far west!" Ramsely screamed into the forest air.

His maps were useless this far west, the trees were too thick to navigate with the sun, the hills and valleys twisted and turned falling into chasms or rivers. His skills proved useless here. The west was too wild. And yet his superiors had set a camp out west, an impossible task, it seemed to him. Maybe if he were to keep walking west with the setting sun he could find his way. But with no horse, any mistake could set him back days.

Fear slowly settled in Ramsely's heart, so he did what he would often do when he was alone in the bush, talk to himself.

"Nothing lives in this wretched forest, I see, not even the birds make noise." Ramsely was closer to the camp than he knew, but the forest had its tricks, and often people who passed through unaware of the twisted paths lost their way. Only the noise of his belt jangling against his side could be heard among the trees. It bothered Ramsely greatly. He had heard of the stories of great animals out west. Large brown bears were said to roam and hunt in these forests. When Ramsely was a kid his father told him tales nightly of great winged beasts that hunted even the bears.

Unfortunately for Ramsely, his life was about to take a turn towards the dramatic. Mages are silent in stalking their prey. It was not great bears or winged manticores Ramsely should've been afraid of. So, with his mind on monstrous animals, he screamed like a little girl when Ralis grabbed his throat from behind.

Ralis covered the scout's mouth instinctively, he could feel the scout's scream vibrate in his hand. He applied force to his arm and the sound stopped as he choked the scout out. In a matter of seconds Ralis had the scout on his back, taking him far away from anywhere close to the camp. He decided to take the scout back to the cliff he had climbed, it seemed like a perfect spot for interrogation. One thing was for sure: it would scare the shit out of him.

At first the dream was nice, Ramsely was being fed cakes by his mom in a nice, soft, plush chair. But the dream turned awfully violent and soon his mother was smacking him straight across the face with bare hands. Groggy and tired, Ramsely was ripped from his dream to realize that the slaps were, in fact, real, but the cake was not. A large man stood looking down onto him, slapping him in the face.

"Wake up," demanded the large, cloaked man.

It then hit Ramsely that he'd been kidnapped by the Rangers. His surroundings hit his senses all at once—the height of the cliff and the stone against his back, his hands tied.

"Oh shit, oh shit, oh shit. Whatever you want, I'll give it to you!"

The man drove his fist straight into Ramsely's nose.

"Shut up."

The man bent down and lifted Ramsely from the armpits laying him against a stone so he was seated up.

"Who do you serve, scout?" Ramsely could see the man's face as he came level to his eyes. His face was bare of emotion, his eyes hardened, his hair, dark and black, spread down the sides of his face. The man grabbed Ramsely by the cheeks.

"Do I look ugly? Answer me."

"Lord Salamon," Ramsely spat through his crunched cheeks. The man eased up allowing Ramsely to speak. "I serve Lord Salamon."

"Good. What I thought. How many camps lie between this one and the eastern faces?" Ramsely shook terrified of speaking, revealing information was deemed treason and punishable by imprisonment or death.

"What would be worse is dying by my hand," the man said coldly.

How did he know what I was thinking? thought Ramsely.

"Because I can hear your thoughts. You're so anxious it sounds as if you're screaming them." The man chuckled lightly as he spoke, as if kidnapping was no big deal to him. "So I ask once more: how many camps lie between here and the eastern face of the Emeralties?"

"There are two more," Ramsely said shamefully as he looked down at his feet.

The man stood up and turned to look out into the valley. Ramsely wondered what he was thinking.

"What is Salamon looking for?" the man asked, suddenly turning around to face Ramsely again. Ramsely knew little about Salamon's plans; it was a little naive of the man to think he knew them. Ramsely remembered what Sebastien had said about the Rangers, how they were nothing but vagabonds, and it gave him something to say.

"We are in search of a group of wasters claiming to be the Wildland Rangers."

"Wasters, huh," the man studied Ramsely with a deep stare as he stood there, his eyes menacing. "Why such a force for wasters?

Armies don't get sent to hunt criminals. There's more to it than that which is apparent."

"That's all I know, I swear!" Ramsely squirmed as he yelled, pleading the man for mercy. The man's boot came down hard into Ramsely's chest.

"What was the purpose of your mission? Why were you on route to the camp?" The man spat angrily, obviously maddened by the hollering.

Frightened, Ramsely spoke the truth. "Word has come in about missing scouts sent from the western camp, scouts from the eastern camp had found soldier's tags. I was to come in to report to the lead captain here and further their investigation."

"Huh, your scouts are good?" The man seemed intrigued about this fact.

"What do you mean 'Our scouts are good'? Have you kidnapped them?" Ramsely said, frightened.

"No, I killed those men."

Marius knocked on the door of Mirane's cabin. Shuffling could be heard inside, and then the door popped open.

Mirane greeted him smiling, she looked tired, but her eyes still had a soft glow of energy.

"I assume you came to talk to Cynthia, she's up and cognitive at the moment, so I won't refuse you," Mirane said as she gestured for Marius to enter.

Mirane's cabin always had a scent of alcohol and herbs. At a lone bed in the corner of the room Cynthia was laid down and slightly propped up, her head and arm were bandaged. She saw Marius immediately as he entered, a smile grew on her face.

"Sorry I missed your match."

"What happened, Cynthia?" Marius asked ignoring the comment. Seeing Cynthia in this state tugged at him.

"Oh don't be mad, Marius, I didn't go down easily, I wanted to win."

"But look what happened!" Marius retorted.

Cynthia could see Marius was angry that she was hurt. It was cute of him, but slightly frustrating.

"We did what Macaro said, Marius, we fought. You can't blame Yuri for my injuries."

"It's hard not to," Marius grumbled.

"What about you? How did it go?" Asked Cynthia, changing the subject.

"I lost." Marius responded shyly.

"At least we lost together, huh?" Cynthia said jokingly.

"At least. I couldn't stand to see you win with my loss," Marius teased. They both laughed together.

"Ok, out now, shoo," Mirane said as she came into the cabin. "She needs rest, Marius, and you should go train."

Marius waved a goodbye to Cynthia and left the cabin with his mind set on training. Mirane was right.

"You thought you could deny my word?" His father's words slashed as they cut the air.

"I am Lord. You are but my son. It does not mean you are impenetrable. A sergeant I'd have hung for not heeding to my command. What should my men think of me if I would punish them and not my own children under the same law?" Salamon paused briefly. "What should they think, Patrick?"

Patrick stood, awkward, unable to think of any response appropriate enough to say.

"I don't know father," stumbled out of his mouth.

"You don't know? Good thing my men think of you but nothing more than a child. They see my teachings not as teachings of law, but teachings as of a father. These are my men, Patrick, they are loyal to me. They will do as I command."

Salamon gazed at his son with disdain. He looked much like his mother, standing there in silence.

"Anything else to say?" Salamon asked his son.

"No, Father."

"Then leave." Salamon looked at his son one final time as he left slamming the study door behind him. *Tsk, children,* Salamon thought to himself. As if he hadn't had enough problems to deal with currently, his son's rebellious behaviour was about to top it off.

Salamon stood up to face the window behind his desk, the view of the city always helped him think. His eldest son Sebastien had been on his mission for quite a while now, but Sebastien always had his way of getting a task done no matter the costs. That's why Salamon admired his eldest son: his commitment to the forces was outstanding. Thoughts came to him as he looked out the window, gazing at his marble city, thoughts of how many men he had lost, how many Sebastien would lose looking for the Rangers.

Frustrated from his cluster of thoughts he pulled the handle on the window and pushed it open, allowing fresh air to fill his study. The war with Arngrimir the neighbouring continent had been having dire consequences on his capital's economy. Anger filled Salamon as he thought of the war, it was never his war, it was never even the peoples of Thenus' war.

As he was lost in thought, a large raven flew into his study out of nowhere and began to flutter around the room. Salamon remained calm and allowed the bird to land on his outstretched hand. He locked eyes with the odd-looking raven, and with the gaze the message filled his mind.

The scout had given Ralis little information, but the little he was given confirmed much. Salamon's men weren't looking for his friends at Highwash. The scout had little preparation or knowledge of the skills Ralis had, which could mean that Salamon avoided informing them of a Mage's ability in fear his men would refuse such a task as hunting down Mages, or that Salamon was not aware of their presence in the west at all. If the latter were true, it meant the Vatican did not know of their position in the west either.

Ralis couldn't know for sure what the reasoning of Salamon was to send troops into the western valley, speculations were the best he had. So he decided the best course of action would be one of three things: either find these Rangers, use himself as bait to lead Salamon's forces out of the west or kidnap someone from Salamon's command chain.

Ralis thought back to when he was interrogating the scout. The images of the scout's thoughts still lingered in Ralis' mind, the sting of someone else's mind still lingered as well. The scout was thinking about the Rangers, how they were vagabonds—someone had told him this, a man. Ralis looked deeper into his memory of the scout's mind. A man told him, he felt respect for this man, *Seb... Sebas... what was it?* Ralis couldn't make out the images of the man's name, but he could remember vividly the face he saw in the scout's mind. That was all he needed: a face.

Ralis hated reading minds. Macaro's lessons came back to him as he felt the scouts thoughts in his mind. He could feel the fear of the scout, the frustration. Whenever Macaro taught Ralis skills of deception, such as mind reading, he often would say "You must first learn the ability to control your own thoughts. If you cannot separate the thoughts of another from your own, you will crumble, like how a mountain crumbles from wind. It's a slow death, but inevitable." Macaro never thought Ralis was ready for such skills, claiming he was too emotionally scarred, too damaged, but Nathaniel thought otherwise and made Macaro instruct Ralis anyways. That was back when Nathaniel was... different.

The scout's memories flickered through his mind, scenes of men, of forests, people Ralis couldn't recognize and then him. He was staring himself straight in the face. Ralis tried to dodge it, avoid it, but the fear struck like lightning with no explanation.

The same fear the scout had filled Ralis, scared, he felt like a little boy. He was back in the tunnel, the silhouetted figure before him, he was just a child. The memories dispersed as quickly as they came. The fear was gone but its deeper effects still filled his mind. Perhaps Macaro was right maybe he shouldn't read minds. Ralis just lay there on the forest floor looking up, he was covered in sweat and still shaking.

"I hate reading minds," he spat out loud. Getting up he recovered his mind and regained his awareness of his surroundings. He regained focus of himself forgetting the panic attack he just had, and turned to the task before him. There was little possibility of finding one man out of a group so large, so hunting this "Seb" figure would be out of the question. Making himself a target would be risky, so Ralis figured that would be a last resort if the army attempted to move further west. So finding the Rangers seemed like the most feasible thing, and the first thing he should start with.

Ralis paused for a moment to reflect. It was midday and the sun filled into the forest where Ralis stood. The forest was big, too big for Ralis to survey himself, and even Salamon's best-trained scouts were having issues finding these so-called Rangers. He needed a lead. He needed a way to see the whole forest, to see through many eyes at once. And as he stood there in the forest, alone, contemplating his course of action, an answer was given to him with a lone bird fluttering down to the ground before him.

"Marius, can you name an animal hierarchy native to the forests east to us?" asked Macaro.

"Well, we have local rabbits that feed off grass, coyotes and eagles feast off the rabbits." Marius answered confidently.

Macaro had been giving another lesson on animals local to the surroundings and how to engage them. He must've caught Marius dozing off and woke him with the question.

"Good. How about you, Reggard? Can you name another relationship?"

"What about the flies eating decomposing animals?"

"That is a fine example, yes. And there is an importance of knowing and understanding these relationships among the living beings. Animals may seem simple in their ways but they are complex, and some are highly intuitive. Recently two of our fellow classmates have had an encounter with a local species native to the west. They should be grateful to be alive, and grateful for the fortune that had struck them."

Macaro gazed at both Yuri and Marius as he spoke.

"Clive, what eats the coyotes and the wolves?"

"Manticores do," stated Clive.

"Tell me about them, Clive," asked Macaro, pacing as he spoke.

"What I've read about them is that they descend from great winged creatures from a thousand some years ago. They are apparently large, varying in size, aggressive in nature and roam both continents. I've also read that they're nothing but folk tales."

"You could ask your classmates if that is the case."

As soon as Macaro remarked Marius could feel all eyes turn to him, he dared not turn to look anyone in the face.

"Manticores are real and very alive. Manticores are large winged beasts, yes, and they are very territorial, enticing them to attack strangers that struggle too close. They also are highly intelligent, capable of memories, many emotions and abilities to communicate. They're a myth to the common man of Thenus mainly because they detest humanity and avoid us at much cost. And the recent encounter has caused us great concern. If there is one, there will be many, as manticores nest in families. We have no way of locating their nest for now. So, I would like to ask all of you to stay within bounds of the village. Please refrain from going past Talun's stables, and please do not venture into the fields alone. A manticore is a vicious enemy, and even I would not like to be caught alone with one."

As the lesson ended and Marius got up to leave the main hall, he could hear Mathius and the others whisper words about him. Nothing bad. Just curiosity and gossip about the manticore. The people scattered the hall departing in groups.

Marius started leaving the hall, as he did so he caught eyes with Yuri. Yuri looked away immediately, obviously still awkward and angry with him. Irritated by this, Marius decided to approach him.

"Yuri."

Yuri glanced at Marius and continued on his way out, exiting the hall. Marius frowned, not wanting to play chase but forced to, and followed after. It was the afternoon but the air was brisk, scattered clouds took the sky and a light breeze swept over.

"Yuri!" Marius shouted as he jogged forward to catch up with his friend.

"Yes," Yuri said, still continuing to ignore Marius and rudely walk onwards.

"I saw Cynthia, she's doing pretty well."

Yuri halted at Marius' comment. "Yeah, and what about it?" His remark vibrated with anger.

"I just thought I'd tell you," Marius responded calmly. "She looks as if she'll be released from Mirane's care soon. I just thought you'd like to know."

Yuri gave a spiteful look at Marius, his face answered all. "Thanks, but I'm quite capable of going to see her myself."

"C'mon, Yuri, why are you being like this?" Marius asked holding out his hand trying to sympathize with his friend.

"You know perfectly well why, Marius!" Yuri's fist clenched as he hollered.

Marius, in fact, did know why Yuri was upset. For the longest time Yuri had the deepest crush on Cynthia, and it was a well-known fact that most of the boys at Highwash had had a crush on Cynthia at some point, she was among the only females in the village.

"I'm sorry, Yuri," Marius said weakly, managing to speak just a simple sentence with his cluster of thoughts storming in his head.

"No, you're obviously not sorry." Yuri stormed off his face scrunched.

A cold gust of wind hit Marius' face and he decided not to bother following Yuri, he obviously needed to be alone. Marius needed to be alone himself, too, after that commotion, so he decided upon heading to the ocean side. The stone granite slab always held answers for Marius and that would be the best place to go. Cold gusts of wind sliced through the air as Marius made his way, the day felt ominous and the air felt thick. Shivers crawled down Marius' spine, the vibes he received from the air were too similar to his dream. He could feel the same feelings. The weird darkness in the energy, the overwhelming feeling.

"Marius! What wonders to happen upon you."

Marius jumped surprised by the voice that spoke. It was Nathaniel who happened to be walking as well.

"What are you doing out here, my boy?" Nathaniel spoke awfully cheerful.

Marius hesitated for a second, feeling uncomfortable by the surprise, but this was his Archmage, Marius thought, so he eased up a bit.

"I'm just coming out to the cliff side to train."

"The ocean has its way of calming you. It does for most, yes. That was my favourite spot in Highwash for a long time, but it doesn't seem to work its charm on me like it used to."

Marius stood still awkward and uncomfortable. What was the meaning of Nathaniel's approach?

"I've heard rumours, Marius. I've heard you lost to Mathius, and I heard you put up a decent fight. But decent is not good enough, is it? One must be prepared to die to truly fight free. To dance with death one must know death."

Nathaniel's words grew heavier as he spoke, Marius started to feel fatigued as Nathaniel spoke.

"But now you have lost, I see. The future seems uncertain doesn't it? Without passing the second task you cannot move forward. You certainly thought you'd move forward, didn't you? But I have a request from you. Since you lost you need not be here at Highwash for the time being. So, I ask you to accompany me east. I need someone, you see, I need someone of your size, particularly."

Nathaniel was a large man, but his request seemed strange to Marius. Marius did not understand what his size had to do with anything.

"So, come with me, Marius. Come assist your Archmage." Nathaniel's eyes penetrated deep inside Marius' mind. He could feel whispers like worms in his mind, he grasped for control.

"I think I should stay here, or at least see what Elder Macaro would think."

"Macaro wouldn't disagree. To assist your Archmage is a great tribute to Highwash."

Marius could feel a deep headache coming on, like if something was attempting to pierce his mind.

"I think I'll stay."

Nathaniel's voice changed ominously, with intense power as he spoke, each word smashed Marius' mind.

"I am your Archmage, to deny me is against our law."

Succumbing, Marius began to speak, "Ye…" and before he could finish his sentence another voice piped into his ears—a familiar voice, one that sounded pure, bringing Marius back to his senses.

"Nathaniel, Marius, odd to see you both out here. Especially you, Marius, as I just gave a command to avoid travelling alone."

Macaro stepped behind Marius, placing his hands on Marius' shoulders.

"Macaro," Nathaniel said through clenched teeth.

"What were you two speaking about?" Macaro asked.

Marius awaking from his deep headache began to speak, "Nathaniel had asked me to journey with him east. I wanted to ask you first."

"No, I can't agree to that. I have much planned for you to learn, and many duties for you to carry out, Marius. I'm sorry, Nathaniel, I can't let you take him. Maybe one of the older students could accompany you." Macaro nodded slightly, and gestured Marius to walk on with his hands.

Deep down Marius thanked the skies for the blessing he had received. The further Macaro walked Marius away from Nathaniel the clearer his mind became, his will slowly came back.

When they were well away from Nathaniel, Marius began to speak, "Thank you."

"Don't thank me, Marius. My job is to protect my students. Now, go be around friends, to be alone is to be unsafe. A darkness lies in Highwash. And, Marius, if you ever need to talk, come visit me in my quarters."

Macaro walked off leaving Marius close to the main hall. Macaro did have a point, he should be around friends, and Marius needed to talk. So, once again Marius went to chase down Yuri, wherever he may be.

"Yuri are you in there?" Marius knocked on the rickety wooden door to Yuri's quarters. The small shack stood silent, nothing but soft chirping from nearby birds made noise. The evening sun cast an orange ray of light on the door. Marius could see his lone shadow placed on the door. Marius knocked again but was answered by a similar silence. Disappointed and without an idea where Yuri could be, Marius just stood there outside his door contemplating.

"Hey, Marius, what are you up to?" It was Clive, he had obviously seen Marius standing there.

"I'm just looking for Yuri, do you have any idea where he is?" Marius asked. Marius liked Clive a lot; he shared many similarities to his sister Cynthia, especially in looks. Both of them had deep brown hair, and a bright green set of eyes.

"Yuri, I saw him last at the dining hut, he was having supper with Mathius and them."

"Cool. I should go see him then."

"Yes, you should, he doesn't seem so fond of you of late." Clive smirked a bit as he spoke. "And, by the way, may I ask you about your encounter with the manticore? It was pretty obvious that Yuri and you were the ones Macaro was referring to."

This is what Marius didn't want, he hated gossip, and even more so he hated gossip he was entangled in.

"What I can tell you is, is that it was accidental and regrettable."

Memories of Ralis burning the creature's corpse flashed into his mind, Marius could almost smell the burning of its flesh.

"And huge," Marius finished, leaving Clive standing there with another smirk on his face.

Shaking his head, Clive thought both Yuri and Marius were two characters, that was for certain.

Marius walked onwards, focused on finding Yuri. He didn't know how he was going to reconcile with Yuri, but he was planning on making his best attempt. He repeated many different lines in his head. None of them seemed to sound sincere after he repeated it in his head a couple times. What do you say to a boy that has his heart broken?

The dining hall was packed with students. The multitude of long bench tables were almost all completely taken, even some of the Elders sat and ate with some older students. Marius hated this time and often avoided it, preferring to eat at less crowded moments.

As Marius walked in, some eyes were on him like a hawk, others appeared to have no interest in him. Marius could make out Mathius, Daniel, Reggard and Yuri at a table close to the entrance. Marius now realized he had never clearly thought out this moment, and the lines he ran through his head were not enough preparation. How was he going to get Yuri alone? He hardly wanted to sit down at the table. Swallowing his throat, he gathered himself and went to sit down at their table uninvited. He had no other choice and standing frozen by the doorway was becoming more awkward by the second. Spoons clattered and mouths crunched, and the discomfort of the walk to the table seemed to last forever.

"Hey guys," was all Marius could muster as he sat down at the table beside Yuri.

The conversation they were having froze in place and all went silent for a second. The only voice that piped up was Reggard, since he was still fond of Marius.

"Marius. The man of the hour, we were just talking about how you two fought off a manticore!" Reggard said pointing to Yuri and him. "It sounds intense, I mean the only thing I've fought off was a couple of coyotes and a black bear—separate events—and

I just scared them away. I've read about manticores, highly aggressive, amazingly fast and strong."

"Yes we heard Macaro say," Daniel piped up, his voice covering over Reggard's. Reggard continued ignoring his comment.

"But, hell! You guys killed this thing? How big was it? Was it a male?"

"I wasn't too focused on the sex of it at the time, but Ralis claimed it was a female," Marius replied.

"Jeez, you guys are lucky, I don't think you would be here if that was a male. Males are supposed to be much bigger than the females," Reggard continued chewing on a potato as he talked.

"Yuri was talking about how you guys fought it. Sounds messed. And what about those crazy creatures you encountered in the caves?" Daniel asked, interjecting Reggard's train of thought.

Marius frowned at Yuri in response to being asked. He was surprised Yuri would talk about that event openly.

"They weren't fun," Marius replied flatly.

"What I don't understand is how you guys got out?" Mathius said finally breaking his silence.

"How did you all even hear about all this?" Marius retorted. The last time Marius had talked to Mathius they had bickered at each other.

"From Yuri."

"What did they look like, I mean the creatures in the caves?" Reggard asked with his mouth half full, interrupting Mathius and Marius with his curiosity. Reggard seemed unaware he had done so as he continued to chew away.

"I couldn't get a good visual of them, but I recall them being covered in grey scales, sort of shaped like a spider."

"No, c'mon it was way similar to a crab!" Yuri said finally speaking, "They had pincers and all."

"I agree with the pincers, but if you're really curious they made a clicking noise, and were sensitive to light," commented Marius.

"Huh, interesting. I'll look around the beastiaries and see if there is any notes on them. Actually, I think that's what I'll do after I eat," Reggard said nodding to himself as he spoke.

"Has Yuri shown anyone the wound yet?" Marius said jokingly nudging Yuri with his elbow.

Everyone chuckled and replied "No." And for the rest of the evening they sat, ate, talked and laughed about Marius and Yuri's journey back with Ralis. How Marius and Ralis carried Yuri for many days, the storm, the only parts both Marius and Yuri left out were the scouts Ralis had murdered and Nathaniel's disappearance. It seemed Yuri and Marius were talking again, and for a moment Marius smiled to himself realizing improvisation had seemed to work the best.

Soon it was just Marius and Yuri, a dark, starlit night blanketed them as they walked back to their huts. They walked silently staring at the moon that overhung the eastern mountains, it glowed a fierce fiery orange.

"Yuri, I have to tell you something."

"Let me guess. You have feelings for me," Yuri said laughing, pushing Marius.

"No, it's serious, Yuri."

"Oh, ok, alright, tell me then," Yuri said, stopping in his tracks.

Marius paused for a moment gazing at the moon, summing up the words to say to Yuri.

"I've been having very weird dreams lately, I can barely remember them and each time something horrible happens in them. During the second task, when I stopped moving, I felt something—that's what made me pause—I felt something, the same feelings I feel in my dreams. And then today, after we had argued after class, I went to go to the cliffs to calm myself. But guess who I ran into? Nathaniel. First of all, that's odd just because of the fact he never leaves his quarters," Marius said.

"Same, I ran into him earlier in the month too, before the second task. Did he say anything strange to you at all?" questioned Yuri.

"Here, let me finish and I'll get to that. He did say something strange, he asked me to join him on a venture to the east. He didn't specify where, but I assumed his intent was to head to the ruins we found him in. He knew I had lost the second task. I tried to say no, I tried to back away from him, but I felt the same feeling again, this feeling of fear, of... I can't explain it..." Marius stopped, putting his hand to his head, he could still feel remnants of his encounter with Nathaniel.

"Marius, are you ok? This is awfully weird what you're saying. What do you mean 'feeling'?" Yuri asked as he placed his hand on Marius' back, "Just try to describe it."

"It was as if I had no control, I almost even said yes to him. But Macaro happened to be there and told Nathaniel no."

"He might have just been influencing your mind. But I can't see Nathaniel using mind control on a student—he's our Archmage," Yuri said in disbelief. He couldn't imagine such deeds committed by the Archmage.

"No, you're not understanding, Yuri. When Ralis and I were carrying you back to Highwash, one night I noticed Ralis had bruises all over his abdomen and chest. I asked him why and he didn't say anything. Later, another time on our journey back, he strongly implied it was Nathaniel who had given him those bruises."

Both Yuri and Marius stood there in silence for a moment pondering on the words said.

"What if you misunderstood him?" Yuri asked.

"I really don't think I did. And who else would have given him those bruises?"

Marius spent the rest of the evening alone, lying in his bed, staring at the ceiling of his shed, afraid to fall asleep. A slight buzz of fear still lingered in his mind, but he pushed it to the side of his mind with good thoughts about how he and Yuri were talking again. Sleep soon took him over and the same feeling, the feeling of fear, crept slowly closer.

The next day Macaro resumed lessons as normal. The students were all expected to wake up before dawn and meet at the cliff side by the ocean for meditation. Afterwards, Macaro led his students back to the village for a quick breakfast and lessons in the main hall.

Macaro ranted for hours sometimes in his lessons, explaining and demonstrating various magic work. Some days lessons would be of the outside world, teaching the children knowledge of political powers in the continent. There was no strict regime to train Mages, each Elder taught his own way of the path. Only the Elder of a group of students could know what his students were capable of and what they were ready to learn. This was the bond to the students an Elder had. His teachings were their path, their way.

Today's lessons were strictly about martial arts. Macaro led his students out of the main hall and into the brisk morning air.

Everything seemed back to normal in most ways; lessons resumed, Cynthia was back to training, Marius and Yuri were getting along. The winter was approaching, cold winds and storms came in from the western sea, bringing about torrents of rain. The mountain peaks in the east could be seen as white jagged teeth, gathering snow on top of them. The days became shorter and the seas rougher. It seemed as if another year was coming to a gentle close.

For the month of November the students trained each day rigorously. Some days left Marius exhausted mentally, from multiple series of energetic work forcing Marius to manipulate the energy of elements in some way. They reinforced old techniques daily, casting fire, shooting lightning bolts and manipulating air to knock each other off their feet.

"Today I shall teach a new skill. Watch and observe," Macaro said. He stood on dark granite rock, the ocean waves beating at the cliff wall behind him.

The students stood before Macaro, clustered in a group. Macaro lifted his hands as if he was grabbing something in the air. His hands moved as if they were grabbing strings in the air. First small twinkles of water appeared underneath his hand, and then, with a movement of his hand, an amount of water to fill a cup appeared floating slightly below his hand. Relaxing his hand, the water droplet that was suspended in the air dropped and splashed onto the rocky ground.

A mocking scoff could be heard among the group of students, enticing the class into a giggle.

"Not impressed?" Macaro said, smiling.

Turning to the ocean side he raised both his hands. At first nothing happened and the class stood waiting. But then, out of nowhere, a massive amount of water appeared in the air over the ocean. And with the flick of his hands the water roared towards the ocean, like a massive tidal wave, the roar in the air rang through the students' ears as the water smashed into the ocean.

"I guess that's good if you want to give your opponent a bath," Mathius said, mockingly.

"Or put out a fire." Macaro joked in response to Mathius' remark. "You see this skill is entirely dependent on the skill of the user. Before all our energy came directly from within to cast an element, now we shall attempt to use the energy outside of us to manipulate the elements. A key to this is to remember everything is the same. One must remember that each element is just energy represented in a different form. When one understands this, he will learn to manipulate and turn the elements into each other."

Some days left Marius physically beat. Bruised, bloody and sore Marius would lie in pain at night. When he was younger, this pain disturbed him and caused him great restlessness. Nowadays the pain had become so common he grew used to it. It almost brought joy to him as he felt the nostalgia of the day's fights. He could hear Macaro lecturing him as echoes in his mind, "Fighting is not a game and should not be interpreted as such."

Marius still always found fighting his classmates exciting, but something still disturbed Marius about the day's events. He stared at his door in wonder. Near the end of the day Yuri and Marius had happened to take a walk. They visited Talun, who proclaimed wonders about how Ralis sent his horse back. "A good man!" Marius remembered Talun shout. On their way back to the village, both of them noticed Nathaniel in the distance, walking the road toward the stables. Both of them agreed they'd rather not talk to Nathaniel, so they dove into a bush close to Talun's and hid. As they hid, Nathaniel approached Talun outside his stable as he washed his newly returned horse. Nathaniel had asked him for a horse and road off west.

The day's event spiralled in Marius' mind. Finally making his decision, Marius shot out of bed, dressed in his robes and left his tiny cabin, embracing the night. The dark winter night proved beautiful, like an icy mistress whose cold touch would take your breath away. Swiftly and silently, Marius walked, heading towards Yuri's cabin.

A gentle knock woke Yuri from a deep slumber. Another pair of knocks came and a gentle whispering voice saying, "Yuri."

"Aw, who is it?" Yuri said, displeased about being woken.

"It's Marius, I've made a decision—I'll do it."

"Damn, Marius, you took this long to come to an answer," Yuri said.

Slowly, he got up. Yawning, he grabbed for his robes strewn on the ground and put them on.

"I was way more excited for this earlier," Yuri said grudgingly as he opened his door.

Marius stood before him outside his shed, gently illuminated by starlight.

"What do we do if he's there?" Marius asked Yuri as they stepped on towards the main hall.

"I don't know, we run?" Yuri said speaking in a low voice as they came closer to the centre of town.

"No joking. If we get caught, this could be mean banishment from Highwash—or worse."

"Marius, we either do this and accept the consequences of what might happen, or we don't do it at all."

The both of them stopped as Yuri said this, he stood directly facing Marius and spoke firm.

"Is this how you justify doing things like this?" Marius said. Yuri could tell he had a scowl on his face even in the dark of night. "But I get it. Let's just get it done."

Yuri smiled, laughing inside his own head about his friend's worrisome nature, "You woke me up for this shit, so, don't back out now," Yuri said with a chuckle.

"Shh, you asshole. Let's not risk being loud for no reason," Marius hushed, looking over his shoulder.

Sneaking up to the centre of town through the tall grass that edged the village, they came up behind Mirane's dining hall, hiding in cover behind the building. Leaning around the corner of the building Yuri got a visual of the main hall.

"It looks all clear."

Marius nodded and followed Yuri as they made their way around the dining hall and towards the main hall. Crouching as they walked, they stayed as low as they possibly could. Sneaking around at night would be hard to explain to Macaro. Only their shadows lit up by the starlit night sky walked with them.

The ground crunched as they walked in the silence of night, it seemed with each step the main hall got further away. After a torturously anxious walk, they got to the main hall. The pair of them huddled close to the building, as they snuck up to the entrance.

The door was shut.

The both of them looked at the door and then at each other, both reluctant to open it. Marius gave Yuri a look, furrowing his brow in an attempt at gesturing "You open it" to Yuri with a facial expression.

Yuri understood and nodded. He reached up for the handle and slowly turned it. The brass bolts inside slowly clicked. With a creak that sounded like a scream in Marius' ears, Yuri pulled the door open.

Inside, the main hall was dimly lit by candles that never seemed to fade. No one was inside, not even an Elder meditating. Sheer luck, Marius thought. The two of them slowly crawled in crouching, attempting to avoid making even the slightest of noise. The walls were lit up from the candles perched on tiny cylinders fastened into the wall, so there was no way of not being seen if someone were to happen by.

Stepping fast, they headed for a door on the left hand side of the hall, which led to a stairway up to the upper levels. That door creaked worse than the main door and the two of them cursed Talun's name as they opened it. He was in charge of taking care of the buildings, so the rusty hinges were from his lack of greasing them.

The boys looked up the stairway and listened for any sounds echoing down. Nothing could be heard but the sound of their own breathing, so they gave each other a nod and started their way up. The stair set spiralled its way up to the third floor.

An ominous feeling overcame Marius as he climbed. A musty smell bugged his nose, the smell of dust, mixed in with the dim lighting of the stair set, the walk up felt almost dreamlike. Approaching the end of the stairway on the third floor, they faced their destination. Standing tall and lonesome, dark and heavy with oak, the door to Nathaniel's quarters loomed. Fear tugged at Marius, an unsettling feeling, one that accompanies you in the dark.

"It's locked," Yuri whispered, pulling down the door handle. "A good sign he is not home, wait while I open this, watch our back," Yuri commanded as he started to tamper with the door handle.

Marius turned to stare down the stairs, nothing but darkness lurked down there.

"When we were younger, an older student taught me how to pick locks, in case I ever wanted to have an extra snack," Yuri said in a low whisper.

"How come I never heard anything about this?"

"I was trying to help you, Marius, didn't want you to get fat. And, anyways, the key to keeping it a secret is to use it only on occasion," Yuri said as he fumbled with the lock.

Marius heard a slight chuckle from behind him as Yuri cracked the door open.

"Gotcha."

The room was creepily dark and absent of life. They entered, fearfully anticipating the unknown that could dwell in the darkness of Nathaniel's quarters. Finally coming to a stand, they lit little fires in the palm of their hands. Their fires revealed the furnishings of the room. It was quite simple, a large bed sat in one corner of the room and a desk with papers sprawled all across it was placed opposite to the door.

"Woah, now I already thought Nathaniel was a creep, but this is creepy," Yuri said, observing the emptiness of the room.

The two of them approached the desk.

"I guess we start here," Marius commented as he started to search among the papers.

Yuri continued to pace in the room, observing the whole of it.

"Yuri come see this," Marius said with a seriousness in his voice.

"What?"

Marius turned and handed Yuri a piece of parchment from the desk. Lifting his hand with the lit fire, he got sight of the words written on the paper. None of the words made any sense, all of them looked like nonsensical symbols scratched on the paper. Some were oblique in shape, finely written to form crescent moons, others were completely illegible, and Yuri couldn't recognize any familiarities between them with languages he had studied.

"What is this?" Yuri asked, muttering in astonishment as his eyes scanned the paper.

"Look, there's more," Marius said as he held up a drawing, which was buried under sheets of notes.

"Woah. I didn't know Nathaniel was an artist."

The drawing was of a large shape made from many shapes, it had cuboidal corners, but round edges, and three peaks of a triangle extended out to three corners. It would've taken the skill of an incredible artist to draw such a piece, Marius thought to himself. Nathaniel was a man of wonders, it seemed.

Marius tossed the drawing aside and the two of them continued looking through the papers sprawled on the desk.

"Some of this is in common tongue," Marius said, gesturing Yuri to have a look at what he was holding. The words were common tongue, but Yuri could hardly recognize them still with the scrawling handwriting that had been formed on the paper.

"Shit, the Archmage needs some of Mirane's writing classes," Yuri said, just after he received a backhand from Marius to his gut.

"Read it instead of insulting our Archmage."

"A spectacular phenomenon the ruins are, I have concluded they must have been built around a millennia or so, they are so old that caves and mountain structures have blended into the ruins, collapsing some portions, fusing others with caverns older than the ruins themselves," Yuri said as he struggled to read the notes out loud in the dim lighting of his fire.

"Skip forward, here, look," Marius said interjecting.

Yuri started to read further down the page.

"The ruins were obviously not built by any human intelligence, the structure is dynamic, yet flawless in its design."

"Why do you always do that? Interrupt me when I read?" Yuri said offended by Marius' way of talking.

"Not now, let me finish reading," Marius said taking his eyes off the paper giving Yuri a harsh stare. "The ruins are older than man himself, and no engineers today could build such architecture. In my time meditating there I have come to realize a great source of energy lies in the caverns. I can feel it, it's tremendous power, it is me. I know it is me."

Marius stopped reading out loud, his eyes scanning the page, reading faster than he could speak. "Though I am prevented from releasing my true form…"

Marius looked up at Yuri, whose face was still crunched angrily.

"Read this Yuri, something's not right at all," Marius said handing Yuri the paper.

"I'm not reading nothing. Why do you always do that? You always interrupt me when we read or study together," said Yuri, clearly irritated.

"I can just read faster than you," Marius said, rolling his eyes.

"You cannot read faster then me," Yuri said scoffing as he talked.

"I was already halfway down the page."

"Are you two just trying to get into trouble?"

Both Marius and Yuri jumped suddenly, frightened by the new voice. Macaro stood by the entrance of the room, his image was a silhouette, a black figure with arms crossed, it was his voice that gave him away.

"Are you two idiots? Your voices carry down the stairwell like echoes, and you left the stairwell door cracked open. Have I taught you two nothing?"

Both of them stood dumbfounded, frozen in place. It was Marius that broke the silence and answered.

"Macaro, you have to read this!" he said as he swiftly gestured the paper forward.

Macaro did not look pleased.

"I will take no part in this, you two are lucky it was me that caught you and not one of the other Elders. Now, go, get out of here before anyone sees you."

Surprised, Yuri and Marius gave each other a look of shock and took off running past Macaro and down the stairs. Macaro could hear them scamper down the stairs, then the fleeting sound of the main hall door creeping open and then closed. Macaro stood there gazing at the desk in Nathaniel's quarters. He chuckled to himself, thinking back to what had occurred, he had lied to them, he did want to take part in this.

The next day proved awkward for Marius. The previous night's adventures only illuminated half-truths, causing him greater confusion. Maybe if Yuri and him had not bickered like fools they would have read further on. What he learned had bothered him more. What was in the ruins Nathaniel desired so deeply? Marius lay there on his bed, staring at the ceiling, lost in a train of thought. Was that why Nathaniel wanted Marius to come with him?

A sharp knock at his door ripped him out of his head.

"Marius. Get up." It was Macaro. His voice was deep and harsh, his command was not gentle.

Without hesitating Marius jumped up and swung on his robes, tying his robe swiftly to then open the door.

Macaro did not make any gesture to greet him, he just gave Marius a nod and walked onward. Marius assumed he wanted him to follow.

The early dawn air was crisp and cold, a sharp wind fluttered by, raising the hairs on Marius' arms. The sun had yet to peek out over the eastern mountains, but the sky was bathed in a deep orange caused by the imminent sunrise. Marius followed Macaro silently, neither of them speaking a word, and Macaro had yet to mention the encounter they had had with each other the night before.

They arrived at Yuri's hut, which was nestled close to tall grass that gently weaved back and forth with the wind. Macaro knocked on Yuri's door and greeted him the same.

"Yuri. Get up."

Groaning could be heard inside, but soon Yuri was dressed and out the door himself. They both followed Macaro as he walked onwards. Glancing at Marius, Yuri gave him a worried look. Marius shrugged in reply to Yuri's gesture.

Macaro led them through the empty village, then through tall grass towards the ocean side. He turned to face them as they came to stand on a large slab of rock, which stood before the ocean. Waves gently crashed into the rock side, while seagulls flew overhead cawing and chirping loudly at each other.

"You two are becoming quite a nuisance. You both know that sneaking around into others' quarters is a great disrespect towards each other. It breaks our bonds of trust. You two are lucky that I stumbled into you. Any other Elder would have you banished, and rightfully they should." Macaro paused for a moment as he spoke, reflecting on his words. Obviously he had brought them here to converse before the others awoke and arrived for practice. "I read what you two read. Now, I don't agree with stealing his notes, but you two obviously read the same things I did. It shines light on our Archmage. Nathaniel is deeply troubled and that is apparent. But this is neither of yours' place to take action. So, I hope you heed my warnings and do not investigate further. I will deal with the rest myself. I ask you both, no more sneaking around, no more games. Focus on your practice. Have I made myself clear?"

"Yes," Marius and Yuri replied simultaneously.

"Good, I trust in the two of you to keep what we have read secret."

The rest of the morning Macaro did not mention the incident from the night before. The rest of the students showed up and started to practice under his guidance. The only one who was curious was Cynthia.

"You two are early," she said jokingly, even though she was suspicious.

Stupidly Yuri spoke without thinking, "Yeah, we wanted to get to practice early."

This only raised greater suspicion in Cynthia—the two of them were hardly ever known to appear to class early or ever really on time. But the class carried on and soon Cynthia had forgotten all about her suspicions of Marius and Yuri.

Macaro's lesson focused on energy work; he had the class practicing the use of drawing energy from outside of themselves and from their environment. Cynthia, Yuri and Marius stood by the cliff edge side by side, each of them attempting to draw energy from outside of them. Each of them held out their right hand in the direction of the ocean.

"Can you feel it, the vibrations that are all around you? The air vibrates with energy. So, inhale and draw forth from it."

Marius inhaled as Macaro directed, but he could feel no energy flow up his arm. Marius was used to channelling qi from inside himself to use magic, but harnessing qi from the outside environment frustrated him.

"One can easily feel and direct their inner qi, but to manipulate the qi of our world requires an understanding, an understanding that we are all one—not as people, not as individuals—but as a whole. You are not separate from anything that is, the air, the water, the ground, all of it flows from the same source," Macaro ranted on, pacing back and forth from either end of his line of students. "I have said it over and over and I'll always say it: Being a Mage is never about you, a good Mage will never find value or enjoyment from our practice. The understanding is that these gifts are for the world. Our strength is our virtue, our skill is from understanding, our nature is compassion. Without compassion, our spirit shall fall and decay, our choices will be blurry and our future unknown. Compassion should guide your every move, your every punch and your every action. And only in this understanding, can you truly master energy and harness its true potential. Now inhale and focus."

Marius raised his arm again, inhaling he focused; he focused on his breath rooting his feet into the ground. He could feel it slightly, the same feelings he got during the first task, a vibration beyond himself. At first when Marius would feel it, it sort of felt as if it was him vibrating. But focusing further Marius could feel that it was, in fact, the air around him that was vibrating. He could feel it wrap around his arm like tentacles, this vibration that would move up his forearm in waves. But it then dissipated as fast as it came.

"Calm, Marius, you almost had it," Macaro said who was now standing behind Marius.

"I don't get this!"

Everyone turned their heads towards Mathius as he yelled in frustration. Chuckles echoed in the air. Macaro shook his head, smirking, and stared on towards the ocean horizon. His students were so young-minded; Macaro feared the day the blanket that covered the realities of life was torn off from them. Gazing at his students, each of them trying wholeheartedly to learn the skill, he thought to himself, *They might just have a chance.*

It was animals that Ralis loved. Ralis had no respect for humankind, but animals he had utmost respect and compassion towards. To Ralis, animals seemed soft-hearted and warm in contrast to what he had received from humanity. The way animals walked without sound, flew with such grace or swam with such dexterity. That was why Ralis tried his hardest to befriend the best of animals, from horses to birds to dogs to cats. He had a hand for it, too.

Ralis wouldn't describe himself as so, but he had had a hard childhood. Growing up on the streets of Palinteer, a beggared boy isn't the most dreamed for life, and it definitely wasn't Ralis' dream. But he became accustomed to living in such a way. The hardest part of being a beggared boy was the fact the townsfolk offered nothing but complete avoidance of him. This left nasty scars, of course, but that's where animals had played their part in Ralis' life. He often found himself talking to seagulls under the pier during the day. Sitting on corralled rock, he would string together many sentences to the seagulls, they would sit, perched, only to stare blindly at him before flying away. It didn't matter though, other animals roamed the streets of Palinteer.

Above its tower of wealth, beneath Palinteer was a city of trash. A city of rats that ate at the filth piled beneath the city streets, of street cats that roamed at night stalking softly as faint as a shimmering heartbeat. The city was a decrepit place, only to ride on the back of the everyday working men to show a false image of prosperity. Ralis was its truth. Now Ralis understood that, but back then he did not.

Since he left Palinteer, the forest had become Ralis' home. He lay down resting, nestled in between branches of the thick forest canopy, staring at the sky above him. The fall nights, if clear, proved a stunning image. Large stripes of red, yellow and orange stars glowed far above in the night sky, as if someone had painted it with colours.

Ralis was enjoying the rest from hiking, the forest night was deafeningly silent, it offered him peace in the ruckus of his own mind. A whooshing sound came down and a nearby branch shook. Slowly, Ralis sat up. It was an owl, one of the many birds he had sent forth to do his bidding. Well, not so much his bidding, more of a friendly favour. The owl was deep auburn brown, its eyes were black as coal, even to been seen against the darkness of night. Ralis held out his hand gesturing the bird to perch on his arm. The bird did so. Its sharp talons cut into him, but he didn't mind it and ignored the pain. The owl's feathers rippled with softness as the owl's head twitched and ruffled its feathers. Ralis looked deep into the owl's eyes, looking deep into the owl's memories.

The beating of wings, the feeling of flight, the nocturne beast took forth to the sky headed in search. The owl's memories soon took over his mind. Ralis only knew where to begin searching but nothing further than that. The eyes of the forest would serve him well. The owl had flown north, riding high above the forest growth, scanning; then it flew east, diving into the forest dodging through trunks and branches in search of signs. Any signs would do, signs of mass movement, disturbance to the forest floor, left over rubbish and equipment from travel, anything that would give away these Rangers' position.

The owl scoured the eastern valley of the Emeralties, but the Rangers had left no signs, they had left not a single trace of their existence or presence.

Ralis looked away from the bird's eyes, removing himself from its memories, and stared off towards the forest canopy.

How was that possible? How could a group of people hide themselves so well that not even owls could find them? Maybe Salamon had got it wrong, maybe they were in another location and Salamon had been misled, Ralis thought to himself. Staring blankly out into the forest, Ralis became aware that the owl had not left.

"Shoo, bud, your task is done," Ralis said flicking his fingers, gesturing her to leave.

The owl stared at him with an odd expression tilting its head.

"What is it? What do you want to show me?" Ralis asked, then, understanding the owl's intent, looked deeply into its eyes again. The black circled voids took over Ralis' vision.

Again he was flying among the trees, dodging and ducking, winding his way among the forest. Leaves brushed against him every so often as the bird flapped its wings. Still Ralis did not understand what the owl was trying to show him. The forest looked empty, with no signs of human travel.

Suddenly Ralis started to descend, the bird diving low, swiftly circling the base of a large cedar. At first Ralis could not make out what the owl intended him to see, but as soon as it perched itself on a branch across from the tree it had circled obsessively, Ralis understood. It was a clue for sure, but for how much it would yield Ralis knew little. Looking down at the base of the cedar, it could clearly be seen that two bolts had been lodged into its bark. Studying closer, Ralis understood that they were not bolts, but in fact arrows. Arrows left behind by a forgetful hunter...

His vision returned to his own as he refocused back on himself. The spot the owl had shown him was far off from any of Salamon's camps.

It's a start, Ralis thought to himself. He thanked the majestic bird with a simple caress of his head and a nod.

It was night time in the forest, but time was of the essence. Ralis could spare not a minute with Salmon's troops mounted in the valley. He could navigate the forest at dark with the risks it entailed. He could hear Macaro's words whisper in his mind, *Only a fool travels a forest at night.* Macaro said many things, at times they were contradictory, but this was one of the things he said Ralis agreed with.

However, with risk comes reward. And so, Ralis jumped down from where he lay among the branches and dropped onto the forest floor. It was cold and damp in the night chill. Darkness lurched around every tree and bramble bush.

Walking in the pitch black made Ralis think back to when he taught Marius and Yuri in the dark that night. Ralis laughed out loud, smiling to himself thinking of it. He had made the lesson up simply to give them a few smacks, but truly it was a necessary skill: to see and stalk like a panther, to glide like a snake, unseen, but all knowing. The animals of the night saw more than just with their eyes. They could feel the heat of creatures against the coldness of night. Any noise rang into their ear. That is how a Mage needed to navigate. Stalking, silently, slithering with skill. So Ralis stepped on through the bramble, which twisted and turned every so often, reminding Ralis to stay on the path with nicks and cuts.

Every so often Ralis would climb high into a tree and chirp to call forth a bat. Blood bats would come in from every direction and Ralis would use them as his eyes in the abyss of the forest night, helping him navigate through the trenches of black.

Dawn crept forth slowly and with it an amber glow slid across the forest canopy. Ralis still paced on, his feet sore and growing blisters, but he was nearing the spot. The journey proved treacherous, the ground sloped up and down many times, forcing Ralis to climb through trees instead. With the new light Ralis could see the forest floor more clearly, it was crimsoned in decay from fallen trees and dead bramble, but from within the dead forest floor more life bloomed. Thickets of cedars and pines reached high into the sky.

No wonder Salamon's troops have had not searched here, the place is a death trap, Ralis acknowledged as he observed the forest floor. There certainly would have been no place to camp out as the forest floor dropped, uplifted and was littered with dead wood, moist from rot within them. No horse could traverse the ground either.

Ralis' feet were sore and knotted by the time he arrived at his destination. A thick cedar tree stood in front of him looming high into the sky. Eye level with Ralis were two arrow bolts lodged into the bark which splintered around them. Coming closer to the tree, stepping over branch and waste, Ralis could see the bolts clearly. They were of a deep red colour.

Odd, Ralis thought. *No men of Salamon use such quills, maybe freelancers? No, who would come out here, and for what? Perhaps it was these so-called Rangers that left these arrows. But what does that give me?*

Ralis took his eyes off the bolts and studied the ground. The soft forest bed was littered with pine needles and deep red leaves. Scanning the area around the arrow-embedded cedar showed no signs of any human footprints, and, if there were any, the newly fallen leaves would have covered them. The smell of a pile of dung alerted Ralis to its presence, crouching to get a closer look he realized the poo had crusted.

It must be a day or two old, Ralis thought to himself, *maybe from the animal the novice hunter had been after? A deer, perhaps?*

The area near the tree did not yield many clues, so he paced north of the cedar tree where he thought the shots must have come from. Looking up, Ralis could see the sky drooped with clouds, a fresh system coming in from the cold, wet western sea.

A storm, great, Ralis thought, letting out a light chuckle. Maybe, by chance, it wouldn't rain, he thought, and continued walking north. The forest was thicker as the hill raised in elevation. Tinier hemlock trees flocked among the large scattered pines and thick belly cedars.

A shot from this area would have been hard, and even further up the hill the shot would be impossible, Ralis observed, gazing at the cedar tree downhill in the distance.

But even the area where Ralis determined the shot had been taken from proved no results, nothing but a thick layer of dense pine needles was to be seen. The rattle of rain among leaves began and tiny droplets of water splashed onto Ralis' head, thickening his wet, matted hair. Looking up at the sky, he was greeted further by more splashes of rain. Ralis stood there, frustrated for a moment among the still trees, as the rain started to pour down on him, beginning to soak his robes.

Ralis hated wearing wet robes, so he took them off, but left on his leather woven pants, tying his robe around his waist. Shirtless, the rain splashed cold against his skin, the wind that raced through the trees raising the hair on his arms.

Ralis started down the hill, navigating the ground back to the cedar tree that had been victim to the two arrow bolts. The ground began to stick to Ralis' feet, the ground softening more with each step. He hated the feeling of mud between his toes. As he got back to the cedar tree, he grasped and tore out the bolts one at a time. Two holes were left in the cedar. It seemed to almost have saddened the tree, giving it a depressing appearance. He held both arrows in his right hand, gazing at them. It seemed his only option was to use the help of the forest animals. Whatever had come here and shot the bolts had left no tracks.

If there truly are Rangers in this forest, it would seem they are hiding on purpose, covering their tracks.

Trailing back slightly, Ralis went to a stream he had spotted the night before. He sat in the rain among smooth rocks in the streambed, filling his canteen with water, drinking the container whole, and filling it again. The stream was only a few feet wide, and about knee deep at its deepest, but the water was fiercely cold. Across the riverbed Ralis spotted bright orange autumn berries. Hopping across some boulders jutting out of the stream, he reached the other side of the riverbed standing on a large rock.

The autumn berry bush grew hanging on a ridge cut out by the meandering river. He plucked a few off their stems. The softness of the berries leaked juice out with the softest touch.

Later, Ralis had a smile on his face as he walked further up the stream in search of birds. Breakfast was good this morning, and in the forest that's something to be thankful for.

Whistling, he called for some crows. The sound carried throughout the forest and at first nothing answered. But suddenly shrill caws could be heard and a flock of five crows flew down, landing on the ground in front of Ralis. He leaned down to greet them as they hobbled about. He looked through their tiny black eyes, and through those mirrors he could see all of their thoughts. He whispered words into their minds and placed an image of the bolts. Cawing, the black birds flew off with the objective to find the users of these bolts. Ralis knew crows were intelligent, they had often been known to steal items and wares from travelling traders. Of all the birds, the crows could find these Rangers, Ralis thought.

A while was spent in the rain waiting for the birds to return. In the meantime, while waiting, Ralis decided to save his energy and spend the day snacking on the autumn berries that grew among the stream side and meditating.

Meditation brought Ralis to the sounds of the forest, the gentle rushing of the stream, the soft echoes of falling leaves, the chirping of birds that flew by playing with other birds. The quietness brought him further inside himself, and soon he was breathing calm feeling his energy spiral in his body. From his toes to his head, he could feel his whole body vibrating at once. Withdrawing further, Ralis' mind drifted to the sight of himself. He could see himself sitting there cross-legged, the riverbed and forest behind him dimmed grey. He could see himself glowing, shimmering, glowing softly yellow, but in the centre of his abdomen a snarling darkness grew and with it came fear. A fear that spread over his whole body. He felt it move across him as he watched the blackness consume his once illuminated body. Darkness covered Ralis, and again he could smell a musty smell of sewer and waste, the dark figure, his heart racing and racing beyond control.

Cawing awoke Ralis. He lay on his back facing up. The hard river stone showed to be a dreadful place to snooze and he could feel the result in his back. Ralis groaned as he sat up. Above him the flock of crows circled, crying shrilly. The crows had brought pictures of a doe carcass in the east of the woods. It seemed like a short walk, so Ralis decided to head there straight away.

Throwing the crows some of the berries he'd collected in thanks, he headed onwards. The rain had stopped, but that left the ground muddy and torturous to walk in, so Ralis climbed among the trees. He swung between branches of large trees, climbed through thick nestles of tree branches and crawled among the canopy.

Hours passed by quicker than ever, and the day soon started to signal its end with the spray of orange that lit the sky. Ralis walked until night time darkened his way. Finding a spot among dense fir trees, Ralis fashioned a sort of hammock with many branches. It was unsightly, looking as if the user would fall through at any moment, but Ralis had practiced building the makeshift hammocks a regrettable amount of times. Hungry and tired, Ralis needed sleep, he would make due with his tree-branch bed.

The sun barely had risen over the eastern mountain range by the time Ralis was up and hiking again. The night before was groggy and sleepless, but Ralis trekked on nonetheless, thankful of the clear skies and the pass of the storm.

It was midday by the time Ralis reached the carcass. The fourth day of hiking left him weary and tired. He had traveled far with little rest among the deep-forested mountains. The constant change in slope of the valley, from up to down, up to down, had taken its toll on Ralis' legs. Approaching the carcass he knelt down, his legs burning. The doe was grey-hued as it lay on its side with its torso ripped a gash. Its intestine spilled forth onto the dirt, mingled with rot and flies. Ralis' throat burned as he inhaled the smell, making him scowl at the carcass before him. He looked at the doe, fore to buttocks—something was off. It seemed too perfect, the way it lay on its side, tongue drooping out of its mouth. The way its legs were together seemed odd. Both the front and hind legs were paired together, as if the carcass was dragged.

It wasn't killed here, Ralis thought. He knew if it had fallen running or died struggling its legs should be spread. The doe also looked as if it had been rotting for a few days, its skin a dry, dull, grey colour. Anxious, Ralis stood slowly, as he did he observed the ground around him.

No drag marks, just slight indentations of footprints, means it was placed here, tied to a stick and carried, placed here, Ralis said to himself in his head as he analyzed the ground. *But why was it placed here?*

Nervously, he frowned, puzzled, and began to turn to leave. But as he turned he came to face a cloaked man who stood before him. Hearing the sound of many bows being drawn around him, Ralis came to realize the reason the doe was there.

"Hands in the air, Mage!" the man screamed. The man before him held a crossbow aimed at Ralis' chest. The bolt was massive and obviously not standard issue.

Ralis could sense about twelve men, at least, in the woods surrounding him and the doe. All of them cloaked, all of them holding bows, strings drawn.

"Hands in the air, Mage!" the man screamed again. Slowly, Ralis raised his hands in the air. Macaro's words filled his mind, *Compassion is our nature,* and Ralis, not wanting more death on his hands, did as he was told.

The cloaked man who held the crossbow approached Ralis in slow steps filled with caution. All eyes were upon Ralis and the circle of bowmen started to enclose.

"On your knees!" the man yelled.

Ralis did as such and knelt. A soft rag tightened around his eyes and all went dark. Hands clasped his wrists and brought them to his back, chains clinked and cut at his hands and wrists as they bound his hands. A hand grabbed his face and forced his jaw open, violently shoving a wet rag into his mouth. Ralis gagged at the smell, and soon consciousness escaped him. The last thing he felt before he passed out was himself slumping onto the dirt floor.

At least he had found them.

The rain had come to Highwash again, but, luckily, this time Marius was in the village, not wandering the wilderness. The streets grew tiny rivers of flowing mud which spread out to all of the buildings. Marius jogged hurriedly through the wet torrent, rain splashing at his heels. Macaro had called him to his quarters, which was east of the main hall. A toilsome journey it was as the rain pelted down upon him. Marius could see others running for shelter but was unable to make them out in the downpour.

Reaching Macaro's shack, Marius was drenched, his robes and pants blackened and dripping. He knocked hurriedly and Macaro, seeming to understand, opened the door immediately, laughing as he saw Marius.

"How was the walk over?" Macaro said, greeting Marius and gesturing him to enter. He slid a tiny stool over to Marius to sit on by the doorway, "I don't want you to get everything wet. Too bad for Ralis, eh?"

"Yes, stiff luck," Marius replied courteously.

Tapping drummed on the roof of Macaro's quarters, little droplets hitting the floor as some broke free through the roof. Macaro paced for a second and then took a seat on his bed. Calmly, he sat stroking his chin, finding his words.

"Your dreams? Any change?" Macaro asked, his eyes focused on Marius.

"They have grown less disturbing in the past while, but I still hardly recall them."

"Strange... so... you lost the second task. I had thought otherwise."

Marius gulped as he heard Macaro speak.

"But that does not mean a cessation of your progression, no, I will still train you, don't worry about that. Though it does tell me you were not as ready as I thought you were. You see, the second task held a great importance: the ability to defend against aggression. Playful sparring is one thing, but you of all people should know all too well the viciousness of the world. Well, anyways, I just wanted to say you shall still be following all the current lessons." Macaro clapped his hands once as he spoke. "As well, I have task for you. North of the village in that little thicket forest an hour from here, there's these certain autumn berries that grow this time of year, and I would like you to collect some for me."

"Today?" Marius asked his face turning into a puzzled frown.

"Yes, today. I certainly shall get hungry."

Marius agreed humbly and left Macaro's quarters. *Why is he sending me on such a simple task, today of all days? Was this supposed to be a joke?* Marius thought to himself as he headed towards Mirane's, the sky careening rain all around him.

By the time he got to Mirane's, Marius was fully soaked again. Macaro said she would be at the kitchen and requested him to lend a bucket from her. Marius mumbled under his breath, cursing Macaro as he entered. All of the students were in the dining hall today, the rain sheltering them inside. Older students sat to the left, near the wall, while Reggard and the rest of his class sat at a long bench in the middle of the room. His class immediately noticed him enter. Giggling, Cynthia waved to him and called his name.

"Marius! You look nasty, come sit down!" she hollered across the room.

"I can't, Macaro sent me on errands today," Marius said as he walked by them.

They seemed to care little and resumed talking. Laughing could be heard as he entered through a doorway covered in hanging drapes that separated the kitchen from the eating area. Mirane was in the back chopping vegetables contentedly, while two other Mages Marius recognized cooked what looked like oats.

All at once they said, "Hi, Marius," as he swung the drapes open and entered.

"Mirane, may I borrow a bucket? Macaro wants me to pick berries."

Her face frowned, her soft face becoming wrinkled, "In this weather?"

She shook her head, confused, and paced around the kitchen. The kitchen was a lot less organized than her medical hut. Pots and pans were thrown, unorganized, in many shelves that edged the walls of the room. A table stood in the centre of the room, holding a variety of vegetables, while straw bags of oats and rice sat lazily in the corner of the room. Mirane had always stated that cooking for young Mages was hard work.

Mirane came back to Marius, handing him a large wooden pail. "This should do," she said, smiling and looking down on Marius. "I don't see why he wants you to get berries in this weather... but better not to refuse him."

Ruffling up his hair, she patted him on the back before he made his way off. Passing his friends the second time was much harder with the bucket. Even Yuri couldn't help but comment, spinning a joke at Marius as he stormed out of the dining hall.

Rain spat down hard, all the while anger was building up in Marius. *Was this a joke? Did Macaro send him out to get berries just to isolate and ridicule him? There was no way, Macaro would never* do that, but then why were his friends sitting having fun while he was left to do... to do—to do this?!

Marius' mind stormed on as he headed through the north part of the village. He passed the main hall, which had tiny waterfalls coursing down its sides. Soon the buildings disappeared behind him and he was among the grass. Autumn's moisture always worked wonders here. Bright green, the grass stood strong and stalky, finally getting the water it so desperately needed after the summer's blistering heat. Marius knew the thicket forest north of the village, it was roughly only an hour's walk.

His time walking alone brought back memories of his journey east with Ralis and Yuri, how even to get to the crossroads took hours. He had not been this far from the village since then. Memories of the manticore shot through Marius' mind. He paused for a moment, clutching the bucket against his waist, listening to the rain patter against the grass, listening. There was no way Macaro would send him into danger blindly. Relaxing with that thought, he took a breath and continued on.

The tiny forest bloomed orange, falling leaves and needles fell amongst the raindrops. Tiny bushes lived in between the separation of trees, covered in a spray of orange and brown.

Time to pick berries, Marius thought, mocking the task in his head. He soon came to discover the berries Macaro described were not rampant among the thicket forest. Marius checked bush after bush, encountered a squirrel that ran off with a nut in its hand, and checked bush after bush again. The rain never letting up.

After a while of searching, Marius came to sit on a lone stone, sighing in frustration. It was midday and he had collected no berries. Convincing himself to continue searching, he wandered through the forest lazily, calling at birds that flew by, chirping, or practicing a flip among the trees.

I guess I will just tell Macaro that I didn't find them. Will he even accept that answer? Marius thought to himself as he turned back, retracing his way home. His mind went about a hundred excuses, but none seemed conclusive. Why did Macaro send him out here? His mind always wondering back to the familiar question. *Was this punishment?* Marius stopped for a moment and gazed at the forest around him. No patch of berries could be seen. The forest around him offered nothing but an autumn colouration. *Could it perhaps be that the berries did not even grow here?* Marius thought to himself, working himself up. Nothing seemed clear to him. Had Macaro lost respect for him? Was this truly his new purpose? Errand boy for Macaro?

The rain tapped on and on as Marius' mind raced. It bothered him so, like a final insult from the skies themselves. He stood still, listening for a second. The rain sounded almost like laughter. But amongst the laughter an almost silent sloshing could be heard, like tiny footsteps in the mud. The sound had blended in with his own steps before when Marius was walking, but now standing still, the noise seemed clear and distinguished.

And then that's when he heard it: a deep snarling, a clasp of teeth.

Turning without hesitation, Marius came to face a large wolf. Its grey fur shimmered wet in the rain. A shock bolt ripped though Marius' spine as he caught sight of it, it was closer than he had heard. Before Marius could position himself to react, the beast lunged. Its giant forelegs lurched for Marius, its jaws thirsting for flesh, the wolf jumped forward. The weight of the animal took Marius to the ground, the impact jarring his skull against the muddy ground. Its jaws clamped around his shoulder. Marius screamed as a sharp pain erupted through his right arm.

"RAAAH!" Marius screamed as he focused energy into his left hand, smashing his fist into the wolf's side. The force smashed the wolf to the side, launching him against a small tree. Marius jumped up as fast as possible, springing with his good arm and landing on his feet. The wolf was up just as fast. Disentangling itself from the tree branches, it shot out headed for Marius.

With no time to check his wound, Marius stepped to the side, avoiding the wolf's lunge. However, the wolf was swift and, swinging its back around, it came to face Marius again in a flash. It launched forward, aiming its jaws for Marius' leg. Seeing this, Marius smashed down the wolf's skull pinning it against the ground. The wolf swung Marius off easily, sending him flying back and stumbling.

Both the wolf and Marius were covered in mud, brown soaked against their bodies. The rain continued to pour.

Quickly Marius summoned fire from his left hand, scorching the wolf. It yelped as it jumped back, away from the flames. Marius would not let it get the upper hand. Losing this time meant more than embarrassment. The fire dispersed into the air as Marius lowered his hand.

The wolf seemed to have disappeared into the bush. Everything stood still. Nothing made a noise. Marius stood solid, listening, his head twitching, anticipating any noise to come. Suddenly the wolf rushed out from the bushes from the side and leapt high in the air. Marius had predicted this and tucked underneath the flying wolf, allowing it to pass over him. The wolf nimbly flipped back to face Marius, then started to circle him, pacing slowly in a continuous circle. Its growl was deep and penetrating.

For the first time, Marius got a clear sight of the beast as it circled. The once caked-on mud, now slowly slid off the wolf's black matted fur, the rain washing his fur anew. The wolf was massive, twice the size of any man, as well as more deft.

Why was this wolf alone? The thought came suddenly as he observed the beast. *And why does it attack so relentlessly?* His thoughts were muted as the wolf lunged to bite again.

First it veered left, chomping nothing but air, as Marius dodged right. With its side revealed, in that quick instance, Marius went to strike, kicking the beast. His foot slammed against the beast's ribs, but the beast reacted quickly, its jaws chomping for his kicking leg. Stepping back, he smashed the wolf's opposite side with his good fist, sending the beast into the ground.

They danced in the rain, a violent dance, splashing mud with each step. Every hit seemed to only anger the wolf more. It seemed to only react faster. At once, fast as lightening, it chomped a bite on Marius' lower tibia. It's massive jaws clamping down on his flesh. Marius yelled in pain as he crashed down into the mud.

Screaming, Marius lit both his hands, embers and flames shot forth. The air reeked of burning flesh as the wolf dashed off him. Marius lay on his back, grunting, mud soaking into his clothes. He felt for his leg, the wound was wet with blood or mud, Marius couldn't tell, but he knew he had no time.

Frantically, Marius scurried back with his arms. But the wolf was there, just sitting in front of him. Marius blinked at the sight before him. But there it was. The wolf sat calm, staring at Marius who shook fearfully.

Marius stared for a second, blinking, unable to believe his eyes. Slowly, he attempted to move into a crouch, his eyes locked on the wolf's, but as soon as he began to move, the wolf started to growl. The beast's face turning from calm to sour and Marius knew what he would have to do: there was no way the wolf would allow him to stand, he needed to bait it.

Starting with slowing his breath, Marius calmed himself, focusing qi into his left hand, letting it build a great force. As soon as he stepped into a crouch, the wolf leapt. But its effort was null. As the wolf leapt for Marius' throat, Marius smashed his fist square in its jaw. The blast of qi sent Marius back, and sent the wolf flying. The yelp from the wolf was so fierce Marius felt it himself. Marius quickly sprawled to his feet. His injured leg gave forward and he crashed down into the mud. Looking up, he saw the wolf ahead of him, lying on its side in the mud.

Was it dead? Marius hoped to the stars he had not killed it. The wolf twitched and got up nimbly. Marius sighed with relief, but fear soon struck over him again. The wolf had not died. The wolf just stood there, gently licking its wounds, and then darted off quick as a flash. The noise of it running soon dissipated amongst the sound of rain. It was gone.

Marius fell over on his side. The rain tickled his face as he turned to face the sky. Surprisingly he felt a surge of happiness and started laughing uncontrollably. The rain had come to feel amazing.

As he turned around and propped himself up, he came face to face with a lone bush. It had dark green leaves, tiny as fingernails, and amongst its branches, large, blooming orange berries hung. Seeing this made Marius laugh even more. Getting up hurt his left leg, but he could walk if he limped.

He looked around the area where he had fought. The ground was massed with footprints, and in the centre of the clearing his bucket lay, smashed into two splintering sections. It most likely got smashed when the wolf had surprised him. Covered in mud, disappointed and without berries, Marius headed back to Highwash.

With the adrenaline that coursed through his body fading, his wounds could be felt clearly. His right shoulder ached tremendously, blood soaked his robes which clearly oozed from the wound. Looking down he could see his left ankle swollen and bloody.

The hike to Highwash was brutal and filled with misery. The rain continued its downpour, and being injured only slowed Marius down. It was almost evening by the time he reached the outskirts of the village.

Marius sighed as he came down the hill and saw the main hall in the distance. It was dark and lonesome as it stood against the grey sky.

Dinner is probably being served, Marius thought bitterly to himself as he closed in on the village. He felt cold and alone now. The adrenaline that had once brought on laughter now left him depleted and despaired. First, he decided to go see Macaro. Marius was unsure where Macaro would be at this time of day, but he thought he should inform Macaro of what happened before visiting Mirane.

"Come in, Marius." The words echoed from inside Macaro's cabin as soon as he knocked. Marius opened the door to see Macaro sitting by the window, staring out at the grass horizon beyond.

"I didn't find the berries... well, actually, I found them but my bucket had broken."

Macaro chuckled loudly, suddenly, his head raised back in laughter. "My dear Marius, you would be the one to mention the berries before mentioning how you were attacked by a wolf."

"How did you... I hadn't told you—" Marius began to stutter.

"Please sit down," Macaro said cutting off Marius, while sliding over a stool for Marius to sit at by the door. Marius sat eagerly, but still confused. "You see, I had sent the wolf."

Hearing the words made Marius erupt with anger. "What? You sent the wolf? I can't believe—did you even truly send me to pick berries? What if I was mauled? I was lucky to have survived, it had caught me off guard!"

Macaro held out his hand, gesturing in a kind way for Marius to stop speaking.

"Marius, do you not trust my teachings? I needed you to truly fight, to truly face fear. I needed you to truly fight for survival. The wolf is my friend, comes from a pack up north I had the luck of running into. You see? The wolf would have never hurt you severely, I just needed you to believe it would. You failed the second task, where I thought you would have succeeded. So, the wolf is merely a gesturing, an offering of sorts, from teacher to student. If you had lost to the wolf, I'd have come to find you this evening. The wolf I commanded would have let no harm come to you as you lay hurt, waiting for me. If you had lost, I'd have known you weren't ready. I would have known why you had lost the second task. But you see, here you sit before me, bloody, tired and awfully dirty, but undefeated. You chose to live. And that's the fire I must see in my students. Now do you understand my actions?" Macaro asked finalizing his words. His face was still and rock-like.

For a second Macaro's usual look of happiness seemed to have changed to a stone cold look. The look of a warrior; a look Marius had never seen in him before.

"I understand," Marius responded.

"Good, now lets go see Mirane and get you patched up."

XI

The second floor of the main hall held a large library, sheltering some of the oldest books Marius had seen.

"This one just reeks," Yuri said as he pulled a rustic-looking book off of a towering shelf.

"Lets see," Marius said holding out his hand for Yuri to pass him the old leather bound book.

Yuri came over to the desk they were seated at and propped it open for both of them to see.

The library was dark and musty. Many books of old sat undisturbed, coated in layers of dust among the endless rows of shelves. Marius hated coming in here, it burned his nose just being by all the decaying books.

"Blech," Marius said repulsed by the waft of air that blew as the book swung open. "That does smell," he agreed. With his left hand Marius awkwardly flipped through the book, his right hand occupied in a sling.

Meanwhile, Yuri went to a shelf close to them in search of more books. The dim candle that sat in the centre of the desk flickered with each flip of a page Marius made.

"There's nothing in here about it, only notes on subterranean chasms north of here that occurred by constant erosion from the sea. That's the closest thing related to local caves in this one," Marius claimed, raising his voice for Yuri to hear among the bookshelves.

"Keep looking while I find another book." Yuri's voice echoed back.

A hush could be heard from inside the room. Frustrated, Marius sighed. It had been Yuri's idea to come up here and search for any references on the ruins Ralis had taken them to. To Marius, Yuri seemed slightly fixated on the ruins they had once visited, but it seemed to make sense at times, and Yuri had been gravely injured during their time in the ruins. And Marius was secretly glad to get some time away from training anyways, his arm still ached from the wolf's bite. At night he could still feel the heavy clamp of its jaw.

A gentle hand placed itself on Marius' shoulder.

"How's your arm?" whispered a familiar voice. Cynthia stood behind him.

"Its getting better, but still aches," Marius said, gesturing for her to sit.

"Clive told me you two would be in here. Surprising for Yuri to actually want to study."

Marius scoffed in agreement.

"Have you found anything?" Cynthia asked, taking a seat across from Marius at the small table he sat at.

"Nothing yet."

Suddenly Yuri clambered out between the narrow gap between two bookshelves holding three books in his arms.

"Check these then," he said, plopping the trio of books on the desk, the force blowing out the candle placed on the desk. Marius relit the flame with flick of his palm. The three books were old and flaccid, barely surviving their own weight. Each was a volume by a certain Professor Frederic, a doctor of biology and mammology. Marius' was titled *Western Thenus*, a portrait and description of western ecology in cold black inscription on the spine. On the front cover, worn and grey, the author's name was titled: *Professor Frederic Hope*.

"How is this going to help me?" Marius blurted.

"I don't know, just take a look. There could be anything in there," Yuri said upholding his resolution to keep searching.

"Yuri is right, Marius. I can't tell you how many odd references and mentions I have come across in these texts. Definitely with this author, he wrote sort of queer."

Marius answered Cynthia with nothing but a scolding stare while she smirked laughingly.

An hour went by, maybe more, Marius couldn't tell in the dim lighting of the library. The three of them sat there flipping through the pages, Marius constantly pointing out the texts relevancy to their search.

"Couldn't you have found a more useful book? This is discussing ladybugs."

Yuri chuckled and finally just shook his head.

"Find your own books then," he joked. At least Marius thought it was a joke. Searching the old bookshelves Marius felt a wave of nausea. The smell of must disgusted him. Each book was grimy to the touch, making Marius hesitant to even search and turn back to the desk his friends sat at.

"I'm done with this, I'm going to meditate in the hall, I'll see you two in lesson."

"Alright, bye," they both mumbled, their heads down in the books. Shrugging Marius started off for the lower hall. He did indeed plan to meditate.

The main hall echoed with the sound of breathing. Its chamber held Marius and his classmates following a lesson on meditation guided by Macaro.

It was evening at Highwash, and evening lessons were always more relaxing than the ferocious lessons that accompanied the day. Often times, evening lessons were focused on topics of discussion, many being about the world itself, the political hierarchies of the outside world, languages of the different cultures among the world, the old world and the new.

Today's focus was on meditation. At moments, Macaro would pace the class, touching each student on their navel and head, realigning their qi with his own force. Marius felt the shock in his body as Macaro touched him, his body vibrating vigorously as Macaro placed a palm on his head. Meditation classes were often held once a month, teaching the Mages how to focus their internal energy, to build it up and to harness it.

With a snap of his fingers, Macaro awoke the class. Light filled Marius' eyes as he opened them. Macaro stood in the centre of the dim room, the rest of his class sat on the circled steps. At first Macaro did not say anything, he simply gazed among his students. He always thought about his first words.

"First off, I would like to congratulate the victors of the second task. You have proven, through focus and dexterity, one's will to survive. The opponent will not always be your friend, that is for certain. You are still young and have not left home. None of you have gone past the eastern mountains. But you are all maturing into bright Adept Mages. As your Elder, I have thought deeply of this matter, I believe its time you all know the truth."

Marius' spine rose to this.

"I have often spoke of others who are our brothers and sisters, but it is time you truly know who they really are." Macaro paused for a moment, clearing this throat. "Imagine seeing your own family hurt each other," his words were raw. "It is something not easily talked about, but long ago, when I was a child, I was raised in another home. It was the same as here, bright and happy, our traditions had carried forth for hundreds of years. It was my home, you see. We had not yet even explored the west of Thenus. Highwash didn't exist. I know that seems hard to imagine as you all grew up here. But there came a day when… when one of us decided to use our power for harm. Convincing most of our brothers and sisters to follow this new path, he took over our home, capturing any who didn't follow his order. I was around your age when this happened."

The hall was filled with a chill, brought in by the setting sun. It seemed to suit the mood. "Nathaniel and a few other Elders took some of us and escaped, I was among the lucky ones to escape with them, the others…"

"They now call themselves the Vatican. They do not worship the skies and the heavens like we do, they worship the pounding of their fists, they worship the cunning of their minds, they worship the opposite of compassion, they worship control. Some of you will want to leave Highwash if you become an Adept. I tell you all this for those who wish to leave. They are everywhere. They watch everything. They have birds in the sky, wolves on the ground and armies in their pocket. That is why we reside here among the western shores. It's a hard life, but we exist in secrecy. It will serve you unwell to flaunt your skills out in the world of the common people, they will not hesitate to kill you or make you their slave. This is the truth of our situation and the reality of our life. We must constantly hide, we must constantly seek the shadows. The darkness and places unseen are our refuge."

"Now moving on from such dire straights. I have chosen the third task to be on the eve of tomorrow. The last few tasks have tested our mental fortitude, our strength and our focus. The third task places a great emphasis on our willpower and our ability to manipulate the elements. For those of you who were unsuccessful during the second task, you shall not be participating. But for the victors—prepare, spend the evening meditating, review your techniques, tomorrow will likely be unkind, so come focused."

The class sat in silence in the awe of Macaro's words. Marius felt horribly disappointed, had he not lost the second task he would have been able to compete in the third.

"That is all," Macaro said as he bowed, finishing his lecture.

Exhausted Marius plopped on his bed and removed his robes. He felt dirty and sticky, a reminder he needed to bathe. *I'll do so on the morrow,* he thought to himself.

The day's events spiralled through his mind. Macaro talked grimly about these members of the Vatican. *Who were they? What were they? Macaro had fled them when he was a child?* Marius tried to imagine Macaro as child, the thought of a bald child seemed silly and made Marius chuckle. The fact Macaro was hesitant to talk of them made him uneasy.

The thought of the day spent at the library with Yuri came up in his mind. It was odd that no texts referenced the ruins. *It must be old,* Marius thought. It must be really old if no one had written about it. Marius imagined somewhere in Thenus there must be a book on those ruins or an old explorer who had climbed into its depths. *Somewhere, there must be,* were Marius' last thoughts as his drifted away.

A swift backhand woke Ralis from his faded slumber. His head pounded. Whatever fumes he had inhaled left a nasty wave of ill energy inside of him. Opening his eyes proved less illuminating than when his eyes were closed. The room, or wherever he was, was pitch black, held in a firm grip of darkness. He felt himself seated on what felt like a chair. Another hand lay a smack across his face. It stung on his cheek where it impacted.

Ralis lurched left then right, attempting to move. He realized ropes bound his hands behind his back and his feet were tied together. A thousand scenarios ran through Ralis' mind. He could free himself easily from his bonds. *But to what avail?* Ralis thought. He had not a clue where he was and wanted no more bloodshed on his hands. His words would have to be his weapon. Plus, conversing with his kidnappers might prove to relinquish some valuable information. Sighing, he stopped his struggle, relaxing in his binds.

Two lights flickered in the distance of the darkness, they seemed to float in the air. They bobbed up and down ever so slightly as the lights came closer and closer, revealing that they were torches held by men.

As the torches finally reached him, Ralis got view of his surroundings and his kidnappers. He was held in a damp rut of a cave. Dark limestone walls surrounded him. The men who held the torches were dressed in grey cloaks with hoods over their heads. The light of their torches revealed a man, rough, tall and boar-like, who stood beside Ralis. He was obviously the one who had laid the smacks across Ralis' face. All three men wore sheathed swords upon their waists. One of the torchbearers handed the gruff-looking man who stood beside Ralis his torch and stood silently observing Ralis. The man grabbed Ralis' jaw, holding his face up to get a clear sight of him. The man had a thick jaw and a rugged, auburn beard with flakes of grey mingled in between the brown. His eyes remained hidden underneath his hood.

"Why did you not attack us, Mage? What is your game?"

"I did not want blood on my hands," Ralis answered.

A hand smacked Ralis firm across his face again.

The boar looking man sneered and began to speak, "Sir, why do we bother with discussion? Everything he utters is coveted with lies, not a word of his we can trust. I say we kill him and leave it at that."

"No," the bearded man replied. Little things like that revealed much to Ralis, the bearded one obviously was in command. He began to speak once again. "Your brothers have shed blood for a lot less, a lot of the blood being blood of my men."

"I have no brothers of which you speak."

Another smack hit Ralis' face, he could taste blood beginning to pool in his mouth. A coarse laugh came from Ralis as he spat out blood.

"You'd better mind to tell your man down, I believe I've been rather sincere so far."

"You're in no position for demands, Mage. Do not lie, we have watched you, we have seen you whisper to the birds, we know of your powers. So, why do you seek us? What does the Vatican want from us? Our quarrel is with Salamon, not your people."

The man's words made Ralis laugh. "You believe me to be a Vatican Mage?" Ralis chuckled even louder at the notion. The pig-looking man raised his hand to strike again, but the bearded man grabbed his arm in mid air, holding him back.

"Why do you laugh?"

"I laugh because if I was a part of the Vatican you would all be dead already. Is that enough evidence to prove my claim of no heritage to the east?"

The trio of men froze, exchanging worried glances.

"Then why seek us?" the bearded man asked again.

"I sought you and your men out because Salamon holds the forest and the valley to the west. I intended to figure out why and change that, but it seems I've found my answer: Salamon seeks you. You've proven it quite adequately with the fact that I am held in a cave against my will," Ralis replied earnestly.

"Yes... I am aware of Salamon's presence in the south. And you're right, they are in search of us. But that doesn't explain to me who you are and why you're here?"

"Look," Ralis said frustrated, burning the ropes behind his back, while shearing the ropes that tied his ankles with the force of his legs and coming to a stand. The three men backed away, unsheathing their swords. "You see, I've had the ability to escape this whole time. I could kill all three of you without breaking much of a sweat, but I haven't," Ralis said as he took a seat back down on the chair crossing his arms.

The men eased visibly when Ralis took a seat again.

"So, it does seem I'm in a position to make demands. It would be better off for both of us if we work together. Don't you say?"

"It seems we've naught much of a choice," the bearded man replied, his sword still held out in front of him.

"So, why don't you put your swords away and we talk like civilized folk. Bunch of buffoons you are. Truly if I was a Vatican Mage, as you suspected, you thought the smartest plan would be to kidnap me?"

"Yield," the man ordered. The two other men gave their commander confused looks and hesitantly sheathed their swords. "We intended to interrogate you, and hopefully send you back to wherever you came with a bargain to leave us be."

Ralis snorted at the comment. "You truly do not know your enemy then. The Vatican carries no sympathy, your plan of action should have been to run and hide."

The man's cheeks went a scolding red.

"Lucky for you three, I am not who you thought I was."

"What is your name, Mage?" the man said, changing the subject.

"Ralis is my name."

"Your family name?"

"I have no family name, I was born a thief and raised a beggar. It's rude to ask for one's name without offering your own," Ralis said. scolding the man in authority.

"My name is Rrillin, and I am lord commander of these men. Some call us Rangers, some call us vagabonds, some call us the men of the forest, but to us a name doesn't matter, title us as you will."

"And did you name yourself commander?" Ralis asked mockingly.

"No, my men follow me out of choice, not fear of a whip."

"I'm sure Salamon would say the same," Ralis jested.

"Our commander cannot be compared to that usurper!" the boar-faced man exclaimed.

"Calm now, Jestin, the man is simply prodding us. Now may you go alert the men, alert them to our guest, so they have time to familiarize themselves with this newly-acquainted face," Rrillin said, commanding Jestin.

The boar-faced man Jestin took off immediately, his torch soon disappearing in the darkness of the cave.

"So where are we exactly? You said Salamon's camps lie to the south of our position. When I had surrendered to you and your men they were west to me, so where are we exactly?" Ralis asked Rrillin.

"Come, and I will show you."

Rrillin led Ralis through the darkness of the caves. The path twisted and turned, each corridor leading to another dark empty space.

"So where are you from, Ralis?" Rrillin asked him as they walked through the black of the cave.

"Palinteer."

"Palinteer? A godforsaken place that is. For myself, I grew up in Salamon's Keep," Rrillin said. His conversing irritated Ralis, but he stuck with it regardless of how he felt.

"A lord, huh?"

"Yes, I once was. But now, as you see, the woods are my home." Rrillin went silent for a bit and nothing was said, only the sound of footsteps echoing in the cavern halls spoke.

"How did you end up here then, Rrillin? With Salamon at your heels?" Ralis asked, curious of the man before him.

"Well, that's a long and depressing story, one I do not wish to tell. But what of yourself? How shall I explain to my men that we have made terms with a Mage?"

"You tell them I am no Mage and I never have been."

Silence overtook their conversation again as both of the men walked on, dwelling in their minds. Light eventually started to fill the tunnel and Ralis could see the exit, cold blasts of air winded past him blown in from the opening.

As they stepped out of the caverns, the sight of a bustling camp greeted Ralis. Makeshift tents stood all around, nestled on the edges of a small clearing in the woods. Looking closer, Ralis could see further into the bush. Among the dense forestry were hammocks and tents made of branches and woven leaves. How natural the tents looked made them blend in like camouflage. Around the camp men, women and children scattered around, each doing what Ralis thought were needless chores. The camp contained people of all ages; the elderly, young children and even mothers clinging to infants.

"How long have you lived like this?" Ralis asked after witnessing a mother breastfeeding a baby who looked no more past two months of age in a tent.

"I cannot say how long for certain, almost thirteen years," Rrillin said. Ralis could sense the distaste on his tongue.

"Thirteen years you've been running? How do you manage to survive winters?"

Seeing the camp brought Ralis into memories of his own childhood; remembering the chill of winter brought a shiver down his spine.

"My men and I are all trained for reconnaissance in the wild. I would not let any of my people come to harm." Rrillin spoke with a drilling tone, his eyebrows crooked, sensing Ralis' unspoken questions.

"If you fear the Vatican, as you say, why have you put these people at risk? These are families," Ralis said challenging Rrillin.

"And why do you care, Mage? Not a moment ago you were my enemy," Rrillin retorted angrily.

"Because I—" Ralis stopped in midsentence, hearing Macaro speak in his mind, *Compassion is our nature, our skill shall be used as a beacon of hope, not fear.* "Because it is my duty to care."

"Why did you come here, Mage? You have had your chance to leave, and you have had your chance to kill me, what is your purpose? To play mind games and destroy us from within?" Rrillin stopped in his tracks shouting.

Ralis spoke sternly but calmly. "No. I came here to help myself. I want Salamon out of my valley. They are looking for you, and I wanted to know why. It seems I'd never understand at this point, and I don't want to. But I see here innocent babes and women who do not deserve the fate both of us fear. I know the Vatican is relentless, I have met them personally. And what I do know is the Vatican will want me more than you."

"So you're saying you have a plan?"

"Well, yes. It just came me now."

Marius' feet pounded into the ground as he ran behind Yuri. Macaro had led the class outside for a long midday run. Within the last month there had been no sightings of manticores, so Macaro allowed the class a run amongst the woods—provided he was in attendance.

A Mage had to run fast, swift as a panther but as powerful as a horse. Macaro led the run through the forest, up and down trails, leaping across small ravines. He was fast, even Marius had a hard time keeping the pace Macaro set.

Later in the evening Macaro held a lecture in the main hall. Today's lesson was about astronomy and the stars.

"It's a clear night tonight, a perfect night to view the stars. Come now," Macaro said, directing his class to follow him outside.

Macaro had delayed the third task to the following week in accounts of Mathius being injured. Mathius remained silent on how he'd come to be injured.

"Honestly, I think he wanted more time to practice his half-ass magic," Yuri joked, whispering to Marius and Cynthia who trailed behind the group.

Cynthia nudged Yuri, gesturing him to stop with the rumours.

Macaro led them just outside the main hall where the ground grew rough and hard from repeated traffic of human footprints. Seating himself here the rest of the class copied, taking a seat on the bare dirt as well. The bright spray of orange and yellow stars illuminated the darkness of night. Marius found Cynthia to look almost angelic amongst the deep hue of night.

"Look up, my children, and see for yourself," Macaro said pointing to the sky.

In the sky above, bright strings of red, orange and yellow stars arranged themselves across the whole peripheral of the night sky.

"With each season, the planet we ride tilts on its axis, allowing us a different view of the stars. And with the change of each season we see different sections of the cosmos. Autumn's colours are orange, red, a deep yellow, it seems to coincide with the change the plants make as well. Each season represents a different element. The bright colours of purple during spring align with the element of lightning and its energy renewing life into the earth. Spring changes into summer, bringing the heat of fire. Fall represents the element of earth and air; the leaves gravitate towards the planet absorbed by the earth itself. And winter, representing the element of water, with water solidifying on our planets surface as snow. Obviously you have all seen these changes of our planet and have witnessed the changes of the skies, but there is a greater knowledge that arises when one understands the view of the heavens. Look, do you see those two massive stars, red and orange?" Macaro pointed towards the sky.

Marius could see what Macaro pointed out, two massive stars, one glowed a bright orange while the other a deep, scarlet red.

"The red one is Virgus and the orange one is Tritus. Astronomers have long used their position in the sky to track the circadian cycles of earth and to track the date as well as year."

Marius found it hard to focus on Macaro's rant of the night sky. Above him the stars shimmered with intense beauty.

After the lesson Yuri, Cynthia and Marius casually walked underneath the stars chatting about the day's events.

"I'm kind of glad Macaro delayed the third task, I'm anxious about this one," Yuri said.

"And you weren't anxious to beat me up?" Cynthia said, laughing as she pushed Yuri.

"Ok, if you put it that way, I was nervous for the second task as well. But that was different. The suspense of not knowing who I'd fight drove me nuts, but this third task relies solely on my skill in magic. And you all know my skill in magic."

"Yuri, you're fine at magic work, and you know that. Remember last week when Macaro was teaching us how to harness qi to heal minor wounds? You picked it up right away," Cynthia objected, trying to raise Yuri's confidence.

"That's only because I saw Ralis do it a hundred times," Yuri said, exaggerating his claim. "And then once Macaro showed us the technique, it seemed easy."

"Well then, apply that same attitude to this task. You can't have any doubt. Doubt will lead to death. And trust me, Macaro will force you to realize it," Marius interjected. Memories of the wolf he had fought raced through his mind.

"I see your point. Its just after that incident with Ralis, I don't feel the same," Yuri held his hand over the scar on his abdomen, a constant reminder of his failure. A constant nagging that would remain forever. "Macaro told me I almost died, whatever creatures had poisoned me gave my body a nasty shock. Apparently Mirane had to spend days clearing my qi and clearing infection."

"But what does that have to do with the third task? Nathaniel tricked us into going down there. I still haven't a clue why, but it wasn't your fault, Yuri."

"Yea, but if it wasn't for you, Marius, I'd have died. You see I failed where you didn't…"

"Yuri, stop," Marius stopped in his tracks, he was tired of Yuri's pouting about. "You didn't fail. If you had failed, we would have both been dead down there. It's our bond of fellowship that keeps us together, that keeps us alive, that keeps us strong. Macaro always says this. If we think individually, we fail, we succumb to our ego. But together we can never fail. And look at the result! You're standing here, alive and well, stronger than ever. Our bond is what kept you alive, and our bond requires an immense effort on your part. So, shut up. You're going to kick ass at this third task."

The three of them stood silently on the dirt road under the stars for what seemed like minutes. Cynthia was shaking, she had not accompanied them to the ruins.

"I had no idea it was that intense," Cynthia said, breaking the silence. And she was telling the truth. Marius and Yuri had not dwelled in the specifics of the incident with Ralis when their peers had pried. The only people who knew the whole truth were Ralis, Yuri, Marius and Macaro.

"It was. We've never really told you much about it," Marius said to Cynthia.

Finding a comfy spot among the grass, Marius and Yuri described their encounter with the manticore in detail, Ralis' odd training sessions, Nathaniel's queer behaviour, the vile insects that had maimed Yuri and the brutal journey back.

"If I knew you two would actually have followed Ralis all the way to the crossroads, I'd have made an attempt to stop you, Yuri."

"And that you should have," Marius said following a deep yawn. "I'm heading to sleep, you two should do the same."

Cynthia and Yuri agreed and they all went separate ways to their quarters. As Marius lay awake in bed, the soft blanket of sleep slowly over taking him, he was greeted by a vision. A vision of a star, bright and blue, thousands of miles away.

Darkness overtook the sky, and with it the Ranger's camp slept. But no sleep was to be had for Ralis and Rrillin. With five of Rrillin's best rangers, they sat huddled in a tent. Smoke and embers softly floated in from a fire being stoked outside.

The tent itself was one of the best quality tents Ralis had observed among the camp. It was made of leather sewn from rough hide and held together by four large sticks in each corner, which connected to angled sticks acting as hip rafters supporting the roof of the tent. It still had space for more men even though seven sat in it already.

"Everyone, our friend here is named Ralis, he claims to have a plan to lure Salamon off our trail."

The five other men shot him looks of disgust as Rrillin introduced him.

Obviously trust is going to be an issue, Ralis thought.

"Yes, Jestin had informed us of our guest," one of the Rangers said, grimacing. He had rough black hair that hadn't been kept for a while. His cool, blue eyes stared Ralis down with distrust and malice.

"I'm not too fond of him either, but he knows more about the Vatican than we do. So we will hear him out," Rrillin said attempting to reassure his men.

Everyone turned to face Ralis, expecting him to speak.

"Well, it's apparent we're off to a great start already," Ralis joked, receiving only blinks to his remark. "I'll start with a question. How much do you know of the Vatican?"

All five of the rangers turned their heads, gazing at their lord commander. Forced to speak by his men, he began.

"We only know that they are a secret organization in which their members have powers no mortal man should possess, and that they have Salamon in their pocket. Other than that, much is just rumours among our folk, for we have yet to meet them."

"Well, then I shall fill in some of the details. They origin in the east, formed back hundreds of years ago. They are everywhere and see almost everything, using the birds and the animals as a way of seeing. Salamon is in their pocket, that is true, and they do possess powers. And you were all naïve to underestimate them. The Vatican will not hold back when you are found. Whoever they decide not to kill, they will maim, beat or turn into a slave. Thinking you could've caught a member of the Vatican could have cost you all your lives and the lives of the innocent in this camp."

"Enough of the lecture, what's your plan then?"

"My plan? My plan is simple. We shall bait them."

All five of the Rangers piped up at once, each offering their own personal argument.

Rrillin raised his hand hushing his men. "Let him speak. I'd like to hear of such an idea."

Ralis continued speaking after the rush of noise died down. "Salamon's troops lie everywhere in the valley, I have observed multiple camps of theirs. A main camp lies southwest of here if your commander speaks true of our location. Obviously attacking them would be futile and only bring further attention to you and your people, and it's not like you have the manpower to do so. But we do have one thing going for us: Salamon's troops themselves aren't very cunning, they're easily tricked and I think we might be able to get them off your heels with a bit of luck and a guise. So, what if we attempt a feint attack, something to lure their attention towards me?"

After a bit of thought with the men pondering Ralis' words, Rrillin spoke. "That's actually not as crazy as it sounds. What are you considering?"

"I know this forest, I've travelled it many times."

"What are you? A hermit or something?"

Another Ranger snorted. Under his hood Ralis did not recognize him, but it was the man he found to look like a boar. His features were quite similar to the animal, a big bushy head of hair, a long nose and an ugly face. A brute of a man this lad called Jestin was, no wonder the rest of his comrades already had a predisposition of hatred toward him. He must have ran his tongue.

Completely ignoring the snide comment, Ralis rummaged through his bag, pulling out a folded piece of paper. It was crumpled beyond recognition, and when Ralis unfolded it to unveil a map, some of it was faded in a wet hue.

"Shit, we have better maps than that, Rrillin," Jestin gibed.

"Then why don't you fetch them?" Rrillin ordered, ill impressed by Jestin's remarks.

While they waited for Jestin to return they used Ralis' map instead.

"What's your best estimate of where we lie currently compared to the valley?" Ralis asked Rrillin, with the map laid out on the ground for all to see.

"Here, slightly north of the valley. Close to this southern mountain face," he said as his finger dragged across the map.

"Salamon has three camps southwest of our position, here, here and here," Ralis said informing the four others. "This one, the one furthest east, is their main force. I predict, if we act with enough haste, we can catch them off guard. They believe you and your men are running, which is partly true, but if we attack we can catch them with their hands down their pants, especially if we attack at night. And for my plan, well it involves a little bit of stealth on our part."

"But how shall we imitate an attack without a major force?" the blue-eyed Ranger asked.

Ralis remained silent for a second, the four other men already knew what he was about to suggest. "Often what accompanies war is an element we can use to beset our needs. Fire."

"So, you're suggesting lighting a wildfire among the woods? This is crazy, Rrillin," another Ranger argued, baffled by what Ralis was saying.

"No, I don't mean to light the whole of the woods ablaze. It is autumn, and with it the west carries many storms, whatever we light a flame, shall be washed out. What I intend is to light the edges of their main camp on fire, the northern, western and southern edges, forcing the camp to scatter and flee east. More so, when they catch sight of one of their attackers, they will charge with all their might, angered. And, I think I will put up a good chase."

"So, you think with this feint attack they will believe you to be one of us and follow pursuit on your trail?"

"Yes, and into the east back towards Salamon's valley. Most definitely if I am dressed as one of you," Ralis said, feeling proud of his plan as the four other men sat running the ideas through their minds.

"They will know it's a bluff if they only catch a single man," Rrillin warned, pointing out a flaw in Ralis' plan.

"That is why I will need some of your men, Rrillin. As for the rest of you, I suggest packing up with haste and moving north, over the course of the year head towards the northern wildlands, they remain unclaimed and Salamon will neglect to search there."

"And you can say that for certain?" Rrillin questioned.

"No, but its your people's best chance."

Rrillin thought in silence for a bit, staring outside the tent at the camp beyond, dimly lit by a tendered campfire.

"I can only give you three of my men if you intend for us to travel," Rrillin said finally decided on his course of action.

"All I need is three. So, you will follow through with my plan?"

"Yes, I will. It seems the best bet to get my people out of reach of Salamon and the Vatican. Either way death stalks us, but the wild will be more forgiving than Salamon. Anyone caught by Salamon will be labeled a traitor and punished as such. The wild will offer us much cleaner deaths."

"Well, if I was you, Rrillin, I wouldn't let any of my people befall such an ill fate."

"To that I agree."

They were warm words, but both Ralis and Rrillin knew the fate of the children and the women would be in the hands of the stars. The wild would prove just as relentless as the Vatican. But it took hard men to make hard choices, and this seemed like the safest and clearest path forward. All of them, including Ralis, sat with sombre looks on their faces. Ralis thought of his friends at Highwash, he could see Marius' face before him, and he could see what would befall Marius and the others if he failed.

"What about the other smaller camps? Even if the main force follows in pursuit of you, Ralis, how will we dissolve the other camps?"

Rrillin answered his Rangers question for Ralis. "Knowing Salamon as well as I do, his army relies on his scouts for communication. Thus, if we attack and the main force moves, the commander posted at the main force would most likely send scouts to inform the others."

"Then I volunteer to go with the Mage, Rrillin," the blue-eyed Ranger announced. "I will not stand idle while Salamon knocks at our door."

Funny, that's what I said to Macaro, Ralis thought to himself.

Later that night, as Ralis lay awake staring at the stars, he realized Jestin had never returned.

Despite his friend's words of confidence, Yuri was still nervous for the third task. The task was to be held at a steep creek north of the village of Highwash; the autumn run off coursing down had been fed by recent rains.

Yuri stood on one side, awaiting Macaro's instruction. On the other side Macaro stood, staring down into the creeks belly. The water of the creek lapped at both sides of its sheered cliff banks.

"Yuri! My child. You have progressed far where others have failed. You have overcome trial and tribulation. But now you must overcome another obstacle, one that I feel will weigh significantly on you." Macaro's voice trailed over the water as he yelled across to Yuri, his voice slightly muffled by the current of the creek. "But first we must talk."

This surprised Yuri. He had not known what to expect for this task, but a talk was the last of his predictions. His mind trailed to each form of magic he'd learned, running through his mind like a list. He remembered how to cast fire, manipulate water, use the force of air, jump electricity between objects and even heal a minor wound, but words... words were unpredictable and never Yuri's friend.

"It seems you have been distracted of late," Macaro said, beginning the uncertainty of the talk.

Macaro's intention seemed quite illusive to Yuri. *Where was this going?* he thought.

"And a distracted Mage is never an efficient one. Tell me, Yuri, what distracts you so." Macaro's words hung across Yuri's mind.

What distracted me so...? The words seemed almost unreal. Yuri's tongue froze as he fought for words.

"I... I have not been distracted, Elder. I have been training often and regularly, I have mastered my forms, my energy work, every night I meditate before sleep."

"Often what distracts one is hidden beyond the veil of his practice. Emotions can be a detriment to a Mage just as much as laziness can. So, I ask you again, what distracts you, Yuri?"

Macaro's words brought him back to distant memories. It was in this exact spot that Macaro had held this task twenty years earlier for another student. His face was clear as day, the rough beard, the long hair and the new wisps of grey that now formed on his head. *I hope Yuri is ready, more ready than Ralis was,* Macaro thought as he stood there observing his young student.

"As you said, Elder, I carry no distractions, distractions lead to death."

From over the creek Yuri could see Macaro shake his head in disapproval.

"As you say, Yuri. You are a strong one then. Even I'd find it distracting if the women I loved, loved another."

Macaro's words stung deep, this was not at all what Yuri had expected. The memory of Cynthia and Marius kissing cut like a knife down his spine.

"Knowing such a truth is one thing, but to witness it. You emanate true strength, Yuri, if you do not carry that with you."

Irritation filled Yuri, what was Macaro's game? Was this the task? Was there something to see beyond, or was this merely a trick?

"I think you're lying, Yuri, I feel your anger, I feel your confusion. She has been your friend from the start, you have given her all the love you could muster, and yet you lack something you could never attain, something unknown to you and she has chosen another."

A fire started to rage inside of Yuri. He did in fact love Cynthia, and it left wounds deeper than graves inside his mind.

"How does it feel, Yuri, to know that she will never love you, never comfort you? Admit it to me. You are angry, you want to hurt Marius. What makes it worse is that Marius saved your life, you're indebted to him, forcing you to stand idle, filled with confusion."

Boiling like a steaming pot, Yuri's mind was on fire, he could see it playing over and over in his mind, Cynthia kissing Marius, their constant stare towards each other, the yearning for each other.

"Stop," Yuri muttered, his voice gravelly with rage.

"Stop what, Yuri? You want me to stop stating the truth? I have seen it within you. The anger, the fire, it will be your downfall."

Macaro had him, he was ripe with emotion, filled with anger, his enemy was fire, and what cools fire is water. Macaro had guessed that Yuri's natural element was fire. He would need water to cool such a rage.

"You are distressed, you cannot even face the truth yourself, you cannot admit it to me. You even left your friend when he needed you the most. I was there, remember? When Marius fought Mathius, you left him, stuck in your anger."

"I said stop," Yuri said through clenched teeth, he could feel the energy building in his hands, his body shook almost to a point of tremors, he wanted to hurt Macaro. But Macaro continued his sermon anyways.

"And then you took out your anger on the one you love. I was there, too. I saw you beat Cynthia down, if you had loved her you would have let her win, but you didn't. Does it bother you she was the only student who needed medical attention after the second task?"

The moment was becoming perfect. From the opposite side of the stream Macaro could see Yuri's face turn beet red.

"But instead of gracing your ego, you stroked it. You hurt her, more than you have ever hurt anyone. I had chosen you to face Cynthia on purpose, Yuri."

"ENOUGH!" Yuri screamed.

In a moment's flash Macaro launched a wave of fire and heat towards Yuri. A wave of fire that would scorch on impact. And with a lurch Yuri used the water of the creek, rising it upwards as fast as the fire spread across the air, consuming the flames, killing the fire and blasting Macaro with a torrent. The remaining steam in the air dissipated within seconds and Yuri could see Macaro standing there, unhurt and smiling.

"Congratulations, Yuri, you have completed the third task."

Yuri stood calm and silent, no longer angry. *It was untrue,* he thought to himself. It was all a goad.

"Water cools the flames of anger to reveal the truth. I hope I did not scar you too intensely, but it was necessary, necessary to see the truth. Your enemies will use whatever they can against you, even your own emotions. But it is your task to see beyond your ego and remember the truth. Emotions are fleeting and intense, but also untrue. The truth being we are beings filled with compassion and light. I commend you, Yuri, I had thought the fire would have consumed you, but you have proven otherwise. Now come, let's get you some good food, I'm sure you will appreciate it."

While most of the students had prepared and participated in the third task, Marius was stuck with the musty smell of the library. Yuri had asked him to continue searching for texts on the ruins they had the misfortune to venture to while he was summoned for the third task. Begrudgingly, he had agreed. Peering up away from the monotonous pages of the book he held, he gazed at Cynthia sitting across from him. Her green eyes glowed with lustre as they scanned pages meticulously. At least he was not alone.

"I've read hundreds of books in here, not one of them mention these ruins," he said, at once breaking the silence, attempting to steer their attention to conversation and not the dreary task of reading.

"Gosh, Marius, can you not read without complaining," she mocked, her eyes never steering away to meet his.

At least someone is enjoying this, Marius thought to himself. Marius gazed down back at his book, the words and letters formed blurs in his vision, his mind fading he began to yawn.

"What are you two doing?"

Finally someone to talk to, Marius thought. Looking back he saw it was Clive. He had also lost the second task, so he had the same unfortunate fate as Marius—left alone to practice or to do duties.

"Reading," Cynthia answered, her eyes still not leaving the page even to meet her brother's.

"Same, I came to study," Clive said as he walked off from their table and into the maze of towering bookshelves.

That didn't last long, Marius thought, craving any form of excitement. Marius did in fact like reading, but the subject of searching books endlessly for a place that seemed illusive to most common scholars bugged the recesses of his mind. The endless search seeming to be nothing but a wild goose chase.

"Has your book at least yielded some knowledge?" Marius asked, almost begging for an answer.

"Actually, yes," Cynthia smiled as she looked up, amused by Marius' frustration.

"You're cute when you're bored, similar to a child nagging his mother for attention."

"Thanks…"

"Here, look," Cynthia said putting her book down on the table for Marius to see. But before Cynthia started speaking her eyes darted upwards to something behind Marius.

"How did it go?" she asked. Marius turned to see who was behind him and, as he suspected, it was Yuri.

Excited Marius asked the same thing, "How did it go?" His voice came out a little more loudly than he'd have liked.

Yuri could see them, his two best friends, how much they cared. Their love for each other was never against him. Yuri started tearing up the instant he saw both of them, seated reading on his behest.

"I passed."

And the moment he said the words Cynthia leapt up from her seat and wrapped her arms around him, embracing him in a hug. Looking past the curtains of Cynthia's hair he could see Marius seated, but turned to face him, with the largest grin on his face. A grin that said "I told you so."

XII

The camp packed up faster than Ralis had expected. It seemed Rrillin did indeed train men and women alike for reconnaissance in the wild. Once the order to move north was issued the camp began bustling about, packing objects such as axes, spears, sleeping mats, cots, food rations, containers of water, and hoisting the gruelling amount of items onto pack horses. Even mothers bearing babes seemed to move faster than normal. Some women complained to Rrillin, fearing the wrath of winter's cold, but Rrillin eased their fears once again.

It seemed Rrillin was more adept at leading than Ralis had previously thought.

"We have done this a many of times," Rrillin told Ralis as Ralis accompanied him through the camp.

Within a day and a night the camp had been deconstructed, any traces of their presence ceased to exist, with Rrillin's own scouts purging the area of signs of human settlement. The skill of Rrillin and his men surprised Ralis, *Who were these people? And why did Salamon want them?* Not many people who dwelt among Thenus had training in the mind of warfare, let alone training to survive in the wild. So, how did these people come across such knowledge?

Over the day they'd dismantled their camp, Ralis observed them. They seemed to know the mechanics and operations of Salamon's scouts, how they searched, communicated, positioned themselves among the woods. This seemed to answer a brooding question Ralis had for quite some time, *How have these people avoided Salamon's best-trained scouts?* But the answer only seemed to bring up more questions, *How have these people learned such skills?* Every time Ralis pried Rrillin to tell him, all he received were cold, blunt words, never revealing any truths. They finished packing by the day's end. It was a late, cold afternoon, and the question began to seem irrelevant.

Ralis stood with three rangers and Rrillin under a woven canopy of branches. Three Rangers volunteered to partner with Ralis on his plan. The first was the blue-eyed Ranger, named Farion, tall and slender, but quick on his feet, he didn't speak often. The second Ranger to volunteer was Jestin. Unlikely as it seemed, the boar-looking man volunteered, stating he wanted to be the one to kill the Mage personally if he pulled a fast one. Jestin's appetite for conflict was as large as the man himself. The third was a Ranger who'd sat quietly during the original organization of the plan named Devin. He was short and stocky, quick and obviously robust.

The three Rangers said their farewells to Rrillin while Ralis walked off to the side and knelt down by a lone evergreen, he hated farewells, particularly one he wasn't a part of. Though far away, Ralis could still hear the words Rrillin spoke not meant for his ears.

"When you come back, follow the mountain ridges north, we shouldn't have travelled far, but I will leave signs nonetheless to point you in our direction. I entrust you three with my life and the lives of our people, so do not fail us. If capture is inevitable, be prepared to take your life, each of you, do you promise this? The enemy must not know of our route."

The three Rangers nodded in agreement to Rrillin's nightmarish order.

"I trust this Mage, but do not forget yourselves, stay alert, and do not let him out of your sights for long. I wish I could accompany you three on this, but I can't, I must stay with our people. So farewell for now, may your purpose guide you."

In the distance Ralis could see Rrillin bow to his men and take off behind the rest of his people who travelled north ahead of him. Soon the woods quieted, and all sounds of people and horses moving deafened among the trees and woods. It was just the three rangers and Ralis now.

They walked south among the woods in quiet, nothing but the Rangers' swords clinking against their waists, and the contents of their rucksacks jiggling could be heard.

"Your name is Ralis, correct?" Devin spoke first, breaking the silence of the woods. Ralis nodded irritably, obviously the man knew his name. "I have a question. So, as I've understood, we are to start bush fires on either side of Salamon's main camp, but how do you intend to start the fire? We have brought nothing to aid us in that."

"Yes, you have, you have brought me," Ralis said with a coarse chuckle, while the three comrades gave each other nervous looks.

"Enough of your jests, Mage. You convinced our commander to march our people north. So tell us, how do plan to start the fires?" Jestin roared.

"You know nothing of Mages do you?" Ralis said as he stopped in his tracks.

Raising his hand towards an open space among the sky, Ralis sent streams of fire out of his palm that reached high into the air. Soon a vortex of fire surrounded the air above them. Stunned, the three men's mouths hung open in disbelief of what they were seeing.

"I am the fire."

The group hadn't spoken since Ralis showed them his ability to conjure flames, though it was quite obvious the men dwelled on the experience. The four of them sat huddled around a fire during the cold of night. The three rangers sat plump on logs shivering, their hands out trying to embrace the warmth of the fire, while Ralis sat undisturbed on the bare earth.

"How did you pull such sorcery?" Jestin finally asked.

Ralis knew the question had been brewing. There was an ounce of fear in Jestin's voice despite the clear despise he had for Ralis.

"It is not sorcery, there was no trick about it."

All three of the men eyed Ralis suspiciously as he spoke, apparently the show had not eased their misconceptions about Ralis.

"Then explain to me what we saw."

Men always bothered Ralis. Their ignorance of the world was baffling, and they seemed to ignore the most blatant of truths that lay in front of their eyes, and ignorance bred fear.

"You saw fire," Ralis said coldly, unsure of how to put it. "And fire burns."

"What kind of ghastly abomination are you?" It was Devin who rose to speak, his eyes reflecting the campfire.

"Sit down, please," Ralis said with a slight implication of a warning.

"Is that a threat?" Devin seethed, eyeing the sword in his scabbard.

"I don't understand you men, did you accompany me only to utter curses at me?"

Farion suddenly spoke, "Sit down, Devin."

Slowly Devin took a seat back down on the log, his eyes cursing Ralis and his superior. *Now two of them hate me,* Ralis thought to himself comically.

"Explain to us how you made that... fire... how did you do that? I can't speak for my brethren," Farion spoke glancing at the two other Rangers, "but for me, I came because, for some reason, my commander believed in you. So, please convince us why we should trust you."

With a deep sigh, and already regretting the words he was about to say, Ralis spoke. "Anyone can do it, even you three. It involves manipulating your internal energy or the external energy around you. To keep it simple one can transmute their energy into one of the basic element forms."

All three of them laughed, "You speak nonsense!"

"As it may be, but Rrillin trusted in me, and so should all three of you. Lives are at stake, so shut up about your worries and mistrust, it won't matter if we're dead."

A dark quietness overtook them for a period. But finally Jestin spoke. "You've an attitude, Mage."

"Lord Salamon!"

The tent flapped open, as the scout ran in, cold with sweat.

Sebastien stood over a desk placed underneath a massive leathered tent held on four giant spokes. He knelt over the table, gazing at maps drawn of the western front.

The scout bowed as soon as he entered the tent, but rambled fast as he stood up. "Major Harding would like a word with you. He sent me to ask permission for your time."

"Yes, send for him."

The scout left as fast as he entered, the entrance to the tent flapping behind the scout.

Pacing as he waited, Sebastien gazed at a mirror standing on a smaller table in the corner, it blended well with the rose colours of the tent. He had grown a bit of a scruffy beard during his time out in the woods. He looked at himself with disapproval, tugging at the mess on his face. Things had not gone as planned. They had spent the spring, the summer and now the majority of the fall scouring the western forest.

Seven months and nothing to show for it, father will be displeased with this failure, Sebastien thought to himself. *No, we have not failed yet.* But still, despite his cold-cut confidence, Sebastien couldn't help but worry. By the time winter hit he would have to take his men further inland, retreating from the mountains and the woods.

"Lord Salamon," Major Harding announced as he entered and bowed, lowering to one knee, his head of brown hair covered by a leathered helm.

"Rise and speak, Harding."

"Some of our scouts have found something, it's not good." Harding looked solemn as he spoke.

"Well then, show me," Sebastien commanded.

"They said they were traversing a ridge just northwest of here, they said they found a burnt corpse and this." Harding passed a chain over to Salamon. It was coated with charcoal stains and burn marks. Laying it out on the table, Sebastien could clearly see it was a signet of Salamon's, the rose burned out by flames. Flipping it over, he saw words that struck his heart. The metal was indented with the name Scout Joseph Ramsely. Sebastien gulped as he read the name, remembering the scout's face.

"He was found burnt? How did this happen?" Harding looked how Sebastien felt—very uneasy.

"We don't know. But we have just cause to believe that it was the same people or person who killed our other three scouts."

"Yes, I remember," Sebastien agreed. He paced relentlessly back and forth, deep in thought. "That means our western camp might not have received his message. So, send three scouts to the western camp, bringing such a message, as well as confirming if he died before or after reaching the western camp."

"Lord Salamon, if I may speak, he was found way off his intended route. That's reason to believe he was kidnapped."

Salamon gave Harding a stern look. "Go," he commanded. And with a nod Harding turned and was out the tent.

It was a dark night, cold but dry.

A perfect night to start a fire, Ralis thought as he and the Rangers sat crouched on a rocky ridge overlooking Salamon's main camp to the south. The embers of torches and fires could be seen as tiny lights in the distance against waves of blackened forest.

They sat together organizing their attack.

"Devin, you're going to head to the southern end of the camp. I've observed their camp, and there you will find their munitions of explosive bolts. I want you to ignite those," Ralis said as he gave all three of them their tasks.

"And how do you suppose I do that? I don't have fire hands like you," Devin mocked.

"Easy, steal a torch from a guard." Ralis' comment brought Devin into a chuckle.

"Shit of a shock that'll give 'em," Jestin said, approving the idea of setting off an explosion.

"You just want to blow shit up, Jestin, why don't you do it then?" Devin spat.

"No, I need him to go with Farion."

"And what do you plan us to do?"

"Well, this needs to look like an attack, and for that to happen, you need to attack."

Jestin and Farion both had the same stunned look on their face.

"You intend for us to just walk in their swords in hand?"

"After I ignite the first fire in the west. Then as you two come in from the eastern flank, I will light the north side of the camp. At the same time Devin here will light the bolts causing the explosion.

That should give you the chance to retreat and then head back north while I head to the southern side of the camp to start a fire there. If you're fast enough they will head east to search for their attackers, assuming you retreated in the direction of your attack. But I will be there to draw their attention, to lure the main force of them east."

Ralis felt proud of his plan after he went over it again in his mind.

"You alone will outrun men on horseback?" Farion questioned.

"Well, I can't see you three faring a better chance."

"Well, it's your death then. Let's get this over with. I want to get back to my babe."

Farion's blue eyes reflected deep thought as Ralis peered in them, deep thought indeed.

Four bodies burned, all of them scouts. Sebastien sat in thought, alone in his quarters. The large tent that was hoisted for him could have easily fit twelve men, it was rather a stupid size, of course, Sebastien thought to himself, but that was the luxury of being a Salamon.

Despite its size and luxurious interior something about the tent still felt off. Outside the roar of laughter and drunkenness went on, but inside stillness prowled. And in the stillness Sebastien could hear only but his thoughts.

It didn't seem like coincidence, four scouts, all murdered, all burned and left to dust and ash. *Did they see something? Or was it happenstance?* Sebastien thought. These Rangers, whoever they were, obviously knew they were here. Obviously the forest was theirs.

Thinking of his next move, Sebastien paced wildly, only to prop himself into a chair and stand back up again. Outside bottles clanked and stomachs bellowed.

If only my men would spend more time thinking than drinking, maybe we could actually get things done, Sebastien thought to himself as he stared at the tent's entrance, violated by all the hollers and insults. *Four dead men and we cant even get a sight on them, they must be laughing at us. Not even a clue we have found. Only if father would have told me more, who are these people?* He was failing and his men knew it, *But out of fear they would never say it to my face, and then they mask their fears with drink.*

He stared down angrily at the map placed on the oak desk before him. He had been doing it the whole day now. On the table beside the map was Sir Ramsely's signet, twirled on it's chain. Grabbing it he crushed it with his hand. Vividly Ramsely's face flashed before his eyes, but faded quickly to fog, a distant memory. *Did he have a family?* Sebastien hoped not. Sending a pile of ash would hurt more than seeing a corpse.

Outside the noises roared. Men yelled and hollered, raucous and loud. *Why do men party oft in the wake of doom? They must know my father's zealous nature when it comes to failing.* Sebastien thought as he listened to the men yelling outside. It seemed rather aggressive for a bunch of troops with drinks in their waist.

The noises were loud and sharp, suddenly a shriek of a horse propped Sebastien out of his seat. The noises didn't seem to be of men celebrating anymore. Quickly Sebastien threw on a tough-looking fur coat, there was no time to don his armour. Grabbing his sheathed sword propped against a desk, he was out the tent, with the entrance flapping behind him.

Outside revealed a state of mania. Men ran past shouting orders in all directions, men struggled with horses, scouts scrambled in all directions gathering armour for their knights, and then a horn.

BAROOOOO!

The forest shook with the thunder of the horn. They were being attacked. In the distance, Sebastien spotted flames spreading across the trees. The flames seemed to consume the horizon of his camp, it spread like an infestation quickly among the trees, with flames licking this way and that. The flames seemed to light the chaos of his camp in a red hue, an evil glow mocking the drunken insanity. No one expected an attack, none of his men did, worst of all, Sebastien never saw it coming.

Suddenly a man slammed into him and grabbed his arm. Sebastien immediately went for his sword, but paused when he saw it was Major Harding, his mop head covered in sweat.

"My lord! My lord, I was in search of you," he was shaking and terrified Sebastien could clearly see.

"It's alright, Harding, what's happening? How many men?"

Yells and horses running by knocked the two of them aside, muting their conversation. Recovering his stance, Sebastien looked towards the noise of yelling. A cluster of men, his men, swords drawn, though Sebastien couldn't see the enemy they were fighting.

BAMMM!

A mighty explosion ripped through the air, smashing Sebastien face first into the ground. His ears rang. His chest thumped, and for a second all he could hear was the rhythm of his heart. Suddenly he was upright and standing. Major Harding had pulled him up and he was yelling something, something Sebastien couldn't hear right, all he knew was the sword that Harding thrust into his hand. Harding raised his hand to point, turning, with his sword clutched in his hand, Sebastien saw them, two men wearing cloaks dark as night. Six of Sebastien's men lay in the wake of the two cloaked men.

All around him was fire, tents lit in flames. Sebastien knew what he must do.

Armourless, he still charged the two men, he would not go down without a fight. The two rangers saw him charge immediately, one was massive and looked similar to a pig roasting in the amber glow of fire, the other looked dark and cold with an icy stare. But it mattered not what they looked like to Sebastien.

Sebastien was a renowned swordsman throughout the continent. He did not earn title of commander with just a name and birthright. Sebastien had fought his way up the totem pole of success, through blood-soaked fists and many shattered swords. To be honest, with himself he moved better without armour.

The larger of the two men took the first swing at Sebastien, lunging forward with a massive swing for his head, but Sebastien easily stepped to the side and parried the blow sideways, sending the man sprawling. The second man came in with a cut aimed for Sebastien's stomach, but lowering his sword in reaction to the second man's move, he caught the blow and pushed the man aside with a heave. Under the second man's cloak, Sebastien could see icy blue eyes, cold as death.

Harding moved into the fight with a grunt, clashing his sword with the other man, while Sebastien traded parries with the blue-eyed ranger. He was fast, moving with the hands of a trained man. After what felt like a blur of a song of traded steel, several men donned in armour came flooding in. They wore the silver mail of Salamon's infantry, they were Sebastien's men.

As his group of soldiers surrounded the blue-eyed man, he glanced over to see Harding collapsed on the ground, guts strewn about. Harding's dead face showed that his final moments were of horror. The larger man seemed to have disappeared. A shriek sharp and guttural caused Sebastien to look over to find two of his brothers lying down, one still clinging for life, while his group of men circled the ranger who fought on.

Enough of this, Sebastien thought as he ran into the circle, delivering the final blow to the Ranger. Cleaving the man's head off brought joy to Sebastien. The sweetness of blood, served as revenge never seemed to disappoint. The scene almost seemed surreal, all around him the woods were on fire, engulfing the remainder of his camp that wasn't damaged by the explosion.

Grabbing a soldier by his collars, Sebastien began to scream orders. Ordering one soldier to grab any horses that lived, another soldier to grab weapons that survived the blast, another to grab maps, one man to grab rations and canteens, and another to take twenty scouts to either camp to deliver an order of evacuation back to the mainland. The camp was done, and he knew it, but one trail was still warm. They had seen a Ranger, and one had fled. Sebastien thought that, if he could gather his men soon enough, he would still be able to catch the one who fled.

Within minutes his orders were complete. Mounting a great horse, armour donned and his sword polished, Sebastien led a force of thirty knights on horseback and fifteen scouts east. This was it, his clue toward finding the Rangers. Or so he thought.

"You fucking idiot!" Jestin screamed in the midst of his cold rage. His face bloodshot and mottled with angered veins.

"I told you to go north, it wont be long until they arrive," Ralis replied calmly despite Jestin's tantrum.

"He's fucking dead, you dimwitted Mage! You sent us into a damn bloodbath! And now he's fucking dead! He had a son, for fuck sakes, but what? Baseborn Mages don't give a lick about sons, do they?" He spat at Ralis as he talked.

"No. I don't. And I also don't give a fuck about men. So back off and do as I said. Go north, now," Ralis said irritated.

The man Jestin insisted on not following his advice. Instead of going north to meet Devin, Jestin insisted on tracking Ralis out east.

How to persuade a fool? Ralis thought as he stared at the man's boar-like face.

"I'm going nowhere," the man growled as he stepped closer towards Ralis.

"Well, you should, because any second now we will be stormed by horses."

And, suddenly as if on cue, a rumbling of hooves could be heard echoing among the trees. The noise made Ralis stand up from being propped against a tree.

"See, you're the fucking idiot," Ralis said sadly, mocking Jestin's ill fate.

"You evil bastard…"

But before Jestin was able to form another word, the sound of hooves and hollers drowned out his voice. Suddenly they were surrounded by horses and armoured soldiers. Ralis could make out almost twenty men on horseback, but he needed to wait, he couldn't run yet, he needed to be clearly seen.

The moment struck perfectly. As the horsed men lined up to form a circle, one man on a great mare came forth out of the line, he had long hair tied in a ponytail, gleaming blonde despite the night, his armour shone bright, and his hard eyes met Ralis. Ralis had seen his face before, in the memories of the scout he had kidnapped. That was the moment, as soon as their eyes had met, Ralis moved swiftly, ducking under a horse, and then bounding off into a sprint into the woods heading east. Ralis could hear shouts and commands being yelled as he ran, and then he heard the trample of horses behind him. The chase was on.

His plan had worked, at least for now. He regretted the fact he had had to leave Jestin. He wasn't supposed to be there—an unfortunate fate it would be for the man. Ralis could only imagine what would happen to him. He was supposed to go north.

"Should we kill you? Should we take you as our prisoner to interrogate you? No, I think we can do both right here," Sebastien said as he paced around his prisoner, while two of his men held Jestin on his knees with blades to his neck. Sebastien knelt down to get a closer look as his captive's face. "Anyone ever tell you, you look like a pig?"

Jestin hacked a spit at Sebastien in response.

Standing, Sebastien smirked and looked to his men. "I thought asses spit, not pigs," he said to their laughter. "And it seems that's all you have the power to do now, spit. Tell me, convince me, why I shouldn't have you burned alive, like you did to my men, instead of taking your head? You're going to die today, a captive is too much work for me. And despite that, you're too heavy for our horses. So, tell me, what do you have for me that is worth a clean death?"

With an empty gaze at the ground Jestin replied, "Do as you must, I have nothing for you but hatred."

"So be it, your head shall serve as a means to break your friend."

Sebastien gave a nod to his men and, with one clean slice, Jestin's head tumbled to the ground. Another man tossed a blanket on top the corpse to stop the spray of blood. Sebastien didn't have time for games, nor did he have time to burn a prisoner alive. He looked out east in the direction the other ranger had run. Nothing but dark forest lay in that direction and the fear of night does break a man's will. Ordering his men to grab the head and round up, making their way east. It wouldn't be long until they found this coward who ran, Sebastien thought to himself.

The darkness of the forest scared Salamon's riders, this much Ralis could tell. Ralis sat perched high in the branches of what he thought was an oak tree. Underneath him, the soldiers who had road off after him at their lord's command, sat in rest.

Ralis had led the men on a massive chase and their horses needed rest, so they decided it would be a good time for them as well. Ralis lurked amidst the leaves, listening to every word the men said, their tongues loose without a commander peering over their shoulder. Overhearing their conversation told Ralis of their plan to wait until the main force had reached them, so they could split up and search the forest in wider groups. Jestin's death would be a waste if it came to that. Ralis would need to present himself soon if he wanted to continue the chase, and he needed the bulk of the horde to follow him for his plan to truly work. But the more the plan ran through his mind, the more doubts Ralis created.

It was true, no commander with even half decent intelligence would send a whole fleet of cavalry after a single man, that would breach all codes of military tactics.

Unless... unless... unless the field commander was somehow provoked enough to do so, Ralis thought, suddenly a plan reformed under the surface of his skull. *And what's the best way to provoke a man? Fear.*

He would need to act fast and soon. No doubt the main force would kill Jestin, his mouth would remain silent for sure, that would send them this way and they would be here soon.

Macaro's voice hung low in the depths of his mind. *Compassion...* The word sat in his mind, floating. *They will have no compassion if they come for you,* Ralis said in his mind, picturing all the faces at Highwash, sweet Mirane, how he'd always liked her, the young children, Cynthia, the damn nuisance Yuri, Marius, and their fate if he would fail. The plan was then set in stone.

Jumping down from his spot among the branches, Ralis landed on a soldier that sat nearest to the tree. He felt the soldier's ribs crack as he smashed down on top of him. Horses neighed sharply, pulling at their hoists, while six other soldiers yelled in shock, utterly taken aghast by the surprise.

Ralis was up in an instant, the man below his feet now unconscious. Quickly, the soldiers clued into what was happening and a few of them grabbed their swords and shields, while others went to grab torches or sticks, whatever was closest to them. Ralis didn't even have time to see their faces before they attacked, but that's what he wanted.

Two men approached him from the front, instantly one went to slash Ralis. With a grin of malice, Ralis stepped with grace to dodge the blow, all the while smashing the man's skull against the tree, the blow clearly ripping him out of consciousness with the soldier sliding to the ground. The second went to strike, but Ralis raised his hand towards him and sent a wave of air colliding into his chest, sending the soldier into the ground. Ralis could hear him gasp for breath, probably collapsed a lung. Three more soldiers ran forth, two bearing torches. But fire was a mere charm to Ralis, and he sent those flames against all three of the men, lighting them ablaze. Ralis preferred to burn dead corpses versus alive, the shrivel shrieks were quite disturbing.

BAROO!

A troop unleashed the howl of the horn alerting the forest.

More men came running in, starting to circle Ralis. Spinning and striking, Ralis dodged blow after blow, some soldiers would get sent sprawling away by massive kicks, some soldiers would drop unconscious from blows to their skull, while some would drop to the ground with their own sword stuck in their chest. It seemed that, despite the numbers, no man was fast enough to defeat Ralis.

A pile of people had started to form around him, now the remaining men stood, awkwardly circled, clearly afraid and hesitating to make a move.

Suddenly the storm of hooves took over the forest. The forest was filled with knights on horseback, every knight was clearly shocked as they rode over the forested ridge and entered the scene. Seeing their comrades, the footmen were given some courage and charged towards Ralis, swords waving in the air. But their fate was the same as their brothers, and Ralis put each and every one of them into the ground.

Now a horde of horsed men stood circled around the bodies that lay at Ralis' feet. Each with spears and swords pointed towards Ralis.

One man rode out of the line, breaking rank, and into the circle. When he took off his helm, it revealed long hair that fell down thick, and deep heavy eyes, with a face too pretty for a soldier.

"What are you?" the man spat in disgust as he ripped his sword from his scabbard.

All around Ralis were men on horses, and at that moment Ralis got the brightest of ideas. Looking around at all the horses, he made eye contact with each of them, all young stallions—they chose only the best for Salamon's cavalry. But, like all horses, they were soft and playful creatures at heart. They didn't understand the mechanics of war and would hate no man. Ralis could feel them, and their thoughts.

Buck, Ralis thought, and suddenly near half of the horses started to buck their riders off.

Some had refused to listen to Ralis' command, but the ones that did caused ruckus enough, slinging the riders off their back or smashing into others as the horses bounded around mercilessly. Even their own commander got smashed to the ground by another horse colliding into the one he rode. It was a mess, if one thing was for sure.

Ralis stood by as the mayhem went on, men got trampled and the commander lay before him on the ground, struggling to get up.

With a yell the downed commander smashed his fist into the ground, grabbed his sword from the dirt and charged for Ralis. Other men followed behind him. A storm of swords headed at Ralis.

The commander can fight better than his lessers, Ralis thought to himself as he danced away from his sword, and with a kick to the chest he sent the commander flailing to the ground.

Blood pooled in Sebastien's mouth. He had fought many times before, but that was the hardest kick he'd ever received in the entirety of his life.

Awareness began to come back to him, the force of the kick wearing off. Sebastien needed to get up, he had to, he would not fail his men. Pounding the ground he rolled to the side to get up. And then he saw the man. He moved as if he was bewitched. He was faster than any man Sebastien had laid eyes on, and fought with a style that he had never seen. *How did a man fight without a sword?*

Sebastien lay there, bewildered, as the man picked off each of his troops, laying waste to each that charged with nothing but his fists. Gulping, Sebastien looked at his sword glowing a deep red in reflection of flames the man sent forth. Grabbing the sword, he leapt into the battle. He slashed left then right, but the man seemed to predict every step he made. With every slash, Sebastien tried to keep his distance so his opponent could not reach him. It worked for a moment, until the man danced around his blade and pummelled Sebastien with a blow that brought him to his knees. Sebastien couldn't tell if a fist or a foot hit him.

A lance swept overhead aimed for the man's head, distracted by it, Sebastien was allowed to recover and stand. As he stood he came to realize his armour was dented, from the impact of the man's fists. Sebastien stood in horror as another two soldiers fell to his enemy's hand.

"Men, form ranks!" Sebastien screamed, hoping some of his men would fall in line amongst the chaos of fire and freaked horses. Behind him he could see and hear the shuffle of his soldiers.

"Archers!"

A few of Sebastien's men ran in to fight the man, keeping him distracted, while, behind, his soldiers took control of their mounts.

"Archers now!" Sebastien screamed, as more felled men ran into the battle. His ranks were getting smaller by the second. Then, after the second command, a wave of arrows were unleashed.

Sebastien yelled curses as he ducked, nearly getting impaled by his soldiers' mediocre shots. The man seemed to dance between the arrows, while pushing half of them aside with what looked like a gust of air, but Sebastien couldn't tell in the midst of all the commotion. It seemed too unreal to be real.

"I'll do it myself!" Sebastien shouted as he grabbed a crossbow from the nearest horse rider, yanking it from his hand. Aiming down the crossbow sights, he could see the man dance between three of his soldier's blades. The moment was ripe, he was distracted, all Sebastien had to do was line up the shot. He aimed for the man's chest and pulled the trigger, unleashing the bolt.

You almost could hear the screech of the bolt as it launched through the air and lodged itself into the man's leg. Not Sebastien's best shot, but a hit nonetheless. The man lurched down to the ground, and Sebastien could hear his cry of agony. Handing the crossbow back to the rider, Sebastien picked up his sword and walked towards the man with a cold, strutting confidence. Despite the bolt in his leg the man still fought on with an awkward limp. Only one man remained of the three fighting him, and he was down before Sebastien even reached him.

The man seemed less witch-like and more manic as Sebastien got a clear sight of him. A bolt in the leg can do that to a man. His brown eyes held crazy, his black strands of hair looked unkempt, and his beard hadn't been shaved in what looked like days. Sebastien almost felt sorry for him as the man hobbled on one leg, collapsing every time he put weight into the other.

"Yield, tell us what we need to know and we will have you unharmed," Sebastien said as he held out his long sword.

A dark chuckle came from the man as he bent down on one knee. Sebastien held out his sword, ready, but the man merely ripped the bolt out from his thigh, baring his teeth at Sebastien. Coming to a stand, the dark strands of his hair fell over his face. Along with the dark of the forest, it made the man look almost demon like. He was obviously not going to go down with words.

"Any last words?" Sebastien asked as he held out his sword.

The man smiled along with his words, "Yea. Fuck you."

And before Sebastien could react a wave of fire appeared out of nowhere, launched with incredible force. Ducking, Sebastien covered his face. Still, he was sent flying back into his men as the force hit him.

With a pinch in his back, Sebastien slowly sat up, observing the scene before him. About twelve men remained of his troops, who were recovering from the blast themselves. In front of them lay bodies of men; some dead, and some sprawled on the ground moaning, as they lay there too injured to move. A few light embers still burned on the ends of dry branches. The scene was an absolute bloodbath.

"What the hell was that?" Sebastien heard a soldier ask, while others agreed just as baffled.

"Mount up, we will not let him escape."

A deep rumble woke Ralis. Frightened, he lurched up, only to find himself nestled among some tree branches high among an aging pine tree.

It's nothing but the wind, Ralis thought as he listened to the emptiness of the forest and felt the tree sway. He'd been running east for days, straight through the narrow valley, a devilish pass that followed a river up into the mountains and then down into the eastern floor and its peninsula. Salamon's riders had been on his back the whole time.

Ralis would purposefully leave tracks and snap branches, giving scent to his direction. He needed them to keep following his trail for his plan to work, although not without some improvisations.

Nights before Jestin had proved unreliable and suffered for it. A bolt to the leg hadn't been part of the plan either.

Ralis felt down towards his right thigh. He couldn't see it clearly, but when he touched the wound it would reverberate pain up his body. He had spent many nights healing it. The wound was sealed internally, but he still needed stitches and he had lost his rucksack long ago. Despite the setbacks, Ralis' hashed up plan seemed to have worked, the bulk of Salamon's force was either burned up among the explosion and fires, dead or injured, or in pursuit of him. How long they would take to return to the west with strength, he did not know. He sighed, looking down towards his leg.

Awake now, Ralis thought to do some healing work. Sending energy from his navel to his hand, Ralis' palm lit a deep orange hue. Rubbing the light against his thigh he leaned back with a moan. Maybe his plan wouldn't work, maybe Macaro was right and it would only bring more attention to the west. Retracing the past events, Ralis could see how that was plausible. If only he could see how the stars could see, observant and all knowing. The stars could answer the elusive question: should a man choose action or inaction? For Ralis that was always his question—action or inaction?—the murder of his father always hanging in his mind. Above him the sky shimmered orange and blue, winter was approaching.

Blue stars were the sign of the approach of winter and the start of November.

Salamon's men must be choking in their sleep, Ralis thought to himself, winter was no one's friend in the mountains. The continent of Thenus was never known for a harsh winter, but the mountains that ridged the continent's western side still proved a mutual friend with the cold. Salamon's troops had taken his bait and followed Ralis up the valley pass, and now they spent the night on one of its highest portions. The cold wind blistered past. If it made Ralis cold, he wondered how men from the fields were faring. Ralis smiled at the thought of them shaking in their boots while they slept.

During the day Ralis ran, and run fast he did. With Salamon's troops on horseback, the pounding of hooves were always close during the day. Sometimes Ralis would even find himself cornered by riders who had caught up with him, many of the times ending with a pile of bodies. Night was the only time Ralis could rest. While he rested, Salamon could regroup and gather strength, sending out scouts, hunt and find water. Plus, their numerable size in men allowed them to carry more rations and gear. Ralis, on the other hand, started to grow tired and hungry. There was no food among the forest during the dreariness of the fall.

At night Ralis would sometimes forfeit a good night's sleep to sneak among Salamon's camp and steal what little he could get from their rations. Eventually, he stopped doing so, convinced the risk was too great.

To sleep, Ralis would nestle himself high in the branches of a tree. He couldn't dare rest on the ground with Salamon's scouts about. Every night he sat, hungry, and each night he got colder as the winter moved forth. His legs thumped with agony, sore from hours of running, and his wound began to fester. But nothing would deter Ralis from his mission. And each night he sat gazing at the stars, unable to sleep, thinking of his friends at Highwash and what was at stake. Macaro would sit idle, but Ralis would take action. Each night he would meditate as well, trying to find answers among the silence. What would he do when he entered the fields of Thenus? They were wide-open grasslands, flat and empty. Once he was there his plan would have worked, but he would no longer be able to hide among the trees and bush of the forest. He guessed he would have to improvise when it came to that. Not everything can be planned, and a Mage must use what is at his disposal. A Mage must adapt.

Marius stood outside the door of her quarters, in debate whether to knock or not. *Would she even be awake at this hour?* Marius hoped so.

He shivered in the cold of night, stuck in decision. In his hand he held a small spherical stone. On one side of the stone was a clear cut-out, made to see the emerald encased inside the stone. Marius could feel the cut-out in between his fingers as he rubbed it anxiously in debate. The emerald felt smooth. It still felt the same as the day Macarò had given it to him.

It was the only thing he had of his father's, Macaro told Marius when he had given it to him. "Your father is a brave man, troubled but brave." Macaro's words echoed in his head. It was the only thing Marius had of his parents at all. He imagined blurred faces of who he thought they would be. They could be anyone. Beggars or thieves or lords or dead, but Macaro had never told him who his parents were. "A Mage has no heritage other than the bond to his Elder, each of you are my children."

Marius had never met his father, any feelings he had towards the stone were fake. He wanted her to have it, it matched her eyes.

Making his decision, he knocked on the rough surface of the door. For a second nothing stirred inside, then a sputtered hello came from her familiar voice.

"It's me, Marius."

The door opened with Cynthia standing there, peering oddly at Marius. Her hair glued to one side of her head from sleeping on her face and her robe was half thrown on, held together by her hand at her breast.

"Marius? What are you doing here?" Cynthia asked, her face furrowed in surprise. Marius had asked himself the same question. "Never mind me, come in, come in," she said swiftly, quickly realizing her manners.

Marius stepped into her cabin behind her, the emerald stone clutched in his hand. Her cabin looked the same as every other students'. Inside the small rickety shack was a single cot and a small nightstand.

Cynthia sat down on her bed and gestured Marius to sit beside her, as she tied her robe up.

"What did you need?" she asked as she lit a lone candle standing on her nightstand. Her eyes gleamed the same as the emerald Marius held in the soft light.

"I... umm... wanted to give you something."

Her face lit up with even more surprise to Marius' comment. "Give me something? Ok, well let's see it."

Nervously, he held out his hand. Cuffing her hand over his she opened his fingers to see the stone. Taking the stone curiously she span it around in her hands.

"Marius..." Stunned she stared at the emerald absorbed by its beauty. "Marius... this is gorgeous... where... where did you get this?" she said stumbling on her words.

"Macaro gave it to me long ago. He said it was my father's. Apparently he knew my father personally."

"Well then, you shouldn't give me this, Marius. It was your father's."

"Cynthia, I never knew my father." He paused for a second thinking of his words, "But I know you Cynthia. And every time I've ever gazed into it, I've never thought of my father, I've only thought of you, and I want you to have it."

Cynthia stared at it for a second with water in her eyes. "I've never been given anything."

"Well then make this your first."

Before Marius could say anything more Cynthia grabbed him by the face and pressed her lips against his.

"Thank you, Marius." She stood up from her bed, and gazed at her new stone. "It is so beautiful," she admired as she put it down on her nightstand beside the candle. She gently placed her hands on his and helped him to come to a stand. She looked more beautiful than ever, he thought.

"Who do you think your father was? I like to imagine mine was some kind of auctioneer or something."

"Why an auctioneer?"

"Because I like the thought of being sold better than the thought of being stolen."

Marius chuckled at that. "If it's up to imagination, I'd like to think my father was the best swordsman of the continent, falling any knight who would dare to face him."

Their hands reached out and caressed each other as they traded words.

"I guess I better be going then," Marius said languidly.

"Well, I was thinking maybe you could spend the night…" Cynthia said, softly.

"I'd like that," he whispered into her ear.

Pushing Marius on her bed she giggled, her robes falling to the ground.

They were closing in on him.

It had been weeks of treacherous running in the forest and Ralis didn't have much farther to go before he hit the fields of the mainland. The forest had thinned tremendously the further Ralis headed east. The thinning of the bush and trees, allowed for flatter ground in the forests of the eastern side of the Emeralties. The flatter ground had given Salamon's riders an advantage of speed, allowing them to almost run down Ralis a couple of times. He'd escaped, but the frequent close calls had exhausted him. He ran mindlessly now, tired and drained, constantly in fear, constantly looking back as he ran listening for the sound of hooves. His wound made him weak, it festered at his side. He almost felt like Yuri for a second.

Salamon's force had grown over the weeks as well. Forces from his other camps had merged with the main one. It made Ralis doubt his survival if he were to be caught.

He ran on through the thinned woods. The ground was softer on the eastern face of the mountains. Flatter than the western face, the ground formed wide passages in between the great trunks of oaks, hemlocks and pines. Weak and tired, Ralis' wound pierced with pain, causing him to fall to the ground, his legs trembling.

Get up, Ralis said to himself. He could hear Jestin's voice ring through his mind, "Out run a bunch of horses?" He would be laughing in his grave right about now, Ralis thought, his face full of dirt. He pushed himself up to a weak run, his legs barely holding him upright.

The current day had been cold and harshly dry. Rivers and creeks had begun to freeze over, and many trees were bare without leaves, and it was only the great pines that provided cover from sight. After barely sleeping the night before, Ralis had cause for an early start, his legs roaring with disapproval. He had not gotten far despite that. As far as Ralis could tell it was currently midday, but the countless days of running had thrown him off course and he had lost the estimation of where he was, Ralis had thought to have reached the forest's end by midday today. It seemed his guess was off. The thought of being lost made him despondent.

The woods of the west were never to be taken lightly; it was said to have swallowed even the most cunning of scouts. *Follow the rising sun*—the adage never seemed to work as well halfway through the day, Ralis thought to himself bitterly, not knowing which way was east. Weariness started to overwhelm him—even a Mage was bound to the physical limits of food and water, which Ralis had lack of. He stumbled often, catching himself on trunks of trees, or narrowly hitting the ground before continuing on. He held on though, like an old, rusted nail, tired and bent from countless hammer strikes, but still holding on through sheer grit.

I must continue east. The thought spiralled through his head as he drudged on. The only thing that held him together was the thought of the people at Highwash. If he were to be caught, their fate would be the same as if Salamon found them.

It was awfully quiet in the forest, Ralis noticed quite suddenly. Not a chirp or flap was to be heard, only the sound of his patterned steps and breath. Stopping, Ralis stood still, listening to the sounds of the forest. Silence. But beyond the silence, a deep rumble. A deep rumble caused by hooves. *That's why the birds have been silent, they've been scared away.*

Ralis picked up his pace and started to run as fast as his worn legs could take him. The sound of hooves grew slowly louder behind him. It wouldn't be long until they reached him. Ralis thought if it came to it he would seek refuge in the comforts of a high spot in a tree.

But before Ralis could make a move to climb one, something caught his leg snug around the ankle and sent him flying face first into the ground. With a jerk on his leg he was hoisted into the air upside down. His head ringing, Ralis came to quickly, realizing he was bound in the air by a rope tied snug around his ankle.

Shit. Ralis thought to himself as he dangled in the air, caught by the trap. *Salamon must've snuck scouts ahead of his position the night prior.*

Reacting, Ralis reached up and sent a few flaming embers towards the rope, it burned easily, dropping him again face first into the ground with an *oof.* Groaning, Ralis got up. His head was in a daze.

"Don't move!" A command shouted from somewhere, Ralis couldn't tell with his head ringing. Suddenly a hand reached out, grabbing Ralis' arm, and within a moment Ralis was breaking a man's arm.

What looked like a scout was bent below Ralis screaming, with the arm that grabbed Ralis twisted and locked under

Ralis' grip. Six other men surrounded Ralis; all of them wore the emblazed red colours of Salamon, a smaller robe and thin mailed cuirasses, the gear of a scout. All of them held blades out, ready to attack Ralis. Coming to, Ralis could hear the sound of hooves on dirt louder than ever, they were getting close, and this was Salamon's plan. To catch Ralis disoriented between his scouts and his horde. Salamon was getting better, but he would not die today, Ralis told himself.

Throwing the scout down, Ralis leapt towards another scout in the circle around him. The scout went to strike, but Ralis quickly disarmed him and sent the blade through his throat. Blood spurted across the ground as the man fell to his knees. The five remaining men ran to attack Ralis simultaneously, but Ralis sent forth a wave of air, knocking the scouts to the ground. Using that energy exhausted Ralis and he collapsed to his knees, drained.

The sounds of the men were even closer, the thumping of hooves, the clatter of armour and blades, and the yells of command all echoed through the forest. Salamon's host had grown.

The five scouts started to get up slowly. All of them shook their head, dazed about what had just happened.

Ralis growled as he got up, he was exhausted, every part of his body ached, his head pounded and his vision was starting to blur. *Run you fool!* Ralis told himself, commanding himself as if his body was another person. He forced himself up and began to run. He made it past a few trees before one of the scouts tackled him down into the ground, his face becoming covered in mud once again. That only angered Ralis, and he broke the scout's neck as they wrestled on the ground. The four other scouts caught up to him as he got up from the ground. They didn't hesitate, slashing their swords at Ralis, forcing him to weave and dodge the blades.

Ralis grabbed one of the men, twisting him into the path of another scout's blade. The sword pierced the man's chest. Ralis could feel the scout's ribs crack as he held him. Another blade slashed towards Ralis' skull forcing him to duck and whirl around, and then hooking a kick around the attacker's legs sending him to the ground.

Swiftly, Ralis grabbed the sword from the fingers of the downed scout and plunged it into his throat. The scout gargled blood as he held the blade, coldly staring the two remaining scouts down. Ralis' guessed their orders were to attack on sight because, despite the fear clearly worn on their faces, they attacked.

Ralis was up again, running and having dealt with the scouts, but suddenly a group of riders were upon him, flanking him from the right side and forcing him to veer left, ducking under the low branches of a pine. The whinny of the horses cried loud as they bulled through the branches behind him.

BAROO!

The wail of the rider's horn bellowed from behind as Ralis ducked under branches and ran.

Not good, all of his horde would have heard that, Ralis thought as he pulled himself up over the gnarled roots of an oak. Behind him he could hear the neigh of horses, stuck behind the line of tree growth. Ralis stood on a path of barren ground nestled in between an oak at one side and two large pines on the other. Ralis could catch his breath for a moment, but he did not know his next move. He assumed he was a mile or less west from the edge of the forest, he could try to run it and make it there if he wasn't seen, but what would come after breaching the forest's edge?

Ralis hadn't put much thought into it earlier. His mind ran circles for a second before he came up with an idea. He could steal a horse from a rider, that would get him out of the forest and into the fields safely, but if the horse should tire… The idea didn't sound perfect, but it was an idea nevertheless.

Inside his little crevice in between the trees he could hear the shouts of men and whinny of horses circling the area.

"He went that way!" Ralis heard shouted from beyond the wall of trees. He could hear the clatter of mail as a few riders dismounted and started to weave through the branches towards him.

There's no time! Ralis thought as he ducked between some branches and started running. He wrestled though some branches of an old pine, but just as he blasted out from the fingers of the pine into a clearing, he saw he was running right into a group of riders.

The riders went to rush him immediately, trying to storm him with their trample, but Ralis jumped up and kicked off the side of one of the horses, spinning in the air and landing agile like a cat then taking off down the path the clearing opened up to. The riders struggled to rear their horses and turn them around.

With their swords ablaze, the riders pounded down the dirt trail after Ralis. He dodged and ducked, turning down the trail in a fury. It had a wider berth, and at its thinnest the trail still formed a rut wide enough for a horse. Ralis could feel the canter of the horses behind him, the cry of men, his own heart pounding.

BAROO!

The horn unleashed again, this time by the riders that currently had sight of Ralis. He despised that horn.

As Ralis ran, more riders came forth. Some joined the group behind him, others came out of the forest without notice, trying to cut him off. One rider who tried to cut Ralis off ended up being tackled off his stallion, and smashed into the ground with Ralis leaving a footprint of mud on the man's face.

Behind him he heard the draw of bowstrings. He could hear the fine screech of the strings building tension, just before the flutter of arrows coursed their way towards Ralis' backside. Ralis ducked frantically as he heard the release of the strings. The arrows flung overhead and Ralis sprawled up to a run and started off again. The riders were closing in, they were so close Ralis could almost feel the breath of their stallions on his back. A few arrows whizzed by, missing their target, and suddenly Salamon's riders were doubling back. Ralis looked back to see what the riders were doing, continuing to run, but abruptly the trail ended and the ground was no longer beneath him. He understood at that moment the reason for their retreat: the trail was about to end and drop off into a grassy hill.

Ralis found himself tumbling down a large steep hill, covered in long reeds and fine bushes, smashing into all sorts of greenery as he rolled down. The hill came to end quickly with the flat ground at its bottom smashing Ralis with an unwelcoming greeting. Dazed, he got up as quick as he could, ignoring all feelings of pain, he tried to run but his legs felt like iron, and before he could get anywhere, he collapsed into the grass. At least he had reached the mainland.

Ralis didn't remember what happened next, but he was unexpectedly standing on his feet, surrounded by a circle of horses. Men sat abreast the mounts, their mail shimmering in the light and their lances pointed at Ralis. Some of the riders dismounted, while others stayed their place with either their lances or bows readied.

As the soldiers who dismounted entered the circle and closed in on Ralis, blades raised, it seemed Macaro was right. Ralis didn't want to admit it, but at that moment, as he was surrounded by soldiers and struggling to stand, he saw everything in one instance. He could see all the blood he had spilled, all of the bodies that lay forth from the start of his journey to now, he could see all the death that would be caused in the future by his hand, and he could see his own death, his own bloody corpse reaped by death, all of it playing out in his head like a play on a screen. Compassion was the answer. Macaro always knew that. But Ralis never understood, and now that he had it was too late, he had picked his path, he had chosen long ago. Ralis could no longer live in the grey, no longer could he walk the fine line of life and death, no longer could he skirt the line of compassion and animosity. He had to choose.

The choice seemed simple to Ralis now. He knew who he was; it was always about just coming to terms with it. So at the moment the soldiers came forth, Ralis didn't hesitate, he didn't hold back, he let loose, he let the darkness inside of him out, he became the fate Macaro feared for all of his students.

He became the vessel of death.

Ralis lunged forward, smashing one man in the chest with a kick. He could feel the soldier's heart stop from the impact of the kick. Whirling underneath another soldier's blade, dodging the sharp, cold steel, he smashed the man's skull with his elbow. A flock of arrows unleashed at Ralis, but he simply grabbed another dismounted rider to use as a shield. The body looked like a human dartboard as Ralis dropped the now lifeless corpse.

Weaving between arrows and lances, Ralis spun, unleashing streams of fire and scorching all the horses that circled him. It swiftly broke up the circle. As Ralis burned the horses, they kicked up and freaked, some of them bucking their riders off, others lit aflame and dropped to their death while some galloped away from the scene, their riders in tow. Men ran at him from all directions, some bearing lances, others with swords or daggers, but Ralis didn't resist. He gave them the fight they so wished for.

Blood splattered, bones crunched and men screamed as Ralis beat down Salamon's men one by one as they continued to run and fight him, weapons ablaze. As their force quickly diminished with even some of the riders now horseless beginning to retreat and flee off into the fields in the distance, their commander screamed curses at them as they ran.

Soon it was just the commander of the force, a few soldiers, a pile of bodies and frightened horses left with Ralis amidst the field of broken soldiers. Ralis collapsed to one knee as he stood there, his breath heavy. He felt worn and tired.

"Enough of this!" the commanding officer screamed as he ripped his sword form his scabbard and pointed its end straight at Ralis. The man ripped off his helm to show once again his lush, long golden hair and toned face. "I am Sebastien Salamon, First Commander of Salamon's fleet and his first-born son. I shall not be defeated like this, not even if the skies had designed my fate so."

Sebastien threw down his helm and began to walk forward, sword in hand. His men followed behind him anxiously as he walked towards Ralis but he stopped and turned his head to them.

"No. You men shall not be one of the bodies today, ride to my father and tell him what has happened here."

His men stopped in their tracks wearing looks of confusion and indecision.

"Go!" Sebastien screamed, and at once his men nodded curtly and turned starting off. Sebastien turned to see Ralis. "Its just me and you now, demon, before you strike me down, at least give me your name."

Ralis began to chuckle at once, blood filling in his mouth as he laughed. He must've gotten hit somewhere along the line.

"Does it matter my name, when your body is piled among your soldiers?" Ralis said as he spat blood at Sebastien. Sebastien stared up towards the sky and its blue beauty.

The heavens are so close, Sebastien thought to himself as he stood there before Ralis kneeling bloody on the ground. *And if they are so close, I hope they see me and help me now.*

Releasing the straps on his breastplate, the sheen metal dropped to the ground with a thump, leaving all but a leather cuirass on Sebastien.

He stepped forward towards Ralis, sending his sword for Ralis' neck. But Ralis stepped aside, easily dodging the blade. All of Sebastien's force had disintegrated and, as he fought Ralis, only Sebastien's lone mare stood in wait for him. Sebastien would hit nothing but air as he swung his steel. All of his teachings and practice, and this man could dodge any blow Sebastien mustered.

What kind of knight is he? Who could fight in such a way? Ralis began to laugh as he dodged each blow.

"It is said in the west that the knights of the east fight like sloths. It seems so," Ralis mocked as he smashed Sebastien across the face with his fist.

Sebastien stumbled forward and dropped his sword.

"And you commanded them to leave. The arrogance," Ralis said as Sebastien got up and reclaimed his sword from the dirt. Sebastien held his sword firm.

"No, not arrogance, just faith," he said as he spun around with a slash aimed for Ralis' gut. Ralis responded eagerly, dodging the blade, and whilst Sebastien was left vulnerable for that second, Ralis jumped and spun into a kick sending Sebastien launching into the ground.

"Your faith is wrong," Ralis said as he picked up Sebastien's fallen sword.

Sebastien lay on his back, struggling, as Ralis walked over to him, the blade he held shone in the light. Sebastien looked up to see Ralis' silhouette approach him, and suddenly realized he was going to die. Here. Today.

The darkened silhouette approached him, with the sun on Ralis' back, his blackened face looked almost truly demon-like. For the first time Sebastien felt true fear. Thoughts raced in his mind; he wanted to live, he wanted to see his brother again, to hug his sister. In his mind he began to beg to the skies.

And they answered.

In the distance over the hill, behind Ralis, someone stood, tall and alone holding a crossbow. Before Ralis could notice, a bolt had already been shot.

Ralis lurched and then fell to the ground in front of Sebastien. Sebastien could clearly see the bolt in Ralis' shoulder blade as he struggled and groaned on the grass. The man in the distance ran over, revealing that it was the soldier Sebastien had ordered to send word to his father.

"I know I disobeyed orders, punish me as you will, sir, but I could not leave you."

Sebastien smiled with relief, it was the first time he was glad an inferior disobeyed an order.

The bolt had penetrated deep; Ralis could feel it lodged in his upper back. He held himself barely on his hands and knees. *Breathe*, he told himself as he sent a wave of energy to the wound calming his fluttering breath. He would not die today.

Sebastien began to get up, coming to a stand while grabbing his sword from the ground. Ralis had dropped it when he was hit.

"It seems you're wrong, demon, faith is with me," Sebastien said as he lifted his sword to swing.

In the sunlight the sword glistened as Sebastien raised it, but Ralis lunged and tackled him to the ground before it made contact. Both of them fell, with Ralis on top. Ralis' back screamed in torture, but that didn't stop him from smashing Sebastien with fists to the face. He had already known pain. Ralis could feel Sebastien's face bruise under his fists, he could feel blood bubble in Sebastien's throat. Ralis was barely there anymore, so lost in anger and pain, his fists were the only thing he felt.

Suddenly an arm from behind grabbed Ralis around the neck, choking him. It was the lone soldier who had stayed. Ralis lurched back, prying the soldiers arm from his neck, then flipped him over his back, smashing the soldier down on his commander. Ralis was on his knees now, the pain was becoming too much, his vision was starting to blur and his mind started to fade. In front of him the soldier and Sebastien squirmed on the ground in pain, both of them suffering and unable to get up. He must have broken the man's ribs when he slammed him, Ralis thought as he knelt in the grass.

Ralis looked around at his surroundings, his vision clearing as he refocused his breath. The field was a desolate mess. Bodies of Salamon's troops lay crumpled everywhere, some sprawled out, moaning, while others were frozen in their death. Among them were the burnt corpses of the unlucky horses who didn't flee. Some of the unlucky stallions were even still alive, struggling amongst the grass, unable to get up, their burnt flesh stopping any movement they tried.

He had caused this, Ralis realized as he witnessed the scene before him. So much suffering and so many dead, all because he chose to help. Did he help? The scene that lay before him didn't seem like much help. Macaro was right. He should never have left, he should have stayed at Highwash, but at the time, Ralis just thought he could help. Macaro's words fluttered through his mind once more, *Stay here, Ralis, you are needed at Highwash.* And now he could never return, it would risk too much. He had made his choice when he left Highwash and now he had to continue down this path.

Among the mess of corpses, Ralis noticed a single black mare that stood out from the rest. The animal was not burned or hurt, and it even seemed unaffected by the toils of war around it as it stood munching on the grass. With all the effort in the world, Ralis stood and slowly started to walk his way forward towards the lone mare. Every step was like moving a mountain and as he walked he realized his robes were soaked in blood. His blood.

Behind him, Sebastien rolled over on the ground, his face now bloody and bruised. He could see Ralis walking towards the horse in the distance, if he got there, Sebastien knew he would get away. Unable to stand, his head in waves of agony, Sebastien started to crawl towards the crossbow his soldier had dropped. With all his might he dragged himself across the grass towards it. It was right there, *so close*, so close. Reaching the crossbow, Sebastien tried his best to sit up on his knees. He could see the man nearing the mare, grabbing the tethers and starting to lift himself on the horse. Raising the crossbow, Sebastien gazed down the sights, it would be a dead shot right towards his back, all he had to do was pull the trigger.

Click.

But nothing came out of the crossbow, just an empty click. Sebastien gazed in awe as the demon man rode away into the distance lurched on Sebastien's own mare. He felt so stupid. The crossbow hadn't even a bolt loaded in it.

XIII

It was a gloomy afternoon, Marius thought as he walked with Cynthia. The morning had been spent training fighting with his class under Macaro's guidance. Clouds had covered the noon sky and it gave Marius a bitter chill. The morning had been worse. Macaro had them training sparring and kicks. Marius was partnered with Reggard and they'd spent the morning battering their shins at each other in the cold of dawn. After Macaro made them all carry water from the well which lay down by Talun's stables; it was a toilsome trek back into the village carrying the pails.

Macaro had then called them all to the main hall for some sort of lecture. The warm rush of air soothed Marius' face as he entered the hall. Taking a seat next to Yuri on the descending steps, the lecture began. Macaro's voice warmed them when he began to speak.

"I hope you all have recovered from this morning. As the rest of this year we shall focus on our trainings, less on learning new skills, but more of a focus on reinforcing all that we have learned over this turn of a year. November's grey is upon us and its time we conclude this year with the final task."

"We have learned much this year—from manipulating new forms of energy like lightning and water, to using the outside forces of qi to conjugate energy to a specific point—we have spent countless hours going over our forms and many countless evenings with our heads in books. I want to congratulate all of you on this, each of you—despite your wins and losses—you have all done an incredible job this year. Each of you strive towards a better vision, each of you are forging your way to individuality. And thus, the final task will strive to spread that as its message. We want to grow, as a Mage, a community and as a world. Nature does so strive to grow, and so shall we."

Macaro paced in the centre of the room, his shadow wavering with the flickers of the candles.

"The final task is an accumulation of all of what we have learned and will test us on the grounds of our spiritual basis. Those of you I name, rise and stand."

The class stilled as he spoke.

"Yuri, you may stand."

Marius gave Yuri a nod, and Yuri rose with dignity stepping off the steps towards Macaro.

"Mathius, you may stand. Reggard, you may stand. Daniel, you may stand."

All four of them stood and made their way to Macaro at the centre of the room.

"You four have made it to the final task, you four proved through will, sheer power and strength that you have the will to represent what a Mage is. You shall prove a vision for your fellow students, you shall be a model of light. There is but one more step to prove your adeptness. Each of you must contribute something of great value to Highwash and its people."

Both Marius and Yuri wore the same expression of surprise, no one had known what the fourth task would be, but this seemed... almost elusive.

"That is all I require: for you to bring something of your own to Highwash, for you to mark your place among us as a Mage, to show us your light," Elder Macaro said continuing to speak. "What you provide of great value should be yours to determine alone. After you shall be Adepts and no longer apprentices, you shall be free to do your own bidding among Highwash, and you will no longer be under my teachings. For the rest of you, may you look on these four with admiration and continue to focus on your training. The time shall come for all of you."

Macaro bowed, finishing the lecture, and the class emptied out of the great hall.

Cynthia and Marius stood by the main entrance watching their classmates leave the hall and waiting for Yuri who stood in discussion with Macaro. When Yuri finally came over to them, Marius asked, "So what do you make of the fourth task?"

"To be honest, I have not a clue. What does he mean 'provide something of value'?" Yuri asked as they started to leave the hall, the gush of air blistered their face as they entered the cold of outside. "Clearly he expects something big, but what's near here other than sea water and grass?" Yuri continued on. They listened to Yuri's rant about what he was going to do about the fourth task all the way until Marius reached his quarters.

His quarters held no warmth inside, so he sat on his bed cross-legged and began to meditate, building warmth with his breath. Yuri's rant had made him think of himself and his own value at Highwash. *What do I contribute?* His thoughts eventually dissipated and he was left in the void of his self, feeling the patterned waves of breath and thought.

Soon it was the evening and, as Marius had promised earlier, he was neck deep in books with Yuri in the library. As he sat among the dust-filled books of the library he began to severely regret offering to help Yuri so long ago. Yuri was head down in a book as he sat beside Marius at a long desk nestled in the deep crevasses of the library. Marius gazed off across the room, staring at the darkness in the distance, the darkness taking random shapes and figures, sometimes floating into a man or others turning into Cynthia herself.

"Marius, I've been thinking," Marius jumped as Yuri began to speak, but Yuri hadn't noticed. "Look, maybe we've been looking in the wrong place, what if none of these books have anything on the ruins? I mean they were certainly deep in the woods."

Marius thought about it as Yuri talked, maybe he was right, maybe none of these books contained anything on it, and Marius would certainly like being done sorting through the endless journals and copies.

"What if we have already stumbled on what we needed to know?" Yuri asked giving Marius an evil stare.

"What's that supposed to mean?" Marius asked cautiously, trying his best to avoid being roped into another of Yuri's awful ploys.

Yuri turned is head looking for any onlookers and then leaned in close, lowering his voice. "Remember the notes we found in Nathaniel's quarters? Well, I think our answer lies in there."

"You mean *your* answer," Marius said interjecting.

"Yes, whatever, but listen, what if our—*my*—answer lies in there? I mean who would be best to have information on that place other than Nathaniel?"

"Well, that's a good thought, but remember Macaro took the notes? How do you expect to come upon them again?" Marius wished he never asked because Yuri simply responded with a mischievous grin. "No, I am not breaking in there." Marius stated bluntly, knowing what Yuri was about to ask.

It was nil for nothing Marius knew, because three hours later, while Macaro sat in meditation with the other Elders, Marius found himself outside Macaro's quarters lurking in the darkness of a bush with Yuri.

"I hate you," Marius said as a branch prodded his backside. Yuri just hushed him as he popped his head out of the bush to peer.

"C'mon, now," Yuri whispered as he waved for Marius to exit the cover of the bush behind him.

Leaving the bush, they huddled against the cover of darkness behind Macaro's quarters. Both of them knew they couldn't access the door to Macaro's, any slight indication the door had been picked or busted and Macaro would know, but Macaro always left the window open. Sneaking up to the back window Marius and Yuri could clearly see its shutters wide open.

Earlier Marius had stated vigorously that he would not enter Macaro's quarters himself. Yuri and him had come to an agreement that Yuri would be the one to break in and Marius would just accompany him. Watching Yuri vault over the windowsill and into Macaro's quarters sent a nasty chill down his spine. If anyone were to catch them...

It felt like minutes passed by in the cold of night before Yuri jumped out from the window, and Marius gave him a cold stare that said, *What took you so long?*

"It was under his bed," Yuri said, as they slipped back into the darkness. Later that evening they sat together in Marius' quarters on his bed. Both of them scanned the page of notes relentlessly.

"A lot of this we read the first time, but look down here," Marius said, pointing to the bottom of the page. "It's here, there, what he wants, what it wants. Whatever it is, it's here, I know it is. Why, otherwise, am I drawn here, drawn here like a puppet tied to strings? I'm unable to see it, but I can feel it pull me closer, I can't reach it, too large, my vessel, too large. My time as its vessel is over, I am forfeit."

It felt cold as Marius and Yuri sat there reading the rest of the notes that were nothing but a jumble of words.

"What does that even mean?" Marius asked, "I hope you don't get us banished over this. Wasn't worth much, got to say." Marius said pleased with himself that he was right about not stealing the notes from Macaro.

"This is everything, Marius, it's what we have been looking for. Don't you see? There is something there in the ruins—something he wants. That's why he wanted us to go down into the tunnels," Yuri said a bit too loud, starting to get excited.

"Yuri, Nathaniel is clearly insane. Look at the notes, they don't even make sense."

"Why else would he have sent us down there, Marius? There must be something down there. And with the fourth task being 'Do something of value,' what if this is a sign?" Yuri said as he paced around Marius' quarters, his face becoming pictures of bewilderment.

"A sign from?"

"The skies, Marius. They are obviously calling us there."

Marius felt stunned for a second by the words his friend was uttering. "You can't be serious?" Marius said standing to meet his friend eye to eye. "You can't go back there. Remember what happened last time?"

Yuri paused for a second and Marius hoped that his friend was starting to see the light.

"But what if I am meant to return there, Marius?" Yuri said to Marius' disappointment.

"No, Yuri, listen to me, you can't go back there."

Suddenly a flash of anger shot through Yuri's eyes.

"Who are you to command me?" Yuri said, his voice starting to rise.

"Yuri, you barely survived last time. This isn't about fate or the skies, this is about your life and schooling here at Highwash. If you go there, and even if you survive, Macaro won't welcome you back here, and you know it."

"He won't have to know I left."

"How the fuck wouldn't he know, Yuri?" Marius said coldly, he was starting to get tired of this truculent conversation. "I don't even think this is about the fourth task, I think you're hurt. I think you're hurt because of the fact that that place had us beat. I think you want to redeem the fact you had fallen." The words sounded more obtuse as Marius ran them through his mind after he said them.

"Had me beat?" Yuri said, pushing Marius onto his bed, "No, I think you're jealous, Marius, of the fact I've gotten to the fourth task in the first place."

And before Marius could say another word, Yuri left with the door of Marius' cabin swinging on its hinges.

Damn, I hope he doesn't head there, Marius thought to himself as he stared at his door. Marius lay down on his bed, sighing. Another fight with Yuri, had they always been this way? His mind drifted away into the deep slumbers of sleep.

Soon Marius reopened his eyes. He was floating or drifting in a black void, he couldn't tell which. The black void seemed endless, and all Marius could feel was his own heartbeat and the rhythm of his breath. It seemed so real as he floated among the blackness. His limbs felt weightless but he couldn't move. It was a dream, Marius knew, but it was a dream unlike any he had had before. Suddenly he couldn't breathe, his lungs burned with fire as he shook and quivered, gasping for breath. It was no relief. And then before him, appearing from nowhere, was this blinding light of blue and white. He couldn't look at it, it pierced his eyes so brightly. But he wanted to look, he needed to look, even though he knew it would blind him. He could feel the warmth of the light, he could feel it grow stronger and stronger around him, until even having his eyes closed provided no cover from it. The blinding light pierced passed his eyelids, and soon all Marius could feel was a deep vibration of light and a solemn feeling of fear. The light began to grow more and more intense, as if it were heading towards Marius, or Marius towards it, it didn't matter much but it was growing more intense with every second that passed. Eventually the light was everywhere and Marius was staring deep into its depths. Inside the depths of the light was a figure, a figure brighter than all of the light that surrounded it. It began to approach Marius, and as the figure drew closer, the fear grew more and more until Marius was shaking and sputtering. The figure reached Marius and he could feel his eyes burn away against the light, but for some reason he could still see the glowing figure in front of him. The figure started to raise what seemed like a hand towards Marius, placing it on his forehead. The pain was unbearable, it felt as if all of his nerves were being plucked out of his body and burned with fire. "Open your eyes," a voice commanded, more terrible sounding than Marius could imagine. And as the voice commanded, Marius opened his eyes, willingly, and before him was a face he knew well, the figure wore the face of Yuri.

Shooting up from the covers of his blanket, Marius panted. He was covered in sweat, and his robes which he had forgotten to disrobe the night before, were now soaked through.

"Fuck," Marius said out loud to himself. Lying back down, he stared at the ceiling. All that raced through his mind was, *What the fuck was that?* Nothing felt good about that dream.

The next day was clear but cold; the bright skies emanated a soft blue while Marius and his classmates trained forms on the cliffs of the coast. Macaro paced back and forth among the line he had arranged them in. He was teaching them new forms today, first by demonstrating, then by getting his students to repeat, but Marius found it hard to focus on the positions.

His fight with Yuri the night before was a nuisance, Marius thought, it irritated him that he would even have to try to convince Yuri out of attempting to go back to the ruins.

Yuri had joined the line at the opposite end by Clive and Daniel; the complete opposite side Marius was on. Marius didn't understand this—why was he so mad? To be honest, he thought it was childlike, but still, Yuri was his friend, and it bothered him much to be quarrelling. *Maybe I had said something wrong.*

Every so often Marius would look down to end of the line and gaze at Yuri. Macaro would notice Marius break his posturing, and just the Elder's simple gaze told Marius enough and to perfect his form. *Lift your left leg, step out to the side, extend your arm, step back,* Marius said the sequence of steps in his head, trying to focus on the task at hand, but every so often his mind would slip and he would find himself thinking of Yuri again. *Dammit,* he thought to himself, Yuri was plainly being stupid and he shouldn't be this distracted by it. Forcing himself to forget about Yuri, he again focused on his forms and movements.

Days past, but Yuri and Marius had still not reconciled. One brisk morning, where the clouds drew long foggy strips in the sky, Macaro had called for a morning class on the cliff side. Yuri had not shown to the class. *Not good,* Marius thought to himself, seeing his friend's absence among the students. When everyone lined up as usual for a morning class, Marius could tell Macaro had noticed Yuri's absence immediately.

"Everyone, good morning," Macaro said slightly bowing. "Has anyone seen our friend Yuri? It's not like him to be late."

The rest of class shrugged and Marius could hear Clive say, "I saw him last night," like what he said had provided insight.

"Well, I'm sure he will show up," Marius found himself blurting out loud.

Macaro gave him an odd stare, but then dropped the subject and started teaching another lesson on using water to disable an opponent. When Macaro had called for them to partner with someone, Marius quickly grabbed Cynthia.

"I said to Clive I'd help him with energy work, the other day," Cynthia said as Marius pulled her over.

"Well, you're with me today," Marius said with a laugh, but to him it wasn't a joke.

"Ok then," Cynthia said somewhat understanding, with a look over at Clive who was now partnering with Reggard. Cynthia walked with Marius slightly away from the group so they couldn't be heard.

"Why are we training over here?" Cynthia asked puzzled.

"I need to talk to you."

"Oh, well then, let's."

Marius could tell Cynthia was worried, but not for the reason of Yuri's absence.

Anxiously Cynthia began sputtering, "The other night if—"

But Marius cut her off immediately. "No, it's about Yuri."

The splashing of water and grunts of students echoed with the shoreline breeze a few feet away.

Cynthia looked around to see if anyone was listening, and then spoke in a low voice, "Why isn't he here?" she asked.

"The exact reason, I don't know, but the reason I think isn't good."

"Well what's the reason you think?"

Suddenly Macaro was walking by, so Cynthia raised her hands and blasted Marius with a wave of water, knocking him off his feet.

"Good job, Cynthia," Macaro stated, "but Marius that could have been an easy block, just manipulate fire or air and the water she sent would've turned to steam."

Marius frowned at Cynthia while he lay on the rocky surface and Macaro stepped away.

Getting up, he continued, "Next time we need a signal, and anyways the other night Yuri and I fought."

"You two have seemed weird the last few days."

"It wasn't just a little quarrel, he started talking about how he wanted to go investigate the ruins again, something about how he thought it was his way of completing the fourth task."

"So, you're telling me you think he might be on his way there now?"

"Possibly," he answered.

"Highly possible," Cynthia said, agreeing.

They gave each other a long, worried stare, but before they could continue talking, Macaro ordered his students to circle around him for a demonstration.

It felt like the class went on for hours, and as the morning whipped by Marius found himself constantly looking over his shoulder hoping Yuri would appear. Eventually Macaro ended the lesson on energy work and took the class for a gruelling run along the cold, rocky, cliff coast of Highwash.

After visiting the bathhouse Marius ventured to the outskirts of Highwash where Yuri's quarters were. Not even waiting to knock, Marius opened Yuri's hut door, revealing nothing but Yuri's empty cot.

"Shit," Marius said out loud. *This wasn't good.*

By midday no one had heard anything about Yuri. Cynthia had searched the coastline, while Marius searched through the library, Mirane's quarters and even the kitchen. But Yuri was nowhere to be seen. After searching, Marius waited for Cynthia by the main hall. They had promised each other that they would wait for one another to finish searching. It was getting cold as Marius waited there, his bum finding the rock he sat on damp and unpleasurable.

"Marius, how are you?" Marius looked up to see Macaro approaching him, his bald head gleaming in the sunlight. But before Marius could answer, another voice piped up from behind Macaro.

"Macaro! Macaro! I've been looking for you since this morning."

It was Talun, the horse master, he looked awfully distressed, his long locks of grey hair hadn't been kept, and his face looked scrunched with worry. Marius thought it was odd to see him by the main hall, Talun rarely ventured far from his horses.

"Good afternoon, Talun," Macaro said bowing. "What may be the problem?"

Talun began rambling faster than a fly. "It's my sweet Stanford! He's missing, there's no way he would have taken off, Macaro, Stanford loves his combing, he wouldn't have taken off—"

"Let me guess, Talun, another horse has escaped. No worries, I'll send some of my older students on a search."

But Talun wasn't relieved with that answer.

"Stanford would never have left!" he hollered. "He was thieved, I promise you, Macaro, he was thieved, it must have been one of your nasty students, or the mean ol' bugger, Ralis! Oh,

Stanford, he needs his combing, Macaro." As Talun wallowed he visibly became more and more distressed.

"Either way I will still send a search party to find… your Stanford. But I'm sure it wasn't one of my students, there would be no need for them to take your horse, and Ralis hasn't been seen in the village since the beginning of fall, so I doubt it was him," Macaro said calmly trying to soothe Talun's worries.

By the time Macaro had convinced Talun to stop fretting and that he'd find his horse Marius was long gone.

How curious, Macaro thought.

"That idiot!" Marius found himself barking at Cynthia in her quarters. "How stupid is he? He stole a fucking horse! I told him 'Don't go.' He is going to get banished, maybe even wind up dead." Marius lay on Cynthia's bed ranting, while she paced back and forth from wall to wall in her quarters.

"May you please calm down, Marius, I'm sure it was just a coincidence."

"You're not understanding, Cynthia, you didn't see how determined he looked, how determined he sounded."

"Are you certain he's headed there?" Cynthia asked, locking eyes with Marius.

"Yes, I'm certain, I know Yuri."

Marius sat up and sighed, worried about his friend. They both stood in silence for a long time neither of them saying a word. In the quiet Marius could hear his thoughts, and he knew what he would have to do.

"I have to go get him." Marius finally said breaking the silence.

"You cannot be serious, Marius. You're going to get banished, too," Cynthia stated, her face in shock.

"It doesn't matter the consequences, I have to go, his life is at stake and I can't stay here knowing I let him go."

"Yuri makes his own choices, Marius."

"And so do I," Marius said, standing. He stood slightly above Cynthia, her eyes showed sadness to the prospect or even the slightest idea of losing two of her friends.

As he started to leave Cynthia grabbed him by the arm. "Well then I'm coming, too," she proposed, stomping.

He turned to look at her. "No. No you're not. You don't know what lies there. Last time I almost lost Yuri, and I'm not losing you. But I am going to need your help to get there."

In her eyes a deep anger and sadness fumed but she couldn't refuse, and Marius was right, "What do you want from me then?"

"I need a horse."

They concocted a jury-rigged plan to steal a horse from Talun. He wouldn't be happy, considering Yuri had just stolen one, but they didn't have a choice. Yuri was almost a day's ride ahead, and Marius would need a horse to reach him in time.

It was the peak of the afternoon. The brisk air blew eastward at their backs as they headed to Talun's stables. His stables were composed of two buildings on the outskirts of the village; one his home, which looked a hundred years old, with wooden panels falling off the side, the second was a large open stable that housed the dozen horses he'd raised over the years.

No one knew how long Talun had resided in Highwash, but it was said that he was here before Mages had even arrived on the western coast. He certainly looked the part, with a balding grey head of hair and a wiry beard to match he looked almost ghostly. But most times, despite his rough appearances, he always held a smile.

As they approached his stables, both of them felt slightly guilty of what they were about to do. Talun stood in the under crop of the stables, combing the auburn hair of a large stallion. Marius waited off at the side in the cover of a large nestle bush while Cynthia walked onward. When he saw her approach, Talun smiled.

"What's ought to bring you here?" he asked.

Cynthia began to speak, "Some others of the search party and I would like a description of your horse. So, I asked to come see if you would like to share."

Instantly Talun looked chided. "His name is Stanford." Not part of the plan.

"Yes, well, Stanford, we need a description to find him."

Marius could see in the distance that Talun had agreed, not enthusiastically, but still he agreed to go. Now for his part of the plan.

When the coast was clear, Marius, remaining crouched, hastily snuck over to the under crop of the stables. There was a lot to choose from, a large black female, a couple brown males, it made Marius wish Ralis taught him how to communicate to animals. He could hear Ralis' voice echo in his head as he chose a horse, *I can't teach how to be friends with animals, that's something you teach yourself, but I can direct you on the right path. Start with not viewing them as animals.*

Unlocking the hatch and opening the half door, Marius entered into a large auburn mare's pen. The horse shook its head back and forth, obviously displeased by the unexpected company.

"It's ok, it's ok, little buddy," Marius whispered as he stroked the horse's side.

The animal calmed with his touch. Marius quickly strapped a saddle on its back, wasting no time. Grabbing the tethers, he began to lead it out of its pen, but the mare pulled back, reluctant.

"Come on, buddy, we're going for a ride," Marius said, pulling harder.

Realizing she was free, the horse left and trotted at Marius' side. Hopping on the horse, Marius squeezed his thighs signalling her to canter and then roar into a gallop. Dust kicked up and the row-style stables disappeared in the background.

"We will call you... Marrow, yea, Marrow," Marius said to the horse. His destination was east and he hoped he remembered the way.

"She tricked me!" Talun screamed at Macaro while Cynthia stood at his side, awkwardly ashamed. "She tricked me, while one of your students stole my sweet Hamilton." Talun looked like he would almost break out into a bawl at any point.

"I would like to believe that's not the case, Talun," Macaro said, giving a sideways glance at Cynthia. "But I will speak to Cynthia here and get the truth. I will come to you in a moment, my friend."

Talun stormed off, fuming, but nonetheless what could he do? Macaro's word was always enough.

Macaro turned to Cynthia, his face was straight and strict. "What are they up to?"

Cynthia had no idea what to say. A few sputtered sentences came out as she stumbled out her words.

"Talun has been a good friend of ours for a long time, I'd hate to see him disrespected like this. So, please, tell me what they're up to."

Gazing at the ground Cynthia knew there was no way to avoid Macaro's all-seeing eyes. By the time his hand had reached her forehead she knew he would have already seen everything.

"So, that's where they're headed," Macaro said commenting on Cynthia's thoughts.

At once Cynthia cried out, "It wasn't Marius' idea, Yuri had stolen a horse to go to the ruins." She was frantic, but Macaro put his hand gently on her shoulder, hushing her.

"I know, Cynthia. It wasn't his fault and he did the right thing. He should've come to me, but I see his point of view." Macaro shook his head as he spoke. "Well, come with me, Cynthia," Macaro said as he started to walk away.

Confused, Cynthia followed behind. "Where to?"

"Well, I'm going to have to ask Talun to lend me a horse, and I'd like you to watch me suffer."

The frostbitten ground broke off in chunks as Marrow pounded her feet forward. Marius squeezed his thighs, signalling the horse to push onward. His inner thighs ached from the hard riding but Yuri would be well ahead.

The eastern trail was long before it came upon the forest's edge, but on horseback the ride would only take half a week. As Marius rode, he followed what he believed to be the prints of the horse Yuri had ridden, the obvious indentations freshly marking the trail. *If anyone followed, the route we took is blatant for them to see*, Marius thought to himself as he looked back behind him to see his own trail of prints forming. He wondered how far ahead Yuri was and if he would catch him soon. The sooner Marius found him, the quicker they would get back to Highwash without anyone noticing their absence.

Almost a week later, Marius had reached the edge of the forest, the dark green waves of trees before him climbed up the slope towards the harsh mountain peaks covered in a thick layer of clouds. The forest looked endless and grim, a part of him barely wanted to step inside again knowing the toilsome trails.

Marius looked back in despair towards the rolling fields of Highwash, he had hoped to catch up to Yuri before the forest line. He had hoped he wouldn't have to enter the forest. Maybe he'd stumble on Ralis, he thought with a warm feeling filling him;

maybe he would stumble into Nathaniel, the thought of that provided no warmth.

Thoughts rushed into his head, *Nathaniel had wanted me to accompany him to the ruins before he left Highwash.* The question had creeped Marius out, and now he worried deeply for what his friend could be walking into. Standing outside the forest's edge, Marius knew he needed to make a decision. And he needed to hurry.

Inside the forest it was cold and dark, the canopy of great fir and pine trees loomed overhead, casting their ominous shadows. It was near evening and the light made the forest swim with ghosts. The slope steepened instantly, and Marrow started to shake her head in displeasure. But, with Marius nudging her on with the tethers, she started to climb up the slope.

Eventually the horse became too disagreeable and Marius had to turn to find a route less steep. He rode until nightfall, up the course of a meandering stream only a few brisk strides wide. By the looks of it, Yuri had followed the same stream up into the mountains. Many branches were snapped along the path up and tracks could be seen following the trail. He eventually found a gentle spot among the streambed to lie, while Marrow lapped up water from the stream. The spot was restive enough, but in Marius' frantic departure earlier, he had completely forgotten to bring supplies. He hoped Yuri had brought more than he had.

He remembered the last time they'd come this way as he lay there in the dark, listening to Marrow's slurps. It was a treacherous journey on foot, but on horseback it wasn't so bad. After having some water himself, Marius cuddled up next to Marrow.

"You're becoming quite a good companion," Marius said rubbing the horse. "I hope Talun isn't too mad I borrowed you."

The next day Marius started at sunrise. Riding Marrow to a trot he made his way up the stream by midday, eventually it led to a small cut-out cliff. Water sputtered off its roof, forming the stream Marius had followed, and small trees clung onto the cliff side for life.

He was way higher in the mountains now, but the cliff had cut off his path. Dismounting, he searched the area for tracks or signs of where Yuri was headed. The lower portion of the cliff showed no signs of his friend, and climbing up to the high portion served useless as well. He had lost Yuri's trail, but he still knew where he was headed.

From what he remembered, Ralis had led them to this stream for water. They hadn't come up as far, but Marius thought that if he followed the ridge northeast he might catch a lead.

Marius climbed through the branches of a greyish pine that hung over the cliff; below him he could see Marrow drinking from the streamside. Jumping down into the streambed, Marius jumped on Marrow and started following the cliff line.

For a while it led nowhere, Marius just followed what seem to be a never-ending ridge of broken granite. Sometimes the path would narrow and pin Marius between the hard face of rock and the lashes of fine branches, forcing him to dismount and lead Marrow through on foot. It was hard to travel through the forest with such a cumbersome mare, it had saved time getting to it, but proved a nasty encumbrance once inside.

Pulling at the tethers, Marrow argued with neighs and complained with spit.

"Come on, you nast!" Marius grunted, pulling back on the tethers and forcing the horse through thickets of bush.

Hours went by, but finally Marius wrenched Marrow and himself free from the bushes' tendrils. He found himself in a flatter, higher portion of the forest where the ground sloped upward softly. Wiping himself free of leaves and thorns, he could see he had climbed up beyond the cliff face. It seemed he still had an hour or two of daylight left, but in the thick of the forest Marius couldn't get a clear sight on the sun. He decided to move on, he needed haste. So, mounting Marrow, he continued up the slope.

The forest darkened quickly before Marius had made it far, but he didn't want to wait until sunrise to continue forward.

He doubted Yuri would wait just because of nightfall, but riding his horse would prove risky and he didn't want to risk the horse tripping in the dark. So Marius led the mare to a soft outcrop of ground among the trees and tied her tethers to the trunk of a tree.

"You stay here for a little bit, I'll come back quickly," Marius whispered to the horse while stroking her gorgeous, auburn mane. Marrow looked oddly stressed to be alone, but she still circled and nestled herself among the needles and leaves on the ground. Making a mental note of where he'd hoisted Marrow, Marius headed off, vowing not to travel too far away.

The darkness of the forest curdled like webs of black milk. Shapes made faces out of the darkness and Marius found himself awfully afraid to travel the forest at night. He didn't have Ralis' cat eyes either, so, in fear, Marius scampered across the ground grabbing dry sticks and tinder and lit it on fire making himself a makeshift torch. It offered little relief from the dark, lighting only a foot of distance in front of him, but still Marius felt relieved. Memories shot forward in his mind like daggers: the wolf's claws and teeth, and the bite that grimaced Marius' shoulder and the way it snuck up onto Marius, silent and undetected. Wary from the wolf attack, Marius now listened and heard. The forest night was always awfully silent, issuing nothing but the faintest of ruffles or dribbles, always leaving the hearer in a state of constant question, *Did I hear that or not?* But Marius' ears were trained from hours of meditation and this time not a noise would escape him.

He continued on for a bit up the slope, stomping into the ground every so often, or scarring the bark of a lone tree to mark his way back. *Marrow is probably getting lonely, and probably a bit hungry as well*, Marius thought to himself, debating whether or not to turn back or continue up the hill a bit longer.

He stood still for a second, his legs wanting to turn back around, but suddenly a whinny called out in the forest.

Marrow! Marius immediately thought, but right before he turned around another whinny called. *It wasn't Marrow, no,*

Marrow was whinier and shriller, and the noise came from up hill, Marrow was tied downhill.

Bolting through the forest with his torch in hand, Marius ran uphill. Whatever was making the noise neighed once or twice more but then went coldly silent. Pausing, Marius hushed his own panting, he needed to listen, he needed to hear whatever made the noise.

Crunch, crunch, snap.

Marius could hear the faintest crunching noises to his left. Snuffing out his flame, Marius crouched and started left, weaving his way through bush and scrub. Marius moved slowly towards the noises, crouched and silent, every step he made was perfect and cautious. As he drew closer, the noises became louder and clearer. It was definitely crunching, Marius thought agreeing with his ears.

Snap

Fuck, Marius thought as he stepped on a branch; the noise he made was indefinitely audible for the creatures of the night. The forest answered in silence, even the crunching had stopped suddenly.

Slowly, with his heart racing, Marius exited the bush he was entangled in and entered a large clearing surrounded by pines and oaks. Lighting a flame in his hand the forest came to life, the trees stood tall, and in the centre of the clearing a horse lay on its side. *A horse?* Marius thought to himself as he investigated the clearing. He could see the tethers of the horse had been torn, as if the beast had tried to escape from something, and its abdomen was ripped open to reveal its internal flesh. Even the ribs of the horse had been pried back.

Marius knelt down to get a closer look. He could feel the warmth of the dead creature. Dipping his finger in the wound, his thoughts were confirmed: the blood was warm and fluid. The horse had been killed recently. *This was some thing's dinner.* Marius thought to himself as he looked around the clearing.

Suddenly Marius knew what the crunching noise was. *If this was some thing's dinner, the noise must have been that something feasting.* Marius' thoughts were cold but accurate. He needed to move, and now, he thought, slowly standing up away from the broken horse. Whatever that had attacked this horse had fled upon hearing Marius, either out of fear, or out of deception. The idea of the alternative shot a cold fear up Marius' spine.

Creak.

His head twitched to the faint noise, but it was too late—the creature had fled out of deception. Turning, Marius came face to face with the ugliest of creatures he had ever seen.

Lit by the dim fire in his palm, Marius could see it. It bore scales black as night, held a long large lizard-like body, wore wings like charred leather that swooped across its back and had three long whip-like tails that extended off its back. Its jaw was long and narrow like a dog's, but, despite being covered in slobber like a hound, the creature was covered in fresh blood. Its hiss was deep throated, and as it reared its back legs Marius could clearly make out its size. The creature was massive—almost as large as a thick brown bear but clearly more nimble. All of his thoughts came together at once, and Marius suddenly knew what this was. It was a manticore, a male manticore.

Almost instinctively Marius held out both of his hands and soaked the creature in fire. The manticore hissed and backed away from the stream of flames, but it clearly wasn't afraid by the show. Immediately it responded by jumping to the side and sending out lashes with its long, barbed tails. Marius ducked and spun back, dodging the long tails, but as soon as he landed, everything went dark with his flames out. In the pitch of black he could hear the manticore's hiss but not its footsteps.

Suddenly he felt the slam of flesh and claw smash his chest and he was flying backwards into a bush, and then he was tumbling down. It took him a second after he bounced up to realize he had fallen down a slope. It was pitch black, and his head now ached; all he could hear was the manticore's deep hiss drawing closer. *It pushed me down here purposefully,* Marius thought, *to disorient me.*

He could feel the gnarl the creature's claws had made in his chest, and now his robes started to soak in blood. Listening to the approach of the hiss, Marius thought of Macaro's words, and Marius said to himself, *I choose to live.*

Darkness ushered itself all around Yuri; he had forgotten how dark this place had been. And now, without Nathaniel's Mage lights, he felt lost without clear direction. His old wounds on his side ached in fear, remembering the place.

Yuri felt the walls with his hand as he walked on. One hand on the stone wall, the other hand holding a ball of fire to light his way. This time the journey in the ruins brought Yuri a deeper appreciation of the walls here. The walls were cut so smooth not even the softness of his fingers found them rough. Last time he had journeyed here with Ralis and Marius he felt such a sense of awe, now, alone in the ruins, he felt a sense of despair and coldness, the place didn't feel right.

The old ruins twisted and turned, sometimes it would lead into a black chasm of a great empty hall of the past, or sometimes the hallways would trick you and run circles that led back to where you'd come from. Nothing seemed like what he had remembered from last time.

It was all about finding the hallway where the floor broke off into the caverns. He remembered Nathaniel guiding Marius, Ralis and him to the opening, but he couldn't remember the exact route. His only hope would be scouring the ruins for the opening.

After what seemed like endless twists and turns, Yuri finally came across a narrow pathway where the floor broke from underneath him. Looking down into the chasm where the floor broke off he could make out the old block of flooring that once stood, but now lay at an angle, leading down into the caverns. The darkness grew even blacker as Yuri stepped down on the broken, tilted floor into the tunnel below; even the darkness seemed to eat at the ball of fire in his hand. At first the path narrowed and Yuri could clearly see the stripes of sediments on the damp walls of dirt. Snuffing out his flame, Yuri crouched in the darkness, feeling the dirt wall with his hand, and his other hand went to the vial in his pocket.

Yuri had read much about starting fires and creating devilish concoctions from his time spent reading in the library. He had asked Cynthia and Marius to research about the ruins, but Yuri had spent time researching on this.

In his hand he held the vial, getting it ready to use. Inside the vial was a hellish mix of liquids Yuri had stolen from the alchemy section in the library, a little bit of the "black shit" and a sprinkle of a powder and Yuri had successfully created his first flammable bomb which, once lit, would *hopefully* explode in flames.

He ventured forth slowly and cautiously, his thumb running circles over the vial's lid. Eventually the hallway split into an open chasm of a room. Yuri could feel the damp air, and, without his sight, the cold feelings of fear crept up his spine. But he calmed his breath and moved forward, ever present and ever listening.

His feet moved slowly and sure in the dark, he couldn't dare make a noise. Old wounds made reminiscent whispers at his side, the shocks of pain reminded him of what had happened here before. This time would be different, Yuri thought.

Oof.

Suddenly he smacked head first into a large, wet object, in shock he jumped back, reeling.

Ding.

The sound echoed like a wave in the emptiness of the black and he quickly realized he'd dropped the vial. He scrambled to pick it up but it was too late, the floor had a slight slant downwards and away the vial went, rolling.

Shit, Yuri said to himself as he stood there, crouched frozen in fear. *What did I stumble into?* he asked himself as he wiped off a hand on his robes, still wet from whatever it was.

He didn't want to do it, but he found himself doing it anyways, raising his hand, a slow ember lit in his palm and the warmth of the light revealed his surroundings. In front of him was a large, decomposing body of what looked like a dog-sized insectoid creature. The same type of creature that had attacked Marius and Yuri before, but this time just its rotting corpse covered in blood, and the kill looked not too old as well.

Slowly standing up, allowing the flame to grow in his hand, the light spread further unveiling what was once covered in darkness. Around and in front of Yuri was not just one decomposing insect, but several, all sprawled across the room, some ripped open and some just frozen, decaying without the look of a single wound.

What had become of this place? Yuri asked himself. Even though the dead creatures had almost killed Yuri at one time he couldn't help but feel a sense of despair for them. Whatever had wiped them out had not known mercy. Softly he stepped forward, over and around the dead; oddly, the corpses gave no smell of rotting.

As he walked on, he scanned the floor for the vial, but it had rolled off and disappeared in the vast chamber. It seemed he no longer needed it, Yuri thought, feeling relieved. Now all he had to do was find whatever Nathaniel had wanted here. Images conjured in his head of what it would be—a crystal chalice, a necklace of gold, or an ancient text—all the possibilities ran through his mind, even the thought of glory he would receive at home from finding such a miracle crossed his mind. He just had to find it, that's all, and he believed he would know what it was when he saw it.

Stepping between corpses and stone, Yuri ventured further into the black of the chamber, it seemed to go on forever, nothing but a black void to swallow victims whole.

Suddenly he froze, he could hear a soft faint breathing in the silence of the cave and it was ever so soft, so soft Yuri could hardly tell if he was even hearing it. He needed to see. With an ounce of courage he relit the flames in his palm and held up his hand to serve as a light. Against the warmth of light stood a black silhouette of a human in the distance. At first the figure was unrecognizable, but Yuri swiftly realized who owned the long braided hair and tall figure.

"Nathaniel?" Yuri asked in a hushed voice, oddly afraid.

The figure didn't stir, but Yuri could sense it had heard.

"No, not Nathaniel. The last echoes of him died long ago, now what you see is nothing but a shell." Nathaniel didn't move as he spoke, but stood there, statuesque, with his back to Yuri.

"What? What are you doing here?" Yuri asked. His voice quaked slightly with shivers, his body frozen in fear.

Nathaniel ignored Yuri's question and just continued his rant, "A useless shell, trapped, and stumbling."

Yuri could see Nathaniel raise his hand, giving his palm a stare.

"He held for a while, yes, yes, he did, but he doesn't serve my needs anymore."

Nathaniel slowly turned and started walking towards Yuri, his gaze was penetrating and chilled Yuri to the bone. "But, fortunately for me, you have come, child, you shall now serve my purpose like you were meant to."

Nathaniel's gaze did not drop for a second as he came towards Yuri. Yuri felt frozen, stuck in the gaze, no matter how badly he wanted to back away and run, he couldn't.

Afraid, Yuri began to yell, "I'm not doing shit, let me go!"

But it was too late, Nathaniel was before him, placing his palm on Yuri's forehead. All went dark, Yuri could hear nothing but Nathaniel's voice.

"Let you go? You chose to come here. I called to you, remember? In your dreams."

Yuri was nowhere, but everywhere, floating in a void of blackness, his whole body felt weightless but his head hurt like an iron was being driven into his skull.

"You chose to seek me out, though I must say you were always powerless in the end, and now you shall serve my purpose."

No! Yuri wanted to scream, but his voice couldn't find itself. Now he was walking, dragging his legs, step after step deeper into the caves. His mind was a blur and his body was just doing, as if he had no control over his limbs at all. Step after step. He tried to resist but it was futile.

AHHHHHHHHHHH! Yuri screamed inside his mind. Nathaniel was in control of him. And the feeling of not having control over one's self, over one's emotions, over one's life, brought Yuri to the brink of emotional collapse. He would not have it. Nathaniel would not control him, just like Marius or Macaro could not control him. Yuri was the fire, and the fire you don't control.

Raggggh! Inside his mind he raged and pulled and broke.

He was there, whole again standing in the caves. Nathaniel stood before him, smiling.

"We do this the hard way. I shall break you then."

Inside Nathaniel's eyes was nothing but the glow of malice.

Marius was afraid. Macaro had seriously ill-described the speed and ferocity of a manticore in his lesson. This was nothing like fighting the wolf, nor anything similar to facing Mathius. None of Marius' sparring practices would assist him either. The manticore moved demonically fast, moving possessed, focused solely on the prey that stood before it, and in the dark Marius had hardly a moment of time to dodge its attacks.

Marius leapt back, the swoosh of the claws rang in the dark, signalling its coming, and then he ducked to the whizzing whip of the creature's barbed tails nearly striking him overhead. Marius had barely time to think before he was dodging the next oncoming sound. In the black of night he often lost his footing, slipping on loose stones or fallen branches, but with all of his might he made sure he would not fall. One misstep—any chance for the manticore to pounce—and Marius was sure as dead.

Lightning! Marius heard in the back of his mind, and with the thought he held his hand out swiftly. Summoning the energy from within his centre, he drew it forth into his hand and shot forth a wicked blast of blue lightning bolts. The bolts whipped ferociously, zapping the manticore; it screeched in pain. The flash of light Marius had created quickly disappeared and the manticore was no longer visible.

Marius listened as deep as he could, he could hear the hiss of its growl, the light steps amongst the leaves, the pound of the creature's heart. The lightning had not done much other than anger the creature more. Marius stood in fear for a second, a cold sweat dampening his neck.

He had tried every trick he knew—lightning, fire—nothing seemed to scare the beast off, and Marius would need to be able to see to face the creature head on.

Suddenly noise from the creature disappeared, and Marius stood frozen, unable to pinpoint the creatures location in the black of night. His ears betraying him, Marius was unexpectedly smashed in the chest by a kick from the manticore's hind legs. It sent him launching back into what felt like a thick tree, the bark of the tree smashed as hard as rock would and Marius slumped to the ground. The hit was unforgiving. Macaro was right, these creatures were intelligent, it had figured out Marius was relying on sound to predict its movements, so in response it had slowed its breath and quieted its steps.

Jaws suddenly gnashed, but Marius reached out, grabbing the creature's pair of massive, slobbering and snapping jaws and preventing them from closing around his chest. The warmth of the creature's breath wafted in Marius' face, the smell was putrid and vile, smelling of old decaying meat and plaque. Quickly lighting his hand in a ball of flames, he sent his arm deep into the throat of the creature and blasted forth his flames into the monster's insides.

Marius could hear the creature hurdle back and spin, yelping in pain. It whipped its massive torso back in place to face Marius, and, with a giant roar, the manticore charged straight at him. Just in time Marius leapt out of the way, landing with a roll onto his feet. The tree had a less fortunate fate and was left with a giant gnash in its bark.

The manticore was already on Marius, its tails whipped and caught Marius in the thigh as he stumbled away. The barbs caught the skin under Marius' robes, and when the manticore pulled back it ripped pieces of his skin right out with its nasty barbed hooks. Marius fell forward in pain, but caught himself with his hands. And, just as swiftly as the barbs, a claw lashed out and connected with Marius' face, sending him flying to the side.

Marius felt his face as he lay on his stomach, the wetness of the leaves now soaking into his already bloodied robes. As his hand felt his face and the slash across his right cheek, he shook terribly. How was he to fight a foe he could not see?

Stop trying to see with your eyes. Lessons of Ralis' from long ago echoed in his head as he stood up from the ground. His feet were suddenly taken from under him as the creature's tails smashed them, sending him into the ground once again.

Now it seemed like the creature was just toying with its prey.

Lying in pain, wet with blood, his face and body screeching, Marius started to wonder grim thoughts. *Is this how I die?* he asked himself. A sudden calmness overcame him and all stood still. In that moment all became clear, all of Macaro's lessons came to make sense. A Mage was meant to die, for his friends, for those suffering, for his Elders, for the world; and the purpose of a Mage was to accept this, accept that your life was for death and you would do all you could to protect others—even if that meant your own demise. That was why they were never allowed to know their own family;

the whole world was their family, all of them to be protected. That was where a Mage found their power: in the act of compassion, in facing their death everyday, facing it with strength, facing it with all of their fight, leaving none behind. Marius would do all he could to save Yuri, not for his own purpose but for the purpose of compassion and the love of the living.

And as Marius stood up, the manticore before him, hissing ready to pounce, he could hear Ralis' words. *If you truly want to see, close your eyes.* And it was as if in that moment he understood what Ralis had meant. *Stop trying to see what you cannot see.*

Coming to a crouch, Marius started to close his eyes and calm his breath. Around him was nothing but blackness and cold air, drafty, moist and clean. The noise of the manticore hissing echoed in the air, reverberating and vibrating. Vibrating.

Vibration.

It began to feel like the vibration he felt during the first task—a slow hum, a vibration of the air around him—but this time it was slower, deeper and more resonate, the cold winter air being less energetic than the summer heat. Marius began to stand. He couldn't see, no, but he could now feel. And what he felt was the world around him—the heat emanating off trees, the heat of life, the manticore's breath, its rhythm of breathing, and the hiss pulsing through the air.

As Marius stood the manticore lunged, its claws out to strike the killing blow, but this time Marius didn't move frantically, there was no need, Marius could feel every movement the manticore made as waves in the air, vibrating against his skin.

Stepping to the side, the manticore flailed, missing its target. As it twisted, spun and launched again, its razor claws poised for Marius' flesh, Marius spun around the lunge and smashed the manticore's face with a powerful blow with his fist. The beast rolled against the ground and flung itself up standing, wasting no time to pounce again. This time Marius charged his fist with energy and smashed the beast's chest as it leapt for his throat.

They both flew back, creature and Marius, into the ground. Marius had underestimated the beast's weight and was sent flying as a result. Flipping up onto his feet, he calmed his breath and focused again. The manticore reared on its legs, hissing. In waves of reddened heat, Marius could feel its musculature flex against the ground, its legs preparing to pounce.

Nothing seemed to deter the beast, and the two of them battled on in the dark of the forest, the creature clawed and whipped its barbed tails at Marius while Marius pounded the beast with fists and kicks and scorched the beast with fire. But the beast's will was impregnable and it would not stop. The vile creature wanted a bloodbath. Marius remembered Clive talking about the creatures often after his first encounter, he'd stated manticore's fight to the death over territory and mates, but Marius was neither of those.

The soft murmur of rain began to fall around the two opponents, its wetness coating both of them in a sheen of cold. Marius disliked the idea of killing the manticore, plus he even wondered what it would take to kill it, but if that were what it would take, he would have to do what was necessary. His life and Yuri's were at stake.

The manticore's tails slashed the ground, taunting Marius as they circled each other in the small clearing of the v-shaped ravine.

Now, more aware of his surroundings, Marius could feel the cold, hard blocks of marble that sat alone at the side of the clearing and the array of trees at either side of them.

The manticore made the first move to attack, lunging at him, but as Marius stepped left to evade the attack, it feinted at the last moment and leapt left at Marius. Caught off guard, the manticore's massive claws took chunks out of his chest and sent him flying back.

The speed of the creature was bizarre, even Marius, a trained Mage, had a hard time dodging such attacks. It felt as if time had slowed down. He lay on the ground, blood soaked, when the manticore leapt on top of him. He could see its massive jaws drooling before his flesh, the rear of the manticore's head before it came for a bite on his throat. But suddenly, before the manticore's mouth made contact with his flesh, his fist was launching up and smashing the manticore in the throat with a blow that sent it flying back, wriggling on the ground in pain.

It had felt as if he had not moved his limb but as if an alien force had done it for him, or his body moved with its own mind. Marius stood quickly, his chest felt like waves of fire and anguish, hindering his ability with his left arm. But it didn't matter now.

Before Marius, the manticore rolled on the mucky, wet winter ground, writhing in pain, its wings beating helplessly against the ground. Marius must've broken the creature's trachea. As it cried before him, panicking in pain, Marius felt a tinge of guilt. If he had been able to convince Yuri not to leave, this creature that was once alive and beautiful would still be alive… and beautiful. *If you can call this beautiful,* Marius thought to himself as he saw the beast struggle.

Marius walked over to the struggling beast, charging his fist with energy. He smashed down on the manticore's skull, putting it out of its misery. The beast twitched for a few moments, its hind legs kicking dirt, but then it went limp and lifeless. There was a beauty in death, Marius thought as he observed the serenity on the creature's now broken face.

But the moment was fleeting, pain rushed back to Marius' body, just as quickly as the thoughts of Yuri returned to him. *Where was he now?* The manticore had caught him off guard way earlier and had thrown him down into this dry ravine. But looking around he suddenly realized he recognized the place, the cold marble blocks, the shape of the ravine and the chasm at the end of the clearing.

Running up the ravine, he found what he was looking for. For some reason the skies had chosen a strange guide to lead Marius. Lighting a flame in his hand, Marius could see the black empty chasm held between two jagged cliffs, the moss growing around the rocky entrance, which had broken in years before. It had been a while since Marius had last visited this place.

And so, stepping down into the black of the caves, Marius had reached his destination, and entered the even blacker abyss of the ruins.

The kick felt like it must have shattered his jaw, Yuri thought as he lay on the stone floor. His face ached from the kick.

"That wasn't fair of me was it?" Nathaniel said as he stood there laughing after smashing Yuri with kicks and strikes from the dark. "It seems you'd not put up a fight at all in the dark here. So, why don't I light this place up? You shall then see what fate besets those who ignore my will."

And so, opening his palm, Nathaniel sent four blue balls of light forth. They floated just above their heads, illuminating the chamber that held them.

Yuri looked around the now-illuminated cavern. Hundreds of bodies lay on the floor, the crumpled insects continued on even to where the last rays of light from Nathaniel's light ceased to shine. The bodies looked like they could go on forever, an uncountable amount of corpses lost in the dark. Nathaniel's face was shadowed, grim under the light of his Mage light, as he stood there before Yuri still grimacing on the ground.

"C'mon now, you have a shot, you can see me," Nathaniel said to Yuri, beckoning him to stand and fight.

Frustrated by his beating in the dark, Yuri pounded the ground with his fist and stood swiftly, raising his hands in the air, one fist out and one fist near his face. Taking a step back he entered his stance.

Nathaniel grinned menacingly as he came forward towards Yuri, throwing a strike for Yuri's head. Yuri extended his right arm to parry the blow but the power of it pushed him to the side, forcing him out of his stance. A knee headed for Yuri's torso, but he couldn't parry downwards with his hands fast enough and was smashed in the abdomen by a hard knee. Yuri jerked forward from the power of the blow but Nathaniel caught him square in the face with a strike, and suddenly Yuri was on the ground, his head spinning.

Nathaniel chuckled loud as Yuri gasped for air. Grabbing the back of Yuri's robes, Nathaniel lifted him up and booted him square in the chest, sending Yuri sliding against the stone floor. Coughing up blood in his mouth, Yuri groaned, the last thing he thought he would be doing down here was fighting their Archmage. Even before they had fought, the idea of winning seemed impossible, but now, beaten and bruised on the floor, Yuri thought even the idea of survival seemed bleak.

But that didn't mean he wasn't going to fight.

Leaping up and dodging a kick aimed for his head from Nathaniel, he spun and struck Nathaniel in the back with his heel. Nathaniel twisted around, fast, undeterred by the blow and lashed out a punch at Yuri, easily being parried. But it didn't matter, the strike wasn't the true intention, as Yuri blocked it, Nathaniel struck Yuri's open chest with a stunning punch. Another blur of blows and Yuri found himself on the ground again, crawling in misery.

"My child, so weak, so pitiful," Nathaniel said as he grabbed Yuri from behind and lifted him onto his legs.

Yuri's limp legs could barely hold him, so he slumped as Nathaniel held him by the collar of his robes.

Nathaniel's fist rained down on Yuri's bare face, opening his skin and jarring his skull. Yuri attempted to block a few but his attempts were futile and his arm was smashed away by Nathaniel.

"Disgusting, really, almost saddening, how stupid you are. To come here alone, waltz into my hands so easily, without telling anyone. I mean you made it too easy, Yuri, at least Marius put up some sort of fight, had some kind of intuition."

His eyes focused on Yuri's and Yuri found himself unable to let go of his gaze, unable to stop listening, unable to stop believing.

"No, but you, so stupid, so easily manipulated, I barely had to try to be honest. A couple of dreams and a stupid mortal believes the skies are calling and beckoning you. Remember your teachings, Yuri, dreams can be evil. I said I would break you, and look at you, limp and broken, unable to do anything, no friends, no one coming to save you. Try to resist again and I will break all your bones, blind you and deafen you, and you will still be under my command, still bend to my will, it really is up to you, Yuri how broken do you want to be?"

It felt like a thousand more punches hit Yuri's face, and he could now barley see, his vision becoming a blurred mess.

There, lifeless, hung under Nathaniel's grip, he could see Nathaniel start to raise his hand, the same hand that took over his mind last time.

It was over, Yuri had lost, everything had been forsaken, he had turned his back on his friends. Marius was right, he should never have come here, he should have listened, but now it was too late.

Then, in the moment he was about to give up and let Nathaniel in, out of the corner of his eye Yuri saw a dark figure step into the light of Nathaniel's Mage lights. The figure was dark, angry, bloody and unrecognizable in Yuri's blurry vision. But suddenly it clicked, and under the mask of blood and dirt he knew who it was.

Marius.

It felt as if a thousand soldiers cheered inside of Yuri. Marius didn't hesitate to act and jumped high in the air, striking Nathaniel with a massive kick from both his feet. Nathaniel flew to the side, dropping Yuri, surprised by the unexpected attack. Marius picked up Yuri and stared him straight in the face. Yuri thought Marius looked how he felt—he was covered in blood, bruises and mud, but behind the veil his eyes glowed a fierce rage. A rage that said, *We fight now, here together.* And that was all it took to convince Yuri. A new glow of hope emerged in his chest, he stood up by himself and gathered his breath. Together they would fight Nathaniel.

Opposite to them, Nathaniel stood laughing, his laugh was dark and without joy. His face glowed an ominous blue from his lights.

"Both my prospects come to me. And I was just saying you were smart, Marius—how wrong I could be! Both of you shall be my vessel, I don't mind breaking you both."

Nathaniel came forward, striking. Yuri took one side and Marius took the other, parrying the blows. Nathaniel was fast and could easily deal with the two opponents parrying their strikes. But both of them worked together and smashed Nathaniel in the chest with their elbows. Nathaniel stumbled back, caught himself easily, and was back throwing a combo of kicks at them. Smashing Yuri to the side with a massive kick, Nathaniel quickly separated the two boys. He spun a kick at Marius—which was dodged—then came in for close chops and punches. Marius held him back, blocking the speedy strikes with his elbows and knees. But Nathaniel kept the hammer on him and kept smashing him with punches.

Quickly Marius ducked around Nathaniel's side, but Nathaniel stepped to face him, quick as ever, moving like a blur, his steps and form beyond perfect. Unable to keep up with Nathaniel's pure swiftness, Marius was caught by an elbow to the skull he narrowly blocked. The blow smashed him to the floor but he rolled, avoiding a stomp from Nathaniel, and was up again with Yuri joining at his side.

"This is getting fun," Nathaniel said menacingly as he came forward again.

Every strike, every combo they lashed out, Nathaniel blocked, countered or parried, his skill way beyond both Marius and Yuri's. Every now and then they would land a kick or strike on Nathaniel, but he would soak the hits up like a sponge and continue fighting. While Yuri distracted him, Marius landed a spinning kick right on the square of Nathaniel's chest, sending him crashing backwards into the darkness beyond the light of his now-fading Mage lights.

The room stood silent for a second while Marius and Yuri caught their breath. When Nathaniel returned into the light he appeared different. Blue streaks of light ran courses and webs across his skin, it almost looked as if his skin was tearing apart from underneath, the light coursing up and out of his body. He was completely covered in the lines of light, almost seeming to glow. Though it did not seem pleasurable.

"Enough of this game, I grow weary of it."

Even Nathaniel's voice sounded deeper as he spoke.

This time Nathaniel moved like a blur. He was on them before they could react, throwing strikes and kicks. Marius and Yuri had never felt power like this before, his speed and strength were inhuman, and every blow they blocked broke their stance and sent them astray. They tried to parry, tried to block, but every other strike of Nathaniel's landed. An elbow and three punches crashed into Yuri, then Nathaniel sent one fist launching into Yuri's chest and one into his navel, sending him crashing into the floor. Yuri's gut wrenched from the blow as he gasped for breath, clutching his stomach. His old wound now pierced his side with pain, feeling fresh, as if it had just been reopened.

It was hopeless, even together they couldn't defeat Nathaniel—his power was supernatural, demonic and inhuman.

Looking up as he cringed on the ground, Yuri could see Marius struggle to hold back Nathaniel, as blows pummelled him. Soon Marius was on the ground, struggling, with Nathaniel picking him up by the robes. Pain shot through Yuri, as he struggled to get up—but he couldn't, his body was broken. And as he watched his friend, held by Nathaniel get his face smashed with punches, Yuri felt a wave of despair. Here he was, defeated, lifeless and mistaken, watching his friend die by his own actions. If he had never come here, Marius would never have followed. He felt almost pitiful as he struggled on the ground, unable to help his friend. All he could do was watch as his friend grew more limp by the second.

Smash after smash after smash after smash. Yuri could almost feel Marius' skull crack. *He came for me, despite my... insolence... and now look, I've caused our deaths,* Yuri thought as all hopes of life diminished from his mind.

Nathaniel glanced over to Yuri who watched broken on the floor and dropped Marius who slumped lifelessly on the ground.

"My, my, Yuri, so pitiful enough to just watch your friend be beat," Nathaniel said as he slowly walked over to him, cracking his knuckles.

And as Nathaniel stepped towards him, he saw a glimmer in the corner of his eyes. Looking to see what the glimmer was, all hope remerged in Yuri. In the corner, barely illuminated by Nathaniel's Mage light, was the vial Yuri had brought, now stuck on a massive block of stone.

With all the power and might that remained, Yuri lit his hand on fire. With a scream, he threw the ball of fire at the vial, hoping and praying.

Woof.

The sound of the explosion was deafening as the room was covered in a sunder of heat, fire and rumble. As the whole room was rumbling from the explosion, a large chunk of stone from the ceiling collapsed on top of Nathaniel, crushing him into gristle. As soon as the ceiling above gave way, the whole flooring they stood on dropped, and all of sudden Yuri was sliding downwards, and then falling, mingled with stone and ash and dirt as the floor collapsed underneath him.

His head hurt as he awoke. His whole body ached, his lips were cracked dry and the back of his throat ached. How long he'd been lying there, he didn't know. As he sat up he saw around him a veil of blue light that lit up the room, but he couldn't see where the source emanated from.

What was going on? Who was he? His head was blurred and it hurt to think. And then the memories came rushing in, playing out like clay unknown figures in his mind. He could see a man, a tall man, braids in his hair, he was fighting him with another... another younger man. Yuri.

Suddenly his memories returned to him like a crashing tide and Marius shuttered deep feeling his head. Around him was nothing but stone, large blocks of fallen granite pillars and hunks of marble flooring.

The room was illuminated by a soft, deep, blue light. '*What had happened?* Marius thought suddenly panicking, remembering fighting Nathaniel with Yuri, but his body ached and he could only move so fast. He sat up, groaning, then propped himself up, standing with the use of a block of marble roughly the size of a child. As he sat up, hunks of dust fell off him drifting to the floor.

Standing, the room came to life for Marius. Somehow he was in what look like a massive chasm of a room. The same blue veil of light illuminated all the walls and ceiling, shining light on what looked like intricate drawings. The indentations in the walls and ceiling spread across like an ivory web, some of the carvings detailed animals and men, so well drawn and proportionate, Marius couldn't help but wonder who made them. Gazing above and staring at the drawings, Marius noticed a large section of the ceiling was cut out directly above him. The gash in the ceiling seemed too perfectly placed over where Marius had woken.

Eventually Marius clued in. He had fallen, or the floor broke through when they were fighting Nathaniel, dropping him deeper in the ruins. That would explain his confusion. A blow to the head could have knocked him out for hours. He could be alone; he might even have fallen alone if he had been rendered unconscious during the fight. The thought of that chilled him. The last thing he could remember was Nathaniel grabbing him the rest was a blur.

I could have been crushed by any of them, Marius thought, grateful he wasn't under one of the massive stones. The thought of Yuri entombed by one of the boulders quickly came to Marius' mind, but he pushed it aside as fast as it came. He would search first, the thought of that seemed too rash to believe, however likely it was.

Starting to walk, he stepped over chunks of stone that looked almost like clay. The room was ominously quiet and there was no sign of Yuri. The blue lighting cast long shadows off of awkwardly placed stones and pillars making Marius see ghastly images of Nathaniel. It made him uneasy. Eventually he found his way blocked by a massive block of marble flooring standing as tall as two men. He had to climb it, but his hands were weak and he had a hard time gripping the rough, almost-sheered edges of the stone. Dragging himself up and over the top of the piece of flooring, his hands now bloody and scraped from the stone, the whole of the room revealed itself to Marius.

It was much larger than it had first appeared and much brighter than where Marius had woken. It was half architecture, half nature. Massive rock formations, stalactites and stalagmites mingled in with the perfectly smooth cut walls. The large piece of marble flooring had blocked most of the light in the room and cast a deep blue shadow where Marius had woken, but now standing on the block, Marius could almost barely hold his eyes open.

The origin of the light came from the centre of the room, shining bright blue and white. It was so bright that even when Marius closed his eyes the veil of light shone through his eyelids. It felt like he was dreaming as he stood there, bathed in light. The room almost seemed to hum with the light, as if when the light shone, vibrations came with it. Whatever was casting that light was unknown to Marius, it seemed to just float there without anything holding it upright or anything for it to be perched on. Nothing he had ever seen, studied or heard about matched any description of what he was seeing. It was as if the sun had been placed in the room before Marius. Not a yellow sun, or an orange sun, but a bright blue sun streaming long rays of white light. Large cracks of blue lightning would rip out from the centre of the light every so often, cracking louder than thunder against the stone walls of the chasm.

Cringing as he opened his eyes and covering them the best he could with his hands, he gazed down to observe what would be his climb down. Below him stood a steep slope of tile, flooring and broken rock. He would have to climb down to reach the flatter portion of the room which looked about the centre of the giant chasm he was in. *Where is Yuri?* he wondered. But it was useless to look around from up here, the blinding light was almost impossible to see past.

By the time he was at the bottom of the mound of rock, his hands were blistered and aching, and his shoulders screamed. He almost slipped once or twice, his body barely able to hold on. At the bottom, he turned to face the light again. It was brighter down at the base of the room and Marius had to look up to see it.

Now, closer to the light, whatever it was seemed immense in scale. If this was what Nathaniel had wanted, it seemed he would have had a hard time dragging it out of here. It sat above Marius on a high step of stone tiles. The light was mesmerizing, its blue waves and white streams seemed to call to Marius, and suddenly Marius found that the light was no longer scorching his eyes and he was able to look at it with ease. He found himself staring at the light, mesmerized and walking forward toward it. The beauty of the light seemed to call his name.

Step after step Marius walked forward toward the light, stepping over loose stone and broken tiles.

As he approached the light, he saw something that brought him back to reality, grounding him.

"Yuri?" Marius called out to a solo silhouetted figure standing way before him, closer to the light. The figure turned its head back slightly.

"This is it, Marius. This is what the dreams had shown me."

Waves of memories of the reoccurring dream Marius had had scorched his mind. The light was so similar to his dream, the white light, the blackness, the dark and empty feelings, and the fear. Slowly, Marius stepped towards his friend, his feet having a hard time lifting as he stumbled over loose stone and gravel. Suddenly a tremendous feeling of unease filled Marius.

"Yuri, let's get out of here," he said, instinctively reacting to his fear.

"No, Marius. I understand now, this was what my dreams were showing me," Yuri said solemnly as Marius finally reached where he was standing.

"What are you going on about? We have to get out of here. This isn't right."

With a look of dark malice Yuri turned to look at Marius. His eyes were filled with an unnatural gaze he had never seen in Yuri.

"No, Marius. You've always wanted to stop me, hold me back, stop me from fulfilling my destiny."

"You're obsessed, Yuri!" Marius began to yell, "You're obsessed, just like Nathaniel was. Let's go."

Marius reached out and grabbed Yuri's wrist, but it was a massive mistake. Before Marius could even think to react, Yuri smashed his chest with a blow so hard it sent him flying back a few feet. As Marius struggled on the ground, he could see his friend turn and begin to walk up the large stone steps towards the light. The closer Yuri got, the more often blue streaks of lightning would shoot out from the light. The stone tile floor would explode in shards of rock and dust as the bolts hit them, but Yuri seemed unaffected.

He's going to kill himself, Marius thought, tired of having to save his friend's life. Pushing against the stone floor and hauling himself up, Marius stood and began to run towards Yuri.

The bolts of lightning started to shoot out rapidly, some towards the ceiling, some bolts towards the ground. It seemed whatever was casting the light was reacting to their presence.

Grabbing Yuri by the waist, Marius threw him aside in anger back down the steps. Yuri's body rolled limply down the steps and smashed onto the stone cold floor. Marius wanted to shout at his friend, tell him to stop, tell him let's go home, but suddenly his voice was gone and all went black and dark.

Yuri quickly fell out of his trance. But for him it was too late as well. He lay on the floor, stunned by what he was witnessing, gazing up the stone steps towards the light and his friend. Bolts of energy ripped towards his friend, the crack of the lightning was so loud Yuri's eyes shut forcibly on their own, all around him the room shook with tremors as Marius was bombarded by what looked like a million lightning bolts. His friend was screaming, screaming so loudly that Yuri could hear his cries beyond the cracks of thunder and drum of lightning. And with a massive bang Marius crashed onto the floor, limp and lifeless.

As his friend fell, a wave of energy that felt like it shook the world through rippled past, the light was gone and all fell dark around Yuri. He was alone, lost, hurt and tired. Worst of all, he had killed his friend.

"What have I done?" Yuri said, sobbing in tears. He was manic as he climbed the steps, feeling his way with his hands and his feet. Reaching out with his hands he found Marius' body, and began to sob harder. "No, no, no, Marius, come on, Marius."

Yuri cried as he shook his friend's lifeless body. He felt for Marius' hand and gripped it hard, but it would not grip back, would it ever grip back? Had he killed his friend? The thought left Yuri in despair. There, in the dark, holding his friend's limp hand, Yuri had never felt so cold and so alone.

Marius was floating, where he did not know, but it felt as if he was dreaming. It felt as if he was floating among clouds, but there were no clouds to see. There was nothing to see, only darkness, only the black, even his own limbs were lifeless and colourless. It felt as if he was floating on a rim of water so still and thick that no movements could shake it.

Then, out of the dark, a figure appeared—a figure of a person. It took on all shapes and sizes. The figure felt inhuman but took on the shape of people Marius knew. It looked like Ralis, it looked like Macaro—and even for a second it looked like Yuri—but it was none of them, but all of them. And then laughter, laughter filled with malice, a malice Marius felt in his bones that crawled all the way up from his insides and into his heart. And suddenly all Marius knew was fear.

The figure came forward, walking on what seemed to be nothing but space and air. As the figure came forward, Marius tried to thrash about, tried to escape the grasp of the veil of water that held him, but it was no use, he could not move no matter how hard he tried.

"Marius." The voice was deep and resonant, but held a tone of beauty within it, so soft and perfect was its tone. Once the figure reached him and stood in front of him, Marius could see it more clearly. It looked as if it was all the people he ever knew, all at once, forming and transitioning from face to face until it froze on one face that struck deep in Marius' heart. The face of Cynthia.

"My child, you touch me, fumbling in the dark, fumbling in ignorance, unaware, unheard, unseen. But here I am, and you face me, but yet to live. Nathaniel served his purpose, however nil his purpose was. He broke, broke fast under my grasp. But you—you are strong, stronger than those who touched me before. And that is what I need, strength from a mortal, strength from a being of flesh. Your flesh shall serve me as tools, your mind shall be my weapon, your voice shall be my will."

As the figure of Cynthia spoke, its mouth did not move, as if the words played on their own in Marius' head. Marius could not speak no matter how hard he tried, his mouth was locked, his mind shut from himself.

"Yet still you deny me, yet still you deny powers greater than you've ever known, your ignorance is baffling, your species is lesser than those you worship, than those you know. You play with fire when you tap into the energy of life, you call yourself Mages yet you still live in the dark, unseeing, unknowing. There is a world beyond your own, Marius, and it lies inside you."

Suddenly the figure's hand reached forth and entered into Marius' chest seamlessly, being engulfed by Marius' flesh. "You are mine and always have been and always will be."

Marius had never felt a pain such as this. Suddenly and swiftly his body was scorched with a burn he could not fathom as the figure's hand wrapped around his heart and crushed. He wanted to scream, but no voice came out, only the pain of all his nerves burning at once, like a spider web of fire, burning through his whole body at once. It was as if something was pulling on all his nerves and his brain like chords on a harp.

"Forever we unite, until you serve my purpose."

Then the veil of black was gone and Marius was flying, flying above a world he had never seen. Was this his world? He could see the forests that stretched on, the mountains that bordered the continent, he could see the oceans crash into the cliffs of Highwash, he could see fields of men training. The whole of the earth appeared as a panorama, with every direction Marius turned his head the more he could see.

Suddenly the figure grabbed the back of his skull with a grasp that burned like fire and his view changed. The world he observed twisted and warped, and before Marius were millions dead, thousands of bodies bloody and burned all lying on a field of ash.

"This shall be our work, you and I together, we shall create."

NO! Marius wanted to scream but he couldn't no matter how hard he tried.

In the field of ash lay all of his friends—Mathius, Yuri, Clive, Cynthia, even Macaro—all of them bloody, lying dead, mingling in with the millions of other corpses. He could see a castle, towns, forests and fields, all on fire, all covered in waves of blood, the blood of the dead.

No. No. No. NO!

"Yes," the figure said as if it heard Marius' thoughts.

And suddenly Marius was back in the void, but not himself. As he floated he gazed upon himself, separate from his own body. His mouth opened and filled the place with his own cries as blue light streamed out of all of his orifices. His skin started to rip open, the blue light separated the cells of his skin, and then he exploded in waves of blue and white light. No longer was he there, the earth no longer stood, nothing stood, all went black and all went dark.

All that was left was fear.

Marius awoke to a soft light. He quickly shut his eyes afraid to look where he was.

"He's awake," he heard.

It was voice he recognized, one with a soft and harmonious tone. He heard the sounds of shuffling, a door opening and slamming shut, and then nothing but silence.

Slowly opening his eyes, afraid to see, he felt a wave of relief towards his surroundings. He lay on a soft woollen cot, in what looked like a wooden cottage. A fire burned in the corner of the room under a fireplace. The familiarity of the room made him laugh. The last time he'd been here he'd vowed not to return, but now the scent of dampness and sight of Mirane's messy medical quarters filled him with a gracious happiness.

It wasn't real, he told himself. Beside the cot he was placed on, he saw a small shelf riddled with used stitches, bloody clamps in clay dishes and many folds of bloody bandages and clothes. Quickly he realized the bloody clothes were his robes, and that he was naked under the bed sheets. Filled with joy, he laughed and teared, alone by himself.

Cynthia was the first to visit, and as the door to Mirane's medical hall swung open her beckoning smile greeted him with warmth. She ran across the hall to where he lay and held his hand, staring deep into his eyes. He could see her eyelids rimmed with an outline of tears.

"Once I heard you were up, I came running. You brought him back, Marius, you brought him back," Cynthia said, her voice quaking under her joy.

"I did," Marius stated trying his best to smile back at her.

"It was said you might not make it, your wounds…" Her hand reached out to touch Marius where his chest was exposed and bandaged, but stopped, hesitant to touch him, not wanting to inflict any more pain. Before they could say anymore, the door swung open abruptly again, and Macaro waltzed in with Mirane in tow.

"Thank you, Mirane. You may leave us, as well as you, Cynthia," Macaro said with a sense of foul in his voice for the fact that Cynthia was there.

She left hurriedly behind Mirane, and then it was just Macaro left with Marius.

Macaro stared at him for a long while, his face blank with judgment.

"You two disappoint me often. Knowing Yuri had left, you should've come to me, not run off on your own to be a hero. And now look at the consequences," Macaro said sternly, glancing at the wounds that covered Marius. "Yuri's trial shall be held tonight. Although no student shall attend, I'd thought you would like to know. Your trial shall be tomorrow eve, if you're able to stand."

Another wave of relief washed over Marius. Yuri was safe as well. Macaro pulled up a stool, and for a while Macaro sat with him quiet.

"I want to know the truth," Macaro said as he placed his hand on Marius' forehead. Marius knew what was to come, so he did his best not to resist. He could feel Macaro twist and weave through his mind, viewing all his memories of the event prior.

After, when Macaro lifted his palm off of Marius' head, his face was nothing but a canvas of shock. Again he sat in silence for a bit and Marius could sense his head was turning in knots from what he'd seen.

"In all my years, I've never thought Nathaniel would do as such, you two are lucky to be alive."

"You saw it, right?" Marius asked Macaro, wanting to know if what had happened was not but a dream.

"The light? Yes, I saw what you saw. But before you ask—no, I do not know what that was. It seemed Nathaniel had sought whatever that was for a while now, and when I found you two in the dark of the dungeons it was no longer there, I had not known of its existence until now, Marius."

"You came for us? How did you know?" Marius asked beginning to clue in how he had come to arrive in Mirane's quarters. He had hoped it all was a nightmare, but it seemed it wasn't—the manticore, the fight with Nathaniel, the unknown light—all had been real and come to life now that Macaro had confirmed them. Only the dream was left to be confirmed as a truth.

"Still don't know? Cynthia. She gave you two away just by the look on her face. It seems you need to get to know your friends better," Macaro joked, lightening the mood, but neither of them laughed. "I'm glad you're ok, Marius, but I'll have to leave you now, my duties are to attend to the other Elders and Yuri's trial."

"What will happen to him?"

Sighing, Macaro stalled to speak. "Nothing good, Marius. Nothing good will come from the trial."

Macaro got up from the stool he sat on, bowed low, and began to leave.

"Elder?"

"Yes?" Macaro said stopping in his tracks. A part of Marius didn't want to ask, but he needed to. He needed to know.

"Did you see anything else inside my mind?" The question slipped out awkwardly and even Macaro seemed puzzled.

"No, no I didn't. Why?"

It wasn't real, Marius thought. *It wasn't real.* "Nothing."

Macaro frowned, then turned and continued walking towards the door, deciding not to pry. But as he reached the door and touched the handle, he paused.

"Marius. I'm sorry."

The door swivelled on its hinges as Macaro left and Marius was left in an awkward silence. At least the dream and the nightmarish figure weren't real.

Evening had come, and with it Yuri's trial. No student was allowed to attend, except one: Yuri himself. The trial was to be held in the main hall, where all matters of betrayal, discussion and importance were decided.

In the centre of the room, under the dim lighting of the candles that surrounded the steps down to the centre podium, Yuri stood awaiting the word and decree of the Elders of Highwash. Standing around him with their arms crossed, each Elder stood at a corner of the steps that led down to the centre of the room.

Macaro stood on the steps above and in front of him; he, after all, was Yuri's Elder, and would be the one to run the trial. On his left stood Elder Mixen, a tall gruff-looking man Yuri knew little about. Mixen had a long black beard, broad heavy shoulders and a face beset by heavy blue eyes to match. To his right was

Elder Carolina, she was short, thin, wired with muscles and, even though she was old, her face showed little signs of aging. Behind him stood Mirane, in place of Ralis who had not returned from his voyage east. To Yuri, none of them looked impressed as they stood with grim shadows under their eyes.

Macaro was the first to speak. "Yuri, my child, my student. We are here today to discuss matters of unfortunate circumstance. Do not speak, for your voice shall be ignored, your voice means little to us now. I had warned you many times, I had given you many chances, and I had oft forgiven you in times where I should have been strict. In other words, this may be a fault of my own. I loved you like my own child, and I had neglected to be serious with you during times I had been soft. I thought you more of this. I had thought of you as strong, unrelenting and a warrior whose voice shall be carried across the waves of your life spreading compassion like fire. But twice now you have risked the lives of those you care for, twice now have you ignored the heeding of those who love you, twice now you have chosen rash behaviour over patience, and twice now you have ignored our rules and betrayed our code. I had told you—I had commanded you—not to return to those ruins, but you defied my word. Have you visited Marius yet? I'm afraid I know the answer to such a question. No. No you didn't. I looked into his eyes and saw your crimes. Marius risked everything, his life, his own teachings here at Highwash to get you to see the truth, and what have you given him in return? Even during the final moments, you turned your back on him, hurting him for your own succession. Maybe you should see his wounds and reflect on your choices. But no matter, your time here at Highwash has come to an end. We have decreed to strip you of your title of apprentice, to strip you of your title of Mage, and to banish you from ever walking the halls of Highwash again. I'm sorry, Yuri, for this hurts me just as much as it hurts you. Letting a child go is my worst of fears, but too often have you defied me and risked the lives of others. You have a month to say your farewells, gather your things and depart from Highwash, but do not expect warmth during that time from us. We will not leave you for dead. We will provide you a map of Thenus to guide you, a compass and rations. But no more than that shall be given, even that is too much. I'm afraid this also shall be the last time we speak, and this will be the last warning I give you: In the world beyond stay your hand and be wary to use the skills you have learned. There are others who watch from the trees and the skies."

Silence filled the room as a deep sadness overcame Yuri. He wasn't surprised of the outcome; he had prepared mentally all day for the worst of outcomes. It was his worst expectation. As the trial ended and the Elders all left through the main entrance, Yuri couldn't help but stare at the ground, embarrassed.

Leaving the great hall behind the Elders, avoiding eye contact with any of the students who walked by, Yuri headed for his quarters. It was evening out, and a low cast sun set over the western horizon; covered by a grey sheen of soft clouds, it gave the feeling as if night was falling early. The air was misty as tiny trickles of rain covered his face and dampened his robes. Happening by Daniel and Mathius, he didn't stop to talk or trade words; he could feel their judging scowls on the back of his skull as he sped up, trying his best to make haste out of the centre of Highwash. Everyone knew what he had done and there was no need for them to gossip. Yuri wore his shame on his face for all to see. The air smelled beautiful though, with the dampness of rain, seagulls cawing and a soft wind blowing. This was his home, but now no more.

Right when he got to his quarters and sunk onto his bed, not caring about dampening his cot with his wet robes, the reality set in for Yuri. It truly had happened: he was banished.

Banished.

The word felt alien as he said it over and over again in his mind.

This was his home, he had grown up here, he had trained here, and this place was all he knew. He had prepared his whole life for the Trial of Apprentices, his whole youth had led up to the moments of this last year, and he had blown it. All for what? That glowing light? A fight with Nathaniel?

Yuri wondered if Marius would forgive him for what he did. He replayed the memory of punching Marius in the chest in his mind. He didn't know why he had done that, it had just happened, as if he had not even been in his own body. But it was too late, all was damaged and not to be recovered. And now where would he go? He visualized himself having to leave Highwash a month from now, alone, and having nowhere to go, no one to go to and nothing to achieve.

Worms crawled in his stomach at the thought of it. He wanted to run to Macaro, beg and plead for forgiveness, maybe then Macaro would let him stay, maybe as a cook or stable boy for Talun. But the thought of cowering at Macaro's feet was too much, and for a second Yuri felt like a little boy crying for his mother, a mother he did not have.

Highwash was his life, and he had cast it aside. And now... and now everything was an unknown. No. *I'm not a little boy,* he told himself as he stared at the ceiling of his shack, as little droplets of water built up under the rain of Highwash. *I am a man and I'll make my own way in this world. I don't need Highwash, I don't need friends, I have myself and that's all I need.* He knew it wasn't true but he told himself so anyways. It helped soothe the regret.

After a bit of time of staring into the nothing of his ceiling, watching drops of water build up and fall, dropping beside his bed, he got up. Upon deciding his best course of action was to make amends with at least one person—the one he held dearest in his heart—he headed for Mirane's cabin to see Marius, but when he got there and swung open the rickety door, no one was inside, the cot that held him was empty.

Marius stood tall, ready to receive the judgment of his Elders. Under the soft light of the candles that surrounded the walls of the main hall, all three of the Elders looked angelic, their faces proud with years of training and studying. He wondered what they would say, and cold beads of sweat trickled down his back as he stood waiting for Mirane, the last Elder, to enter, so the trial could begin. His eyes met Macaro's who stood in front of him, above on the steps before the centre of the hall. His eyes held sympathy, but Macaro always had a tinge of sadness on his face so Marius wondered if that was just the way he looked or if something bad was about to happen. He would have to be patient and see.

Soon Mirane entered the hall, apologizing to the other Elders for her lateness, bowing low at Marius, and signalling Macaro with a bow that she was ready to begin. A deep quiet grew and no Elder spoke, all of their eyes peered at Marius and Marius could feel even Mirane's stare on the back of his head.

Under the awkwardness, suddenly Marius found himself speaking. "I'm sorry for leaving, Yuri had just left so suddenly. I know I should have come to you, Macaro."

Macaro raised his hand, interrupting Marius from speaking. "Please, there is no need for you to speak or apologize, we are all well aware of what you did and why you did it." Macaro looked around at his colleagues with a sly smile on his face. "Marius. It was a very unfortunate circumstance that you were entangled in and I'm sorry you had to be a part of it. Yes, you should have come to me, but both you and Yuri are alive and well, and if it wasn't for your decisions, that would be otherwise. We have met and discussed for a while about the choices you made."

A chill ran through Marius; here it came, he knew it was coming. He had heard Yuri was banished, that was sorrow news enough, and he knew his banishment was coming now, too.

"And after a while of discussion we have decreed that you shall no longer be an apprentice, and shall be raised to the higher standard of Adept."

Marius' jaw dropped in awe as he heard Macaro speak.

"The sacrifice you made to protect your friend from harm shows a great valour in you. This is a quality that all Elders wish their students to show, to go to any length to protect a life, to stay true to friendship and to fight for others, sacrificing our own life in their stead. You have shown those qualities. Not only that, you have impressed us greatly with your skill, I saw your memories, and I saw the body of the manticore. Even us, as fully trained Elders, would not dare to risk challenging an adult male manticore, and you were faced with odds that would have killed most. Yet you succeeded, yet you chose to fight and live. It seems you truly learned the lesson I had wanted to teach when I sent the wolf for you to face. I'm proud of you, Marius, and to say you are my student gives me much joy and gratitude. So, we would all like to announce you as an Adept Mage."

All four of the Elders went to one knee lowering their head in respect. They all spoke at once.

"Marius, child of Highwash, student to Macaro, you have honoured us to give you this title as Adept, you represent all that we strive to be, and we thank you for that. You honour us and all Mages that have gone and all the Mages to come. No longer shall you be bound to your home of Highwash, you are free to go as you deem. If you choose to stay, your training shall continue, but if you choose to leave, may you spread light through the world, showing mankind, nothing but compassion and kindness. May you protect the living, protect the weak, honour justice and strive for truth. We know you shall, as you are our student. If you choose to leave, know that we will always carry you in our hearts and you are always welcome back here at Highwash to continue your studies. Thank you, Marius."

Their voices finished echoing off the walls of the main hall.

Marius didn't know what to say. He was in awe and stunned by what had happened. Dropping to both his knees, he thanked them.

"No, Marius, thank you for showing that our teachings have not died and that light shall always burn true in those who value the living."

The Elders stood and congratulated Marius one final time. Mirane, Carolina and Mixen left through the main entrance, heading to attend to their own practice, but Macaro stayed obviously wanting a final word with Marius.

"Why did you pass me? I failed the tasks, wouldn't that not be fair to the rest?" Marius asked as Macaro walked down the smooth stone steps into the centre of the circled podium where Marius stood.

"Why do you believe that you failed? It seems to me every objective the tasks were meant to teach, you learned, and not only demonstrated, but did so through example. As a Mage, we don't care how the lesson *is learned*, only that the lesson is learned."

Macaro came forward and embraced Marius in a hug. Marius had never been hugged by him before. Stepping back, with his hands on Marius' shoulder, he gazed at Marius up and down.

"My, you've come a long way. I remember when you were first brought to me, and now... There is a level of sincerity in you, Marius, I wouldn't even find in myself, or even in the Nathaniel I used to know. I'm sorry you had to go through what you did, I know I've said this before, but I am very sorry. I should have been more aware and seen through Nathaniel's façade."

For a moment they stared at each other. Marius had never known his parents, but at that moment it didn't matter anymore, Macaro was his father, his mother and his guide.

"Have you seen to Yuri yet?" Macaro asked.

"No, Mirane had me spend the day with her, recovering my wounds. But I have heard."

"Yes, it is true, I'm sorry, Marius, it was not my choice. The other Elders had made their decree. It might be best if you find him, he may be avoiding contact with anyone. I'm sure he carries much shame after the incident."

"It wasn't his fault," Marius said saddened by hearing the truth from Macaro's mouth. Before it was a likely rumour, now it was all too real.

"I know, Marius, but it wasn't my decision. I care for him just as much as you do, and I always will. Now go rest, you've been through much."

Leaving the main hall, Marius was in awe of the beauty of Highwash. It always seemed to leave him breathless. The ocean in the distance, the golden fields, the blue skies waving their strings of cloud, the mountains to the east and the cold wind that blew past his face. He thought he might never see this place again. Heading off the bare dirt trails of the village and into the grass fields that rimmed them, Marius wandered for a bit as dusk turned into dark.

He thought and thought and thought. Yuri was his friend through and true. And to see him go would be too much a punishment. He had not risked everything to save him for nothing. Finding a lone birch tree that sat by itself in the golden fields, grabbing its branches and pulling himself up to its top, he stared out at the Emeralties to the east. Even from so far away, and with the setting sun, Marius could see the mountain peaks covered in a soft grey sheen of snow. *How beautiful,* he thought as he gazed at the marvel of the mountains. They always stood, forever holding their ground. It was as if the mountains were warriors, never breaking and never giving in. They always stood tall, and even in the dawn of the next morn they would be there, standing tall and strong and unwavering. Staring at the mountains, Marius made his decision, he knew what he needed to do.

He stood outside of the door, hoping he was in there. Worn wooden panels hung loose on the side of his small cottage, and under the door a soft light from candles could be seen coming from underneath. He knew his decision was the right one, but still, it made him anxious. Knocking on the door he stood there, waiting.

"Marius, come in," Macaro said at once, and Marius entered to find Macaro sitting in his usual spot, on a small chair, staring out the window and into the fields beyond.

"How did you know it was me?" Marius asked him, surprised by his cunning.

"I know my students well, haven't you learned that yet?" Macaro chuckled. "I've raised you since you were a babe, I think by now I can predict your movements."

"So then, you also know why I'm here."

Macaro turned to look at him, removing his gaze from out the window.

"I have my predictions, but I'd rather you tell me than us play a game of guessing each others' thoughts. Please sit. I hate when you stand in my home."

Marius sat on a small stool by the door as Macaro asked. Marius didn't know where to begin, but he had to say it somehow and he had a feeling Macaro already knew what he was about to say.

"I'm going with Yuri." There it was said and off his chest.

"I thought so," Macaro replied to his statement. "But you didn't have to come to me. Thank you for the thought, but you're an Adept now, Marius. You may leave as you like."

Marius felt relieved by Macaro's support.

"I just wanted to let you know myself."

"And I thank you for that. A word of advice though, the mainland may prove unfriendly, and I suggest you not be too tempted to use your skills. The birds have eyes, Marius, and our enemy watches from the skies."

A thousand times Macaro had warned them of these "enemies" called the Vatican. Marius had yet to meet them, and he would rather not encounter them at all.

Marius nodded acknowledging Macaro's word of advice, and stood from the stool, bowing towards his Elder. Just as he turned to leave Macaro's quarters, Macaro began to speak again.

"One more thing, Marius. I have something for you."

Macaro got up from his chair and walked over to a small, ancient cupboard in the opposite side of his quarters. Opening it, he pulled out a note curled up many times and handed it to Marius. In Marius' hand he could see the note was crumpled and old, it was folded many times and was tied by a single red string.

"What is it?" Marius asked.

"I found it crammed underneath Nathaniel's bed when the other Elders and I were clearing out his quarters. I opened it and, once I saw that it was addressed to you, I didn't read the rest. It's rightfully yours."

Marius nodded again, wondering what Nathaniel could have possibly wrote to him. He would read it later he decided. Thanking Macaro, he went to leave again.

"Marius, what you're doing for Yuri. It will save his life."

"I know," Marius responded, and he was out the door.

He had one last thing to do.

She opened the door as quickly as he knocked, it seemed as if she'd been expecting him.

"Marius! You're recovered!" Cynthia exclaimed as she held open the door to her quarters and gestured him to come in.

She planted a kiss on his cheek, her lips felt soft and warm. He had forgotten how soft they were. It made him hate what he was about to say.

Marius came in and sat on her bed beside her. Her quarters were the same as all the other students, a small shed with no insulation, made with simple wooden framing, and a small trussed roof that barely hung onto its framing at some points. Inside were just her small wool cot, and a tiny table with a drawer. It was cold and drafty but he felt a sense of warmth with her presence, and even though her quarters were the same as everyone else's, for some reason Marius liked Cynthia's quarters more than his own. He would miss this place.

"Tell me, what happened with the trial?"

Marius could tell she had worked up the bravery to ask the question, fearing the worst.

"Guess," he said jokingly.

Her face lit up like a beam of light, realizing he was not banished.

Cynthia slapped his chest and scoffed at him. "Tell me, no games."

"Ok, ok. Well, at first I thought I was going to be banished, but… they graduated me to Adept."

Cynthia's jaw dropped to what Marius said. In excitement she got up and spun in circles, laughing joyously. Grabbing Marius, she lifted him off the bed and embraced him in a hug.

"Marius!" she yelled. "How so? Why so? I can't believe this. I thought you would be banished, definitely after Yuri was…"

She went silent realizing what she had said. "Oh, that's terrible. My—Yuri is going to be crushed. He came to me today. He told me what had happened and that he has one month left here at Highwash."

Her face suddenly became distraught and she sat back down on her bed looking solemn and sad. They sat silently for a bit deep in thought about their friend.

"That's why I came to you at this hour," Marius started to say.

"What do you mean?" Her eyes started to grow heavy and Marius knew that she was clueing in fast.

How do I tell her? Losing not just one, but two friends will hurt her more than anything.

"Cynthia, I have to leave as well. I've decided to go with Yuri. I haven't told him yet, but I've made my decision. I just finished telling Macaro." He could sense her choke on her words, a ball of sadness building in her throat.

Dammit, Yuri, the things you make me do, Marius thought to himself as he sat there sensing Cynthia's grief.

"I understand... I would tell you to stay, being stuck here with Mathius and them will suck, but I see you have already made your decision."

Her eyes turned away from Marius and she stared at the door. Marius wrapped his arm around and her, and the soft strands of her hair tickled the exposed part of his arm.

"Cynthia, I have to go. I can't let Yuri leave home all alone, it would be the death of him, he needs me. You know how he is, he can be rash, angry and kind of stupid at times. Without someone there, what will he do?"

"I know, Marius, you're right."

They lay on her bed for a bit, cuddling in the darkness and not speaking.

"I'm going to miss you," she whispered, as she scratched the surface of his head.

"I'll come back, Cynthia. I will need to come back at one point to continue my training."

"You know that's untrue, how can you predict what will happen?"

"Well, you're right in that, I can't tell you the future for certain. But I promise I'll come back. And, hey, I still have a month left here."

Later in the evening, Marius walked back to his quarters under a star-covered sky. The stars rippled in blue strands weaving across the black of space. The stars of winter. The year had ended and with it much had changed. It was hard to say goodbye to Cynthia, and as Marius walked under the stream of stars that lit the village of Highwash in a gentle blue, he thought it would be really hard to say goodbye to his home as well.

I will come back, he promised himself, *I will come back.*

The day was bitterly cold as the whole of Highwash gathered on the granite cliff coast for Nathaniel's funeral. Elder Macaro, Elder Mixen, Elder Carolina, Mirane, the whole of Marius' class—including Yuri—and many older students Marius had known had come for the funeral. All of them gathered in a clump before Macaro and Mirane who would lead the ceremony.

Marius stood beside Cynthia on the side of the clump of people. Beside him, a rough cotton sack sat on the ground. Inside was everything he would need to depart form Highwash; an old metal canteen Macaro had dug out of the confines of his own quarters, an extra pair of robes wrapped around rations of dried nuts and a loaf of bread. He had also packed a couple maps of the mountain ranges of the Emeralties, a knife, a compass and the note from Nathaniel, which he had delayed to read. He could see Yuri standing a few steps behind everyone, trying not to make eye contact with anyone. He, too, had his bag packed, though his was slung over his shoulder. Every so often Mathius or some of the older students would glance back at Yuri with distasteful looks on their faces.

More than a month had passed since Yuri was banished, but Macaro had permitted him to stay for Nathaniel's funeral. When Marius told Yuri he was accompanying him on his travels, Yuri had argued and argued, stating that Marius shouldn't leave Highwash just because of his own mistakes.

A World Beyond Our Own

Memories of the conversation past by vividly in Marius' mind as he looked at Yuri standing there, obviously discouraged to leave.

"Yuri, I'm coming with you," Marius had said after he found Yuri alone, meditating on a large rock in the depths of the fields.

"No, you're not," Yuri had replied like if he had a choice in the matter.

They'd bickered back and forth for a bit, but finally the conversation ended with Marius saying he would simply follow Yuri if he must. That ended the argument but the two of them hadn't talked since.

Noise brought Marius back to earth as a few children ran amuck, running in circles between the small bushes that grew between the cracks on the surface of the granite cliff. Their childlike minds still stuck on playfulness and not fully aware of the situation at hand. No one minded though, the kids seemed to add some humour to the seriousness of the event. Nathaniel had been Archmage for many years, and the only Archmage Highwash had known. It was a grim day to see him pass. Only Marius, Yuri and Macaro knew the truth of what had happened in the ruins a month ago, and, to not spite Nathaniel's reputation, they had kept the truth to themselves.

Macaro raised his hand, and the group hushed, silently awaiting him to begin speaking. "We have gathered here today because unfortunate events have passed and we must say goodbye to someone who was a friend to all of us. As you all know, our Archmage has passed away. It saddens me greatly to say goodbye, and I imagine it saddens all of you. Not many of you had met Nathaniel, nor spent much time with him, but, still, he was our Archmage and his loss is one of tragedy. We could not reclaim much of his remains, but what we did reclaim we turned into ashes."

Mirane held out the urn she was holding and gave it to Macaro. Macaro held out the urn for all to see and began speaking again.

"To ashes and ember we fall,
To ashes and embers we crawl,
For all of us our fate lies beyond the wall,
May we remember his teachings,
May we remember his voice,
For he was once one of us, after all,
To ashes and ember he crawls,
To ashes and ember we all shall fall."

All went silent in respects to Nathaniel.

Opening the lid of the urn, Macaro turned to the ocean and flipped the urn upside down. Nathaniel's remains poured out in a dusty wave, caught in the wind and slowly his ashes drifted down into the ocean, returning to where his heart would always rest, his eternal home of the earth.

A few of the eldest Adept students came forward, dropping bundles of stalk-like, white thistles off the cliff side as well. They were Nathaniel's favourite flower, though Marius cared little about that knowledge.

Soon the crowd dissipated after many paid their respects by dropping flowers or stones off the cliff into the ocean. In the corner of his eye Marius could see the solemn-looking Yuri start to walk off in the distance, northwest towards the fields.

It was time for Yuri to leave, and time for Marius to leave as well. Looking over to Cynthia, who was hugging Clive, Marius knew he would have to say goodbye now or he could never gain the heart to leave again.

"Cynthia," Marius said, calling out to her as he walked over to her.

Clive left her embrace and nodded at Marius greeting him as well.

"May I talk with you, Cynthia?" Marius asked, glancing over at her brother. "May you leave us, Clive?"

Agreeing, Clive walked off to join Reggard and the others who were headed towards the dining hall.

Everyone knew Yuri was banished, but they preferred not to say goodbye to him, as betrayal and banishment weren't on friendly terms with students of Highwash. However, no one knew that Marius was preparing to leave today, and the only person among his classmates he had told was Cynthia. Marius decided that saying goodbye to all of his friends here would be too hard, and would most likely dissolve his will to leave. They'd of course be offended, but he was leaving for Yuri's sake, not theirs.

"You're leaving with him, aren't you?"

Words stuck in his throat, so Marius nodded and embraced Cynthia in a hug. He held her longer than he should have, knowing he would not feel the warmth of her arms for a long while. Finally, when they finished their embrace, Marius could see tears streaming down Cynthia's face. Her voice cracked and she cried out suddenly.

"Don't go, Marius, I need you here," she suddenly begged, putting her hands on his chest.

"I have to go Cynthia." *Damn, she is making it harder than it has to be.*

"No, you don't, it was Yuri's mistake. Don't risk everything for him, don't throw away all your friends because of his mistakes." She leaned in close and put her head on his chest, hiding her tears on his robes.

"I'm sorry, Cynthia, but I have to."

And, pushing her away, Marius grabbed his bags from the ground. Looking back at Cynthia one last time, with her eyes clouded in tears he said, "Goodbye, Cynthia. I promise I'll come back."

After he spoke he ran after the dot in the distance which was Yuri. He knew that if he looked back he would end up running to Cynthia and leave Yuri to his fate, so he did not. He stared forward, running towards his friend.

Cynthia stood there with cold tears streaming down her face. *Damn him,* she thought. *Damn him for leaving me.*

A cold wind blew by as she watched Marius run off towards the fields after Yuri. When he would return, she did not know, and she couldn't bear to think of how long of a wait she would have to endure.

Out of nowhere, a hand was placed on her shoulder from behind. It was Macaro.

"I'm sorry that he had to leave, Cynthia. It's not that he does not love you, he loves you greatly, but he loves Yuri as well. That was a hard choice for him, but he knows you will not be alone here. You will be among friends, but Yuri will have no one other than Marius. Forgive him, for you shall always be in his heart."

Hearing Macaro speak of him was too much for her. Breaking out into a sob, Cynthia stormed off.

Macaro felt a wave of sadness that ripped through his heart as he watched Cynthia run off crying. Too much suffering had occurred this year. Ralis had left Highwash for what seemed like good, Nathaniel had died, Yuri had been banished and Marius... Marius had left as well. Macaro always had favoured Marius.

Joining him by his side, and taking his hand was Mirane. She had seen what happened from afar and felt Macaro's despair. For a while they stood there, until the sun started to burn the ocean orange.

"Did you ever tell him?" she asked, breaking the silence.

"No. I never had the heart to tell him."

Macaro looked Mirane in the face. She had aged tremendously he thought, her blue eyes now held bags and her face had soft lines of wrinkles around her lips and cheeks, but, still, Mirane was beautiful as ever.

"How could I tell him, Mirane? It would break his heart knowing that he never told Marius himself."

Mirane nodded in agreement, and they both watched the sun set beyond the horizon of the ocean.

Marius could hear the items in his rucksack clamber around as he ran up behind Yuri. Yuri had gotten far ahead as he said his farewell to Cynthia, so the sprint up from the coast and into the fields left him coated with a sheen of sweat.

"Yuri!"

Yuri turned with an expression of shock hearing Marius behind him. Panting Marius exclaimed, "Yuri, wait, I'm coming with you."

"You really want this, Marius?" Yuri said with a blank tone.

Catching his breath before he answered he rested his hands on his knees, then began to speak.

"There is no way I'm letting you go alone."

Standing straight they both gazed at each other. Marius had barely seen Yuri this month, and his long locks of black hair had grown now beyond his neck, scruffy and unkempt, but his brown eyes still held a sense of joy.

"So you're telling me you plan on betraying everything Macaro taught you, for me? You realize if you leave they will never accept you back... like me. I can't let you do that, Marius, you saved my life twice and I won't let you throw away everything for nothing. So, turn back," Yuri said with a tone of regret as he turned away from Marius and started walking again.

"Listen, Yuri. I never got the chance to tell you, but I won't be betraying anyone. Macaro passed me to Adept. I'm allowed to leave. I'm not throwing away anything. I'm choosing to go with you out of choice."

Yuri stopped, hearing the words.

"Do you hear me? I want to go with you," Marius said reaching out for Yuri.

"Even after all I've done?"

Stepping in front of his friend, Marius raised Yuri's chin with his hand so their eyes would meet. He could see Yuri's eyes waver under guilt.

"Yuri, I didn't go after you the first time for nothing, and I'm not letting you leave alone. You're my friend. You're my friend no matter what. I forgive you. I know you didn't mean it. Both of us saw what was in there, it wasn't your fault."

Immediately Yuri dropped his bag and wrapped Marius in a hug. "I'm sorry, Marius, I never meant to strike you."

"I know, I know. So, come on, pick up your bag and let's go."

The two of them walked on for a bit as the sun neared the ocean's edge. They talked about their plans of how to navigate the Emeralties in the midst of winter. Yuri told Marius of his plan to head northwest along the coast until they reached the mountain pass that cut through the Emeralties east. Yuri had been studying maps for the last month, and figured it would take at least three months to hike to the mountain pass, allowing much time for the spring melt to occur. Marius agreed the plan was sound, as the southeast valley way through the Emeralties was most likely closed from the forces Salamon had laid there. So they hiked on northwest, friends again.

Later in the evening, as the sun was setting beyond the veil of ocean, they sat around a fire they had made on the rocky coast far beyond the village borders.

"So, this will be the last I see of Highwash, huh?" Yuri said as stoked the fire with a stick.

"I imagine you'll be back one day."

"Don't bullshit me, Marius," Yuri scoffed laughing, "There's not a chance Macaro will let me back."

They went silent for a second, then Yuri spoke again.

"So how did Cynthia handle the fact you were coming with me?" Yuri asked with a smirk.

"Not well. Not well at all. And, to be honest, neither did I."

"Well, this is your last chance to head back, Marius, are you sure you're going to want to spend the cold nights beside me in bed?" Yuri said with a wink.

They both chuckled at that. Another solemn silence overtook their camp, both of them thinking of the friends they were leaving at Highwash.

"Well, I should get some sleep," Yuri said as he lay down on the stone ground. "Long day tomorrow. Miss my cot already."

Marius watched Yuri lay down on the ground and soon pass into slumber. Marius didn't feel tired, so he sat up tending the fire. After watching the sunset roll past the curtain of water and staring at the blue, starlit night, he remembered the note Macaro had given him.

Grabbing his bag and rifling through it, he found the crumbled piece of paper at the bottom of his bag under the rations and his extra cloak. Untying the string and unfolding it he began to read it.

Marius, my time is little and precious here, but I need to warn you, warn you of him. He had chosen Yuri and you, for reasons unknown to me. I have seen the future, and I am sorry I cannot do otherwise to change your fate. He will try to break you, bend you to his will, but whatever you do, don't let him in. Do all you can to see past his tricks. And whatever you do, do not speak to him. Never speak to him.

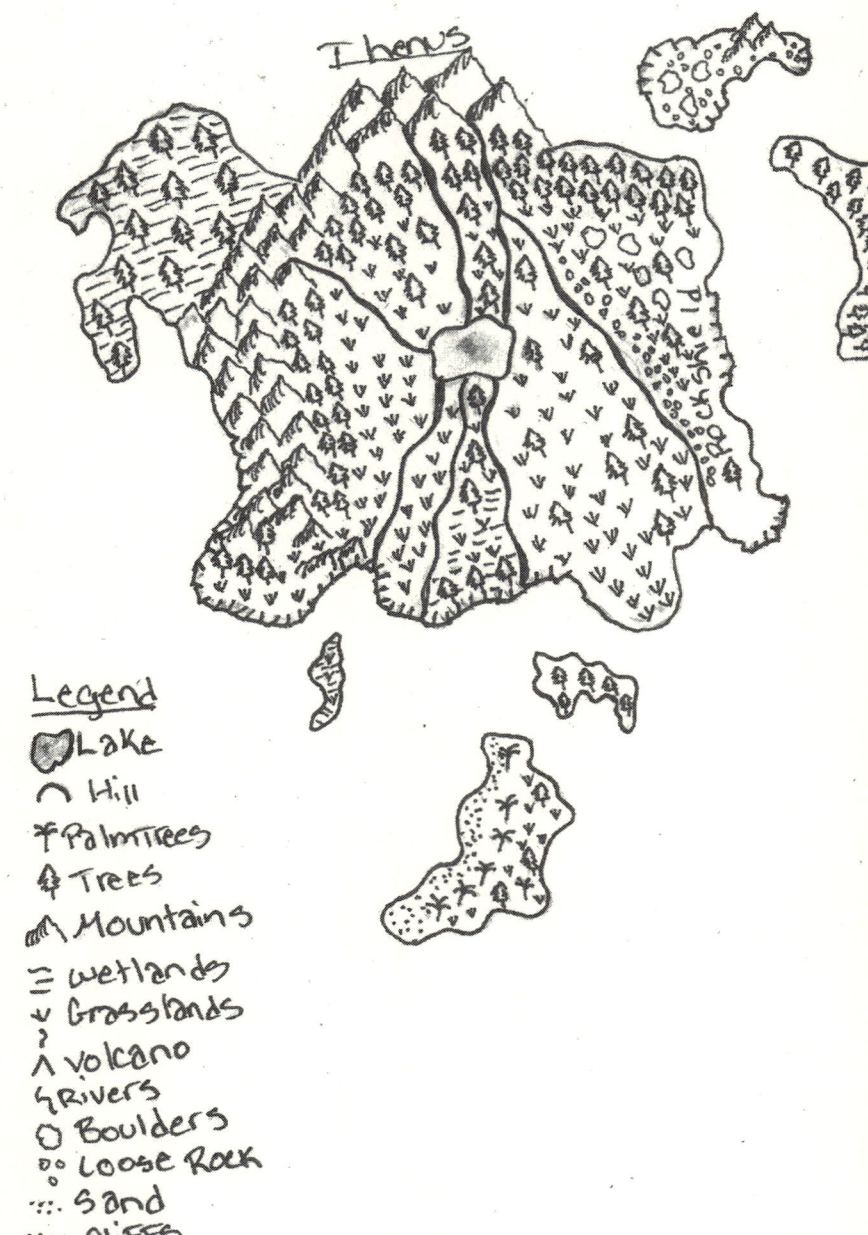

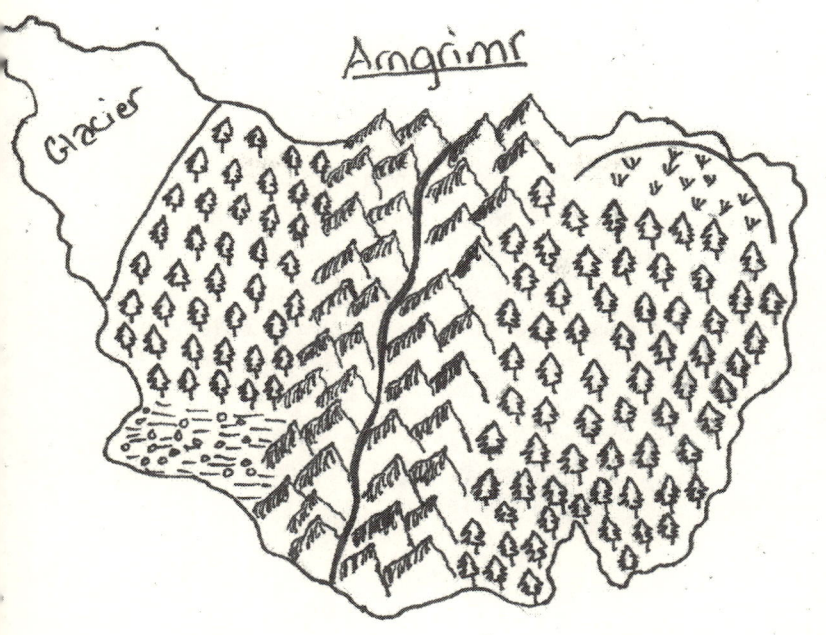

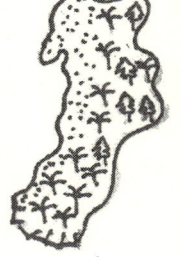

the Black Abyss

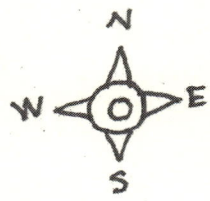

When I first started writing this I never had the intention of publishing it. It wasn't until about halfway through the book that I realized how much fun I was having writing, and that I wanted to try to publish it because it was bringing so much joy in my life.

Thank you to every author out there that inspired me. If not for their dedication towards their own works, my book wouldn't have come to pass. Thank you to every athlete that has kept me inspired to keep working at strengthening my weaknesses, and thank you to Ashtanga yoga.

Finally, and most of all, thank you to my lovely other half, Angelica. Without your continual support and work this creation wouldn't have come to exist.

And, of course, a second book is coming.

Manufactured by Amazon.ca
Bolton, ON